A HISTORY OF BURNING

A
HISTORY
OF
BURNING

JANIKA OZA

GRAND
CENTRAL

New York Boston

Copyright © 2023 by Janika Oza

Cover design by Albert Tang
Cover illustration by Simone Noronha
Cover copyright © 2023 by Hachette Book Group, Inc.

Grand Central Publishing
Hachette Book Group
1290 Avenue of the Americas, New York, NY 10104
grandcentralpublishing.com
twitter.com/grandcentralpub

First Edition: May 2023

Grand Central Publishing is a division of Hachette Book Group, Inc. The Grand Central Publishing name and logo is a trademark of Hachette Book Group, Inc.

The publisher is not responsible for websites (or their content) that are not owned by the publisher.

The Hachette Speakers Bureau provides a wide range of authors for speaking events. To find out more, go to www.hachettespeakersbureau.com or call email HachetteSpeakers @hbgusa.com.

Grand Central Publishing books may be purchased in bulk for business, educational, or promotional use. For information, please contact your local bookseller or the Hachette Book Group Special Markets Department at special.markets@hbgusa.com.

Library of Congress Cataloging-in-Publication Data
Names: Oza, Janika, author.
Title: A history of burning / Janika Oza.
Description: First edition. | New York : Grand Central Publishing, 2023.
Identifiers: LCCN 2022053116 | ISBN 9781538724248 (hardcover) | ISBN 9781538724262 (ebook)
Subjects: LCGFT: Domestic fiction. | Novels.
Classification: LCC PR9199.4.O97 H57 2023 | DDC 813/.6—dc23/eng/20221104
LC record available at https://lccn.loc.gov/2022053116

ISBN: 9781538724248 (hardcover), 9781538724262 (ebook)

Printed in the United States of America

LSC-C

Printing 1, 2023

For Manu-dada and Bhagwati-baa

PART ONE

1898–1958

Pirbhai, 1898

THE LAST DAY PIRBHAI SPENT in Gujarat was ignited by a sun that could not last. The heat was a dry beast, scorching the fields yellow as gora hair. He eased himself onto a step by the water's edge, letting his chappals graze the foam. Jamnagar offered him nothing. For as long as he could remember, every day was the same. By foot, or sometimes hitching a ride on the back of a cart, he wandered the streets, pleading for work. Today the landowner barely raised his eyes, and he knew he was probably one of many boys turned away. *Look around you, dikro*, the man had muttered. *Do you see any rice, any grain? Dry, all dry. Come back after monsoon.* When Pirbhai pointed to the white buds bursting across a field, the man laughed until he coughed. His lips cracked and blood pulsed on his stained teeth. *Those are for British exports. Not for us.*

That morning, Pirbhai had watched his ma ask the gods for forgiveness, praying over his middle sister, whose bones clacked as though loose inside her skin. For days her body had expelled water—sweat-water, wiwi-water, chee-water—and now she was limp and dry as the crops outside. When his ma had turned to him and told him to try Jamnagar today, that a neighbor's son had found work there last week, Pirbhai had imagined saying no. He had thought about rolling over on his sleeping mat, refusing to leave home and playing gilli danda with his siblings in the deadened grass instead. They would fight over who got to be striker and who fielder, and as the eldest, Pirbhai would get first pick. He would strike the gilli all the way to the sea, and his siblings would whistle, Ma looking on in awe.

But he was thirteen, the oldest son, no longer a boy. If he returned bearing nothing again, Ma would suck in her cheeks, then silently scrape her portion onto his plate; a reminder of the strength he would need for tomorrow. *Bhai*, his mother always called him, *brother*, reminding him of who he was, to whom he was responsible.

The reddening sky warned him to start his journey back, but the wind pulling off the water stilled him. He pressed his palms to his face, the imprint of the sun behind his eyelids a single ember. When he opened his eyes, there was a man. A merchant, his belt buckle polished and skin supple and oiled so that its brown shone almost gold. The man shifted a lump of tobacco in his cheek, exposing teeth like chipped bricks.

"Looking for work, dikro?"

Pirbhai nodded, eyeing him, too weary from the day to believe.

The man opened his fist for a second. It was long enough for Pirbhai to spy a pile of coins, grimy but solid, winking in the late afternoon light.

"You and I, we were meant to find one another," the man said, and pressed a coin into Pirbhai's palm. Pirbhai closed his fingers over the skin-warmed metal, unable to resist its unnatural weight.

"You have work?"

The man pointed out at the water.

"I'm looking for boys just like you. Young, tough, hardworking. You'll work hard, na?"

Now Pirbhai focused, aware that this was his chance. He raked a hand through his hair, relieved that he still appeared strong and capable, even as his stomach curled around itself. He smiled to show the man his teeth, that they were straight and square, his best feature—a sign of inner health, his ma always bragged.

4

"I'll work the hardest," he said, and he meant it.

The man clapped him on the shoulder and fished into his pocket, drawing out two things. First, a small tin of tobacco, which he flipped open and offered to Pirbhai. Tentatively, Pirbhai accepted, taking a pinch and dabbing it inside his lip as he'd seen so many men do: languorous restless men, hungry-eyed. His heart leapt knowing that he might no longer be one of them.

Beneath the tin of tobacco, the man shook out a long strip of paper. It was crisp and covered in small black etchings. Pirbhai's spirits sunk. A test. He had hardly been to school, never learned to read. Now he would have to prove himself smart enough for the job, and he would fail.

The man passed him the sheet of paper. He didn't ask Pirbhai to read the words, or to recite a poem like the wealthy boys could, or to take up a pen and write. Instead, he produced a small cap of ink and tapped it open, gesturing to the line at the end of the page.

"If you want to work, you just need to put your thumbprint here," he said.

Marveling at his luck, Pirbhai let his right thumb sink into the pool of black, all the way until it hit the bottom.

It was nearly dark when they climbed onto the boat. The man hadn't said where they were going, only that Pirbhai should wait until night-fall, when they would begin. Briefly Pirbhai imagined his ma worrying where he was, but he had asked a cart driver who was traveling through Porbandar to send word to his family. He pictured the driver calling to his ma from the cart, how his eldest sister would rush to offer him a glass of salted chaas for bringing such prosperous news. How proud they would be.

The dhow was small and wooden, and it creaked as Pirbhai and the others slotted themselves into the narrow hull, side by side like sacks of lott. Some were boys who looked no older than ten, others fully grown men, bearded, speaking of wives and children. Pirbhai recognized them all, though he knew none of them. Like him, they were all thin, dusty, made twitchy from months, perhaps years, of searching. The air glimmered with possibility. Pirbhai felt a greasy fullness, having bought some batata bhajias with the paisa the merchant gave him, upon the man's insistence that he would need energy for the journey. The oil had curdled on his tongue as he thought of his middle sister, who hadn't swallowed food in days, but he forced the thick mash down, sucking away the salt that burned his lips.

Now, Pirbhai didn't see the merchant. Instead, three goras stepped onto the dhow, their shoulders broad and uniforms crisp. Captains, Pirbhai thought, British. The men were speaking, laughing, but the words that tumbled from their lips were unintelligible. He knew only a few words in English, gleaned here and there on his searches for work—*hello, thank you, country, bread*—and he heard none of these now.

"I heard there's work in Karachi, that's maybe where they're taking us," the boy beside Pirbhai said, scratching at a constellation of mosquito bites on his forearm. His name was Jameel and he had skin like midnight. Pirbhai's was more like water-soaked wood. Pirbhai's lungs swelled with relief to know he wasn't the only one unaware of their destination. Not that it mattered: by morning he would be working, pocketing rupees to bring home to his ma, enough that they could buy medicine for his sister, maybe even call on a doctor, enough that they could buy milk and lott from the shop without having to sweep the floors and clean the toilet pit for a discount, or worse, buying the items on credit that his mother repaid later, at night, in secret, though Pirbhai had always known. A breeze lifted the hair from his forehead, and he tasted salt as a spray of seawater covered the men like a shroud. As the dhow groaned into the water, Pirbhai watched the oil lamps on the shore of Gujarat flicker, then fade.

Pirbhai could not remember how many men started out on the dhow, but there were fewer of them now. One, a boy who reminded Pirbhai of his friends in the village, became sick, the hot white of his eyes rolling as he wheezed. When he died, the captains made some of the stronger men haul him overboard. Pirbhai could still see the curve of his forehead, pale as bone, slipping beneath a black wave. Another, a man with henna-red lips, lost his senses, screaming into the wind, swearing at the goras who hadn't bothered to learn even a word of Gujarati to tell the group where they were going. Or perhaps the goras were just feigning ignorance. The captains beat the man, much and often. One day the man clambered on deck and wrestled the wheel, that fiery circle that never ceased its spinning, from the captain's grip. Chalo, he shrieked, time to go home. He sounded like a father at the sweetshop, and also like a child who'd lost his mother. The goras knocked him to the ground, beat him until blood caked in his ears. That was the last time he fought back. The next day, Jameel woke Pirbhai and asked him if he wanted to see a dead man. Against the crack of waves, the man lay lifeless or maybe just defeated. This time, the captains hauled him overboard.

They might have been at sea for a month or three, Pirbhai wasn't sure. Nor did he know if his ma had given up hope of his return, or if his sister had drawn her last breath. All he could be sure of was the rot snaking up his thighs and bottom from sitting in a damp dhoti all day, the cracked sores lining his lips from mixing water with flour or rice, from eating only this. It was as if the ocean had emptied him of everything. He was gutted. The black waters, the men began calling it, we're crossing the black waters. Whatever parts of himself he had lost, the kala pani absorbed. Some mornings, he had trouble recalling his own name.

It was Jameel and Ganesh's turn to cook that day, and between them they lugged a dented pot. Ganesh's arms were peeling from the sun and salt and winds, his brown skin now a chapped grey. Pirbhai groaned, throat tight with thirst, but Jameel, strangely, grinned. Then Pirbhai caught it, the sweet and the tang, a smell that wrenched him back to his family in Porbandar. The shock of smelling something that wasn't shit-sweat-piss-salt or the occasional acid stench of seasick that didn't make it overboard was so acute that he lost his balance, clutching the railing. There was saliva on his lips, streaking across his chin.

The men were laughing, but not at him so much as with him. They were jahaji bhai now, boat brothers bound by the water whether they chose it or not. Those who were still alert enough to notice raised their noses to the air. Pirbhai found himself howling, and the others barked along, hooting, their own pack of dogs.

Jameel raised the metal ladle, where congealed rice dripped in thick globs.

"Onion," he said.

Pirbhai had never been hungrier. The slivers of onion were sparse and thinly diced, but their flavor permeated his entire body, the entire boat. Ganesh joked that they would all be sweating onion for days—the sweetest sweat, he said.

One of the goras emerged, binoculars hooked around his neck. The group grew watchful, the water shushing around them. This one was the big malik, the one with eyes the color of the sea. The captain showed his teeth. "Enjoying, boys?" he said.

Some grunted appreciation, others cursed quietly in Gujarati. Over the journey they had all learned a little English, picking up phrases from the captains, joking over dirty words when the goras were slack with daru.

The captain was speaking slowly now, emphasizing his vowel sounds like he truly wanted them to understand.

"Land," Pirbhai caught, and his heart stopped.

"Land?" he repeated in Gujarati, loud so the others heard him, so that they stopped too, eyes bulging, tongues stilled.

The captain was saying something else, a word Pirbhai didn't know. But he kept repeating it, pitching his voice above the slap of waves. Pirbhai watched his mouth open and close, a fish out of water, moved his own mouth to match the sounds.

"Mombasa," he was saying.

When Pirbhai crossed paths with Jameel or Ganesh or any of the men from the boat, he averted his eyes. It had been two years since he stumbled down the docks at Mombasa on sea-weakened legs, and since then he had learned what it took to survive. Pausing for too long or wasting time to chat was discouraged, punishable if any of the rail police noticed. He pretended it was this that stopped him. But it wasn't, not really. It was the gnaw of guilt, that they had all ended up in this servitude entirely unaware. That they had hopes, had really believed they were sailing somewhere better. How greedily they had snatched the chance.

He kept his head low as Jameel's voice receded, his nose thick with the sweet rot of soil. By now he knew the trees above him, their tangled heads bursting with pungent yellow blooms. Better not to look up at all, to tune out the drone and sting of the tsetse flies, to keep all senses trained on the work. The men were clearing out, drifting back to their camps in clots of two or three so as not to be left alone as the night closed in. Pirbhai lingered, working a rusted sleeper key into the soft mulch and hoping the masters were watching, though he did not look up to check. He pressed down on the sleeper to test its stability, the cool metal a balm on his torn palms. The earth had stained his fingernails— wide, twisted—a muddy red, so that he sometimes recoiled from his own hands.

He brushed soil from his forearms, where dark hairs wound across his once-smooth skin. In the years that had passed, his voice had cracked and plateaued, and he barely recognized his own odor. He had grown too, so that his toes spilled out across the lip of his chappals, but already his shoulders were curved in like an old man's, his knees knobbed and shins bowed so that his walk was more like a limp. The weight of the railway tracks was warping even the sturdiest of men. Whatever they had carried over, they were burdened with a new weight now: they were here to stay. The only way out was forward. They were bound, to one another and to this land.

He'd started smoking beedis, and his lungs crackled in the moist jungle air. But the momentary relief of it, when the smoke hit that tender place between his eyes, was worth it. He craved it now as he followed the muffled voices toward the camp, threadbare tarps that let in all the sun.

At the tent, he eased off his sandals. Many worked barefoot these days, preferring the grip of their toes on thistle and crushed stone. Feet or boots, the important part was the mind. A slight misstep, a single twitch of the shoulder when laying down a track, could lose you a limb. Early on he found himself distracted by thoughts of his family, dreaming of the day he would return home to his sisters, and if one of the other workers hadn't shoved him aside he might have lost a hand to a wood saw. Since then, he had trained his mind to banish such tempting thoughts and focus only on what lay ahead.

It happened not long ago to Sohum, one of his tentmates. A momentary lapse in the cloudy grind, and Sohum's foot was crushed, ankle down, the remaining flesh pulpy and rank with dirt. The foot had to be cut off entirely. An infection crept up the stumpy leg, the skin mottled and purplish all the way to the groin. One night he screamed so long that a man appeared at the tent, a native with eyes like river rocks. The native workers slept in separate tents, or else out in the open with sheets tucked up to their noses against the macchar. In the mornings they set out first with their scythes, slashing away brush and thistle, crushing stone and hauling it down. Only then would the jahaji bhai approach, with wood and saws and metal. Beneath the fierce sun their skins took on the same hues, but the difference was in their hands: black hands, thorn-bloodied and nails split by stone; brown hands, rigid with splinters, oozing dirty pus where infection took root. And all the while the pink-skinned masters watched from the shade, blowing their whistles if ever the workers were caught speaking, ensuring their camps were far apart, even lunchtime quarters split into black and brown. Pirbhai sometimes caught a whiff of the natives' mahamri frying as he slurped at his sorghum porridge and was hit with the deep desire to walk over and dip his fingers into their bowl.

Against Sohum's wails, the native worker spoke fast, but the words were lost on them. The brothers hollered when he approached Sohum's quaking body, but his touch was gentle as he guided Sohum's mouth to a flask, sharing his water rations. He was not a medicine man, just a man with a conscience. Pirbhai watched the flicker of his eyes and remembered his ma the last time he saw her, bent over the shell of his sister. When the man slipped out into the night, Pirbhai followed him and offered him a beedi, which he accepted with a word that sounded like *sorry*. Pirbhai repeated it, sawa, sawa, sorry. He repeated it on the nights the man came back, and to the others who came too, exchanging food and medicines and fragments of language between the barracks and the endless dark.

Even still, Sohum died in a fever. They were shaken, all of them, but the masters used it as a warning. No dawdling, no dillydallying, no willy-nilly, they said, these strange English words that Pirbhai repeated as he worked, part mocking, part earnest. Of course, none of them needed a warning. Men died with every mile of railway they laid down. Lately, Pirbhai had heard rumors of man-eating lions stealing workers away at night, leaving only a tooth here, a turban there.

They were building a railroad to Lake Victoria. Pirbhai had no

11

idea where this was, and when he worked up the nerve to ask one of the railway police on watch, the man said, "Uganda," and Pirbhai was reminded of that moment on the dhow, the first time he heard of Mombasa. For now, he saw no lake, no town or city, just a flat strip of nothing surrounded by every shade of green. If he stared long enough, he forgot which way was laid down and which way they were headed, direction dissolving into sticky air.

Sometimes he envisioned the track complete, a red engine slicing through the trees. But he couldn't imagine who would sit on these trains. Not his kind, he was certain, who the mzungu called *coolies*, whose bodies were breaking under the weight of the task they were indebted to fulfill. And surely not the natives, who carried makarai of smashed rocks to lay down so that Pirbhai and the others could build on their land. "If we ever get to ride that train," one of Pirbhai's tentmates joked, "it'll be British in first class, Indian in second, African in third." Pirbhai laughed along, but he couldn't imagine them all sitting level like that, even if they were apart.

Kind mattered less than order. He knew that now, after the merchant who tricked him, after the Indian railway police who meted out the British punishments, after the natives with their trades of cowpea leaves and mhogo, with their word for the colonists that captured just how the white spirit hovered, relentless, above them all. *Mzungu*, Pirbhai now said instead of *gora*, and marveled at how certainly it thrust off the tongue.

Two of his tentmates were bickering. Rakesh, older than Pirbhai but much quicker to laugh, peeled off his shirt and snapped it at him so that Pirbhai gagged at the stench. Sweat, blood, urine, heat, the jungle's decay mingling with their own. But it was something else too, something so mortal and intimate that his eyes moistened. A grin rippled across Rakesh's stubbled face.

"Moody again?"

Pirbhai scraped a wrist across his eyes, smearing the day's grime.

"You're one to talk," he shot back. A few days ago, Pirbhai had found Rakesh slumped against a musizi tree, his head lolling against the blanched bark. When he managed to rouse him, Rakesh's eyes were dark, squinting as if blinded, a blankness that worried Pirbhai. Back at the tent, Rakesh told the men that he'd caught the sleeping sickness. The tsetse got me, he said, miming a fly pinching his neck. Pirbhai said nothing, but he couldn't forget the deadened stare. That night he forced himself to stay awake, glancing every few minutes at Rakesh's silhouette curled atop his sleeping mat as if Rakesh were his own brother.

Back home, they said that crossing the kala pani washed away your caste. They were all here now, a new creed. Not family, but still jahaji bhai. No one wanted another Sohum. It became duty to watch out for each other, to feed, to slap alert. At night, they kept each other alive with stories. Sitting close enough to the fire that their hairs singed, they told tales of their homes, their pasts, their tentative futures. Pirbhai never talked about his family, or at least, not his real one. When asked, he invented fictional relatives, a sister who danced kathak, her body full of breath, a mother who made a living cooking tiffins for the local laborers. His ma had once told him that they were descended from royalty, and though he'd never been certain if this was true, he claimed it in this new land. He wasn't ashamed of his roots; most of the men here came from villages like his, farming families driven to leave by drought and famine, by the relentless search for work in a country starved by its rulers. But summoning their names in this jungle was a sordid reminder. He had left home to work, and indeed, he was working, and yet he hadn't sent a single rupee back.

If he was indebted to the British for his passage here, he was even more indebted to his ma, to whatever pain his leaving had caused her. He would work harder, until he could atone for his absence. He would work until he became enough.

Pirbhai walked with Rakesh to the side of the tent to wash up.

Runnels of brown water cut through the soft ground. Around them, men shivered against one another. They hadn't spoken again about the incident by the tree. They didn't have to. Pirbhai knew it was no sleeping sickness, no mere trick of the body. He had seen it in so many of their stares: the bewilderment, the disbelief. The inability to trust anymore, matched with the ceaseless drive to do better than the next. That loss of something innately human.

Tonight, as they did most nights, they were making khichdi. Pirbhai dug the hole in the ground and Rakesh mixed the lentils, rice, and water in the aluminum pan. Now Pirbhai nestled the pan inside a turban, a ratty one that had belonged to one of the men who had disappeared, and placed the whole turban in the ground. Together they covered the hole with leaves and soil and lit a fire above, holding their faces close to the flames, counting the seconds, waiting, wondering how long they had done this for, and how far off the lake could be, and at what point does the body decide it's had enough, and how long does it take for fingernails to grow back, and could the lions sense when a man fell asleep, and how long could a person go without sleeping, and what did the masters eat tonight, and what had that sheet of paper said, and would it have been better to let the kala pani swallow them, and how many more nights like this could they survive.

In the damp grit of morning, the sky was torn with bloody shreds of cloud. Pirbhai huddled with the others in his group, torquing his back straight when the colonel's grey eyes swept over him. Out of earshot they had a name for him, the Cockerel, for how he stuck out his backside as he walked. He was the one in charge of their wages, ticking off how many yards each worker covered in his leather notebook, deducting the yards not laid, then making some magic calculation that docked more rupees off their pay slips. When one of the workers protested their food rations, the calculation magicked his entire wage away.

By now, there were rumors among the jahaji bhai that the British would give them land if they chose to stay after their contracts were completed. Pirbhai himself had heard two overseers discussing it while he worked. *Dangle the carrot*, they'd said, a phrase that Pirbhai couldn't make sense of despite his growing grasp of English, but unmistakable to his ears was that same word he'd heard on the dhow: *land*.

"Over the next stretch," the colonel was saying, pulling his lips over blackened gums, "there are some obstructions. Abandoned huts. Most of you will stay here to lay down the groundwork. Two of you will come with me to clear the path ahead."

Again, he met Pirbhai's eyes. Pirbhai sucked in his breath, thinking of the extra yards he might earn, letting it go only when the colonel summoned him with a flick of his head.

Soon after, Pirbhai stood beside the colonel and Rakesh. Upon choosing them, the colonel had handed them a packet of matches and an oily jug, which they clutched clumsily as they cut through the thicket of branches, the colonel two steps behind. Only now, at their destination, did Pirbhai realize what they were expected to do.

Before them, in a wide clearing, was a cluster of huts. They were small and round, their walls constructed with a combination of wood and reeds sanded into poles, brittle hefts of spear grass thatched into roofs that hovered above like malnourished hair. By the nearest hut, an overturned bucket waited beside a blackened firepit, the surrounding ground packed smooth by the pounding of feet. A line of fabric was strung out to dry, a salmon kanga and a series of worn white singlets drooping like dead fish.

The colonel cleared his throat. "Like I said: empty."

Pirbhai risked meeting his eyes and saw a flicker of unease there. A dark heat was building in his chest, the matches and jug by his feet. Rakesh was glaring at the laundry, his shoulders slumped.

The colonel eyed the roof of the nearest hut. "Rickety things, anyways. No Indian engineering in sight, hey?" He nodded at them, and in that instant Pirbhai understood what he was meant to believe about himself in order to plow through these lands that were not his.

Sweat pooled in the creases of his elbows. Neither of them said a word; Pirbhai didn't dare. For one dazzling second the face of the man on the dhow swam up before him, the ropes of hair plastered around his neck, the desperation in his eyes as he wrested the wheel from the captain's grip.

The colonel slapped his thigh, making them both jump, and tipped his head as if addressing a pair of schoolboys. "You have one hour."

Behind his back, Pirbhai tensed his fists. Yes sir, he heard himself say, though when the colonel walked away he felt his jaw loosen like it had been clenched for hours.

When he turned back to the clearing, Rakesh was staring at him.

"Let's get out," Rakesh hissed, moving so close that the fog of his breath warmed Pirbhai's cheeks. Instinctively, Pirbhai stepped back.

"Su? We can't—" he began, but Rakesh dropped into a squat, cradling his shorn head in his hands.

"You realize what they're asking us to do? Kill for them. Do their bloody deeds. We're their dogs." He looked up at Pirbhai, his eyes glassy, a sickly sweat pulsing out across his temples. "Dogs."

Pirbhai felt the specter of the colonel behind his back, a ghostly shackle. Before him, he watched his friend tussling with the dirt.

"Rakesh," he murmured, his voice soft, "where would we go? There's nothing around here. We'd die by ourselves—"

"We'll die either way." Rakesh spat between his feet. "We're dying now. Bhaiya! We're dying every day." He scrabbled his fingers in the soil, came up with a fistful of pebbles and red clay. "I can't stay here. I can't stay here. I can't stay. I can't."

Pirbhai dropped to his knees and grasped Rakesh's shoulders, murmuring to quiet his blubbering. He had been waiting for something to break since the day he'd found Rakesh by the tree. Above, a monkey howled.

"You go."

Rakesh opened his eyes, his brows gathering.

"You go. I'll tell them I lost sight of you in the fire."

He could see the understanding settling in Rakesh's face. What he was offering and what he was still planning to do.

"They're not abandoned," Rakesh said. Pirbhai gritted his teeth. Why say it? They knew well enough what happened to men who disobeyed. And if he refused, was Rakesh so naive as to believe that it would make any difference? He thought of his name in the colonel's leather notebook, how these huts would turn into numbers in an equation that might let him send money back home.

"We have nobody. No money. Only this."

Rakesh backed away, scooting on his bottom in the dirt like a child.

"Bhaiya, you don't have to do this, you can choose something else," he pleaded, his voice barely a whimper.

For a moment, Pirbhai believed him. He imagined burying the gasoline, running until their legs gave out, the only fire he'd light being the one to keep the lions away as he watched Rakesh soften into sleep. Then he remembered where he was. The only way to survive was to last the longest, to prove himself the most loyal of them all. *Like I said: empty*, he heard the colonel say over and over. He stood and brushed the soil from his knees.

"I'm staying," he said with intended finality, though his voice came out ragged, weakened by the thought of losing his friend. Rakesh hesitated, his hands hovering around his throat. Pirbhai grasped the damp packet of matches. He watched Rakesh's expression fall, the instant he understood he was alone. Then, kicking his heels, Rakesh was gone.

Pirbhai did not let the moment linger. The sun had grown sharp on the back of his neck, clocking the minutes. He had passed countless settlements like this one as they laid down the tracks. All the occupants would likely be working their farms, tending to cattle, laboring in British cotton and coffee fields. And yet. He coughed twice and waited a minute, two, for someone to hear him and come forth. Legs trembling, he broke into the clearing and circled each hut, peering through the doorways, expecting a face to surface, to meet his eyes and change his mind. But there were none. Pirbhai said a prayer for the small mercy that the colonel was half-right: though the huts were not abandoned, they were empty.

He unscrewed the jug and began to pour the gasoline, soaking the bases before launching the spout up toward the bundled grass. The smell scalded the inside of his nose, stung his eyes. His face was wet. He tossed the empty jug between two of the huts. His bowels loosened. He struck a match.

The dry thatching snapped into flames. The fire roared, cracked against the muggy air.

Pirbhai stumbled backward, falling on his elbows, cowering. Smoke choked his lungs. From behind the ashen plume he saw the outline of a hut, the yawning mouth, and instinctively he knew what lay inside. The sleeping mats rolled neatly in a corner and the brimming water jug and the steel pot hanging on a nail on the wall, the sagging sack of grain and the bar of red soap and the worn clay floor; he saw his mother holding a tin cup to his sister's lips, every detail he had grown up with, every part his own. Something splintered, a roof caving in, and he leapt to his feet. Chest heaving, he watched his home burn before his eyes.

Sonal, 1902

WHEN THE COOLIE ARRIVED AT her deddy's shop to ask for a job, the first thing Sonal noticed was his arms. They were long, lanky, but tight balls of muscle strained against his dirty cotton shirt. She wondered what kind of work he must have done to get arms like those, but then she saw the missing middle finger on his right hand, the nub puckered and flayed like it never properly healed, and the way he hobbled in his too-small chappals like an old kaka though he looked barely twenty, and she knew his line of work.

Deddy was knee-deep in a mud pit out back, piling scraps of torn packaging and rusty tin cans to burn. It was garbage day, and Deddy was never in a good mood on garbage day. He had put Sonal in charge of both the shop and several of her siblings for the morning, while Mummy rallied the youngest few to feed. At the counter, Sonal peeled a worm of dirt from under her fingernail and clicked her tongue at her brother Nanu, who was pretending to twist open a jar of pickles, rolling his eyes back in fake pleasure.

"If Deddy sees you," she warned, but it was ruined by her grin.

Nanu, buoyed, plucked a small sack of sugar from the shelf and hefted it over his shoulder.

"Don't," Sonal said, the smile gone, but she was too late. Nanu tossed the sack toward her, but his arms were reedy and his calculation off. The bag smacked the counter, and sugar ballooned in a golden

19

cloud, the grains settling into every surface like sand. Nanu stared at Sonal, aghast.

Sonal heard the clank of Deddy's shovel and knew there was no time for scolding. She grabbed the rag from the counter and got down on the floor, the crusty granules grating her bare knees. She heard Nanu fetch the broom from the corner, and when a pair of hands appeared next to her, she assumed it was another one of her siblings come to help. But then she noticed the missing finger, the muscled arms, the skin like date palm bark, dark and scarred.

"Almost there," the boy said, as if he knew her, showing his wide, straight teeth. She stood and folded her arms, waiting for him to say who he was, but he just kept working, his head down.

By the time Deddy came back in, Nanu had resacked the dusty sugar and the boy had his hands behind his back as if he had just strolled in to browse. Behind him, out the open door, rows of corrugated iron shanties crowded around the railroad tracks, Kisumu Station coated with a blanket of ocher dust. When no one was looking, Sonal brought a finger to her lips and licked, the shiver of sweet settling thick on the back of her tongue.

The boy's name was Pirbhai. Usually, when traveling Indians wandered into the shop, Mummy would serve them a hot plate of rice and tea and Deddy would order one of the children to pack them some biscuits and soda before they left. Most of them were like her family, sailing over after hearing of the economic prospects here in Kenya, better at least than the high British taxes and the famines that came and went in India. Here, like Deddy, they set up shops or were hired by the colonials, staking out a place between the natives and the mzungu, though they couldn't own land. Sonal's family had come over around the same time the railroad construction began, knowing that the British liked their comforts—matches, tea, canned fish, cigarettes, toothpaste—all goods the dukan now sold. This boy with the grubby shirt and quick eyes was the first coolie to come in.

Deddy was sucking on a date seed, his gaze fixed on Pirbhai, appraising him like he was a horse.

"You're a Hindu?" was the first question Deddy asked him, in response to his plea for work. "You're honest?" was the second. Sonal held her breath even as he answered yes to both, knowing as one of nine children that they could scarcely afford another mouth to feed.

"You'll sleep in the back of the shop, keep an eye on it overnight. I can't pay you but there'll be a roof over your head and food in your stomach," Deddy said finally, inspecting the dirt in the creases of his palms as if he didn't care either way, even as Pirbhai bowed and breathed a hungry "Yes."

For a moment, Sonal was shocked. How Deddy had beaten her when he caught her adding a spoonful of sugar to the watery dal, screaming that he was not a rich man and she was no rani. Every shilling the dukan made, Deddy scrimped and poured right back into the shop. Their own food came from the land, the soil they worked until yams and ginger nosed up, beans and okra flowering around their quarters. She looked back at the boy, his eyes lowered and lips blistered as if he'd been sleeping many days under the sun, and wondered what Deddy had seen to let him stay. But then Deddy turned around and swiped a finger across the counter, and when he lifted it, grains of sugar clung to the pad.

"Show him where he'll sleep," Deddy instructed her, a bent smile on his face as he walked away, and she knew then that he had seen it all.

As far as Sonal could tell, the coolie's arrival changed little in their home. He came with almost nothing—a few shirts and a scroll of paper—and demanded even less. Deddy still lashed out at them and cursed; Mummy still pulled in her lips like she wanted to swallow them as she whisked the little ones away. Sonal wasn't sure how much Pirbhai saw: he kept to himself, taking his meals in the storage room where he slept on a gunnysack, not even a mosquito net or a rope mat to his name, and working quietly as he restocked the grain or sharpened the display of knives. She was impressed with how easily he slipped between English, Swahili, and Gujarati depending on the customer, how he didn't hesitate in switching the prices. This was something Deddy had trained them to do for as long as Sonal could remember. Triple the price for the whites who could afford much more, double the price for the Africans who knew no better but couldn't afford as much. By Deddy's rules, only fellow Indians got the actual price.

Pirbhai had worked out quickly which natives they were friendly with, how they'd swap a sack of millet for a bunch of matoke, how they'd share tinctures against the macchar and cart each other's wares inside in the harried moments before the rains. Like her, he'd learned how to slice the cake of soap with a thin string and what it meant when someone wanted kawaida—for the white men, a cigarette that Pirbhai rolled with his good hand, for the local children, simsim or coconut mandazi freshly fried in leftover oil until they pillowed—though unlike her, Pirbhai never snuck himself a bite. She had seen, too, how he chased the dogs from the neighbor's store cupboards, swatting at their toothy snouts with his bare hands, and when a British man walked in and barked orders like Pirbhai was a dog, he did something spectacular: he passed the tub of kerosene over and, in perfectly inflected English, quadrupled the price, the calculation effortless behind his blank eyes.

On several occasions Sonal overheard Deddy chiding Pirbhai for using too much water, although he only bathed once a week, and when Mummy dropped boiling chai on him once she did scarcely more than toss him a rag. But Sonal knew it was all a show, because they couldn't complain: he was careful, focused, and his work was good.

But his arrival changed something for her. She felt his eyes on her sometimes, the way she did now, as she pressed labels onto jars in

22

the storage room while he swept. Cartons of salt and rolls of tobacco cluttered the shelves, kept high to guard against rats. She noticed him squinting at the label she'd just pasted to a jug, his lips moving ever so slightly as if trying to make sense of her handwriting.

"Cooking oil," she said, and saw the recognition spark in his eyes. It only now dawned on her that he couldn't read. On the next label, she wrote the letters larger, as if for a child.

"Cloves," she said deliberately as she stuck the label down. Then, afraid she'd been too obvious, she added, "Good for toothaches and for keeping out the bugs."

"Fire ants everywhere," he agreed, swiping the broom in steady, even strokes. Sonal adjusted her misshapen dress over her knees, for the first time wishing Mummy would stitch her something nicer.

"There are ants out there where we sleep too," she said, jerking her head toward the mats lining the extension behind the shop. She wanted him to know that it wasn't intentional, him sleeping with the ants and with rats gnawing his toes every night.

Pirbhai shrugged. "It was worse before."

"On the railroad?" she blurted, then bit her lip. Mummy had warned her not to ask about his work before the dukan, and he never brought it up himself. The furthest back he had spoken about was the day he entered the shop, when a sympathetic Indian stationmaster at Kisumu Station had directed him to Sonal's family, where he'd said he might find a hot meal and a roof for the night. Kind helping kind helping kind, Pirbhai said when he told Sonal this story, with a glimmer in his eye that surprised her. Sonal supposed she understood: her memory of the time before her arrival in Kenya was fickle, a blur of cousins and cramped Dhrangadhra streets and a softly spotted cow that her family had owned. But Sonal had seen the mounds of red earth dotting the tracks, graves that she convinced her siblings were termite mounds, and the questions about what came before bubbled up every time she saw Pirbhai's nubby finger.

He nodded slowly and stilled the fugyo, his injured hand wrapped loose around the handle. Sonal took her chance.

"At the end, when the mzungu said the coolies could go back home. Why stay?"

He glanced away, though she kept her focus on him.

"A lot of my brothers from the camp went back," he said finally.

She remembered the crack of the sea against the ship that had brought her family over, like concrete meeting bone. When their steamer docked in Mombasa she'd seen the weedy dhows rigged up beside it, water pooling as they bayed against the rocks. Wobbly-legged, sick-stomached, she'd wondered how anyone could survive the kala pani in one of those.

Sonal tried to keep him talking. "They're brave, to go back."

He met her gaze. "Brave, hanh. I was afraid of what I might find if I returned. My family..." He drifted off, thumbing the nub of his finger.

She wouldn't let herself look away. "They must be missing you?"

Pirbhai had been slouched against the broom, but now he resumed scraping the fronds across the floor, faster than before.

"It's my duty as the eldest...and soon I'll have land. I'm taking care of it." He turned his back to shake the broom over the doorstep. She had said the wrong thing. Standing, she swatted the dust from her calves, then stopped.

"I'm the eldest too," she said, fixing her eyes on his poised neck, as sunbaked and cracked as a cow patty. "There's a lot for us to watch over. But sometimes I wonder, who's watching out for us?"

He did not turn around, but the swish of the broom stopped. From her pocket she pulled two sticky dates that she'd filched from the box that Deddy had bought from the handcart in the morning. She peeled the dates apart, the syrupy flesh clinging like fingers, and placed one on the shelf near his sleeping sack. Again, she felt his eyes on her as she walked away.

It was a year later that Deddy came to Sonal with his proposition, shaking her awake before the sun. Mummy was already up too, skimming the malai off a pot of milk. Sonal's eyes were gummy and her head pulsed. She had forced herself to stay awake the previous night until all her siblings were asleep, humming low until their faces melted. It had been cold, the ground hard beneath them, and Deddy was not yet on his sleeping mat. Those evenings, her body thrummed like a vulture above the brush. On bad days she would hear Deddy careening through the shop, cursing as he took inventory, as he counted the money they didn't have. Nine children was enough to sustain a business, but too many to be sustained. As the eldest, and a daughter, she often took the blame.

Even now, she could feel the wobble of her left canine, knocked loose by Deddy's palm. That time, Sonal had blamed Mummy. "You don't care about me," she cried, "you never have." She was indignant, blazing with the injustice, not that she had been hurt but that she hadn't been protected. Mummy said little, merely smoothed a paste of crushed leaves soaked in oil over the bruises, her heavy hands working fast. "Don't touch," she cautioned as Sonal winced. When Mummy walked away, Sonal wiped off the warm oil, not wanting to give her mother the satisfaction of doing so little and believing it enough. Her fingers came away stinging and bitter.

This time, the night air was still. When Deddy emerged from the shop, adrenaline simmered under her skin. But his step was light and careful as he trod around the small bodies lumped under the sheets. When he passed her, he paused, meeting her eyes through the dark. "Sleep off, dikri," he murmured, and walked to his own mat.

It was so early when Deddy woke her the next morning that only the loneliest birds were calling out, their fragile cries piercing the indigo sky. Then Deddy told her that she would marry the coolie and move with him to Kampala to work in Deddy's cousins' pharmacy and send money back here. They would cross the border from Kenya to Uganda and make a new life.

Immediately, Sonal looked at Mummy. Here, finally, would be a sign that her mother cared for her, and she waited for Mummy to fight to keep her as Deddy tried to send her away. But when she met Mummy's eyes over the steaming pot, a plea burned there instead, bright and sure. She knew then that it had been Mummy's idea. And she knew, too, why Deddy had woken her before the birds, before the neighbors, before her brothers and sisters—so that she couldn't yell, couldn't even ask questions, could only sit with her tongue frozen in her mouth, as silent as her mother.

Days later, Sonal overheard Deddy speaking to Pirbhai. She was bathing her sister with a bucket at the end of the yard, her arms soaked to the elbow as wet trails of dirt trickled down the girl's shoulders. Whenever Sonal passed Pirbhai she'd wondered if he knew. She had heard that Kampala was orderly, neat streets of whitewashed government buildings and the whole city split up into different quarters— European, Asian, African—so different from the tangle of banana and cashew trees here and the way Indian groundnut sellers mingled with African barbers, trading this for that and chatting under the long shade of the mbuyu tree. She couldn't imagine what it would be like to exist apart like that, to draw lines through the same soil. She wanted to ask if he had thought about marriage before, if he was imagining it all those times she caught his gaze lingering on her, studying the small stud in her left nostril or the white half-moons of her fingernails. She too had found herself roving his face, the way his top lip protruded when he focused, how his shins were scored like mango bark. But she feared sounding childish, worried she'd make him laugh in that way he sometimes did when Mummy-Deddy poked fun at him, a hacking sound peeling from his throat, his eyes black pits.

She watched now as Pirbhai approached Mummy, who was crouched over a pot on the fire. She poured chai into a tin cup, but when he turned to take it back to his quarters, Mummy slapped the wet spoon against his shin.

"My husband wants to talk to you," she said gravely. Deddy emerged from behind the dividing wall at the back of the compound, where the toilet pit collected black flies, and squatted beside them. Sonal worked suds into her sister's hair, not wanting to show that she was listening. Her sister cooed and slapped at the water, and when Sonal next looked up, Pirbhai was clawing his fingers into the rusted ground.

"Uncle, I can work harder, I'll wake up earlier—" he was stuttering. Sonal paused, confused about what Deddy had told him to make him act this way. Deddy held up a hand.

"Bas. You have served us well, but you can't stay here any longer. I have watched you, and I see you are a careful worker, and becoming a good man."

Pirbhai's face drained of color. Deddy blew on his tea.

"Thank you," Pirbhai finally croaked.

"Look at him, so scared." Mummy snorted. "Straighten your back, son. These coolies, always looking down."

Pirbhai's spine snapped straight. Deddy laughed with Mummy, but their expressions were warm. Then Deddy boxed his shoulders and told Pirbhai what Sonal knew. She watched, not bothering to look busy, even as her sister tugged at her hair and dribbled water down her kurti.

"But...why?" Pirbhai asked.

"You told me you were honest, and you've proved yourself true. You may be simple, but you are noble. It's time for my eldest to marry, and together you can increase our family's fortunes. You can help us more if you leave, make a life for yourself and my daughter." His eyes twinkled. "I'm a businessman, see? I know a good investment when I see one."

Sonal was holding her breath. Pirbhai gazed from one parent to the other, both silent now, their faces expectant. Then he turned to her. His forehead was heavy, but when he saw her the lines softened away.

Instead of looking down as she knew she should, Sonal stared straight back. His eyes searched hers, unmoored. Something in her opened. She wiped the hair off her forehead and left a wet smear there, glistening like sand in the sun.

When Sonal and Pirbhai were ready to leave, only the children cried. Weighed down by a satchel that Mummy had packed full, Sonal lifted her chin as she said goodbye. Pirbhai toed at a bristled caterpillar in the dirt. Deddy planted a light kiss on Sonal's forehead, then mumbled an excuse about checking on the shop and disappeared inside. Several of the children clung onto them, mashing their snotty faces into their clean traveling clothes. Sonal stroked their hair and whispered soothing words, promising to be back. Sniffling, they turned to the dukan.

Nanu stood to the side, holding the muscles of his face tight as a mask. Standing there with his arms behind his back, taller than Sonal now, he appeared almost a man, but the round of his cheeks betrayed him, as did the anxious waver of his eyebrows as Sonal approached. She wanted to fold him into her arms, rock him to sleep as she had all those years. Instead she cupped his chin and said, "You have to take care of them now."

A boyish fear slid across his face; then it was gone, and he tipped back his head and shrugged. "Don't worry, sister," he said.

When it was time to go, Mummy made no move to embrace either of them. Hands hidden in the folds of her sari, she stood before the door, legs wide and feet planted into the soil as if to say she would never leave.

"Aawjo, Mummy," Sonal said.

"Thank you for everything," Pirbhai added.

Still, Mummy said nothing, her lips pressed together, her breath whistling through her nose. She was solid, unmoving, and she held her posture as they turned toward the road. When Sonal glanced back, she was still there, watching them, and for a moment Sonal considered Pirbhai's mother, and wondered if she too had gone silent with the loss of her child, powerless to do anything but stand and wait for their return.

The wind cracked against the tarp above their heads, the only separation between their bodies and the night. An owl crooned and Pirbhai shuddered at the feral sound. As they moved inland toward Uganda, past the reaches of the railroad, Pirbhai had receded further into himself. They were traveling west, following the curve of Lake Victoria, hitching rides where they could on donkey carts transporting pumpkins and sacks of cassava. "If only the train went this way," Sonal had joked once, to which Pirbhai had not responded.

The sun held them apart, his skin darkening next to her wheatish brown, but in the moonlight they were the same. Sonal stroked her thumb against his breastbone.

"It's okay," he said, to her, to himself, she wasn't sure.

Sonal laughed. "What else scares you?"

Her hair was matted where it had slipped out of her braid, and there were bluish smudges on her shoulder from carrying the bags, which she had refused to let him take. She wondered if her demeanor surprised him now that they were alone, but away from her family she felt loosened, the voice she had scarcely made known in the dukan now liberated. *A married woman*, she kept repeating to herself as they walked, her mangalsutra a new force between her breasts.

"Having nowhere left to go. And ... " he faltered.

"And?" When he spoke she could focus on nothing else, his words rising to her from some cloudy place that she desperately wanted to know.

"Being alone," he finished.

She nodded, remembering the panic in his face when he'd thought Deddy was kicking him out. Then she sat up, her tunic shrugging off one shoulder, and grasped his hands in her own. She traced her thumb over the stub of his middle finger, which he'd admitted had been sliced clean from a rock hammer on the railroad. He winced, though he'd said there was no pain anymore. But the gesture was intimate, as if she could feel the memory that lived in that space, as if by touching it she was absorbing some of the past.

"My family too," she said. "We had to leave them."

Pirbhai touched her cheek, his eyes urgent. "What your family did for me. When so much was taken—I didn't deserve their kindness. They gave me a home."

Sonal was moved by his disclosure, so vulnerable it had the air of a confession. "Listen." She pressed his palm against her so that he might feel the blood surging beneath her goosefleshed skin. On the previous nights they had touched, their curious mouths finding each other in the dark. But this was different: the insistence of her hand on his, the desire to bear something for him, not offering but simply taking what she could, so that now, held between them, its weight lessened.

"We'll keep carrying them," she murmured, and Pirbhai squeezed her hand back, and she knew he would do everything he could to hold on.

Sonal, 1917

SONAL EYED HER DAUGHTERS FROM the outdoor hearth down the lane from their home. Blue tongues of fire licked her bare arms as she slapped a bhakri over the flame. The ground beneath her chappals was littered with foil candy wrappers, the marketplace reclaimed from the swamps. She shifted her squat, the weight of her thickening belly grinding down on her knees.

The girls were playing war with the neighbors' children, hollering and kicking up red dust. A fair-skinned boy had smudged charcoal under his eyes and shouldered a niimu branch like a rifle. Some of the other girls were clasping their fists and crying, playing abandoned wives, but Sonal's two girls had tied Pirbhai's handkerchiefs around their heads like nurses. Her eldest, Sarita, was smoothing a paste of mud over another child's calf, the flick of her wrists reminiscent of Sonal's own hands as she worked. Sonal chuckled. Sarita was practically born in the pharmacy, and now at ten years old she was methodical, attuned to the smallest shifts in the wind. But not Varsha. Sonal watched now as her younger daughter tore the kerchief from her hair and stamped it into the dirt, then grabbed for the rifle in the boy's arms. The boy jabbed the branch into her flat chest and yelled, *DSHOOM*.

"Mumma!" Varsha screamed, clutching her heart as if a wound really bloomed there. The smell of burnt lott surged. Sonal pushed to her feet, but the bulk of her belly rocked her back and the ground swam.

Inside her, the baby kicked in protest. When her vision settled, she saw that Sarita had already collected Varsha in her arms, covering her sticky hair with kisses. She glanced at Sonal with a stern eye that seemed to say, *you stay there.*

Sonal sighed. Most days she couldn't believe she had another one on the way. Their room was stuffed full, partitioned from the next family only by a row of shorn gunnysacks pinned to the ceiling. Between sending money back to Sonal's parents in Kisumu and to Pirbhai's family in Porbandar, they had barely enough for themselves. But Pirbhai was adamant that they send money to his mother every month, his brow furrowed as he slowly drafted the letters. The previous month he had sent a little extra to support the marriage of his youngest sister; though he was often private about what he wrote in his letters—out of modesty or embarrassment at his fledgling script, Sonal wasn't sure—this time he'd asked Sonal how to write *many happy returns of the day.* "Our girls matter too," Sonal had snapped, but she too felt the tether of her siblings' lives.

It was mere weeks after Varsha's birth when the neighbors began bringing around ghee-soaked gund pak rolled with poppy seeds to encourage the womb to conceive a boy. Sonal had thanked the doting kakis, then buried the sweets in the yard. They never spoke of it, but Pirbhai seemed to agree that they would stop trying. Maybe when things are easier, they thought. After we get our land, Pirbhai once said. This pregnancy, years later, came as a surprise. But Sonal caught the glitter of hope in Pirbhai's eye when she told him, the shine that only the prospect of a boy could elicit.

She dusted ash from her fingertips. The fair-skinned boy had abandoned his gun and was squatted beneath the matunda vine with the rest of the children, playing seven stones. What good was it to bring a boy into this world? It was wartime. Sonal had watched boys with skin as hairless as babies heading to the front line in Tanganyika, looking like mules laden with their tin debe and sleeping bag. Maybe

32

once, a boy child meant permanence, continuity, but now it meant only heartbreak.

Sonal tucked the bhakri into her kikapu, brimming with leaves and berries she'd collected to brew dawa, and signaled to her girls that she was heading home. She passed the whitewashed walls of the pharmacy, a chalky replica of the buildings in the European quarters, marked with shaky English letters that read DRUG-STOR. Behind it, Kampala's hills rose high, their dense neighborhood hidden between their verdant folds. A mzee on a bicycle sped past, the air in his wake scented like salted groundnuts. She paused to retch into the bush before realizing she was ravenous. When she reached the stoop of their home, the women gathered out front shuffled to make room, clucking at her sweaty cheeks and pulling the kikapu from her arms.

"It's peak sun, Sonal, come sit," Meena said, dabbing her hairline with her dupatta.

Sonal obliged, her knees on fire. The women could often be found here in the afternoons, taking refuge from the heat and their responsibilities for a few moments of gossip and cane juice. Afiya, who Sonal had first met at the pharmacy when her son had malaria, pulled a guava from her wrapper and held it out. Only once Sonal had swallowed the pulpy flesh, scraping the skin until no white remained, could she speak.

"This baby thinks I'm a rich woman," she said. "Always wanting me to eat."

Afiya laughed and spat her own guava peel into the dirt. "You're looking low. Surely a boy."

"Ndiyo, girls always sit higher in the womb, closer to the heart," Shilpa kaki said.

"Let's just hope your husband is around to see him," Meena said.

Sonal cocked her head. The sun poured over her face and she squinted to see Meena's mouth forming a grim line. "Where would he go?"

Meena exchanged a glance with the others. "The compulsory service order for all men in Uganda, na? Announced today."

Sonal spun to the group, bewildered. Their faces were poised between tired and pitying. Afiya's husband had voluntarily enlisted earlier that year, Meena's husband would be above the age limit, and Shilpa kaki was widowed. Sonal shivered with the sickening realization that Pirbhai might leave them. Shilpa kaki brushed her knuckles over Sonal's belly straining against her kurta. "You'll have us all here to help you," she said.

Sonal stared at the pharmacy across the lane, where Pirbhai was surely restocking the shelves or tending to a customer. The sickly sweet taste of guava scorched her throat. Though the British were fighting the Germans, most of the soldiers were Africans and Indians, so it was really kin being made to fight kin. Devastating their own land and people for a war whose outcome didn't matter: it was domination either way. As far as she was concerned, there was no need to participate in a battle that wasn't theirs. But she knew Pirbhai would see it differently, not as his war but his duty, an extension of something he had long ago begun. His loyalty to their family had kept him from enlisting thus far, but she knew he wouldn't resist if they came for him.

"He's too sick," she said. Pirbhai's body had never recovered from toiling on the railroad, the details of which he still rarely spoke of. But his lungs crackled all night like an ill-tuned radio, and his limp had grown more pronounced each year. Sonal brewed medicines specifically for his combination of ailments, boiling ajmo into his morning tea and massaging his legs with a mixture of roots and herbs every night. Between her time working at the pharmacy and the years spent watching her mother concoct her remedies, she knew what fed pain and what softened it, what cooled the body and what could drive it into a hot, unrelenting fever.

"You're right, the recruiters will see that," Meena said, though her expression was more of mercy than belief.

Sonal stood abruptly. Pricks of white light clouded her eyes, but she stilled herself and turned to the door. "Tell my girls to come soon, hanh?" She didn't bother to look at their faces as she hauled herself up the steps, waving away the hands that reached out to steady her.

Sonal sent Sarita out to collect what she needed for a new medicine, describing the markings on the leaves and the red shine of the berries in precise detail. She knew exactly what to do, and it surprised her how easy it was to brew harm rather than healing. By the time Pirbhai returned, Sonal had steeped the herbs in oil, stripped the twigs of their bark, and boiled the berries to a bloody mush. Now the room smelled sweet and grassy, the balm waiting in a scooped-out tin of Zam-Buk, because despite all that Sonal had learned about medicines, Pirbhai still preferred the official treatments sold at the pharmacy, the ones stamped and sealed in English.

Varsha was sliding rice around the plate when Pirbhai arrived. She flew toward him and smeared yellow dal on his pants. Pirbhai tickled her chin, but her velocity seemed to throw him off balance, and his left foot dragged as he ambled to the mat.

Sarita nudged the plate forward. "Pappa looks hungrier today," she said.

Sonal swiped a dot of mango athanu from Sarita's cheek. So young, and already taking care of her parents. Sonal felt a pull of gratitude for her eldest daughter, who would surely help when the baby came, especially if Pirbhai were gone. She pressed a fist to her ribs to still the nausea. It wouldn't happen, she reminded herself. He would go nowhere—she'd make sure of it.

Pirbhai plucked at the charred edge of a bhakri and licked the crumbs from his thumb. "Fit for a queen," he murmured, pushing it across the plate toward Sarita. Sonal shook her head. It was something he had begun doing when the cost of food rose with the war, pretending he was full although his stomach caved in.

Sarita adjusted an imaginary crown. Some days Pirbhai told the girls they were descended from maharajas, other days that his ancestors were warriors, dancers, cooks. In truth, Sonal didn't know what to believe. She had found the scroll of paper that he had carried from the railroad to Kisumu to Kampala, and read it while he was out. It was a copy of the colonists' ledger prepared on Pirbhai's arrival in Mombasa, detailing his years under contract to work. But whoever had filled it out had mistaken his first name for his full name—*First Name: PIR / Surname: BHAI*—and thus erased his family name from existence. He seemed to have absorbed the mistake into his persona.

Pirbhai prodded at a peanut in the sweet-corn shaak.

"Eat na, before I finish everything. This baby is hungry, I tell you," Sonal said.

Pirbhai smiled, though he made no move. "That's my boy. Eat up."

Sonal eyed him. The work caught up with him some days, though he'd never say so. "Ja, lie down. I'll keep you some batata aside for later." Her breath was quickening, the baby flipping inside her giddily. She trained her eyes on her daughters. "I'm going to give dawa to your pappa. He needs his rest tonight. You don't stand up until this whole plate is empty." Varsha pouted, Sarita nodded solemnly.

On the mattress, Pirbhai had removed his shirt and was knuckling his chest through his faded singlet. Sonal approached with the pot of Zam-Buk. She'd added some mint at the last minute to mask the smell, but the perfume hadn't sunk in. If he was tired enough, he might not notice.

He grunted as she began to work the balm into his leg. Sonal bore down into her knuckles, pushing deep, oiling the place between muscle and bone. Pirbhai's eyes fluttered closed.

"Nanu's still refusing marriage. My sisters wrote to me asking that I speak to him," Sonal said, aiming to distract.

Pirbhai chortled. "Your brother's married to the shop. In his next life he'll be a rat in the storage room."

Sonal tutted her tongue. "He can't only work. It's lonely, na?"

"Word got out about the pharmacy's headache remedy. People coming all from the African and Asian quarters now. A line around the block."

On a normal day Sonal might raise the fact that she was constantly tending to neighbors arriving at their door for her home-brewed medicines—tick bites, heartaches, babies who refused their mother's milk, she had seen it all. But today she said nothing. The paste slipped into the cracked skin around her nails and burned. Already her fingertips were growing numb.

"We're doing well here," Pirbhai said. He spoke sluggishly, as if already asleep.

Sonal sniffed. In a way, this was a dream. Them together, their little life. It's all she had hoped for: a small place for her family, on stable ground, without debts. The herby scent flooded her nose as she worked, floral and bright like Kisumu's trees, like the sting of her father's slap, like her own mother's fingers spreading crushed leaves over her wounds. She felt it then, the power of her mother, what she had hoped to heal by sending Sonal away. Sonal rubbed in the medicine that would weaken Pirbhai's body and understood what it took to take care of a family. *I see now, Mummy*, she wanted to say.

Pirbhai's eyes shuttled back and forth in a dizzied sleep. Sonal wiped her hands on her dupatta and blew cool air over his cheeks. "Just for now," she whispered, "until they're gone." He wouldn't survive a war. Sonal had seen his face when men in the market spoke of the troops walking hundreds of miles bearing heavy loads, when they brought news of lives lost and villages burned. No doubt his body wouldn't carry him through, but the true battle was in his mind. She could see that deep within him he wanted to stand up and claim his fight; that he believed he had something to prove. But his determination to measure up threatened to overtake his good senses. This was for the best, a temporary pain for a life undisturbed.

She crossed to the kitchen, where her daughters were swatting at one another with the fugyo. The baby was calm, and Sonal drummed her belly with numb fingertips, whispering to him her secret, her action that was her love. She whispered: *Let them come.*

Let the recruiters see her, bloated with pregnancy, her daughters, rail-thin and mewling, the shared lot of their home. Let them see her husband, numbed from the knees down, unable to walk, unable to prove what he believed he could do.

Let them come. They would think him incurable, and they would leave. They would come looking for potential, and find none. But they wouldn't look close enough, their attention turned only to him. If they kept looking, they might see hers.

Vinod, 1926

V INOD CHARGED TO THE FIELD, the happiest place he knew. From the edge he could see his house, on the outskirts of the Asian quarters, with only the field separating it from the African ones. He plucked his shirt buttons loose until he felt the hold of school and rules slacken. Some of the other boys showed up in loose clothes spattered with mud and dried dal, but Pappa always made Vinod wear these stiff button-ups like he was one of those European children traipsing to their schools in pressed uniforms.

At his school, the boys teased Vinod for dressing the same way as Pappa at the pharmacy, or joked that Mumma made him drink ng'ombe pee as one of her medicines, and once, Pulin spread a rumor that Vinod's pappa came into the mandir to pray for enough money to pay rent. Pulin's pappa ran the mandir, which meant people believed him. But the boys on the field didn't care about any of that. These boys saw only one thing: Vinod could play.

Vinod and his schoolmate Yaksh arrived at the field, sweet and free. The grass was yellowish in patches and some parts were torn up, pocking the pitch with muddy ruts, but it was theirs. Well, really, it belonged to the boys they met there. Moses, the oldest of the lot, was the one who'd first invited Vinod to play and convinced the others to share the pitch with the Indian watoto, since more bodies meant better cricket matches.

"Eh, Twiga, you made it at last," Moses called. He had given Vinod the nickname because his teeth were straight and wide as a giraffe's. If Vinod was once embarrassed by the name, now it made him proud. He craned his neck and bugged his eyes and bared his twiga teeth.

Moses slung his arm across Vinod's shoulders, bone hitting bone. When Vinod first met Moses, he was surprised to see that their skin was the same shade. Their brown was deeper than Yaksh's, but lighter than the brothers Simon and Joab, who looked like twin bumblebees in the navy shorts and yellow shirts of the mission school kids.

"You come later every day," Moses said. "That school of yours must be nasty."

"At least we don't have to sit at tables and learn to sew like the mzungu," Yaksh said. They all knew the rumors, of the white children sitting in chairs and learning things they could learn at home. It sounded exotic and silly, and they all laughed, although none of them had ever seen a European school in real life.

"Or wear an ugly thing like this," Simon chimed in, plucking at his vomit-yellow shirt. Of all the African boys they met on the field, only Simon and his brother went to school. Their teachers wore something called bloomers, Simon told them, and sometimes they were released from class early because the mzungu's pink skins couldn't take the heat. But aside from those two, the others practically lived at the field. Vinod would see them practicing their back spins when he walked home for lunch, and most of them were still there when he was let out.

"I heard in your muhindi schools they teach you voodoo. Dancing around flames, worshipping monkey gods, eti?" Joab said.

Yaksh jutted out his chin so that he looked like a baby. "Who told you that?"

The brothers exchanged a look. "Our teacher."

Yaksh opened his mouth, but no words came out. Moses huffed a laugh through his nose. "What, they teach you voodoo but they don't teach you how to talk?"

Yaksh's eyes shrank red. "At least I go to school."

Moses sucked in his cheeks. It was no secret that he wanted to go to school too, but his parents couldn't afford the fees. Mostly, he acted like he didn't care, but some days when Simon and Joab peeled off before roll call, his eyes sparked hot.

"I don't need lessons to teach me how to dance around a fire," Moses shot back.

Yaksh balled a fist, but before he could speak, Vinod cut him off, throwing his arms in the air and ululating, shimmying his hips like he'd caught a fever.

"All hail the fire god!" he yowled. Yaksh's eyes popped. Simon cackled and made a show of bowing down until his fingers grazed the dirt. The air simmered. Moses shrugged and looked out at the line of banana trees.

Somewhere, a popat cawed like a referee's whistle. The sky was purpling, reminding them of their precious sliver of time. Joab tossed Vinod a stick. They had enough to go around as bats, and a few prized golf balls, scuffed but still impossibly white, that Moses had snatched from outside the Kampala Country Club. It was Moses and the others who first taught Vinod how to bowl, how to dance down the pitch, and what it meant to deliver a bosey. They were fast and funny and good, and Vinod knew he could play like them if he practiced more. As far as he was concerned, Moses was lucky. Vinod didn't see why he couldn't be here with his friends every day instead of in Teacher-ji's dull, cramped classroom.

The boys fanned out across the pitch. A grasshopper spiraled up from the grass and Vinod bent low, fixed his eyes on the ball in Moses's hand. Tapped his stick one, two, three, against the dirt.

That night, Mumma told Vinod he wasn't to go to the field again. It looked bad, she said, his playing with the African boys and coming home streaked with dirt and sweat. Why stand on the edge, she said, when they're already trying to push you out? Vinod protested, and Mumma said Pappa would explain why when he got home. Vinod thought this impossible: most nights Pappa came home from the pharmacy so tired you could hear his bones creak. He'd puff a beedi in silence by the window while the rest of them ate, retreating to bed while Sarita and Varsha washed up and Mumma forced her dawa down his throat. For years he'd promised to play a match with Vinod, but by now Vinod knew it was more likely that Sarita would come to the field.

But Mumma was right. When Pappa arrived, his whole face beamed. Then he broke the news: he got a job working for the government, repairing motor parts for the mzungu. "We're on our way up," he said through mouthfuls of bhaat, eating like it was Diwali. "Like our people—we come from a long line of rulers."

"I thought we came from farmers," Varsha said.

"Landowners?" Sarita added on.

Pappa batted their words away with his hands. "Doesn't matter, na? We're here now."

When Vinod asked about the field, Pappa said they all had to act the part, show everyone in the community where they stood. Vinod pouted through dinner, flicking mustard seeds to the floor until Mumma whacked him with the bhatiu. But then Pappa sprung up from the ground, his limbs elastic and loose, and retrieved a gunnysack bloated with purple matunda and waxy madaf and a paper cone of boiled sweets. "All for tonight," he announced, before cracking open a matunda and passing it to Vinod. They ate like that, the tart juice fizzing their mouths, until Vinod's belly ached from the sugar, and the sesame brittle glued up his teeth, and all the fruit skins were heaped between them. That night Vinod went to sleep with coconut meat under his nails and a smile on his lips, the field as distant as a forgotten dream.

The living room of Teacher-ji's home smelled like too-ripe ndizi. Sticks of agarbatti smoked and crumbled in the corners as if Teacher-ji was trying to cover the smell. Vinod fidgeted, sweat sheening the foreheads of the twelve other boys.

Pinned to the front wall was an indigo flag, the Union Jack stretching across one corner like an overeager spider. To its right was a small crested crane, sky blue and encased in a beige bubble. Vinod wondered why it was confined to that tiny sphere rather than roaming free across the wet marshlands it loved. At the start of the year, Teacher-ji said that the flag was created because Britain had spread its control all through Uganda, fixing its borders into one united something—a word Vinod didn't understand but that sounded like *protection*, a word he knew. Teacher-ji explained that it meant the British had extended their authority, which made Vinod think of a long fence penning them in, and all the jackals and gorillas straining against it, the cranes trying to hop over with their vast dusty wings.

And schools. *Authority* must mean hundreds of schools mush-rooming up over the country, stale and dreary. Vinod let his pencil go slack.

He jumped as Teacher-ji slapped his workbook. "You've mixed up your *b*'s and *d*'s again."

Vinod squinted at his lines. This never happened when he wrote in Gujarati, but these English letters peeled off the page and shook their spindly legs. In Gujarati every letter was small and equal, and pressed together as if their arms were around each other's shoulders, but in English they stood apart, some letters bigger than others, like a teacher at the front of a room. Still, Pappa insisted that Vinod focus on learning English. He said that speaking it opened the world, and reading it could save lives. When Vinod asked why, Pappa only grew misty and far away, his face puckering as if he were a small boy.

"I can't focus over the hot-rot-banana smell," Vinod retorted. A few

of the boys clucked; Yaksh pinched his nose. Vinod couldn't help it—
he laughed.

Teacher-ji pulled her back straight so that she towered over him.
Yellow flowers of sweat bloomed from the armpits of her salwar.

"Ah, our star comedian. I guess you'll be completing your work
at home."

Vinod groaned.

"Say you're sorry!" Pulin whispered. A red chandlo was freshly
applied to his forehead, and his belly puffed out over his shorts from
all the mandir prasad. Pulin was Teacher-ji's favorite, and adored by all
the neighborhood aunties for playing the cymbals in the mandir band,
but Vinod thought he was a chaplo and a nakamo.

"Gadhedu," Vinod goaded Pulin under his breath. The boys next to
him cackled. Teacher-ji gasped, waiting for him to explain himself, but
Vinod held in his lips. His legs felt jittery, aching for the feel of grass.
He hadn't been to the field since Mumma forbade it.

"Bas! You want to waste your time, then go, play with the African
boys all day. See where that gets you, hanh? Your classmates will be
driving their autos and you'll be carrying your things with your dark
hands. Who will be the donkey then?"

Vinod made two fists, the tears hot behind his eyes. He willed them
not to fall. He knew he wasn't supposed to talk about the field anymore,
but he felt protective. Before he could stop himself, he blurted, "But
Pulin *is* a donkey. He thinks he's better than everyone but he couldn't
score a run if he tried. Not like me. Not like my friends on the field."

The room was quiet. No one ever spoke back to Teacher-ji that way.
They wouldn't dare, because she lived in the neighborhood, knew
all their parents, their aunties and grandparents. Everyone who could
punish them if they were bad.

Teacher-ji leaned back, her eyelids heavy. Vinod thought the ruler
must be coming now, the *crack* sting across his palms. Then she said,
very calm, "I will accompany you home today, Vinod."

Vinod sunk into the floor, the creases of his knees soft with sweat. He would be walloped, by Teacher-ji and then by Mumma.

"Sorry," he choked out in English. Teacher-ji sniffed, but the corner of her mouth lifted in satisfaction.

When all the children were filing out of the classroom, Vinod kicked out his foot, crushing the incense stick until it fizzled.

The heady smell of banana yeast baking into bread wafted from the African quarters as they walked home. They turned up his lane, where the air stunk like fried mhogo. Aunty was settled on a low stool by the door. She lived in the rooms below Vinod's family, as did an older nana who wore knit sweaters in the peak sun and napped on the stoop.

"All okay, beta?" Aunty whispered when she saw Teacher-ji. Vinod kept his eyes low as he slipped off his chappals. They had to walk through Aunty's apartment to get to his own, and Vinod hoped Teacher-ji wouldn't notice the scrolls of yellowing paper peeling off the walls or the floorboard on the second step that had worked loose.

The sounds of Mumma clanking dishes traveled down the stairs. "Eh, gadhedu, what did I tell you about coming inside without washing your hands first?" she called. Vinod held in his delight. As they entered the room, the scowl dropped from Mumma's face. She stretched her spine but her eyes still only reached Teacher-ji's chin. Varsha was crouched by the window, shelling peas in a woven basket.

"Kem cho?" Mumma said, the loose ends of her usual speech cinched in.

Teacher-ji bowed slightly, though her eyes scanned the room. A dishrag had slipped from the table onto the floor, and a mist of flies pulsed around a softening orange. A breeze rustled the string of herbs drying over the window, and an oversweet smell, like something had ripened and split, clung to the room. Beside him, Vinod felt Teacher-ji hold in a breath.

"Bit hot in here, no?" Teacher-ji said, hooking a finger into her collar. Vinod wanted to remind her that it was she who kept them wrangled inside for their lessons every day. Mumma's mouth pinched into a tight, buttonhole smile. She only smiled with her teeth when she was relaxed, her wonky canine snaggling over her lip.

"Is something the matter?"

Teacher-ji's eyes came to rest over Mumma's shoulder. "It seems your son has lost sight of who he is. He thinks he's better than the other boys and that he'd rather be playing. And today, well. He chose to call Chandrabhai's son a"—she paused, cut her eyes straight at Mumma—"gadhedu."

A flush swept up Mumma's throat. "I see," she said. Vinod hung his head, wishing Pulin's pappa hadn't been named.

Teacher-ji waited, as if expecting Mumma to whip out the cane like they did at school. Mumma didn't budge. "We weren't so lucky, my husband and I. We always tell him that he must work harder than anyone else. Don't we, Vinod?"

Before he could respond, Sarita emerged from the stairs, a kikapu of bark slung on her shoulder. Her long hair was braided but a few curls flung about over her forehead, soil smudging her cheek and forearms. Vinod knew she'd been foraging for Mumma, picking from the niimu tree down the road. On seeing Teacher-ji she pressed her hands together.

"Been at the market?" Teacher-ji asked, eyeing the bundle of pointed leaves, the tiny white flowers clustered like mites.

"Just some neighborhood trees," Sarita murmured. Teacher-ji's face shifted from alarm to pity. Vinod wanted to crank her neck to show her the cupboards filled with rice and lott, the makai drying on the stoop. Mumma was always longing for land of their own to plant all the herbs she ever needed.

"Neem, it's excellent for controlling pests," Mumma said. Vinod smiled because he knew she was proud of this: how the neem oil they smeared behind the cupboards made the bugs leave without killing them, simply drove them out. It's a Hindu poison, she said.

Teacher-ji coughed like she'd inhaled a mosquito. "Well. I don't have much need for that in my own home. Thankfully."

The glow in Mumma's smile dimmed. A look transferred between his sisters, Sarita clawing the dirt from her face. Teacher-ji nodded as if something had snapped into place. She spoke to Mumma in English. "We're a small community here. We mustn't forget our place, na? What will people say if they learn how Vinod behaves, who he associates with, and now he's calling other children, *good* children, names?"

Mumma stiffened. Her fingers snaked her pallu into a taut coil as she told Vinod in English that he must listen to his teacher.

Vinod grimaced. The words sounded strangled. Then Mumma turned to Teacher-ji and switched back to Gujarati. "Vinod is a *good* boy too. He will learn what he needs to." She said *good* in English, making a hard *T* sound at the end. Vinod almost expected Teacher-ji to correct her.

Teacher-ji's bun was fastened to her head so that not a single hair moved. Vinod counted the pins, six gleaming millipedes in wet dirt. "He just needs a firmer hand. Usually the father would handle that, but . . ."

Mumma's nose flared. The stud burrowed in her left nostril flashed. "My husband is very busy these days, working for the Transport Department."

The sneer slumped off Teacher-ji's face. In the corner, Varsha stood and stretched. In the last year her kurti had gone tight around her hips, even though her arms were still neem twigs. Vinod wanted to tease her about it, but he held it in. Her face was determined, something brewing between her eyebrows.

"Pappa barely has a chance to drink his chai, the mzungu keep him so busy." Varsha laughed, a sound like a bell. "We always tell him to slow down, he'll burn his tongue. But he says it's the price of success."

Teacher-ji's eyes were calculating. She brushed down her salwar, then turned to Vinod and brought a tentative hand to cup his elbow.

"Well, beta. You tell your pappa I just dropped by to say congratulations."

Vinod noticed the new gentleness of her touch. Mumma grabbed a pot, her name engraved on the side the way everyone did so you'd know who to return it to. She spooned fresh curd into it now and handed it to Teacher-ji. "Homemade," she said, and nodded to the door, her feet rooted wide, hands steady on her hips.

Once Teacher-ji left, Vinod wanted to play, but Mumma snapped that he'd brought enough trouble home for one day. Still, she boiled ginger and hardar in milk and made him drink the whole cup.

"She was impressed with your work," Mumma said when Pappa arrived home, her sari hiked up over her calves as she scoured a pot with a coconut husk. "That woman thinks she can weed us out."

Pappa tapped his nose. "No use worrying about rooting down. Just focus on growing upwards."

Vinod peered into his drink, the bits of black pepper floating like dead macchar in a yellow river. He still didn't understand what had changed for Teacher-ji to slip out that way. And why he had to suffer in her classroom while his silly sisters stayed home and his friends tore down the field. "She said to tell you good job. But I still hate school."

Mumma sucked her teeth, but Pappa beckoned to Vinod. "Look. Your pappa's work for the mzungu has raised our family up, and now your teacher is noticing. So you don't fight it." He snapped his fingers with his whole hand, so loud it echoed. "I've told you, an education is something they can't take away."

Vinod sniffed. "But I—"

Pappa brought his face close to Vinod's, his eyes sharp the way they were only after a smoke. "Diku, you don't like the work, you know what you do?"

"Su?"

"Put your head down. Work harder." Vinod tried to wriggle away, but Pappa kept going, his voice dogged. "Work harder, so that they see you. The more they see you, the less they'll watch you. And when they stop watching, that's when you're free."

For the next week, Vinod stared at the English letters until they blurred. While the other boys were clowning, he focused on pointing his *b*'s away from his *d*'s. At the end of the week, Teacher-ji hovered over him. Still, he refused to lift his head. He heard her murmur *good* as she walked away.

He let his feet lead him after school. The field was lush and waiting. Buttery flowers kissed his ankles as he leapt toward the other boys.

"I'm back!" he yelled. His gut swooped, the sweet punch of soil in his nose. He clapped Moses's shoulder, rubbed his knuckles over Yaksh's hair. It flooded back, that full, unfettered joy. He caught the stick Moses tossed him, the wood slipping into the old grooves of his fingers.

"Let's play a full game," he said.

They settled into natural teams, African and Asian, an invisible line dividing them. The heat was a pulsing, living thing, the sky god-skin blue. Vinod gripped the stick, and that's when he saw him. Pappa, hobbling up the lane toward home. But his dancing legs were gone. His shoulders caved forward, his chin dipping with each painfully measured step. He could have carried on without noticing Vinod, so curved was his spine, but something about his posture moved Vinod to call out to him.

Pappa looked up, blinking into the sun. Vinod held his breath, aware that he stood where he was no longer meant to be. Then Pappa pivoted into the field, stumbling over the pebbled edge. His hair was dislodged from its usual slick parting, one shirttail hanging limp over his belt. Vinod felt suddenly conscious of his own outfit: the mud on his shoes and the brown of his chest peeking through his unbuttoned shirt. He met Pappa's gaze and saw that the earlier glimmer had dulled, his eyes a waiting cloud.

Whatever had happened at work, whatever was wrong, Pappa said nothing. Acting on instinct, Vinod turned to his friends and splayed his arms. "My father, the prime minister," he announced.

A few of the boys cheered. Simon tipped the rim of an invisible cap. Moses lifted his stick with two hands, holding it like an offering. "You play too, sir?" he said.

For a moment, Vinod thought Pappa might accept. But he shook his head, face impassive. "Hapana, better not."

As they fanned out, Vinod was aware of Pappa still standing there, clutching his briefcase, close enough to play. But the others seemed not to mind, whistling and laughing as if nothing was out of place. Vinod sunk his weight down his hips, locked his eyes on Moses's bowling arm the way he'd taught him to. He imagined the strike of bat against ball, felt in his fingers the tingle of scoring a winning run. Then a white flash, and the game was on. The golf ball sliced the wind, and he thought of the crane floating in its tiny allotment. He imagined the wings unfurling, taller than any teacher, the bubble breaking clean. When Yaksh missed the ball, Pappa stooped to grab it, leaving his briefcase in the dirt. Then he threw it, so far they all stumbled to save it. As Vinod's hands closed around the ball he heard a laugh behind him. He turned just in time to catch Pappa's face breaking, sun winking off his bared teeth.

Vinod, 1935

ON THE DAY OF VARSHA'S wedding, neighbors filled the house. Sarita was back from Kenya, where she had moved after marrying her husband, and Vinod had spent the better part of the morning entertaining her toddler with endless rounds of seven stones. Nanumama was visiting too, along with some of Mumma's other siblings and their families, drinking chai on the stoop and fussing over Varsha's hair. Varsha herself exuded an air of radiance that was perhaps due to her pithi ceremony the night before, her skin scrubbed fairer, the yellow paste still staining all of the aunties' fingers.

When Vinod came in from the yard, Sarita's little one slung giggling over his shoulder, Mumma shot him a glare so sharp he nearly dropped him. The boy scuttled off down the hall as Vinod faced Mumma in the kitchen.

"The brother of the bride has duties," she huffed, as if he were a child, though he was now eighteen. She had been on edge for weeks, the prospect of her second daughter leaving home setting in. All morning, between pressing her best sari and feeding the guests, Mumma had returned to her squat above the stove, stirring a pot of something emerald.

Vinod reached to take over her stirring and make himself useful. She elbowed him away.

"Find your father, see what he's up to. Both of you, disappearing like you're too big for all this!"

Vinod wrinkled his nose at the pot, which had begun to froth. "Su che?"

Mumma opened her mouth, then shook her head firmly. "A women's matter."

Vinod remembered the morning of Sarita's wedding several years ago, when he had walked in on Mumma giving Sarita a vial of liquid, a tangy scent trailing between them. Mumma was whisking now with the kind of intensity that told him she would be entertaining no more of his questions.

He found Pappa among the crowd on the stoop. Since the guests began to arrive, Pappa had played host with a rare display of vigor, constantly refilling plates and slipping in morsels about the wedding: how the groom, Naren, was an accountant at a cotton ginnery, how the silk for Varsha's bridal sari was imported from India, how he had personally met the flower vendor to handpick the blooms for the ceremony. Many nights, Vinod had heard Mumma cursing Pappa for going above their means, and Pappa repeating that he was the bride's father, that it was his duty. *I will do no less*, he had said. Sarita, the level-headed one, had always been there in the past to calm their tempers, but without her around, their fights had escalated, Mumma shrieking, Pappa slapping the table. In the next room, Vinod and Varsha would exchange looks, neither of them wanting to confront their battle the way Sarita would. Vinod was shaken by how the absence of one sibling could change everything.

Upon seeing Vinod, Pappa splayed his arms. "Ah, my son."

Vinod was disconcerted by the attention. In the months leading to this day, Mumma and Pappa had been so busy they'd scarcely had a moment for him. It had allowed him a kind of freedom he'd come to relish, playing cricket with his friends until the sun blinked out. The independence of these last few weeks had opened a space of possibility inside him, though what might fill it he wasn't sure.

"You're next, isn't it," an auntie giggled, reaching out to pinch his cheek.

Pappa looked about to respond, but Vinod laughed and flicked his eyes away. "I've yet to graduate."

Just then, Nanu-mama bobbed up, clapping his back. His hair was pasted to his head with gel, and round silver buttons clasped the sleeves of his patterned shirt. "Don't start on him. I'm sure he's got much more exciting plans."

The auntie flushed at Nanu-mama's attention. There was a shine to everything Nanu-mama did, and if he bestowed his gaze on you, you shone too. Vinod had always admired him, all the times he had come to visit. Now he leaned into Vinod's ear and whispered, "Your pappa asked me to pick up his suit from the tailor's. Walk with me?"

Relieved to escape the commotion of home, Vinod matched his uncle's stride down the narrow street, skipping over a scrawl of pink puppies squirming across their mother's exposed belly. His uncle had taken over the dukan that he and Mumma had grown up in after their parents died. The shop, he told them, had prospered with the cities along the railroad, turning from a gritty shack into a thriving fixture in Kisumu.

"Don't let the marriage talk bother you. It's just what people say at weddings."

"It's not that I don't want that..." Vinod trailed off. The wedding preparations had made him realize that he wasn't ready for such a thing. All the girls in his community knew his family too well; they knew where his father worked, had come for his mother's medicines, had eaten his sisters' food and heard them bicker through the walls. Between all of that, Vinod himself disappeared.

Nanu-mama cut his eyes to Vinod. Only now did Vinod notice how his uncle walked, with chest thrust forward and elbows back. Instinctively, Vinod lifted his chin.

"You've always been like me. Doing things your own way."

Nanu-mama himself had never married, and even Mumma seemed resigned to his bachelorhood. And yet Vinod had always thought him to be happy, moving about as he pleased. Nanu-mama stepped aside to let two boys piled on a bicycle pass. "Don't let them limit you. You could do anything. Go away to college. Become a big man. A film star!"

Vinod chuckled. "I have thought about college." It was true that he had, though not with much seriousness. He'd heard of it happening— boys heading to India or winning scholarships to study in England and America. He had never much enjoyed school, but college held the promise of more than just studies: it meant somewhere with room to dream. It was a path his parents could be proud of, the way they were proud of his sisters' marriages. He imagined reading beneath the polished white columns of a library somewhere, blundering with his friends in the mess halls. The idea had always seemed far off to him, and yet walking beside his uncle it felt within reach.

Nanu-mama tousled Vinod's hair and then gently patted it back into place. "That's more like it," he beamed, and Vinod couldn't help but grin back.

Inside the tailor's shop, motes of dust swiveled in a shaft of sunlight. Africans and Asians alike came to this tailor, since his work was higher quality and cheaper than anywhere else, though gossip said that the African tailors were growing resentful. Standing from his green Singer whirring on the floor, the tailor peered at Vinod. He had a tape measure draped around his neck and a series of pins embedded in the hem of his shirt.

Vinod pressed his hands together. "We're here for my father's suit."

The tailor grunted. "So he sends his son to do his deeds. I hope he sent you with the money too?"

Vinod exchanged a glance with Nanu-mama, who was running his fingers absently over a sheaf of crushed silk. They had paid for all the wedding outfits up front, months ago. Vinod said as much.

The tailor snorted. "Oho, is that so? Did your pappa not tell you that he came in here last week, wanting an English suit made new for the wedding? I'll pay on receipt, with extra for the rush order, he says?"

Vinod gulped. Despite his height over the tailor, he felt small in his gaze. Pappa had mentioned no such thing; as far as Vinod knew, his father would be wearing a cream kurta pajama to match Vinod's own. "He didn't—how much..." Vinod wanted to shrink into the racks of musty clothes.

The tailor stated the price. "I made it fast. My finest work, the finest fabric. No loan, no credit. Not this time." He raised both hands in defense.

Vinod couldn't speak. What had Pappa meant by this, buying a new suit without warning them?

Nanu-mama stepped around Vinod, his billfold outstretched. "What is this nonsense, 'not this time'? Good man, you've become suspicious in your age. We're here to pay, not to cheat you. It's all there." He held out a stack of bills. After a moment, the tailor accepted with both hands.

Nanu-mama brushed a scrap of fabric off his lapel, his silver cufflinks glinting. He raised a hand to the tailor, then turned and strode out. When he was gone, the tailor flung the suit at Vinod. His lips were twisted, eyes hard.

Vinod raised the suit in an awkward gesture of appreciation, averting his eyes when the tailor shook his head in disapproval. He was still his father's son. By the time he hurried out, Nanu-mama was already half-way down the street, red dust marking the hems of his crisp trousers. Even still he looked elegant, striding with purpose, a man people paid attention to.

"See?" he hissed when Vinod caught up to him, slapping the dust from his shins. "Become a big man."

In the lane outside home, Varsha was practicing her bridal walk, staring boldly ahead until Sarita snapped her fingers. "Head down! You should be demure." Varsha shrugged. "I have nothing to hide," she said with a laugh, but she tucked her chin a little lower, swept down her gaze. They were radiant, Varsha's sari kumkum red, Sarita in peach stitched with mirrors. Vinod wanted to tell them they looked beautiful, but he felt embarrassed, as if they had grown and he had stayed a child. He pulled himself inside instead, clutching the suit.

By the dresser, Vinod shoved his legs into his kurta pajama, twisting the rust-colored chunni around his neck. Only as he was attempting to rake down his hair did Pappa enter. With the comb lodged by his ear, Vinod jerked his chin to the suit draped across the bed. He watched Pappa caress the stiff material, then lift the suit like a sleeping child.

"Mumma said we're leaving soon," Vinod said, unsure how to address what had happened.

Pappa nodded. "I'll just be ek minute."

"The tailor said— You're not wearing the kurta?" It wasn't what he'd meant to say. The comb was jammed in his fist, the tines pricking his palm.

Pappa swept his eyes over Vinod in his fitted outfit buttoned to the neck. A smile pulled at his lips. "Look at you. Remarkable. We'll all be our best today. Everyone will see."

"But Nanu-mama had to— Did you know?"

Pappa's eyes grew unfocused. "Your uncle was returning a favor. I helped his family once, long ago." He began to unbutton the suit jacket, fumbling slightly with his hand that was missing a finger. "We take and return. Sometimes we must take more, and sometimes we can give more. It's all just...balance." He slipped his arms through the jacket, tugging at the lapels. It was exquisitely crafted, tapered to Pappa's thin frame, softening the hard lines of his body. He stepped to Vinod, and a shadow of apprehension flickered in his eyes. "Is this all right?"

Through the bars on the window behind Pappa, Vinod could see his sisters resplendent in the sun, Mumma hastening to meet them, sweeping Sarita's son onto her hip despite the heavy drape of her sari. All of them, being their best. Pappa wanted it not just for himself, but for them all. Vinod reached out and picked a stray thread from Pappa's collar, a remnant of the tailor's shop. "Forget Varsha—everyone will be looking at you," he said, and though Pappa waved the thought away with his hands, for a moment the shadow that always followed his father, the fear that he was not enough, vanished.

Flowers of every shade draped the mandap in the mandir courtyard, tiny bells tied to the ends of the garlands so that the air was filled with a gentle chime. Vinod brought plates of food to the elders and nudged candles from the paths of trailing saris, heeding Mumma's warning about his duties. He felt his life shifting. He was the youngest, and a boy, and so had always been doted on. Now, as he tended to the guests, he couldn't help but imagine that this was his future, as the only child left at home, as the son who would have to provide. Nanu-mama's counsel to go to college and make something of himself had grown in weight since the incident at the tailor's. He didn't want to be in his fifties and still snatching favors from his juniors; to disappear beneath the life that was waiting for him, never to be known.

The pandit droned on as Varsha and Naren fed palmfuls of rice and rose petals to the flames. Guests watched from the shade of the cashew trees, children flitting between legs with heat-flushed cheeks. For a moment, Vinod wished he could join them. But then the couple stood to begin the pheras, garlands rustling as Naren led Varsha around and around the fire, and by the seventh time they were married, the crowd vah-vah-ing and Mumma laughing and the pride on Pappa's face so vast it seemed at any moment it might burst.

If Pappa had wanted to show them at their best, he had succeeded.

The tent sparkled, the sky glorious with early evening sun. The long table sagged beneath all the food cooked by Mumma, Sarita, and the aunties in the neighborhood, jalebi gleaming orange with saffron, the air sweet with roasted maize, the sufuria of steaming white rice large enough for a child's bath. In his suit, Pappa seemed to walk straighter, and though Mumma's neck was ringed with sweat, she shone with grace. Vinod watched the joy stretch across Varsha's face, the twinkle in Naren's eyes as he took her hennaed hand, and imagined himself standing on the deck of a ship, skin salty and cool as he sailed off to university. A delicious shiver spooled down his spine.

After the ceremony, as the guests ate and roamed the shaded court-yard, Vinod spied Pulin and some other friends lolling around the mithai table. There was a girl among them, a lily wound through her braid and chandeliers in her ears. Vinod strode over and bowed.

"Brother of the bride at your service," he said. The group laughed and murmured their congratulations, though not the girl, who was dusting pollen from the shoulder of her blouse.

"The pressure's on for you now, na?" Pulin said.

Vinod shrugged at his bare toes. The grass beneath his feet was coarse and prickly, reminding him of the field he'd once loved above all else. "I'm not thinking about it yet."

The girl met his eyes. He had seen her around the mandir before, he now realized. Her family owned a trading business and was building a new house farther up the hill. From up there, Vinod's neighborhood would barely be a smudge.

"It's good to have other plans," she said. "You have the freedom."

One of the other boys was nodding, the silver threads sewn into his kurta glittering. "That's right. I'm sitting my exams to go abroad. There's a ship cabin with my name on it waiting in Mombasa. All I'm figuring out is where it will take me."

The girl raised her eyebrows. The chandeliers in her ears swung against the curve of her necklace. Only beside her did Vinod realize that his sisters' necks were bare, the jewels in Sarita's ears the same ones Mumma had given her on her wedding day, taken from her own ears. A group of uncles jostled past them, and Vinod noticed that most of them were wearing English suits like Pappa's, grey and formfitting. In the sea of custom-made suits, Pappa hardly stood apart.

Before Vinod knew it, the words fell from his mouth. "I'm studying in India next year."

Pulin swiveled to face him. Vinod took pains not to meet his gaze, keeping his voice even. He'd said it now; he had to continue.

"Hanh, I'll be at one of the universities there, reading math. We're just sorting my passage over..." He'd been nervous that they might see through him, but as he spoke it became real, the ocean clear and infinite behind him as he stepped off into a new land, one he knew only through language and blood. The boys hummed their approval and the girl angled her body toward him, raising her chin as if admiring a statue.

"Your parents must be proud," she said.

Vinod flushed with hope, but just as he was about to respond, Mumma jutted in and tapped his cheek playfully, her bangle knocking against his jawbone.

"Meena-kaki hasn't eaten yet, she's looking faint," she said, before naming a string of other guests who were near catatonic by Vinod's neglect. Vinod shrugged his apology to his friends, who waved him off unfazed. His heart beat hard through his kurta. Their reactions had crystallized what he'd felt earlier. He could become something more, someone to be proud of.

When they returned home that night, Vinod entered as if after years away. He wondered how the little concrete stoop would look to him after the intricate Indian architecture, whether the machungwa and matoke trees were different over there. Beside him, Mumma sighed and Pappa kept blotting his nose with his handkerchief. Varsha was gone from their home. Where Sarita had been solemn on her wedding night, her brows drawn as she swiped the dust from her elders' feet, Varsha had been lighter, kissing Vinod goodbye on the cheek and giggling as Naren led her away. Though Mumma was silent on the walk home, Pappa had leaned so heavily on her arm that she huffed that she was a woman, not a walking stick. "You remember the difference?" she teased as Pappa dabbed at his eyes.

Now, without all their friends and family packed in, their home somehow felt smaller. Still, Vinod was buoyant with the knowledge that he too could leave soon. He floated into the kitchen and seized the pot dramatically from Mumma to boil tea.

"Taking his responsibilities as the only child left seriously," Mumma sniffled, though she dropped the knob of ginger and sunk into a chair.

When he came to the table with the cups, Mumma and Pappa both seemed bereft, the glow from the kerosene lamp flickering across their faces. Pappa took a small sip, then pushed the tea away. Mumma put down her cup with precision before taking Pappa's hand in her own. She worked the point of her thumb into the soft tendon in his wrist, massaging until Pappa closed his eyes.

"She's in good hands," Mumma said.

"Both our daughters are secure now. We made sure of it." Pappa let out a sigh and leaned back in his chair. "What more could we wish for?"

Mumma nodded. "The gods granted our highest wish. And today—" She glanced at Pappa's jacket draped over the back of his chair, a little rumpled but otherwise spotless. If she'd been angry about the suit, she'd let it pass. Her face sagged, the poise she'd exuded all day giving way to a softness she rarely let show. "It was more than we could have hoped."

Vinod blew on the skin of his tea, listening to his parents console each other. He wondered what other desires they had allowed them-selves, shared between them and alone.

"I've been thinking more about my future," he said.

Mumma slurped her tea. "All the aunties today saying you're next, you're next, na?"

"Don't worry about that, dikro. You have time yet. Better things on the horizon." Pappa winked knowingly.

Vinod nodded, encouraged. "Right. And I've been thinking, I'd like to pursue a degree."

"There's no colleges here," Mumma said distractedly, slapping at a macchar.

"That's right. I mean, in India." Vinod ground his thumbs into the rim of the cup, the tin sharp against his skin.

The quiet lengthened between them. Pappa cleared his throat but seemed unable to find words. Finally, Mumma said, "Who gave you that idea?"

Vinod sat up. "Many people are doing it. Sailing to India, England, America even! There's scholarships for it. And of course I'd come back and work here—"

Mumma cut him off. "Which people?" Vinod paused. "Which boys?" she repeated. He realized she wasn't asking for names. He thought of the shimmering threads woven into the boy's shirt, the student who arrived at school in a beetle-black Bentley. He thought of Nanu-mama, so sure of himself and yet untethered—no parents, no children—gliding through the world with ease. He slumped in his seat.

"No one," he mumbled. The pandit's voice broke into his mind, narrating the seven duties as the couple glided around the fire: *nourish-ment, responsibility, devotion, loyalty*...Mumma watched him, and her face was not angry but disappointed. He felt chided, as if he'd exposed his most selfish wants.

When he looked up, Vinod had the sense that they were both seeing him for the first time. He wanted to be himself, steady and rising. But he knew it now, with a certainty that caught his breath: if he was his own person, it would always be in relation to them.

Vinod pressed his toes into the rug, on the only ground he had ever known. He had let himself get caught up in a fantasy that wasn't his own. This was his home, where he would always be. "I just thought it could be good for us," he said, but hearing it out loud, he knew it wasn't true.

Pappa and Mumma eyed each other. Mumma had undone her bun so that her hair trailed over her shoulders in gentle waves, and just then Vinod imagined his mother as a girl, the eight younger siblings she'd cared for, and Pappa as a boy, before he lost his finger, traveling the other way across the very sea that Vinod had been imagining, his fate unknown. His father had never spoken of India, and now Vinod was unsure how he'd imagined Pappa would respond, if there was something in his memory that he couldn't touch. He had been foolish to even speak his hungers. For the first time in a day of weeping, his eyes stung.

Pappa's voice was strained. "I talked to someone at the mandir today who offered to set you up with a job. He runs a big tea-coffee trading company. I meant to surprise you."

Vinod couldn't raise his eyes from the table. He recalled the girl at the mandir, whose father Pappa had likely been speaking to at the very same time. His skin seethed—at the thought of the girl learning of his lie, but even more so at the knowledge that he had revealed his ugliest belief to his parents: that he wanted more than they could offer, that he thought himself better. And yet his father had secured him a job; his mother had sent her two daughters off with salves to ease their passage into married life, or perhaps to save them from trouble. His face smarted. They were here now—no suits, no flowers—bared only to themselves. Whatever his dreams, he belonged here, with them. He bowed his head and silently vowed to never again take for granted what he had. He would not be the one to diminish them.

He looked up. Their faces were taut, softened only with hurt. He remembered Varsha gazing at Naren that very morning, her face bright and serene, and Mumma's and Pappa's, dazzling in their pride. To make a face shine like that, Vinod thought, even as his own fell: that was an ambition on its own.

Pirbhai, 1946

I T WAS UNSPOKEN BETWEEN THEM: Pirbhai wrote the letters to his sisters in Gujarati, and Sonal addressed them in English to mail to India. He had never mastered writing English, even after studying Vinod's childhood workbooks by the light of the window each night. But Sonal made nothing of it when she sealed the envelopes, and like this their marriage carried on.

He drained his chai and dabbed his mustache with his handkerchief. Sonal had hinted that he should shave it off now that his hairs were growing in more white than black, but he liked the distinction it gave him. He would mail the letter on his way to work. His stomach fluttered as he pictured his eldest sister reading his request. He hoped she would take it as a sign of his deference, a hint that he still needed her after decades of sending money back home.

He hadn't seen his family in nearly fifty years. His mother was gone, his middle sister too. What remained between them was a thin thread, just the occasional letter with significant news—weddings, births, deaths—and the money. The leaps in life always surprised him, how one letter announced his nephew's wedding, and the next would reveal the birth of his first child. For a long time Pirbhai had sensed the thread thinning, unable to sustain itself. He needed to ask for something, to spool them a little closer, make clear that he was still theirs.

A marriage for Vinod. It was time. It had pained Pirbhai to hear of his son's wish to sail away all those years ago, and shamed him that he couldn't fulfill it. He had wanted to shake his son, and also promise him more. But he hadn't needed to. Vinod had spun around and set his eyes on where he already was. How steadfastly he committed to expanding their life. After ten years at the tea-coffee trading office, he could afford to rent an apartment in a compound midway up the hill, with yellow frangipani spilling over the gates and more rooms than they needed. Room, Vinod had said when he first brought them to see the place, to grow.

His son's salary had led them forward, while his own salary linked them to the past. Pirbhai had realized this the first time he sent money home, while working at the pharmacy after moving to Kampala. It was an event that passed without ceremony, Pirbhai embarrassed at how late and small his fulfillment of his duty, Sonal aware that they were expected to send money back not only to his family but to her own. They understood then that they were moored. Wherever they went, whatever they became, they would always remain tied to the homes that had borne them.

For decades he had harbored a resentment toward the Indian recruiter who had tricked him onto the dhow. The memory eclipsed the ones that came before, the man's oily skin, the weight of a coin in his palm, the moment his life shifted course irreparably. And yet, with time, he had seen—begrudgingly—that they were not so different. The recruiter would have made money for each thumbprint he inked, just as Pirbhai had for each yard of railroad laid. Perhaps the recruiter, too, had had to adopt the belief that he was more deserving—how else to commit such cruelty, to rob others of their homes?

Some days still, Pirbhai recalled the morning he had watched the huts burn. It came to him most frequently in sleep, the match between his fingers, the crackle of thatching, the tongue of heat searing his own skin. But in his dreams, he saw the aftermath too, what he hadn't lingered to witness. The ash supple as sand between his toes. The steel cooking pot in the dirt, blackened like charred remains. The villagers returning to no village. The silence of the forest after the last embers died, every creature fled and gone. Perhaps once he had entertained the thought of returning home, but he had made a choice to ensure his survival here, and though he still carried the weight of that calculation in his heart, he was determined that it would not be in vain. However many letters he wrote, it was here, on this land, that he too would turn to ash.

Pirbhai and Sonal scarcely spoke of their pasts in India. How could they, when it was their leaving that had brought them together? If they were to return, it was only to each other. Working beside Sonal in her father's shop, and in all the years since, Pirbhai trusted nothing more than what she nurtured with her hands. Even the way she clipped the children's toenails, locking their legs in her lap and pinching the small toes so they felt no fear at the blade, astonished him. He was always afraid his hands would slip, and too often he gave in to the children's squirming, their pleas to be let free. Perhaps they too sensed his apprehension. Some days his wife's sheer force grated on him, and he feared that her aptitude only signaled his lack. But however much they quarreled, he could never begrudge her. She had led him away from the site of his pain and offered him another life.

Pirbhai laced his shoes and plucked the envelope from the table. The mouth flapped open—she hadn't sealed it after all. He brought it to his lips to lick the glue but stopped short, noticing a smaller scroll of paper tucked behind his own. It had been torn hastily from a yellow notepad and filled from margin to margin with Sonal's tight, even hand. Curiosity stirred him.

My dear sisters, she wrote. Pirbhai paused. His wife had never met his family. And yet it was distinctly like Sonal for that not to matter. Since they left Kisumu he had never known her to withhold anything— advice, bitterness, love. Pirbhai scanned her pleasantries, questions about this niece and that cousin, names he himself scarcely recalled. Then the ink darkened, as if in seriousness. *I am writing to tell you what my husband will not, being the humble and unassuming man that he is. We are doing well here. Our son, Vinod, has lifted our family in a way unimagined to us both. We hope the match will reflect the place where we now stand.*

Pirbhai read it again. It was bold, yet sly, both her request as well as her secrecy. Who was she to barge into his affairs, challenge his authority with her precise, barefaced words? His skin prickled at her defiance. He considered crumpling the note, pitching it to the wind.

His eye fell on a line she had squeezed in at the bottom: *we hope for many happy returns.* And he recalled, then, how it was Sonal who had taught him to read and write when he worked in her father's dukan. Even then she had attempted to protect his ego, never saying she was teaching him outright, instead reading the labels in the storage room aloud and dropping a pencil by his sleeping mat one night. He had known what she was doing, of course, but it was the fact that they'd never spoken of it, that she expected no praise or reward, that let him trust her. She had allowed him that dignity. When he wrote his first letter to his family on his own after years of asking his railroad mates to do so on his behalf, he felt in her gaze a quiet pride, and in himself, a bud of possibility. More than any tool, she had given him that.

He read those words again, *my dear sisters*, and imagined her writing them. And he saw in them what he'd always known of her, her honesty and her loyalty, the twin to her unreservedness, how shamelessly she fought for what she believed. Here it was, plainly: she wanted more for Vinod. Their family was proof that such mobility was possible in Uganda, unlike in India. She believed him, all of them, worthy.

He knew then he wouldn't mention the note. If he did, he would have to reprimand her for undermining him. Anything less and he would be forced to contend with how she had called him *unassuming*, when on another day she might have instead chosen to say *meek*, or

67

spineless, or *a coward*. Indeed, his cheeks flushed remembering past fights, how in their last moments she would thrust these insults, as if stoking the final embers. *My dear sisters.* He wondered how many other times she had tucked a note into his letters, when else she had trailed after him, demanding more where his resolve faltered. He wondered, as he pressed the envelope closed, what other fortunes in their life could be traced back to her.

Rajni, 1947

I N HER MOTHER'S BEDROOM IN their Karachi home, Rajni outlined her eyes with kajal. Behind her, Ma scraped her hair into a tight plait that reached her waist, braiding a string of jasmine into the last few inches. The radio announced something about a Hindu mandir set aflame, but Ma shot out her hand and clicked it off. Rajni caught her own gaze in the polished tin mirror. Aged by the makeup that Ma had swiped across her face, her resemblance to her mother was more striking, the same wide, flat nose and deep-set eyes.

"Ma." Rajni winced as she tugged at a loose strand.

"Don't move so much," Ma snapped back, raking coconut oil through the halo of fuzz that framed Rajni's temples. "You need to impress today."

"I always impress." Rajni laughed, catching her mother's eyes in the mirror. Ma swatted her on the shoulder.

"Modesty impresses," she said.

Rajni ran her finger along the border of her emerald sari, which was puckered with deep blue embroidery. When her parents came to her about yet another suitor, she shrugged. Though several boys from the mandir community had made visits, so far Rajni's parents had turned each one down, their reasons obscure, not that Rajni minded. She'd barely glanced up when they raised this next one, Vinod something or

69

other, who would arrive for chai on a Saturday afternoon. What was one more?

"If I'm going to marry this man, shouldn't he see me as I am?" she asked, a smirk at her lips. Ma scoffed.

"You expect a man to respect you if he first sees you in your nightdress? Maybe you shouldn't take a bath, either."

Playfully, Rajni shimmied out of Ma's grip, dabbing at her makeup with the back of her hand. "Let me just wipe this all off then."

"Arre," Ma growled, yanking Rajni's braid back so that her scalp sang. When Rajni searched for Ma's eyes in the mirror again, her expression was stony. Unsettled by this new gravity, the smirk slipped from her face.

"It'll be okay, Ma. I've done this many times before."

Ma cracked the elastic around the bottom of her braid. Rajni felt the sting at her hairline. "And how have those worked out? It wouldn't hurt you to take this more seriously."

Finished, Ma wiped her fingers against her stomach and stepped back. She glanced out the window to the street—once, twice—then noticed Rajni watching her and sighed. Ever since the riots began, Ma kept close watch on what time Bapu left the house, hovering by the window when it was nearing the time he should be back.

The night before, Rajni had heard her parents whispering in the kitchen as she lay on her pallet with her youngest brother curled beside her, arguing about when was the right time to go. "Leaving is as unsafe as staying," Ma had said. "Don't pretend you know nothing of the blood trains." And her father's response, muted behind steady palms: "There will come a point when we have no choice."

"Chalo," Ma said now.

Rajni stood and felt the weight of her best sari on her shoulders, the gold bangle threatening to slide off her wrist. Ma straightened a wayward pleat, then looked back at the window. The sky was slate grey, the clouds masking an early moon. Across the harbor, fishing boats flecked the rolling water, the light from a cargo ship illuminating their fragile masts. In the distance a cow moaned, a deep, despairing sound.

"He just went out for milk and bread," Rajni murmured, hoping the simplicity of her father's task would be reassuring against the reality of the riots that were spreading since the dissolution of the British Raj. Rajni's family lived in the Hindu quarters in Karachi, and though they'd always lived alongside their Muslim neighbors with mutual respect, if not kindness, even close friends were turning on one another in the wake of Independence. Sooner or later, their neighborhood would be targeted.

For a moment, a shadow passed over Ma's face, as if she might cry. But as quickly as it appeared, it blew past.

"Yes," she said, "it's just that I need that milk to make the tea."

When Vinod's family arrived—two aunts and a young cousin—Ma ushered them into the sitting room but did not close the door behind them. Rajni stood in the hallway, waiting for her cue to enter. She watched as the two aunts perched themselves on the flowered settee; the girl settled on the floor by their feet. The older aunt's hair was ragged, her sari a washed-out grey. Rajni brought a finger to the jewels pulling at her ears, noting that all their ears were bare. The younger aunt shifted her hips on the settee, then lowered herself to the floor beside the girl with a grunt. Her skin was pocked and sat loose on her bones. Rajni smothered her laughter against her hand. Surely her parents were thinking the same thing, that this family couldn't be the one.

The very thought of leaving her family home to share a bed with a stranger was frightening. Her friends and cousins had not been so fortunate as to be given time, but Rajni's parents were particular. They had never treated her like a burden. As a child, she remembered passing Bapu in the courtyard of her school where he was the headmaster, how he would wink at her or feign a bow, and how it made her feel special, like a gift. Even now that she no longer went to school, Ma would insist that the cooking was finished so that Rajni could go read. Book in hand, Rajni would hear her mother's knife slicing hard against the table.

Rajni trusted her family. In all her nineteen years, her parents had scarcely given her reason to doubt them. Each time another hopeful suitor was turned away, she felt this trust widen around her, like the ever-growing rings around a tree's core.

Ma and Bapu were looking from one sweat-flushed face to the next, and Rajni tried to guess at who would be the first to ask the obvious question. Finally, Bapu said in a timid voice, "And are the men on their way?"

The older aunt broke into a smile, revealing evenly spaced teeth. "Not today." The girl on the floor stifled a giggle behind her chunni.

Rajni craned her neck to see the women's expressions, wondering if they were being mocked. Bapu perched himself delicately on the frayed wicker stool. "Forgive me, will Vinod and Pirbhai be joining us soon? My daughter is just readying the tea."

In spite of what was happening before them, Ma and Bapu appeared meek, their voices reserved. Rajni wanted to catch their eyes, to share a knowing glance as they often would minutes into a meeting, a quick exchange that let Rajni know they were unimpressed. But both Ma and Bapu kept their faces angled away from the hallway, their shoulders held stiff. A current surged through Rajni's body, a desire to yell or smash a cup, something to make them react.

"Tell the girl to bring the tea," the eldest aunt said. "The men will not be coming."

Hearing her cue, Rajni tore her gaze from her parents and entered the room, her footsteps slow and eyes lowered like a bride, a tray laden with teacups balanced in her arms. As she approached the settee, she couldn't help but stare at these bold women. The marriage meetings all blurred together in her mind—the preening, the questions about what she could cook and how well she could mend a shirtsleeve, the rough grabbing of her elbow as she poured tea, proclaiming her too thin. Finally, here was something memorable. She offered the silver box of sweets to Vinod's cousin, who eagerly stuck her fingers in and pulled out a pale shard of kaju katli. The girl broke the diamond into three and offered it to her aunts, who each accepted a piece.

"Na, na, take your own, dikri," Bapu said, nudging Rajni to offer the box again, but the younger aunt shook her head.

"Times are hard on all of us right now," she said. "Who knows when the next shop will be looted, when our own houses will be attacked?"

She said it so earnestly that Rajni gazed down into her rheumy eyes.

"Just yesterday, my neighbor's daughter was taken by armed goondas. When her brother tried to fight the mob off, they stabbed him on the spot, in front of his family. She was fourteen, a pretty chokri. A great difficulty, to have daughters at this time." The aunt looked straight at Ma and Bapu, her eyes narrowed as if challenging them to disagree. That same reckless urge pulsed through Rajni and she clenched her fists, daring her parents to notice her. To her surprise, Ma nodded.

"Yes. A great difficulty now."

The deference in Ma's voice, the surrender in it, shook Rajni. She thought of the bite in their jokes that morning and wondered who was this tame woman beside her. Her wrists trembled as she set the tray down, and the elder aunt raised her eyebrows, likely thinking she was frightened by the story of the kidnapped girl. Beside her, Bapu glanced up at the small brass statue of Ganesh perched above the doorframe, his burnished trunk curving up in greeting.

They had heard similar stories of women being stolen, raped, killed, of pregnant women disemboweled, of babies snatched from their mothers' arms and smashed against the road. Men, too, beaten and burned and hung from trees. All in the name of nationhood.

Bloodshed erupting on both sides of the new border. Hindus in Muslim-dominated areas, Muslims in Hindu-dominated areas: divided as they were, their future had become the same. Uncertain. Expendable. Rajni's father had instructed her to carry mirchi powder at all times to fling in the eyes of potential attackers, though some of Rajni's friends had been bade to do much worse to themselves to protect their honor. Still, Rajni felt her mother's words as sharply as the sting of hairs pulled that morning, without warning, from the root.

The younger aunt stood. Her knees bowed outward and seemed to sag under her slight frame. Rajni had seen many adults like this, their bodies appearing at once young and old, as if they hadn't fully outgrown the vestiges of their childhood.

"Times have been hard for so long," she began. "We lost my sister during the drought. It happened not long after Pirbhai left us." She took a long, audible breath. "And it will only become worse with Partition. Already, many in our community have left for Hindu country. The lucky ones have a way out."

Rajni bit her cheek to stop herself from speaking out of turn. An uneasy feeling coiled in her gut as Bapu clasped his hands in momentary prayer.

"Yes, we've been making arrangements for my wife and sons to cross first, but..." His words trailed away.

"But even then, you know the risks. Girls, especially young, lovely ones, are the greatest risk of all." The elder aunt was watching Rajni as she spoke, and Rajni fought the desire to stare back and reveal her immodesty.

Ma made a noise in the back of her throat. Bapu wrung his hands. In tandem, both aunts leaned back and raised their chins. Even the girl seemed to inflate, a smug smile creeping across her face. Rajni felt as if she were still in the hallway, her family on one side of the wall and she on the other.

The young aunt fished behind her blouse and pulled forth a small

74

square of paper. A photograph. She passed it to Bapu, who peered down for a moment, then handed it to Ma.

"That's Vinod. He just got a promotion at the coffee-tea export company where he works. Pirbhai started from nothing, and look what his son has made for himself. Uganda's rising star. The only thing missing now is a wife."

Rajni's body lurched. Finally she felt the heat of Ma's gaze, but her eyes were locked on the aunt who had spoken, and who now regarded her pointedly, a smile rising on her sallow face.

"Uganda?" No one admonished her for her question.

"There are many Indians there, many opportunities. Vinod is well respected in the mandir community. And best of all, none of this violence and corruption. In Kampala, you will never have to fear going outside."

The impulse flooded back, and this time Rajni couldn't control it. She spun to her mother, expecting to see her own horror mirrored on the face that so resembled hers. Instead, Ma's expression was as calm as the pond behind the house. Only her bottom lip betrayed a sadness, quivering as she spoke.

"A good opportunity for our only daughter," she whispered, voice tight with restraint, as she passed the photo to Rajni.

When Rajni examined the faded black-and-white image, she saw a boy of no more than eight in starched shorts and a button-down shirt, his thick hair parted at the side and swooping low over one eye. It was always like this with the pictures: families rarely had more than one photo to show for their children. At one marriage meeting, Rajni had been presented with a photograph of a nearly naked baby.

Rajni searched the background behind the boy for some clue about Uganda. What she saw seemed familiar: a dusty street, banana trees arching high into the air, the sky clear and cloudless. Just like India, she told herself, though her stomach churned.

Rajni drew her toe through the red dust, drawing a line between herself and her two brothers. Harish squatted on the ground, prodding at an injured moth by his bare feet. Mohan hopped from one foot to the other, his voice rising into a squeal.

"Rajubhen's going to marry without a husband," he tittered. Harish giggled, pinning the moth to the ground with his thumb.

"Don't say that," Rajni said. Mohan spun in a circle, spraying up dirt. Rajni swatted at the air and coughed.

"No-men-in-Uganda, no-men-in-Uganda," Mohan sang, wiggling his slim hips left and right. He was rarely serious, his gap-toothed grin a constant, his laughter erupting with a force too great for his size. Rajni tucked her lips into her mouth so as not to smile and delivered a kick to his bottom. Harish cackled as Mohan rubbed the seat of his shorts.

"Ow."

Rajni wiped her hands on her thighs, dirtying the cotton kurti she had changed into after the meeting. "You deserved it. How can I be a wife without a husband? And anyways, I'm not going."

Harish looked up from his perch. "You don't have to go?" he asked.

Mohan had recently begun going to school, and Harish, alone at home with Ma and Rajni all day, had grown serious in his brother's absence, a wrinkle developing between his brows. Rajni crouched down so they were level.

"It's too far..." She trailed off as the sound of metal tearing shattered the still evening air. Mohan glanced anxiously over his shoulder, though Harish hardly flinched. Rajni wondered how much her brothers understood of all that was happening around them. That this soil they had always played in had been given a new name, and that it was only a matter of time before they were all forced to leave home.

Something in the distance caught her eye. A burning spike spitting sparks into the dim street, voices rising into one tremulous cry. *Pakistan zindabad!* Mohan stepped toward Rajni. All traces of his teasing from earlier disappeared; he was only a child, looking to her for safety.

"Chalo, inside," she whispered, trying to keep her voice even. Mohan hurried toward the door, Rajni behind him. At the entrance she turned and saw Harish still crouched low, his nose close to the moth flipping in the dust.

"Let that go!" she snapped. Startled, he leapt up and ran to join them. His chin trembled as he squeezed past her into the house. As Rajni shut the door behind her, she saw that one of the wings had detached from the moth's body, white as ash in the pale moonlight.

Rajni, Ma, Bapu, Mohan, and Harish sat on the floor around the low table, a steel pitcher of water and a pot of rice between them. Outside, the crickets groaned. Several hours had passed since the visitors left, hours in which no one spoke of what had happened, Ma dicing bhinda in the kitchen and Bapu listening to the neighbor recount that day's crimes and killings like a shopping list.

Rajni tried to imagine the family in Uganda, splicing characters to the names she had gleaned. She tried to picture their home, and herself in it, but the background escaped her, and each time she found herself imagining her own house, the orange bougainvillea creeping across the metal awning like a curtain of sun.

But now, as had been the case each time a suitor visited, the hour had arrived when they would sit together and discuss, reaching their final decision before they would eat.

In the past, it had been easy, Bapu always making the first judgment. *Kumar's son has a club leg, he could do much worse than our daughter. Did you see how Shankar's mother looked at Rajni's ears and neck, like she was buying jewelry? Wouldn't want her as a mother-in-law. That boy has no prospects, his family business is dying. Better to find a boy with a good modern job, no?* Taking his cue, Ma would pile on: *This one has no ambition. That one's too short.* And Rajni had only to listen, quietly relieved.

But today's meeting stood apart. Those other boys came polished, skin flaxen and collars buttoned, their mothers draped in lush fabrics, their fathers flashing their family's merits like jewels. Those other boys all lived here in Karachi, where Rajni was born, or at least in Gujarat, their family's roots. These women were coarse, and yet they were self-possessed, unconcerned with their appearance, arriving without any men. Almost as if they knew that those other boys, shiny as they were, lacked the crucial merit they could offer.

It was Ma who spoke first, digging the heels of her hands into her lap as if kneading the lott.

"Bharat uncle has known that family for a long time. Good people, he tells us. We mustn't judge by how they appeared, sari and hair and all. Over here they might be village folk, but in Uganda they've moved up. Made a name in the city."

Rajni waited. How could she be expected to decide on a man she had never met? The aunts, enthralling in their brashness, hadn't seemed fazed by that detail.

Bapu picked at a loose thread in his sarong. "Bilkoobhai told me today that his shop was raided last night. Men with daggers nearly killed his wife behind the counter. Tore down her images of Lakshmi and made her swear that there was only one god." He winced.

Rajni knew it was happening the other way too, Hindus burning Qurans and ambushing innocent Muslims. She also knew that as a woman, it mattered little which side she belonged to.

"In Uganda, none of this," Ma said.

Rajni looked between her parents, taking in their misted eyes, the way her mother kept glancing out the window, an impulse even when the entirety of their family was in the room. She thought she could feel the ground shudder with the procession of people outside, hear the crack of kerosene torches against the wet fog.

"You knew they lived in Uganda," she blurted. She hadn't known it until she said it, and now she saw that it was true. She had heard Bapu's words, that Ma and the boys would cross over first, but only now did she see how she wasn't part of that calculation. They had planned to ship her away all along.

Her parents exchanged a glance, though Ma quickly averted her gaze. After a long pause, she said, "Yes."

Rajni recoiled. Everything around her only made her angrier: the hurt in Ma's eyes, the outline of a question on Bapu's face, the way Mohan gasped as if it were a radio drama, as if he understood any of it at all.

"How could you send me away?" Her voice rose as the betrayal ballooned in her chest.

As if in answer, a howl rippled through the window, raw as cracked skin. Mohan clutched at Rajni's arm, his nails pinching her flesh.

"It's a djinn?" Harish whispered, the crease reappearing at the bridge of his nose.

The smell of smoke mingled with the haze of the agarbatti sticks burning in the corner of the room. A series of blistering pops ensued like giant stones cascading over metal.

"Just a drum," Bapu said to Harish, the muscles in his jaw held still. Rajni squinted at him, but he refused her gaze.

Ma's face was set in a scowl. "You think this is easy for us either? You think this is what we want, to be away from you?"

Rajni shrank against her anger, Harish cowering by her side. Bapu stayed silent, mashing his lips as if trying to trap something alive inside his mouth.

The quiet after the scream was too empty. A pressure was building in Rajni's skull. She emptied her lungs of breath, and as she did, she felt her certainty slipping away.

"But what about all of you?" The question emerged before she had time to think, and her voice broke.

Tentatively, Ma slid her hand across the table and kneaded the skin between Rajni's thumb and forefinger as she had done since Rajni was a child.

"Dikri," she said, "you don't need to worry about us. That isn't your duty."

Bapu nodded. "We will be fine," he added, "and better if we know that you're safe."

Harish began to whimper, and Rajni cupped his small face against her side. Feeling his pulse beneath her fingers, she understood that her parents were making a sacrifice. That she had been a part of their calculation, but the equation itself had shifted, skewing safety above all else. That they were offering her a survival surer than any they could give themselves.

Bapu met her gaze. "If you say no, we won't force you."

Ma's head teetered from side to side, even as her eyes swelled and spilled.

It was this final tenderness that broke Rajni. The grace of being given a choice. She thought of the blue suitcase that had lain untouched beneath her parents' bed for years, soon to be filled with her belongings. *No*, she wanted to cry, *I won't go, I won't leave you*.

Instead, she dipped her hand into the pot of rice and scooped a mound onto their shared plate, pushing it toward her parents.

Bapu and Ma understood then that the discussion was over, the decision made. Wordlessly, they reached toward the plate and began to eat.

Rajni, 1948

HER FIRST CHILD WAS BORN to rain. Mvua. In Swahili the word lacked the softness of its Gujarati counterpart, the hushed sounds that mimicked raindrops on hot stone, though perhaps it was not a fault of the language but of her own lack of fluency, the new words falling heavy and malformed from her tongue. Binti. Mtoto. She realized that her child would always know the language of this land better than she did. With this consciousness came a deep loneliness. Part of her child, the one whose fluids still coated the insides of her thighs, would always be unknowable to her.

The moment the nurse laid the baby on her breast, she knew. A girl. Her hair was dark and plastered to her tiny scalp, her pupils so dilated she looked more animal than anything else. At her bedside, Vinod whispered as if afraid to disturb the baby, but Rajni couldn't hear him over the beating in her head, and this annoyed her, that he was already more attuned to the child's needs than to her own. She wanted only her mother. The baby opened her mouth, her tongue startlingly pink. A darkness swooped through Rajni's core. She turned her face to the window, the rain cutting patterns through the ocher dust.

Then the baby was gone, the ceiling fan soothing the sticky imprint left on her skin. "She's just tired," Vinod said to the nurse, sounding apologetic. Rajni had watched Vinod bring his lips to the baby's eyes, and when he came up, his own were wet with love. He was a decade older than her, and though she had worried that this would be a source of difficulty between them, she had found him to be lighthearted and untroubled, so that she sometimes felt like the elder one. And yet now, watching him hold their daughter with such seriousness, her own body fragile and yearning to be nursed, she had never felt more like a child.

She was already pregnant when the telegram arrived. She had held the near-translucent page in her swollen fingers, eager for the first word from her family since her arrival in Kampala, and read it over and over until her knees gave. In six words, the telegram notified her that her two brothers had been killed in the migration out of newly formed Pakistan. MOHAN & HARISH PERISHED EN ROUTE.

She remembered how Mohan would look to her as if she could dispel all danger, the shadow of a grin on his lips. How Harish had played in the dirt, oblivious to the threat around him, until she called him to safety. She would not forgive herself for leaving them.

She hadn't known she wanted a son until the girl was laid on her breast. Then it was clear. She had a daughter, and her brothers were gone. Even with all the power of her body, she couldn't bring them back.

She arrived into a home that wanted her. Yet she herself had never before felt so alone. The journey from Karachi to Mombasa via steamer took one month, the longest time Rajni had ever spent on her own, although the ship was packed full, the saris strung between the bunks the only separation among them. Though she made friends on the ship, taking her meals with a group of young women who were all traveling unaccompanied or with small children, each night she went to sleep feeling a little more hollow, as if a part of her were leaking into the dark sea. In that untethered space she felt another self flickering inside her, splintering apart.

Her new family met her at the station in Mombasa—Pappa, Mumma, and Vinod—and the four of them sat together on the train to Kampala in near silence, Pappa squeezing his hands as if to keep them from trembling, Mumma gazing wistfully out the window, and only Vinod making small attempts at conversation, though mostly they revolved around her needs—was she thirsty, could he buy her some oranges, had she slept well on the ship?—as if she were merely a body to tend to. She sat subdued, wondering how much of herself remained.

Vinod, it seemed, had made a choice to accept her from the moment he laid eyes on her. He was sensitive to her, if a little nervous, and she got the feeling that he had resolved to do what he could to love her. She supposed that was marriage—resolving to care for another. Yet she herself had made only the choice to leave, though she had done so for love of her family, not of Vinod. The first time he touched her, gingerly stroking her arm before asking if she would prefer lemon soda or orange, she knew she too would have to find the resolve to love him—that to build a passage across the void she felt would require attention, work.

In her blue suitcase she had carried jewelry, her best clothes. Knotted into the sari she departed and arrived in was a dark river stone Mohan had given her before she set sail, ridged on one side as if carrying the ghost of an ancient body. Harish, not understanding the permanence of her leaving, had asked as she gathered him in her arms if he could accompany her to the market the next time she went for vegetables. Of course, she told him, unable to say anything more.

Though the rest of her belongings were unpacked into cupboards and shelves, the stone she tucked into the inner flap of her suitcase. She could not bear to erode it with her fingers and blunt its surface. It carried many ghosts now, not just her brothers but the land they had all left. Like a fossil, it bore only a fragment of the life they had lived.

Vinod took pains to compliment even her simplest morning chai, met her at home for lunch no matter his work schedule, and on Saturdays bought her hot mandazi or groundnuts roasted in salt as they wandered through town. They would walk beyond the row of stuffy Asian shops until they reached the wide European ones, guarded by doormen who made sure the customers were as white as the mannequins, and though Rajni was surprised by the segregation in this city, her consciousness felt so pinned to Vinod by her side—*her husband*, she kept thinking, *here, forever, with her husband*—that the world beyond them took on the hazy quality of a dream. She stiffened at his advances, though she softened one afternoon when he asked her what she wanted. Seeing the line of street vendors, she answered that she wasn't hungry, only for him to laugh and say, *no, matlab, in life.* She sensed then that something within him truly had hopes for their life together, beyond duty and daily comfort. And she saw how hard he was trying—that what she had mistaken for advances were really kindnesses.

Her mother had told her that the Indians who crossed the black waters to East Africa had become a new caste, and Rajni saw that it was true. They had foods she had never before tasted—lemon chili mhogo and peanut stew, their own blended language and customs. But their mandir smelled the same, like warm ghee and sandalwood, and they too slept beneath mosquito nets and poured water over their front stoops to calm the roiling dust. For every startling difference, she found a likeness that soothed her. She began recounting these observations to Vinod, who, having never been to India, responded with enthusiasm and wonder. She felt she could say anything and he would believe her. "But back in India, the men are much better-looking," she told him once, holding her face straight at his shock until she broke into a mischievous smile, and they both laughed.

Still, it was only at night that Rajni fully loosened. In those strange hours before dawn when even the crickets had taken rest, when the emptiness threatened to swallow her, she turned to him. She would tug anxiously at his drawstrings, unable to move fast enough, and he would wake and kiss her hands and guide them beneath his clothes. They would make love urgently, silencing one another with their mouths, the sheets growing warm with breath. Over time, the line between an amorphous yearning and desire began to blur. She would clamp her legs tight around him until she felt her own power, rising as a wave, filling what was hollowed with greed.

Those mornings, she would wake as if from a dream self, one who was brash and open to the world. A past self, perhaps. Her mother-in-law had told her once that her own marriage had granted her freedom: that in marrying Pirbhai she was given the chance to move, speak her mind, build her own future. But Rajni could not relate. Back home, she had already been free. Her parents had made certain of it. It was as if the choice she had made to leave them was the final one, or at least the only one that now mattered. In their letters since her brothers' deaths her parents had grown distant, a formality seeping in where there was once intimacy, one more loss than she could bear.

For months after the news of her brothers, Rajni turned away from Vinod at night, her mangalsutra constricting her neck. It was simple enough to blame it on her pregnancy, and he never spoke a word against her needs during those months. But she knew that it was not just a baby growing inside her, but a new resentment, as solid and expanding as the child itself. It was Vinod who had taken her from her family, Vinod the reason why she would never again see her Karachi, her brothers. Those nights she would grow cold with fear: at the ferocity of her own bitterness and at the knowledge that she had nowhere else to turn. She could only swallow it down and keep trying.

Now here she was, a mother. She had lost her family and gained another. Her departure had borne this child. But there was no balance, no restitution. One would never heal the other. There was merely loss alongside love.

When she was eight months pregnant, Vinod took her on an outing. By then her feet were permanently swollen and her breasts tender. She couldn't stand the thought of plodding down the streets to the pili pili bazaar, even the suggestion of the scent of jackfruit and nutmeg turning her stomach. But Vinod was adamant, a glint in his eye. They arrived at a hairdresser's. The shop was small and pink-tiled, bustling with Asian women and a few Africans, the walls pasted with magazine cutouts of white women with blonde ringlets, though it was doubtful a European had ever set foot in there. A woman named Nazira shampooed Rajni's hair and rubbed her temples with prunish fingers. The women shot looks at Vinod, perched awkwardly by the entrance, until he complimented one of them on her new cut. Then they fawned over him, batting their eyes. "My husband leaves me here to play cards with the men. Make your own way home, he says! But this one, so protective." Hair soaking in warm water, Rajni allowed her eyes to drift closed. In Karachi her hair had always been cut by her aunt. This felt like a luxury. The muscles of her back eased and she forgot the ache of her ankles. She grew so relaxed that she had to squeeze her thighs together to hold in the wind that threatened to whistle. She thought then of her brothers, how delighted they would be if she just let it go. She rocked with such laughter that Nazira sucked her teeth and held her head straight. Rajni left the shop lighter, her hair no longer weighed down by grease, her spirits buoyed by the caress of memory and the goodwill of the man walking beside her.

Later, once she'd been stitched up, once the nurse had let her sip a glass of sugar water and the cutting pain had dulled, her mother-in-law came to her bedside. Mumma's eyes glittered in the sun through the curtains; the rain had left.

"You will love her," Mumma said. Rajni couldn't tell if it was a command or a promise. She supposed it was both. It was Sonal who had cradled her when she received the telegram, stroking her brow until she slept. Their desires in marriage may have been different, but they were women; they both knew what it meant to leave.

When Mumma found her hand beneath the hospital bedsheet, her grip was firm. No coddling, no whispering, no treating Rajni like a broken thing. *You're strong*, her hands seemed to say, *and you'll do what you must*. In her grip, Rajni felt intact. Before she left Karachi, her mother had tucked into her suitcase Rajni's school certificate—signed by her father, the headmaster—to enable her to make her own living as a teacher in Kampala, and a pair of teardrop earrings, to wear or sell if ever the need arose. They were rafts to weather whatever storms might come. But she saw now that her parents had already given her the truest security they could. They had told her what she was worth. That fortitude would always live within her.

By the time they left Mulago Hospital, the ground had soaked up the rain, the yellow dirt now maroon. Rajni wobbled as her footsteps sunk down, gasping as pain shot through her core. In her arms, her daughter slept, sucking her own lips for comfort. Mumma and Pappa ambled behind her, Vinod to her right. They had told her the baby's rashi moments ago, and between the placement of the moon and the planets at the time of her child's birth, Rajni felt a name bubble to her lips: *Latika*.

Rajni sensed the cave from which this baby emerged, and the other one, buried deeper, from where her brothers, her home, had been torn. She steadied herself. If she'd been ripped apart, she was still walking. Pamoja. She was whole enough to go on.

Vinod, 1954

VINOD SAT IN THE PARK with his two daughters in his lap, thinking about his mother. Latika chewed out the juice from a stick of sugarcane, Mayuri burbling. An African mzee sat on the other end of the bench, and a young Indian couple stretched out beneath the moringa tree, enjoying the cool breeze that had just blown in. He'd awoken with the early call of the muezzins, dressed the girls to the sound of the church bells, fed them a breakfast of malai on bread as the bhajans rose from the temple, a prayer on his lips each time.

His mother had not risen from bed in two weeks. Eyes tinged yellow, urine running red. It was malaria, the doctor said. He prescribed Mumma pills that, even in her weakest state, she refused to take. She'd grown more stubborn with age, suspicious of anything that she herself hadn't made. Pappa hovered around the bed, but even he had given up on convincing her. "Some people, you cannot break," he said.

Vinod had moved Pappa to his own room so he could catch some rest, though most nights Pappa refused to leave his wife's side, while Vinod and Rajni made a bed of the kitchen floor. Their new apartment—in a compound of about thirty apartments halfway up the hill, mostly other Asians, with a Nandi flame tree in the courtyard and a rusted gate—had a separate room for their two daughters, whose door Vinod lined with bedsheets each night to muffle the sounds of coughing.

VINOD, 1954

When Vinod sat with his mother the previous night, grey spit collected in the corners of her mouth, and her eyes flicked left and right, following an invisible story. Rajni entered with a tray of watery khichdi, spooning it to Mumma's lips and catching the dribbles with a handkerchief. It was Rajni who pressed soaked rags against his mother's forehead and spoke to her in a low, steady stream, the only presence that seemed to calm her. Vinod had needed to leave the room, unable to bear the sight of his mother becoming like a child.

He was at a loss for what to do. Rajni was barely able to speak to him, her face drawn with exhaustion, her breasts heavy with milk, still nursing Mayuri, who was nearly one. He rankled when Rajni suggested he call on his sisters: they had their own families now, and this one, he wanted to remind her, was hers. But he could hardly articulate such thoughts. Instead, he pulled away, moving between work and home in a fog, stopping by the mandir to pray for good health, red powder marking his forehead morning and night. His mother had always believed in fate, and he took comfort in the assurance of a plan. With his knees cool on the mandir floor, amid the smells of marigold and agarbatti, he recalled the sensation of arriving at the cricket field as a child: that same solace, to be welcomed just as he was.

The previous Saturday had been chaos, his daughters sensing the scarcity of their mother's attention and latching on to whatever remained, rejecting Vinod's attempts to entertain them. Spurned by their refusal, Vinod had walked to the Snack Bar for the afternoon, playing cards and listening to Jim Reeves on the jukebox with other Asian and African men. The outing had eased him, and he'd returned ready to do more, only to find his dinner congealed on the countertop.

Now Vinod held his daughters in the park, pleased with himself. "I think she wants some," Latika said, touching the macerated cane to Mayuri's lips. Mayuri sucked the sheen of sugar and bulged her eyes, making Latika laugh. She had kicked off her shoes and now flexed her bare toes. Vinod was glad to see her joyful. He worried that the heavy air at home was weighing on her, that his daughters would feel their mother's neglect.

Even at the best of times, Rajni's attention was split. She had begun teaching at the local school and spent the afternoons with their daughters. She grew weary often. Losing her brothers had diminished her, and when she received letters from her parents she would take weeks, sometimes a month, to respond. She mothered efficiently, but often needed time to herself, slipping into the courtyard after the girls were in bed, or once leaving Latika to bathe Mayuri while she lay out on the charpai under the orange tree. Vinod knew she still wanted a son, though he himself was not too bothered with such longings. His daughters were bright and full of life, and the love he felt for them so sharp that he couldn't imagine any greater connection with a boy.

In their first year of marriage, Vinod had wondered if Rajni's withdrawal was a function of her upbringing, her parents educated and her childhood more prosperous than his own, and he had worked harder knowing that she was used to more. He had gone to Mumma about it, embarrassed to air his marital problems but hoping she would tell him what he must do to encourage his wife to step up. Instead, Mumma had wrinkled her nose. "She has sea legs. You wouldn't know the feeling, na? She's still finding her feet."

Vinod was stung that his mother had taken Rajni's side over his, her loyalty stronger than blood. He had wanted to goad her. "Sometimes I wonder if this marriage business is right for me. Nanu-mama never married."

Mumma had snorted. "Your uncle has a secret mistress in Kisumu and a half-caste child."

Vinod's mouth hung open. He could see from Mumma's face that she had not meant to tell him, and she clicked her tongue as if to signal that it was no matter. "If you're wondering why we haven't seen him in some time, that's why. Does that life sound better to you?"

Vinod could think of nothing to say. But he supposed that the trials of life were easier to endure when surrounded by your people. He had wondered then if Rajni's detachment was not about the privilege she carried from her old life but the anchor she had lost upon entering this new one.

Latika slid from his lap and balanced on the tree's exposed roots, too far for him to reach if she were to fall. Mayuri began to fuss, pushing away from Vinod with her heels in his belly. The mzee on the bench eyed him with pinched lips, not unkindly but perhaps knowing. He was a father, only. He had begun the morning in control, but now it was slipping away. His mother was sick and he, like his father, could not think what to do without her direction. His only impulse had been to leave. He stood, hoisted Mayuri to his shoulders, and called to Latika with one sharp bark. She peered around the base of the tree, then trotted over and took his free hand. Breathing a small sigh at this mercy, he nodded to the mzee and led his daughters away. Only when they were nearing home did he realize that Latika was still barefoot and limping slightly on the hot road; he had forgotten her shoes beneath the bench.

At home, Pappa reclined in the shade of the flame tree, a green peel tossed in the grass. When they approached, he split the machungwa in three.

"Your mummy's fallen asleep, at least."

Vinod chewed his orange. He could hear the neighbors congregated on the veranda to swap stories and sip tea in the shade. Unprompted, Latika began to knead Pappa's toes, something she had perhaps seen her grandmother do. But her fingers were small and ticklish, and Pappa roared in mock menace and scrabbled at the bottoms of Latika's feet.

The heat was oppressive, and Vinod was consumed by a memory of his mother dousing herself from the communal spigot when he was a child. He'd approached her and was shocked when she flicked water at his face with a wicked laugh before wrapping him in a soaking embrace. Only later did he overhear her telling Pappa that she'd attempted to go to the public swimming pool that afternoon, forgetting, perhaps willfully, that they were barred from entering.

Rajni emerged from the apartment, dusting her palms. The lines of her forehead had smoothed and she looked like she had bathed, a fresh streak of vermilion gleaming red in the parting of her hair. Vinod exhaled. Perhaps the quiet had done her good after all.

"The men always come home in time for lunch, not a second earlier," she said, almost smiling.

"It's a talent," Vinod agreed, a boyish pleasure filling him when she chortled.

Rajni beckoned them inside. But as Latika climbed the stairs next to Pappa, Rajni froze. Both of them were hobbling. She swiveled her head, scanning the grass, the pathway.

Vinod's cheeks grew hot. He was hoping she wouldn't notice the missing shoes. But Rajni was squinting at Vinod with such accusation that he stepped back.

"Had so much fun at the park she forgot," he said unconvincingly. He felt a prickle of shame for blaming Latika when it was his own carelessness at fault, but he wanted to remind Rajni that he had done well. Rajni's eyes grew livid, but it was the disappointment in her voice that shook Vinod the most.

"I suppose I have to take care of everything," she said, snatching the orange peel from the dirt and turning away.

He had hoped for the day to go differently: to prove himself useful, necessary. Instead, he felt more helpless than ever. He thought of Nanu-mama, who had once advised him to become a big man. Vinod had always known his uncle to do only what he desired, even if it troubled those around him. No matter the scorn the community might harbor against his choices, he would never be considered weak.

It was this that propelled Vinod to intercept Rajni as she prepared Mumma's dinner that evening. She startled as he seized the tray from her. "I'll feed her tonight," he said, shaking his head firmly when Rajni began to protest. He had been too meek with her, a habit he'd acquired in the early days of their marriage, not wanting to frighten her, young and grieving as she had been.

In the privacy of the bedroom, he used the bottom of a glass to crush one of the pills from the untouched bottle and stirred the chalky dust into the bowl. Rajni had soaked rotla in thinned dahi until soft, and now the yogurt took on a faint blue hue. Vinod crumbled extra gur in the bowl, hoping the sweetness would mask the bitter taste.

Mumma eyed him doubtfully as he helped her sit up. "You?" she murmured, the faintness of her voice dampening her sarcasm. "You're hallucinating," he replied. She snorted, her eyes sharp in spite of it all. "I wish your sisters were here to see this." If she weren't so sick, Vinod would have rolled his eyes. Instead, he raised a spoonful to her lips and watched with satisfaction as she swallowed it down.

That night, he was unable to sleep, restless with the knowledge of what he had done, and yet buoyant, he realized, with hope. He had taken matters into his own hands.

When Rajni reached for him, he grasped her shoulders. "Wait," he whispered. A quiet courage flooded his limbs. He couldn't remember the last time he had felt this way. Perhaps the first time he laid eyes on Rajni, long-haired and slim but with sturdy legs and eyes carrying a wisdom beyond her years. Now her hands in his were hardened, the nails hewn down and the knuckles rough. She had come here and built their home. She had learned a language, raised their children and taught others', fried gathiya for the whole street. She was taking care of her own. He had been waiting for her to stand up—but what of himself?

"I have to tell you something," he began. His eyes focused in the dark and he noted the surprise in her face. It alarmed him too, this desire to speak honestly, but he was coasting on a revelation. He told her what he had done.

Rajni turned to the ceiling. Her hands made shadows over her face, rubbing into her eyes. She was sobbing. His mood dampened—what had he done?—but then she slid to his side and held his face and he saw the creases of her mouth. She was laughing. Her nose was against his, her fingers in his hair, but playfully, without insistence, simply there.

"I'll do it tomorrow," she whispered. Her lips twitched. She said it like a secret between them. Vinod scooped an arm around her waist. He sensed that he had earned something: respect, or at least attention. It felt good to invite her in, and to be invited back.

When, one rainy morning, Mumma rose from her bed for the first time in nearly a month, Vinod winked at Rajni. Mumma's hair had become coarse like coconut husks, the fat hewn from her face, but her gaze was clear. Pappa nearly choked on his chai toast when she sat across from him. "You're not getting rid of me yet," she drawled, pushing the carafe of water toward him. The corners of Pappa's eyes grew wet, from coughing or relief. When Rajni came to pour the tea, Mumma stilled her hand. "The food while I was sick—you made it very sweet," she said. Indeed, the jar of jaggery had diminished over the last weeks, the brown mass grated down to no more than a few grainy lumps. Vinod caught the panic crossing Rajni's face, but just as quickly she laughed it away.

"True Gujarati style," Rajni replied. Their people ate everything sweetened, kathu-mithu and mithu-murchu, the sour and spice always paired with sugar. "They say gur is the best medicine, no?"

Vinod nodded. "It worked, didn't it? Raju, you've certainly made this house sweet."

Rajni's face lit up. "We should call it that—Gur nu Ghar."

Even Pappa chuckled, rolling the words in his mouth. Only Mumma remained serious.

"You were there, every day," she said. "You made me better."

Rajni found Vinod's eyes, and hers glittered, summoning him into their private knowing. He smirked back. Between them the pill bottle was emptied, Mumma returned, their family intact. He wanted to hold on to their secret triumph. But his mother was observing him, and her vision was shrewd. He wondered then if she knew. If she was directing his attention to all that Rajni had done, telling him to be thankful too. He drank his tea with his mother, and he knew that she was right.

Pirbhai & Sonal, 1956

THE DAY THEIR THIRD GRANDDAUGHTER was born, they found a portrait of Queen Elizabeth scattered in the street. They were on their way to make a donation at the local Asian school, its rusted roof collecting magpie droppings. They had done so for their first two granddaughters—Latika, then Mayuri—and now Kiya. Each time, the envelope was a little fatter.

After each birth, Sonal anointed the pearl-pink soles of the baby's feet with a paste of kumkum, then pressed the feet into a white sheet laid across the floor. The red stains looked less like footprints than split soil, fractured and river-veined. She saw their family's fate there, carved into the place where their bodies met the earth. She was thinking of this when they came upon the portrait in the dust.

The gilded frame was chipped and a long crack ran up the glass, contorting the Queen's pale face. They were accustomed to these images: they were in every shop and office, sometimes garlanded with red and orange blooms. But they were used to seeing her tacked high on the wall, gazing out and down. They had never seen her from above, and from this angle her features flattened so that she looked feeble and incongruous, her hair outdated, her expression almost dead.

Sonal kept walking, stopping only when she noticed that Pirbhai wasn't behind her. He was bent over, grasping at the frame.

"Su kare che?" she said, though it was clear. He pawed at the dust, then propped the frame against the curb, shifting torn newspapers aside. The Queen's eyes flashed in the sun. When he turned back to Sonal, a bead of blood pulsed on his fingertip.

"Let's go," Sonal urged, afraid someone had seen. The country was rearranging beneath their feet, along with the rest of the world. India had shown it was possible to wrest free of Britain's grip, and the ripple had crossed the ocean. Next door, in Kenya, freedom fighters were rising against the colonials, sovereignty blazing in their eyes. Uganda was next, everyone said.

Pirbhai sucked his finger and squinted up at Old Kampala Hill, where Fort Lugard sat like a crown. His shirt was still as starched as on his first day of work at the Transport Department. When the whispers of independence passed across the country, he reminded his family that it was owing to his government salary that they had first afforded a home for their growing clan. That the British had established it this way for a reason, reserving jobs for the Asians between themselves and the Africans. Their own apartment sat halfway up the hill, the British mansions with their trim hedges at the top, the African shanties and tin-roofed shacks clustered at the base. Once, Pirbhai had struggled to imagine how the Europeans, Asians, and Africans would sit level on a train, even if in separate carriages, and now he saw that he'd been correct.

"Whichever way, we'll be fine," Pirbhai said.

Often Sonal reminded him that their salaries were capped as Asians, their donations to the school more an appeal to the gods than a marker of wealth. As much as Pirbhai had once believed the British would honor their promise, they still could not own land.

"Think about Rajni," Sonal said. Independence had spat her across the ocean and into their family. Sonal had seen enough to know that the British left curses in their wake. She felt righteous in her fear, that the stability they had worked so hard to secure was soon to be plucked loose.

Pirbhai waved the thought away. He had worked for the British most of his life, climbing his way up. Now his son worked in trade and his daughter-in-law was a teacher, lifting them into the civil servant class. Their family had risen to a place where they need not fear the tremors. "It won't happen that way. We're one of them."

Sonal had the urge to contradict, but Pirbhai's voice was breathy. She had never forgiven the British for ruining her husband's body, his ailments beyond the powers of even her strongest medicines. After her bout with malaria, she too felt the weight of her own limbs. She wanted to get back to the baby and sit with a cup of chaas. She turned to her husband and his face was determined, but distant too, reminding her of that first journey from Kisumu, before the bowl of her womb held any child.

"You'll see," Pirbhai murmured, to her or himself, she wasn't sure. She had always sensed that a piece of her husband was unreachable. How hard she had tried to revive that part of him, yet it was all futile. She'd learned to grant him his silences. Only lately, with the awareness of time passing that age magnified, did she see that none of it mattered. Love couldn't depend on fully knowing a person. It flourished in the absences. If it was strong enough, it would withstand the gaps. She took his hand, the blot of his blood imprinting her thumb, and tugged him on, Queen Elizabeth propped up and watching.

At three months, Kiya was ready for her first outing. They would visit the mandir for her first darshan after seeing the sun. Sonal and Rajni planned the meal to follow, but Pirbhai had another idea. A picnic, he told them, all of us together, at the Botanical Gardens in Entebbe, with Lake Victoria stretched at their feet, imported trees high above. They would bring containers of batata bhajia and sandwiches spread with lemon pickle, suck on fresh madaf and Vimto in glass bottles. While Sarita still lived in Kenya with her family, Varsha and Naren and their watoto had moved into their compound—now affectionately dubbed the "Gur nu Ghar"—not long after Sonal's recovery from malaria, propelled by Pirbhai and Sonal's growing frailty, living just a few apartments down. They too would join in today. It pleased Pirbhai to imagine their children and grandchildren in one kempt garden, serene and orderly, where they belonged.

That morning Rajni crouched over the Primus stove, the ghosts of her pregnancies lingering in her thickened waist. The smell of burnt sugar singed their nostrils as she piped tendrils of batter into crackling oil. In the vat, the jalebi glowed translucent, sticky nets floating on a honeyed sea. Sonal stood behind her for a moment, approving of the way she twisted her wrist to pour the batter, the final upward flick, quick so as to avoid waste. Rajni's arms were pocked with burns that mirrored her own. She had always liked her daughter-in-law's hands, sturdy and too large for her body. She'd noticed them right away.

The baby lay on a mat near the doorway, eyes flickering in sleep. Mayuri watched Rajni from beneath the kitchen table until Sonal beckoned her over. Sonal had noticed her middle granddaughter's curiosity whenever she brewed medicines, but she could already tell that Mayuri was more content observing than acting. She wanted to encourage her interest, let her take the spoon when she was ready.

Latika sat at the table next to her father and Pirbhai, who had donned his finest shirt. It was the kind of quiet morning they had always longed for. And yet Sonal felt it as an omen, a luxury to which they shouldn't grow accustomed.

There was a knock at the door, which swung open before Sonal could reach it. Probably one of the neighbors coming for a cup of flour, or more likely a child lured by the sweet waft. "Not ready yet," she admonished, but then she saw the man at the door. She almost didn't recognize him, he had aged so gracelessly, the skin of his cheeks pulling down to his chin in deep, papery lines. But she found the boy she'd known in the turn of his hands as he lifted Kiya from the ground and cradled her like a sack of sugar.

"Nanu," Pirbhai exclaimed. He stood and grasped Nanu's shoulders. "What a surprise!"

Nanu's shirt had taken on the muted red of dirt and he had lost much of his hair. Bewilderment swept Sonal back. Nanu had always arrived with treats, stiff-limbed dolls for the girls and plastic-wrapped packets of the simsim that Sonal had grown up stealing from her father's storage room. Even now, she could only eat them in private, breaking off a bite to savor in the early morning hours before anyone awoke. But his arrival had always been an event, anticipated for weeks, not just by the grandchildren but by Vinod, who looked up to his uncle, and by Sonal, who communed with her own childhood in Nanu's presence: the siblings they had lost, their parents long gone—all her ghosts returned home.

"You didn't say you were coming," Sonal blurted. She couldn't move past his dulled clothes, the emptiness of his hands.

Nanu shrugged with one shoulder, a gesture so childlike Sonal shuddered. For years she had wondered how he managed on his own. It was only on her last visit to Kisumu, still badgering him to settle down, that she had learned of his secret affair. She had never seen the woman or the child and had tried to put it out of her mind. But a vision of the little chotara followed her on her return to Kampala—did he have coarse hair or silky? Did he prefer steamed matoke or khichdi?—and she found herself unable to communicate with Nanu, leaving his letters unanswered and deferring his requests that she return. They wouldn't speak of it now, she knew, the silence having hardened with time.

"Thought I'd drop by. Goodness, the watoto have grown." His eyes fell to Kiya sleeping in his elbow, as if just realizing she was there.

Latika eyed Nanu. She was perhaps too young to remember his last visit five years back, when she was nearly four, but her face was open to him. "You came for the picnic, didn't you?"

Nanu squeezed her chin, though his eyes grew uncertain. "Clever girl."

Rajni poured another coffee and Vinod shuffled over to make room. The room felt festive with the smell of sugar and Nanu coddling the girls, as if he were just another neighbor dropping by for tea. But Sonal was an old woman—she no longer had the time, or the patience, to pretend. She tried catching Pirbhai's eye, but only Rajni seemed to notice. She grasped Sonal's arm briefly as she pinched rice into tiny mountains to feed Mayuri, and the glance that passed between them was full of a mother's anxiety, though Nanu was no child.

"You're looking hungry." Sonal clapped a plate of bhajia on the table, dolloping mint chutney until flecks of green speckled Nanu's shirt.

"Mumma," Vinod grumbled. Sonal arched her brow and dropped the spoon onto the table. Pirbhai glanced up and caught her stricken face.

"Eat a little," he said. He too had noticed the weariness of Nanu's stance. But who among them hadn't felt beaten down by work and responsibilities, hadn't needed to quietly slip away? Some food and a hot bath, he thought, that's all it took sometimes.

"Yes, eat first," she said, "and then you'll tell us what brought you here."

Nanu looked at the plate queasily. He jerked his head to the side, indicating the children: Latika reading on the floor, Mayuri prodding at her rice, and Kiya now back on her mat.

"It's no matter," Vinod offered.

Nanu lifted a coin of batata to his lips, then set it down unbitten. "I had to get out for some time, is all." He wiped his oily fingers on his already soiled shirt.

Pirbhai grunted his understanding. "Out of the shop, na?"

"Out of Kenya."

Pirbhai sat back and motioned for Nanu to go on.

101

"The British air attacks—you wouldn't believe. Dropping bombs like rain. And they think everybody is a rebel. Everyone is suspect."

Sonal was breathing heavily. BBC Radio was always parroting this or that about the Mau Mau rebellion, how the British were suspending civil liberties and sweeping Kenyans into camps. She remembered her childhood in Kenya, how her family could never own the land they worked, and how the farmers her father traded with complained of cash crops taking over, coffee fields obliterating all the good soil. She twinged at the memory of the mbuyu tree out back where they would gather. "It'll be ours again one day," one mzee had told her with a wink.

"But surely you'll be all right?" Pirbhai said. A darkness had settled over the room. Pirbhai felt a flare of annoyance at Nanu for showing up unannounced on the day of the picnic with his gloomy news. Overreacting, he thought.

Nanu tugged at his collar and unwittingly unclasped a button. "One of my workers in the shop was detained in the camps. People say if they don't confess, the mzungu cut out their—" He stopped and glanced down at Latika, who was watching him with all her attention, then pushed away his untouched plate.

For so much of his childhood, Sonal had been the one to comfort him when he was afraid. She wished now she could tell him it would be over soon, the mzungu would end their massacring and leave, but the words wouldn't come.

"So you find another worker. One who isn't a Mau Mau." Pirbhai chuckled. He wanted to lighten the mood, but his joke fell into silence. He felt the stirring in his gut of a long-ago inadequacy, one that he, with British nails and a damp matchbook, had once tried to blister away. His throat tightened as it sometimes did when a memory brushed past, as if to protect against inhaling smoke. He had come a long way since that teenage boy, and yet a piece of him remained, the part that believed unflinchingly in his own survival. The boy who would cross an ocean, break his fingers, devour his pride, to grant his family more. He wanted them to see him plowing ahead without doubts. He wanted his grandchildren to believe not only that he had risen, but that they too could rise. And yet here was Nanu, flying into their kitchen and making them think they had something to fear.

"Can you blame them for wanting self-rule?" Vinod said.

"But at what cost? Look what happened in India. Madness, after the British left," Pirbhai snapped.

A chill slid across the room. Sonal glanced at Rajni, who had bristled over the stove. It felt too close, then, Nanu in their home to escape his own, and Rajni too, both swept ashore like debris carried on an indifferent wave.

"None of this matters." It was Rajni. She was clapping lids onto the picnic containers, the silky burns on her forearms glinting. "Whether you want the British gone or not, whether you think the rebels are good or bad. You can fight over it all day and you still don't get to control what happens. None of it."

Sonal grasped Pirbhai's cup and swallowed the lukewarm coffee down. Her lips curled with the bitter dregs. Rajni was right. Nanu was here, shaken and in need. Her face softened. "So you'll stay here," she said. In the end, it was the only part that mattered.

"Just for some time," Nanu answered, staring into his hands.

"Well then, lucky us," Sonal said, and she meant it. She glared at Pirbhai, who had fallen silent. He met her eyes, and in her gaze he felt a drop of shame.

"Yes, yes," Pirbhai said, waving a hand between them, "it'll be like old times." He remembered kicking around a banana fiber ball in the wash behind the dukan, Nanu screeching when he scored a goal. A feeling of benevolence surged through him. He had this home, had planned this day. Perhaps it was just what they needed, to remind them of their blessings and dust away their fears. Perhaps Nanu had come on just the right day, after all.

They arrived at the gardens flushed with sweat. Though he knew his legs would stiffen over the ride, Pirbhai had insisted on driving. He ground his teeth as he stepped from the car, which he had bought secondhand and repaired himself. The landscape had shifted from cramped markets with laundry flung from every window to endless stretches of coffee and tea farms along the paved road. Pirbhai eyed the fields of cotton, the railroad carrying their white heads across the scored land, and felt a throb in his absent finger.

They peeled out, Mayuri chirping with excitement, Latika holding the baby, the rest of them juggling the boxes of food, the cushions, the Primus stove. The air was drunk with the smell of jasmines and ripe fruit. Varsha and Naren pulled in, their teenage sons Biju and Ishan tumbling from the back seat. Outside the gates, a pair of African women sat on a dyed sheet, beaded trinkets splayed before them. The pair eyed them as if assessing whether they were foreigners, then called out, motioning to their wares.

For the first time, Pirbhai walked ahead of his family, his head held high with purpose and his legs working hard against his limp. At the gate he barely glanced at the guard, a Baganda man in a cotton kanzu and blazer, though Sonal did, and saw the moment when a question formed in the guard's eyes.

Behind the gates, the ground was carpeted in a trim grass, so soft that Mayuri and Latika kicked off their shoes. The paths were lined with furze hedges bursting with yellow flowers. As they walked, Latika read out the little English placards fixed to the bases of trees and bushes: EGYPTIAN COTTONSEED, INDIAN ASSAM TEA, CRIOLLO CACAO. Sonal praised her pronunciation: she was the one who had suggested they alter Latika's papers so that she could start school a year early, and her mind had astonished them all. Mayuri tottered behind her, grazing her fingers against the bony stalks of the sunflowers and breathing her awe.

A young British couple strolled past, the woman dewy beneath a lace parasol. "Hullo," Pirbhai said as they crossed paths, and the man smiled politely and tipped his head. Perched on a wooden bench nearby, an elderly fellow with white hair feathering over his forehead held a pair of binoculars to a small boy's face, angling them up to a nearby branch. Beside them, two white-bread sandwiches waited in a clear bag. Pirbhai followed the line of their gaze to where a bat hawk rested in the tree, ogling back at them with its yellow eye.

They laid their blankets down in the shade of several rubber trees, the trunks distended with silver tendons. Rajni lit the stove as Varsha piled plates with kachumber and dhebra, cold dahi rice, and bhakris still warm from home. On her mother's instruction, Latika mixed water into the tinned milk that Rajni had insisted on buying for Kiya ever since she began going to the English Women's Institute's child-craft classes, where the English nurse taught the Asian mothers to forget their natures. Sonal told Rajni she was wasting two things: her own milk and her money. Nanu chuckled into his drink, the color returning to his cheeks. The air was cooler near the water, light on their skin, the heavy floral perfumes replaced by the crisp scent of eucalyptus.

Seated on an upturned crate with a plate of food resting on his belly, Pirbhai felt the fullness of his family. They had made it. This was all theirs to enjoy, the day spooling out before them.

Vinod funneled peanuts into his bottle of cola and smacked his lips. Charged with sugar, Biju leapt barefoot through the grass, tossing a conker at Ishan. The bushes rustled, and Latika emerged with an orange globe gleaming in her grasp. "I found a tomato!" she cried, her face radiant.

Pirbhai regarded Sonal stretching her toes, flush with gratitude. From his earliest memories he had learned to fear the future. He had crossed the ocean as a boy and arrived, unwillingly, as a man, his past out of reach and his present not guaranteed. It was Sonal who had taught him not only that a future was possible, but that it could be good. She met his eyes across the blankets and for a moment it was just the two of them, ascending a great peak and surveying all that would continue through and beyond them.

They could spend the day here, the breeze mild, the afternoon light filtered through the broad rubber leaves. The tension from the morning was less than a memory now, swallowed into full stomachs, fading as their eyes drooped with heat. They needed nothing else, just a nap perhaps.

They were awoken by the babble of a radio. Their eyes snapped open, aware of being watched. The stove was off but it emitted a ring of heat, a black tendril of smoke that traveled on the breeze. A European man stood before them, radio clipped to his belt, bucket hat shading his face.

"Excuse me, please. We don't permit fires or cooking of any kind on the garden property."

Immediately Rajni knelt to the stove, dismantling its parts and slapping the smoke away. Mayuri shrank to Sonal's side, shy in the presence of strangers.

"We've cooked here before and it wasn't a problem," Vinod said, his speech slurred with sleep. Sonal tried to shoot him a glare, but he refused to look her way. Nanu rose to his knees, eyes sharp.

The man drew his hands from his pockets, revealing open palms. "Those are the rules."

Pirbhai felt the unease radiating off his family. He stepped forward with an acquainted smile.

"Very sorry for the mishap. But come, we're only resting in the shade. No food left." He tried a wink as he gestured at the rumpled blanket, the containers of lunch scraped clean.

The man swept his eyes over the remains of their afternoon. His gaze fell on the tomato, plump as a fist, dribbling juice onto the sheet below.

"And this?"

"From home!" Sonal exclaimed, at the same time as Mayuri and Latika both pointed toward the furze, where a tangle of tomato vines peeked from a gap in the hedge.

The man leaned back on his heels. His straight nose twitched like a cat catching the trail of a rodent.

"Straying off the paths or harvesting of any kind is not permitted on the garden premises." He raised his voice and slowed his words. "I'm afraid I'll have to ask you to leave."

A colobus monkey cackled above. Pirbhai reached his right hand toward the man, then remembered his finger and clenched his fist before reaching out with his left.

"Chalo, let's just go," Nanu whispered in Gujarati. Sonal squeezed his arm, seeing in her brother a new fear, that perhaps what he was running from had followed him here.

Latika was squinting at the man as if learning him, her gaze unafraid. Despite the commotion, Pirbhai was caught by her stance, poised and resolute, but with a defiant edge. So like his wife.

He turned back to the man and forced a laugh. "Just a child exploring," he said, but the man was unmoved. Sobering, he dropped his voice conspiratorially. "Listen, I've worked for the Transport Department for years, a government servant just like you. I know the importance of our rules. We're just a family out celebrating—I'm sure you can appreciate that."

His face was upturned like a son appealing to a father. But the uniformed man had stiffened at his words. He took a step back, his tan boot sinking into the spongy grass.

"I'm not at liberty to make exceptions—for anyone. As I said, I'm going to have to ask you all to leave." He was no longer looking at them but past them, his eyes barely grazing the tops of their heads.

Sonal stood and yanked the blanket, bits of grass and cotton fluff surging around them. As they exited the gate, Pirbhai stumbled against the hedge, sending a ripple down the row of yellow blooms. The guard shot out a hand to steady him, and between them the flowers shivered like flame.

On the drive home, Pirbhai stared out the window, the cotton fields a stark reminder of what had never been his. A thorn from the hedge had nicked his finger, and he licked it absently, recalling the Queen's photograph overturned on the street. There was another photograph, once. An image in the newspaper, in 1931, the year the East Africa railroad reached its final destination of Kampala. Pirbhai had flipped the front page and there it was, ink smearing like soot.

The last sleeper key driven into the ground in Kampala, the caption read, and Pirbhai remembered another decade, another sleeper key, the soil beneath his fingers red and ripe as burst flesh. In the photo, five men stood around the tracks, their white faces obscured by the shade cast off their hats. A woman in a long white dress was using a metal pole to drive the key into the ground. When Pirbhai saw the picture, a jolt tremored his wrists, originating in the middle finger of his right hand. He scanned the grainy horizon for something familiar: brown bodies twisted over the tracks; turbaned heads sloped against tree trunks; huddles of boys around the fire, faces turned to the stars; men exchanging medicines behind the canvas tents, speaking with hands where words failed; knots of thatched huts between the trees, some empty, others brimming with life. But he saw none of this. He noticed only how, in the left corner of the photograph, two dogs watched from behind the crowd of men, one black and one tawny, both with hungry eyes.

Pirbhai, 1958

He WANTED TO RUN. Was running, running. He and Rakesh flying, pinkies linked as they flew, bare feet opening to the dirt, blood spilling and still running, together they ran. Then moving too fast to hold on to each other but still knowing they were side by side, the forest held them close, each other the reason they could run, the love of the other enough to go on.

She was at his door. The hard woman, the wife. The stud in her nose light in her heavy face. She had come to ask his help cleaning the storage room. Perhaps to help him write a letter. But no, she was walking to him with a tin cup in her yellow-stained hands, and he was not sleeping on a gunnysack but a bed, and she was stroking his hair with her palm that was not smooth but calloused, old. She was old. His Sonal. Her rough hands, but she was soft when they were alone. He remembered this and reached for her. Her lips parted and he remembered the children, three of them. The memory surfaced more memories, never spoken aloud, swimming up from the blackest waters of his mind: an unnamed boy with a face like his cousins slipping into the kala pani; the beating he'd known after claiming Rakesh vanished in the fire—every bruised step a prayer that his friend was free; how the wife drank cassava tea after the birth of their son to close her womb, no more children; how his son read him a letter saying that Ganesh from the railway had returned to India and taken his own life, how when his

109

son asked who that was he said he didn't know, not knowing how to say that it was also himself. He had taken away people's homes, though he knew not whose. He had hoped, believed, it would secure his own. Had it? This sweet house, this house of sugar—they had once given that name to this place of rest. His wife brought the cup to his lips and he smelled bitterness and ajmo and too much clove, which he knew she added to mask the unpleasant, though she would never say, but he knew it in his deepest self, so he drank.

He remembered a girl. A baby in his arms, eyes so large and black and wet, moving like the sea. But in his memory his arms were trembling and sun-pocked; not long ago then, so not his daughter. Granddaughter, he said. The wife nodded. Yes, yes, we have three of those now, such relief in her face. She recited names that sparked no light. Latika, Mayuri, Kiya. But he heard a voice outside that opened a shadow of a thought, a girl at the foot of his bed, tickling his toes through the blankets, a girl who turned her head to every sound, a girl unafraid to bear witness. He had seen in her that curiosity—no, hunger—for the truth. The eldest, he said, not knowing her name. Bring her to me.

His wife eyed him uncertainly, hesitating, but then she relaxed, as if understanding something, and nodded. He relaxed too. This good woman, who built a home in the unspoken parts of himself, how lucky he was to be seen by her, how lucky to be seen in life, to have had a true friend.

The girl stood by his side. Close enough that he could see, through the film of his eyes, her dress damp with sweat from playing outside. Close enough that he saw the tilt of her chin, the seriousness of her eyes. Eyes older than her ten years. But she held herself a little apart, not touching the bed, and he had the thought that she was afraid of him. The nub of his missing finger, the bristled hairs of his ears, the ridges of his spine pushing through his singlet like river stones. The smell of him, medicine and curdled breath and clove. Perhaps he

110

had become something alien to her, ugly. He remembered then what his mother always told him, how his teeth were his finest feature, his inner strength, and he bared them now, wide and milky, gums black from years of beedis, crackling at the girl. She did not flinch or look away. He knew then that this was the one he remembered, the one he hoped for.

Sonal-baa said not to tire yourself out with talking, the girl said. He laughed. Of all the ways he had tired himself through his life, saying what he wanted had not been one of them. But I don't have much longer here, he told her, and saw her take this in, how a child grows still when an adult offers the unveiled truth.

He asked her if she knew what happened when someone in their community died. The rasp of his cough between them. She looked at the ceiling in thought. Finally she said, They sing. And cook. And wear white.

He grunted. They turn the body into a fire. They burn it away until there's no body left.

The girl regarded him with interest. He tried to raise his head from the pillow, but it was heavy, full of water; his eyes spun. He closed them, said, Can you imagine that? Everything inside that body, all its bones and memories, erased. All the stories. Its heart.

The girl was quiet. Perhaps picturing his body—so close to skeleton, the hair fine and white as plucked feathers—melting into fire, orange flames slithering over arms and torso, shirt crumbling to ash. The crack of kindling and sting of sparks against his legs. He felt it and knew peace.

Pir-dada, the girl whispered. It was the first time he had heard her voice so small. He opened his eyes. Her wet cheeks, eyes like night sky after rain. He reached out his hand and she took it, her finger filling in the space where his was gone.

He wanted to tell her about all the mercies he had been granted in this life. How his wife had allowed him his secrets. How his children had allowed him to forget. How forgetting was the greatest privilege he had known. How he had forgotten the pain of being alone. That first act of tenderness, when he was still a boy, lost and wandering in old chappals, suffering in the dark burden of what he had done, only to be given a home by Sonal's family. Where would he have gone otherwise? He wanted this kindness to live on. And he needed to tell her what he had learned that day he struck the match, how quickly all can be lost, how nothing is certain, how you must, above all, hold on.

I want to tell you about another fire, he said. His voice was hoarse, so she leaned in. He told her. Her hands held him in place and for the first time he did not turn away. He told her of his bravest friend, the one who ran, who had the courage to say no.

The girl was no longer crying. On the bed now, one leg tucked up under her, the heat of her small body against his. He did not want her to be alone with this, to carry it unaccompanied. He hoped she would share it how she needed to. She did not strike him as someone afraid of going on.

You won't feel it when they burn you? she asked.

No, he said, I won't. But I have felt it all my life. He wasn't sure if he spoke that last part out loud. She was but a child, and despite himself he wanted to protect the softness of her heart. But she was nodding, her chin defiant. Is it better to feel nothing? she said.

He didn't know. He could not remember what had passed between them, where they began. His lungs grew cold. He heard sounds from the doorway, voices familiar beyond name, a family continuing on. He felt only the grace of a hand in his, he could not remember whose, but he knew that it was there, that it had never left, never would. He knew this was what mattered. He heard the sky open, another door, the rain hissing as it met the scorched land.

PART TWO

1962-1972

Latika, 1962

B Y THE TIME LATIKA DRESSED herself and her sisters for the Independence Day parade, the sun burned white. Pappa hadn't let them attend the midnight celebrations at Kololo Stadium, but Latika had jolted awake to the sound of trumpets and registered that it was happening—the Union Jack lowered and the Ugandan flag raised at that very minute. The house smelled like cooked milk, Ma having stayed up late rolling penda for the friends who would stop by throughout the day.

"It feels like Diwali," Kiya exclaimed. She and Mayuri had shaken Latika awake that morning, doubled over in glee as they told her through their guffaws that they'd snuck into the kitchen and eaten Ma's sweets before she was up. Latika could smell the sugar on their breath and knew Ma might blame her for not stopping their greedy fingers. But as she watched them stagger around the room, giggling so loud they were sure to wake the whole Gur nu Ghar, she'd wanted nothing more than to be their co-conspirator. "Arre, hyenas," she'd said, "did you save any sweets for me?"

Now Ma and Sonal-baa were crouched side by side on the veranda, hulling stones from red dal. Against their colorful parade outfits, Sonal-baa stood out in her white cotton sari, the widow's garb she'd worn for four years. Dark red chilies were spread across an old dupatta in the courtyard to dry, and a golden weaver flitted in the branches of the guava tree.

Ma clapped as Kiya twirled in her pink skirt, then looked at her sternly. "Don't get lost in the crowd. Mayuri, don't start dreaming and wander off. Latika, hold on to your sisters out there."

"Hanh, hanh," Latika said. Each day she collected her sisters after school and set the rice to boil for dinner while Ma was tutoring, squeezing her own revision in somewhere between. It was she who gave them their weekly Dettol baths and cajoled them to take their cod liver oil each morning. Some days she felt like their mother, the age difference vast between them.

"You're not coming?" Kiya gasped. Together, Ma and Sonal-baa began to list reasons: the heat, the crowds. Age, Sonal-baa added, pinching Mayuri's cheek.

Kiya's shoulders hiked toward her ears. "But…it's *Independence Day*."

Ma found a pebble in the dal and placed it beside her, where she'd formed a small collection. "Independence, Uhuru; in India we called it swaraj. Everyone has a word for it."

"Swaraj," Latika repeated. She associated the shouts of "Uhuru" with the bang of fireworks and the smells of roasting meat in the marketplace. She wondered what Ma associated with "swaraj." While the rest of them couldn't stop chattering about Independence over the last few weeks, Ma remained oddly quiet.

"Ja, go now, and don't hurry back. Baa and I are having our own independence party at home." Ma shot Sonal-baa a wry smile.

Kiya's mouth dropped open, envy building in her face.

Pappa emerged from inside, cheeks shining from a fresh shave. The day before, Latika had listened to the radio with him in the kitchen, the BBC World Service broadcasting various Ugandan officials speaking about Obote's new presidency. *In the new Uganda, there will be no room for differences*, one official said, and Latika recalled how Pappa's

116

forehead had creased just as Kiya's was now, a shadow darkening his brow.

Pappa turned to Ma and Sonal-baa. "You're sure you won't come?"

Sonal-baa stretched one leg out from under her, cracking her ankle. "I've seen enough change in my lifetime," she said.

As they walked to the gates, Latika turned back for a moment and saw her mother and grandmother scooting something between them on the stoop. The flick of Ma's index finger, the distinct click and roll. They were playing marbles with the stones from the dal. The last thing she saw before Kiya dragged her away was Sonal-baa slapping her thigh with delight.

I've seen enough change in my lifetime. It was this phrase Latika recalled when Sonal-baa passed away a year later. And it was this phrase she thought of the day of the funeral, when Pappa couldn't light the funeral pyre.

Sonal-baa was wrapped in a sheet, the wood mounded high over her slight frame. She had always had thick arms and a solid waist, but she was a small woman in the end, five feet tall and shrunken from her last bedridden months. Latika could see the white cloth peeking through the wood, holding the outline of a foot, the curve of ankle bone. She knew that ankle so well, had seen it every time Sonal-baa hiked up her sari to pull yams from the garden, or when she reached down and massaged her own feet at the end of a long day.

Pappa was the eldest son, the only son, and so he would light the pyre. The priest beckoned him forward and together they chanted, reciting words that Latika couldn't hear over the static of grief.

Mayuri and Kiya were at the Gur nu Ghar with some aunties, too young at ten and seven to witness the funeral rites. At sixteen, Latika was now a woman, and she took her place beside her mother, whose face was chapped from old tears, though she shed none now. Since Sonal-baa's passing, Ma had grown more silent. Quieter than Pappa, who was occupied by the practicalities of death: calling on the priest, organizing the rites and the cleaning of the room and the body. And yet Ma's sorrow filled every room the way a river cuts a new tributary, slowly and steadily, inch by inch, then all at once. For the first time, she told them of her brothers, Harish and Mohan, the boundaries of her grief flooding over.

But Pappa could not do it. Maybe this was too much, maybe he felt that if he accepted the lit stick it would be in his power—to disappear his mother, to accept the truth that both of his parents were now gone. Latika didn't know. Her father was not one to voice such sentiments. She knew only what she saw, which was the tightness of his face as the priest approached, the hitch in his shoulder as he tried to reach out, and then the crumpling, mouth agape, stumbling back. *No*, he said. *No, no.*

There were whispers. The priest murmured encouragingly, but Pappa had said all he could bear to. The priest did not appear worried; he must have seen this before, a grown man returned to a child for the final moments. Pappa stood alone. Then his sisters moved forward and he was enveloped. Latika shut her eyes. It did not scare her, the body itself. She knew it was just a shell now. She remembered her grandfather telling her so, that the body would disappear but the stories, the heart, they stayed on. What had been Sonal-baa was already skyward, nowhere and everywhere at once.

The priest turned to the mourners. Who would it be? his eyes were asking. Latika felt a tug inside her, soft then insistent, a hand reaching in and lifting her up. She stepped forward. She was the eldest child of the only son. A bird whistled and Latika said, "I will."

The priest did not meet her eyes. A girl could not light the pyre, not even a daughter or granddaughter. A hot hand jerked her away, and it was Ma, no longer shrunken but fuming. "Get back," Ma hissed, "you're making a fool." The hand kept her there, bound. She swiveled her head to avoid the stares and found Pappa's gaze. Held between his sisters so that his feet floated above the ground, he looked at peace.

In the end, Sarita-foi's husband lit the pyre, the husband of Sonal-baa's eldest daughter. They carried on: the body turned to ash, the smoke blueing the sky, the fragments of tooth and bone collected from the rubble. Then homeward, aunts and neighbors cramming the room with food and song. Latika rocked her body with the bhajans. Kiya came to her frightened: she didn't understand the event but understood the sound of sorrow. Latika folded her into her lap and rocked her too, drawing her fingers through her tangled hair. She would have to teach Kiya how to tie her own braids, they were always flying loose. Mayuri sat by her side, moving her mouth with the chants. Her voice set against the others was smaller but somehow stronger in its rawness. Despite the loss they were warm and close, the house thronging with their sounds, infusing the day with a kind of bliss.

Gradually, as the bats darkened the horizon and their voices wearied, their home cleared. Pappa's sisters slept on mats on the floor, even though Varsha-foi lived a few apartments down. But instinct held them together. Latika's eyes drooped. Salt, potatoes, dhebra, rich undhiyu and rice drenched in ghee—they were fed everything to bring on sleep. Latika ate and ate. Pappa's plate magically refilled; he ate with his eyes almost closed, his cheeks slack, simply filling the hollow. She noticed Kiya listing sideways over her bowl and took her hand gently, Mayuri's too, and led them to bed. Small bodies heavy with the weight of the day.

Her sisters were soft with sleep, but when Latika tried to leave, Mayuri's hand tugged hers back. She waited a little longer. She remembered how she'd been late to collect her sisters every day last week, taking her time wandering down Kololo Hill from her school to theirs, basking in the space between that demanded nothing of her.

Each day Latika waited for a letter from the university, where she'd applied to the journalism program, and each night she thought of her friends who were acting in the school production of *The Taming of the Shrew*, the first integrated play since the Black students began attending the school following Independence. She yearned not to have to switch from her student-self into her home-self, her sister-self, and daughter-self, to have the freedom to choose. To be an *I* apart from her family's *we*. She could be free only in secret, in the hungry expanse of her mind.

She recalled the reproach in Mayuri's eyes when she was late for the fourth day in a row, and felt a sudden remorse. Next week she would take them into the market for some peanut brittle from the mithai shop, as she sometimes did when she had a coin in her pocket. She would let them revel in the stolen time away and, with their teeth cemented with sugar, make them promise not to tell their mother.

When all the house had fallen asleep, Ma summoned her to the kitchen table, where she sat in the dark. Her pale sari from the day was gone, her nightgown puddling around her waist.

"What you did today," Ma said.

Latika tried to sit but Ma grasped her arm, keeping her standing.

"I didn't mean to upset anyone," she said, "I meant to help."

Ma's jaw was stiff. "Not like that. Help with your sisters, prepare the food, wipe off the spills. You help quietly. That's how it is."

Latika had crouched with Ma and the aunties to scrub the pots clean, had portioned out the leftovers to all the guests, washed the smoke from the day's clothes and clipped them up on the line to dry. In the moonlight, through the leaves of the flame tree, she could see their outlines flapping on the line. She did these tasks every day, she the eldest daughter of the only son.

Latika couldn't see Ma's eyes in the dark. Was she awake or dreaming? Was she here or not here? The herbs Sonal-baa had braided whispered above the window.

"I do all of that," she snapped. "You don't notice how much I do."

Ma released Latika's arm so quickly that she stumbled back, her ankle twisting sharply on the tile. Latika caught the moon in Ma's heavy-lidded eyes.

"You know, I had wanted a son," Ma said slowly. "Maybe we both would have been happier if you'd been a boy."

The static burst open, as if the world had split apart. Ma turned away and Latika wished for light, for sun, for her mother to see her, for once. But she never would. A feeling swam up to her, less a memory than a reminiscence, of reaching up for her mother, her hands small and brown and yearning. She wished more than anything, in that instant, to close her fists.

The door to Pir-dada and Sonal-baa's room stayed closed. They shifted around it, sucking their stomachs in when they passed, though some nights Latika unconsciously reached for the knob, thinking to bring her grandmother a glass of tea. Each time was a small tremor, to confront once more what was gone.

Then one afternoon Latika found the door ajar, Ma wrestling with the bedsheets inside. Mayuri stood with pillows piled in her arms. Although the windows were thrown open and the curtains clawed back, the air held a trace of clove and sour sweat, of Sonal-baa's medicines. Latika pulled the scent deep into her lungs, amazed at its persistence after all the months that had passed.

"We have company," Ma said, snapping the flowery bedspread into place. Her lips were puckered with effort, the back of her blouse dappled with sweat.

Latika tried to picture someone sleeping in this room, hanging shirts in the closet and untying the curtains at night. The blood rushed to her head.

"Who?" she demanded.

"A university student," Mayuri answered. "Kiya's writing him a welcome speech."

Latika reached for the blanket in Ma's hands, but Ma swatted her away. "It hasn't even been a year," Latika said.

Ma grabbed the pillows from Mayuri, patting them into place. "He's a paying guest," she said. Latika bit her lip, feeling admonished. Ma hustled Mayuri out, but at the door she turned back, the stiffness of her face easing for a moment. "And Latika," she murmured, "life goes on." Her shoulders dipped, her arms heavy with old sheets. Latika grew still. She had the feeling that Ma was not chiding her but instructing her. Then Ma was gone, and Latika stood alone in her grandparents' room.

The guest arrived just as Ma was beginning to grumble that the dal was growing cold. When he walked in, Kiya whispered, "He looks like a filmi star!" too loudly to Mayuri, who appeared mortified as the guest let out a startled laugh.

His name was Arun, and he was a university student at Makerere, in his first year of law. His skin was the color of honey and taut around his cheekbones. He was tall and sturdily built, the kind of man who looked like he'd been raised drinking fresh milk in the mornings. Though Latika had been intent on ignoring whoever was moving into the room, when he introduced himself, her breath caught in her chest. His eyes were liquid and intense, thick lashes obscured by smudged glasses that sat on the strong slope of his nose. He had been staying in a hostel for the first months of the university term, but his mother had put out word through the mandir that he was looking for a family to live with in Kampala. Latika noticed how Pappa took pains to call it the spare room.

Kiya took to him instantly, energized by the new presence and even drawing a wet finger down the seam of his starched shirt when she lost his attention. Mayuri grew more reserved, but her eyes remained on him throughout the meal. They sat around the table, all their knees just touching. Arun told the girls stories of his home in Jinja, where the Nile emerged like a rippling snake, and where the electric plant from the dam filled the air with a constant hum and the sugarcane tasted extra sweet.

The table sagged with fried mhogo and black-eyed beans and more rotlis than Latika could ever remember rolling. "He'll be used to this," Ma had muttered as she slit the okra. Arun's family owned a soap factory, she told Latika. They would have servants, a cook.

Arun tore into a fresh rotli that Ma had slipped onto his plate. He ate indiscriminately, swallowing fast and speaking at the same time, almost as if he didn't see the plate before him. Ma looked on as he chewed, satisfied. Latika had hardly touched her food.

"Latika's hoping to attend Makerere herself," Pappa mentioned between mouthfuls. "No such opportunities here in my day."

"I could take you to campus for a tour sometime," Arun said.

Latika made sure not to meet his eyes, still wanting to dislike him but feeling a hope surge within her. For so many months she had lived with dulled senses, the static overwhelming everything. She felt her fingers waking up, sparks tingling at the tips.

Ma coughed. "Is it safe? I heard there was some commotion." She didn't elaborate, but exchanged a glance with Pappa.

"Oh, you'll see—Makerere right now is the New Uganda. Real liberation. This is life after the colony." He flicked his eyes to Latika. "I could take you tomorrow if you like."

"I have to collect my sisters from school."

Arun glanced at Mayuri, who was swirling her rice. "I could help with that," he said. "It's no small task to accommodate a guest."

Kiya shot up from her chair, nearly knocking over her bowl. "You can meet my friends!"

Even Mayuri's eyes grew round with excitement. "We can show you around the city," she said shyly, forgetting that he had already lived here for several months.

"He'll be busy with his schoolwork, na?" Ma said, but a wrinkle in her forehead softened, and she spooned more dal onto Arun's plate. Latika felt an opening in the fabric of her life.

Kiya slithered under the table and emerged next to Arun, throwing her arms around his neck. He laughed in surprise but didn't push her away.

"You can see that she really understands the concept of space," Ma said, and Arun let out a whistle.

"We hope you'll be comfortable here," Pappa said, smoothing an invisible crease on the tablecloth with his thumbs. "We hired an askari for the complex. And if there's anything else you need..."

A few days earlier, on their way home from school, Latika and her sisters had found themselves face-to-face with a Black boy at the gates. Pappa had spoken of pooling funds together with the neighbors to hire an askari as a safety measure, though it was hard to believe this boy could ward anyone off. His shirt was almost see-through with wear, and whiskers of dark hair sprouted above his lip as if he hadn't yet learned how to shave. When Latika asked, he told them his name was West, that he'd previously worked for a European family who gave him that name upon learning that his village was out west. Kiya had offered him a yellow date from her pocket that she'd picked on the walk home, but he'd declined.

Arun waved his hands. "Oh, don't worry about me. Uhuru, na? It means we're in charge of our own destiny." He winked at Pappa, who glanced at the shrine on the kitchen shelf and chuckled nervously. But Latika laughed loudly. She liked how he spoke to them, as if they were his colleagues, and how he carried himself with such ease. She could not imagine anyone denying him a thing. She envisioned walking through campus with him. the doors opening before her.

That night, when everyone had gone to bed, Latika found Arun smoking on the stoop. She couldn't sleep, her body alert with new promise. A jackal called somewhere out of sight. She hugged her bare arms, the night air carrying a chill.

"The winds of change," Arun murmured. He met her eyes and grinned, then offered her his cigarette. She shook her head, though she moved a step closer so that she could smell the waft of peppery smoke mingled with the sweet musk of his body.

"It's nice of your family to welcome me," he said.

"Well, you are paying," Latika replied, then bit her tongue. The gold face of his wristwatch glimmered as he tapped his cigarette. She suspected he hadn't considered that her family was simply grateful for the extra income. But to her surprise, he tipped back his head and laughed.

"You're sharp." Latika's cheeks grew hot. She swept her hair behind her ear and noticed how he watched her, sensing his eyes lingering even after she'd turned away. "I hope I made a good first impression," he added.

Latika doubted he ever made a bad one. Somehow he was both boyish and sophisticated, and her family had certainly fallen under his charm. But she said, "Arriving late isn't a promising start."

He twirled his silver lighter and told her that he'd gotten lost on his way over, walking too far up the hill. Latika had climbed the hills countless times and knew how the houses grew larger and whiter the higher you went, with pearly columns and signs on the gates warning MBWA KALI, and where the askaris carried both pangas and guns. She listened as he described how he'd paused to watch a pair of movers maneuver a waxy rhinoceros head into a truck, how a white woman had supervised from the window of her mansion, how in the distance he had seen the black-and-gold flag flapping in the breeze and felt a sense of satisfaction. The colonials were fleeing and the Asians and Africans would band together to shape the future they deserved.

"You speak as if you're on a stage," Latika said. The smell of his cigarettes reminded her of Pir-dada, the scent that had lived in all his clothes, the tips of his fingers when he pinched Latika's cheek.

Arun shook his head at himself, drawing deep on his cigarette. "That's how we speak in the student union, I suppose. Since Uhuru it's all different. We have so much potential now, so much power to drive change." He cocked his head at her. "You'll get to see for yourself, when you come."

Latika's chest fluttered. It was the third or fourth time he had mentioned Uhuru that night, and the word swam in her mind, taking on a new meaning. She whispered it under her breath now. It was what she had wanted, all this time. Listening to Arun speak of the possibilities of self-rule as the Empire crumbled, she began to imagine the shape of her own freedom.

Arun hummed a tune, and after a moment Latika realized it was a Beatles song. She swayed her hips slightly. His eyes were fixed on her, half a smile on his lips. The next time he lifted his cigarette, she plucked it from him and breathed in the blue smoke. It surprised her that it was so sweet.

The nights became theirs. Latika saw little of Arun in the daytime— he was on campus and she at school—though some days she would find him waiting at the primary school gates when she went to fetch her sisters, and the four of them would walk through the market, Kiya bounding with energy and Mayuri lingering by Arun's side. They would stop for a bag of kachi keri slick with chili, or make a detour before home to climb up Kololo Hill instead of down. They would ogle at the marbled mansions and gaze at the view, her sisters flush with excitement and Latika seeing the landscape anew through Arun's eyes. He pointed out Makerere Hill and described it as a haven where men and women of all communities dwelled in peace despite the ethnic tensions brewing through the nation. Sometimes Arun would forget himself and fall into political diatribes, and Latika would jerk her chin toward her sisters and mouth, *Later*. Then they would meet after everyone had gone to bed, whispering in the shadows of the veranda or ducking behind the flame tree to avoid the prying eyes of the neighbors.

She told herself it wouldn't last, that he would soon be swept up by his friends at university, but each night when she emerged, he returned to her. She felt herself unfurling. Love was its own kind of static, saturating everything. She relished the way he regarded her, as if she was magic, a full person. She was not just a sister and a daughter but a woman, a mind, someone with prospects. With him, she sensed her own power.

He told her of a rally his union was organizing on campus, standing against the rise of Obote's regime, as the military surged into the cracks that Uhuru left behind. The British had carved arbitrary borders that spread tension along tribal lines, and left behind a flawed hierarchy that needed to fall. It was informal apartheid, he said, the way the country remained divided, the wealth consolidated in the hands of the Europeans and wealthy Asians, the rest of the population fighting for meager jobs. He asked her what use it was sitting up on that hill if you weren't using your place for good.

She had seen crowds of protesters congregated in the streets, sunworn men cursing and schoolchildren hurling stones, and later, neighbors gathered on the veranda to whisper of whose son was injured, whose husband dragged off. But always she had carried on, never expected to join, her mind lingering on the inflamed faces long after she walked away.

Arun had taken her to Makerere once, introducing her to the union, and to Daniel, his best friend, who spoke to the room with such vigor that they burst into applause. "In here, we live our politics," he said. "Class and ethnic divisions are our colonial inheritance. That's what the army defends. But our diversity is our strength. I promise you, it's stronger than their guns." That first time Latika met Daniel, she felt a deep understanding between them, as if they'd lived a previous life side by side. His determination for a better world went beyond belief, beyond even desire. It was a need. Like Ma, Daniel's mother was a teacher, though he was raised as one of six children in a rural town before moving to Makerere. Latika would be joining him in the journalism program next year, having received her acceptance just days before. It was within her grasp now, to join the union and fight for justice alongside Daniel and Arun. In the meetings they would all be equal, a democracy, unlike out in the world. As the time approached she was overcome with the knowledge that this was what she had always needed, scarcely imaginable until now.

Arun told her the rally would be big, bigger than anything he had ever done. His voice broke and for the first time he seemed delicate, his lips bitten red and the moonlight catching the amber in his irises. She stroked his cheek, smoothing his sideburns. He turned into her palm, kissing the thin skin. Goosebumps shot across her body.

"I'll come with you," she said. His eyes held something between surprise and concern, but he didn't tell her no.

"But your family—"

Latika scoffed. "My mother thinks I should have been a boy." It was the first time she'd said it out loud. Her whole life she'd strived against a ghost. Nothing she did could satisfy her mother. She wanted only to be enough as she was. And yet here was a boy who saw all the parts of her that her mother couldn't stand, the daring parts, the parts that wanted to step forward and grasp the torch. He would not hold her back.

Arun touched a lock of her hair. "I'm glad you aren't," he said with a chuckle.

Latika tried a smile. He didn't understand. But what he did understand was freedom, independence, a life of possibility.

The rally was on a Tuesday. Latika left school at lunch to meet Arun at Makerere, planning to return in time to collect her sisters. She untied her braid on the way, shearing her fingers through her hair until dark strands twined her fingers. Her lunch was untouched in her bag. Her mind was sharp, her body empty and clear, poised on a great precipice. She was stepping beyond the bounds of her family, and with that came the realization that she would not return home the same.

They packed into the field, voices and signs and fists rising in a wave. She had fought to be up front with Arun and the rest of the union. "I'm not a child," she snapped, "I can take care of myself." Arun refused. She wasn't yet in university. Her family didn't know where she would be. None of the other women felt the need to be front and center. "How will it look if women get harmed for our cause?" he pleaded. She didn't have answers. Instead she lanced her voice with the rest, bellowing louder to be heard from the back. Every sensation was heightened, every color enhanced, the pitch of the megaphones, the touch of the breeze on her skin, and she felt herself coming into focus among the crowd. She had become part of a bigger vision, and she would not look away.

From her vantage point she was quick to notice the green army jeep keening toward the pitch, the soldiers packed inside, the rifles, the second jeep, the third. The cardboard sign fell from her grip. She wanted to yell, but her voice caught in her throat. Then the ripple across the crowd, the collective shift to awareness. She craned her face to the front of the stadium and searched him out. Arun stared back at her, his lips mouthing, *run*.

Canisters of tear gas ripped through the air. Batons smashed down on shoulders and legs, students falling over one another as they scrambled to get away. Latika's escape was fast; Arun had made her stand closest to the nearest building, the escape route should anything go wrong. She grabbed whoever she could, locked hands. She wrenched the doors open and found herself in the old auditorium, quiet as a cave. Her mind spun. She tried to leave and a student threw his arm across the door.

In the hush she remembered the day Pir-dada died, when he'd summoned her to his bed. She considered his story, of a fire he'd started long ago. She did not know why he had confided in her, why he had chosen her to take on his memory. But she was certain it was not so she would remain quietly on the wrong side of the door.

The back exit was unlocked. She slipped out into the sun, blinking like a creature emerging from a long slumber, not knowing if she'd been absent for minutes or hours.

She found Daniel picking through the ravaged pitch. A line of blood clotted against his hairline, red-black, blending with his skin so that she only noticed when he turned to the light. His shirt was ripped at the shoulder, his pants thick with mud. But his face, when he saw her, fractured with relief.

Arun was nowhere. They scoured the campus, coughing against old gas. Their eyes streamed. Bags and cardboard were strewn endlessly, students pressing stained T-shirts against fresh wounds. The heat stifled as the hours passed. The grass beneath their feet was spongy, and when they walked away their shoes trailed red. Latika ran without direction, desperation taking over. Daniel caught her arm, pulled her to stop.

"They were dragging people into the jeeps. Maybe Arun..."

He couldn't finish the sentence. Latika searched his eyes. She wanted reassurance, certainty that all would return to normal—that understanding between them that had never needed words. But she saw only his fear.

A car honked behind them. They both startled. Then Latika heard her name, her father's voice. Her mother's grip on her elbow, dragging her away. Daniel held her gaze, his shoulders heaving. "Who *is* that?" Ma muttered in her ear. She couldn't leave him. She had no choice.

In the car, Latika bit her cheek until it bled. Her parents kept their faces forward. "Not what we expected," Ma spat, each word dropping like a stone. Latika didn't know if Ma was referring to Arun or herself. Behind them, Makerere faded in a haze of smoke. When they reached home, Ma wrenched Arun's bedroom door open and flew at his closet, stuffing his belongings into bags: his clothes, the transistor radio, books and notebooks and a tangle of ties. Pappa watched from the doorway, face tight.

"You can't, how can you—" Latika sputtered, but Ma shot her a look of such ice that she stopped. Kiya began to cry.

"He's l-leaving, he's l-leaving me?" she wailed, snot clogging her voice.

Pappa tugged at his collar, struggling with his words. "Not. In. My. House."

Ma whirled around, shouting over him. "Your sisters walked home on their own. Do you realize what could have happened?"

Latika swallowed. It was the first time she had ever missed picking them up from school. But she had planned to reach them in time. She didn't want to picture them waiting for her. She hadn't wanted to betray them that way.

"I didn't mean to," she said, her voice cracking.

Pappa slapped his hand against the wall and stalked away. The door clanged and from the window Latika saw him pacing the courtyard. Mayuri appeared in the hallway, her face drawn.

"Where is he?" she whispered.

Latika glanced at her. Her mind was blank, her body drained. "In prison." She no longer cared about protecting their innocence, as her parents tried so hard to do. What good did it do, to be raised in such unknowing?

Ma scoffed. "We were wrong about him." She tore a cargo jacket from a hanger and shoved it into his suitcase. The smell of Arun was overpowering, his cologne and the smoke from the curtains, the musk of his unmade bed.

"He's better than the rest of you, pretending you're above it all."

Ma looked up from the closet, a glint in her eye. "Has he told you about his family, hm? All this business about standing up for the little people, and do you know what money he comes from?"

A chill slid over Latika, to think that perhaps Arun's candor had been curated. But she shook off the thought, because however little she might know him, he had seen all of her. She stared wordlessly back at Ma. Satisfied, Ma tore the zipper closed and slung the bags across her shoulders. Kiya was sitting in the doorway, snot dripping onto her shirt. Ma stepped over her and looked at Mayuri.

"And don't pretend you didn't know this all along. Whatever nonsense you heard from him, banish it from your head. I don't know what he was thinking, talking protest-protest around a little girl."

"You?" Latika gasped. "But how?"

Mayuri dropped her chin, then raised her gaze slowly. A tear threatened at the rim of her eye. Latika gaped at her sister. She had thought they'd been so careful, a secret world of two, but all this time she'd been exposed. Nothing was hers alone.

Ma whipped around, one of the bags spewing dirty socks onto the floor.

"Don't you dare blame your sisters for this. You let this go on in our house. If anything happened to my babies, it would be on you."

Latika felt the sting of her exclusion. Hadn't she just sprinted from soldiers as they dragged her friends into army trucks? Hadn't she been the one to witness batons cracking down on unwitting bones? Hadn't she picked through the wreckage of cardboard and shoes and blood in fear that her love was lost? But Ma's care did not extend to her. Even in danger, Ma treated her less like a daughter than some wayward girl. And perhaps that's who she was, who she needed to be.

There was only Daniel, who had limped by her side. And Arun, who whispered plans into her ear at night, who searched for her across the stadium, his lips mouthing a single word.

Latika glared at her mother. "Are you saying that because you couldn't protect my siblings or your own?"

Ma dropped the bags. Latika wished her sisters hadn't heard. It wasn't them she wanted to hurt. But she knew where she stood. In Arun's bedroom, the sunlight caught the framed death portraits of Pir-dada and Sonal-baa, and the glass flashed gold.

Arun, 1965

W E FIND OURSELVES AT A turning point," Arun murmured, his breath choppy as he mounted the hill toward campus. "We can carry on in these worn tracks, or we can unite to build a nation rid of colonial hierarchies. A future for all." He paused, his mouth dry with worry.

From here, he could just see Northcote Hall, the cramped dwellings where he now lived. He was set to deliver his speech later that night at a gathering of student unions, young people traveling in from Kenya and Tanganyika, ready to fight. It was a nearly unanimous decision by the union that Arun should deliver the speech. The arrest last year had landed him more recognition than he expected. On campus he was revered, the imprisonment a mark of his commitment. Latika was in his dorm room waiting to run through his speech one last time, radiant with purpose. And yet, Arun felt his own resolve waning.

In the valley below, the corrugated roofs of the Kisenyi slum winked out of sight. Standing at the university gates, it was possible to forget such places existed. Arun surveyed the landscape, fiddling anxiously with his lighter—silver engraved with his initials, a gift from his father. If he delivered the speech that night, he would be cementing his role as a leader in their cause, a spokesperson and an activist. He would be making a public promise, inspired by Pan-African movements, to fight for land, freedom, and education for the people.

And if he didn't give the speech, if he listened to the churning in his gut and gave it up, he might lose Latika.

His mother's last letter had urged him to return home. Arun's parents, like many in their community, had held on to their British status after Independence, conscious of their growing alienation from this country and clutching onto an escape route. Now their fears were materializing.

The workers at his father's soap factory were striking, citing Uhuru, claiming that this was their country and they need not answer to foreigners. Never mind that Arun's family had lived in Uganda for generations. They were still reeling from the nationalist boycott of Asian businesses a few years back when the factory was almost run to the ground. Now the violence of the post-Independence revolution in Zanzibar had reached across borders, as centuries of anger against the British erupted, only the targets were Arab landowners and Asian merchants, who were murdered as if they were to blame for the country's poverty. It was always the minorities who were attacked when the masses grew frustrated with their lot. Power to the people, they said in the union, Arun himself proclaiming an Africa for Africans. Only now that they had come for his family did he see where he stood in that equation.

But it was when Latika handed him her draft of the speech that his concerns coalesced. She had offered to write it for him when he couldn't find the words. It was powerful, stronger than anything he himself could conjure. And yet he could tell from what she'd written— avowing that it was collective liberation they must strive for, not individual success, that the privileged must relinquish their wealth for the good of the masses—that she was implicating him. But he no longer knew if he wanted a life of sacrifice.

The watery posho and rice that he'd eaten in the canteen tossed in his stomach. A year ago, his belief was so strong that it shook rooms and sucked strangers into its orbit, Latika included. But she had surpassed him, blazing forward with the union, while he was ready to pull back. He felt a flash of regret at the knowledge that it was he who had set it all in motion.

"A Uganda for all," he repeated.

A hand grasped his shoulder and he turned to find Daniel in a white button-down and plastic sandals. He had begun to grow out his Afro, like many on campus, inspired by the Civil Rights Movement in the United States.

"Where's your mind, ndugu?" Daniel said. Arun grinned sheepishly.

"Tonight." He straightened his shoulders, not wanting Daniel to sense his apprehension. Before the union, he'd never had friends he looked up to in this way. Daniel was passionate but measured, always making room for new members, limitless in spirit. Latika, on the other end, was ardent, her devotion to the cause relentless. And yet they seemed to complement one another, Latika corralling the group when Daniel was too restrained, Daniel calmly laying out the steps when Latika's ideas charged ahead. Arun wondered where he landed between them. He sometimes sensed that they were both gazing over his head toward some intangible future that he couldn't see.

Arun and Daniel fell into step through the quad, where groups of first-years lounged. A clot of students dressed in olive green shuffled past; the resistance had been growing since decolonization, as unemployment rose and the military presence in the government expanded. Arun recognized the hooded gaze of one green-suited boy. They'd been herded into the back of the jeep together after the protest last year, both scraping at their streaming eyes.

Arun remembered little of the hours after that treacherous ride, the two nights in prison that followed. The sharpest memory was of his emergence, the warm air a balm, and how Rajni and Vinod greeted him at their door with faces of stone. He didn't see Latika again until she arrived at Makerere. After all that had happened with her family, he imagined she might want nothing to do with him. Instead, she wanted him more. He could recall nothing when she pressed him for details about those nights, and when he finally admitted to her about the bruises that had striped his calves for weeks, she grew still. "This is why we didn't let you join," he said, breaking the silence. It felt like the right thing to say. He wasn't prepared for the look in her eyes, as close to hatred as he had ever seen in her. "You don't get to decide that," she said, and Arun was suddenly uncertain about what was upsetting her more: that he had spent two nights in prison, or that she hadn't gotten to be there.

"Charles doesn't think we should write about tonight," Daniel said. He was vice editor at *Makerere Today*. "*Too divisive.*" He spat on the grass path.

Arun raised an eyebrow. "But you'll write it anyways."

Daniel beamed. "Once they read it, they'll want to print it."

Arun let out a short laugh, even as his skin warmed. Knowing Daniel, lines of his own speech would be scattered throughout the article. *The British wanted to turn us against one another. We have seen this happen across the continent, the world. But we will rise with the poorest among us, with the smallest tribes, with those who labored on this soil for us to stand here. Where diversity is seen not as disloyalty, but as power.*

A current shivered through his limbs. They had been preparing for this night for weeks. All the long Saturday afternoons with the union, the room blue with smoke. The gathering had been Daniel's idea. For Arun, the union had meant more time with those he so admired on campus, the thrill of brotherhood among them, always ready to wax political on the nation, independence, revolution, justice. If only he could still feel the glow of those early days now.

The back of his collar was damp with sweat, and he welcomed the shade of the library. He did want the spotlight, the thrill of his own voice stirring a room. But after last year—the imprisonment, the fallout with Latika's family—his nerves were running wild. And now, with the strike at the factory, his mother's distress, with the newspapers regularly publishing anti-Asian articles, he had to admit that he was afraid.

"This is where I leave you, brother," Daniel said.

"Wait, Daniel," Arun spluttered, realizing what he was going to say only after he'd begun. "Me giving this speech, with the climate now, I'm just worried, as an Asian and..." He trailed off, unable to risk witnessing his own fall in Daniel's eyes.

Daniel squinted at him, then nodded slowly.

"Ndugu," he said, squeezing the back of Arun's neck, "you may not be African, but you're certainly Ugandan."

Arun continued past the library, taking comfort in Daniel's remark. He thought of Latika waiting for him and felt the urge to unburden himself to her in the same way. When he considered it, what he wanted was simple: a life with Latika, a house with several fruit trees, friends nearby, and two or three children. He imagined fading into the background of the movement, leading an ordinary life. At the end of their first term, he'd convinced Latika to spend the day with him at the Botanical Gardens in Entebbe, and despite her reluctance, by the day's end she was looser, laughing openly and shrieking in glee when they spied a crocodile by the water's edge. This was who they could be together, he as the cold compress to her undying fever. *We could have this every day*, he'd wanted to tell her, *just you and me, free.*

"I'm scared that if I tell you I'm afraid, you'll leave me," he said out loud. A student sipping a cola on the steps smirked at him, and he hurried away.

Frequently, Arun thought back to those early weeks with Latika's family, Rajni reusing oil to fry gathiya and Vinod quiet after a long day at work, Mayuri and Kiya filling every silence, all of them pressed around the table. He longed for that closeness again, an intimacy in their home that he had rarely felt in his own. His own parents were at best cordial with one another, and more interested in Arun's accomplishments—in what they could brag to the neighbors—than who he really was. The care he'd witnessed in Latika's household had felt both precious and hard-won, something worth protecting.

And yet Latika was reluctant to speak of her family, and he gleaned that they had grown distant. The few times he had tried to encourage her to make amends with them, he was startled by how staunchly she refused. Though he'd since dropped the matter, Arun had the sense that every step they took toward a life together was a step away from her family.

But away from home, Latika was electric, sneaking into his dorm room or skipping class with her closest friend Brendah to plaster inciting posters around campus. She kissed him in front of their friends and always lingered when it was time to return to her family at night. With so much at stake in their world, from the movement to their families, their love took on a new urgency, and Arun cherished the moments when it seemed that all she desired was him.

Passing the chalky-blue administrative building, Arun ran a finger along the bottom of his front teeth, feeling the jagged edge from some childhood accident that he couldn't remember. His mother told him it was a fall from a jackfruit tree, though if anyone asked, he said it was from a schoolyard fight when he was a boy. Wishful thinking. He was raised in the way of wealthy Asian children in Jinja, his school uniform pressed and sea blue, the maid and the cook always there to pick up after him.

His mother liked to remind him that her own parents had worked in a carpet shop, and that she had spent her childhood slapping dust from old wool until she was old enough to manage the till. *We worked for this*, she would say. He resisted the impulse to repeat this to Latika, to remind her that the British had built the system this way, where Asians couldn't own land and so had to become traders, while Africans couldn't own businesses and so had to work the land.

But every time he found himself defending where he came from or justifying to himself why he was stepping away from the fight, he could think only of Bwambale, his family's driver. He was the one who had shuttled Arun to and from school every day, who chased a pair of thieves away from the house with a kitchen knife, who kept quiet when he witnessed Arun sneaking out one night, never betraying his trust. Bwambale had lived in a small hut at the corner of Arun's family's land with his young son, who Arun sometimes saw wearing his own handed-down shoes, the sweaters he deemed too frayed.

One night the little boy had a seizure in his sleep; Bwambale, petrified, had taken the family car, the very one he drove each day, to rush to the hospital. He returned to find Arun's father fully dressed, late to be driven to work; Arun strapped into his backpack, late for school.

Arun had never seen his father so angry. *Sala kala*, he spat, *dirty Black, you're a thief like the rest.* Arun remembered watching from behind the pleats of his mother's sari as his father wrenched the keys from Bwambale's hands. As he stormed into his hut, tossing Bwambale's possessions into the mud: clean shirts, a miniature radio, two painted clay bowls that cracked like eggshells when they hit the ground. But it was the anguished look on Bwambale's face, as if he had just understood that their love had always been conditional, that made Arun run—not toward Bwambale, as he later imagined, wrapping his arms around the man's long legs, nor toward his father, pleading with him to stop, picking the broken things from the dirt, but back into the house. He was ashamed to remember his relief at being out of Bwambale's line of sight.

It was only later that Arun realized Bwambale's son had not been with him. Hastening to get back to his job, he must have left the boy in the care of the hospital, likely believing he would be granted the small decency from his employers of being allowed to take the car back to collect him. When Arun asked his mother how Bwambale would get back to the hospital, she hushed him and placed another rotli on top of his barely eaten one. *No need to think of them now*, she mumbled, glancing at her husband, but the hitch in her voice betrayed her.

It was this image that Arun returned to: Bwambale walking to the hospital to collect his son, the dirt from the road gathering in Arun's father's old flip-flops.

In the years that followed, Arun brought up Bwambale every chance he could. A way of assuaging his guilt, though it was too late. But the neighbors had their own stories. *Look what happens when you trust one*, they whispered, *did you hear he stole money to pay for treatment for his deaf-mute son, when Uncle-sir was already paying the boy's school tuition, the ingrate, chi chi, that's why you can't let them get too comfortable, how can so much harm come to such good people?*

The new driver was younger, rarely spoke, perhaps having heard the story of Bwambale through his own channels. On the trips to and from school, Arun missed Bwambale's gossiping, the questions he asked so earnestly that Arun giggled.

"The new driver doesn't listen to me," Arun said to his father one night. "So rude. Bwambale was never like that."

He thought it was a barb against his father, to wave Bwambale's obvious virtues in his face. The next day, the new driver was gone; a round, tobacco-chewing man was in his place. It was then that Arun began to understand the precise power of his words.

He reached Northcote and entered his room. Sitting on the edge of his bed, Latika wore a skirt the color of lemons, her long hair tied in a knot at the nape of her neck. She cared little for beauty, but the plainness of her clothing only emphasized her striking features, the large eyes and delicate chin.

"Have you been practicing?"

There was an edge to her voice, a smudge of kajal on her cheek. He made to thumb it away, but she turned her face to the wall.

"What's wrong?"

She shook her head. "The speech. What do you think?"

"The—your speech," he said, catching himself, "I..." In his pause he saw her eyes harden. He had the sudden desire to please her. When he had told Latika about Bwambale, she gently suggested that the issue was perhaps not his father's behavior that day but the fact that they saw themselves deserving of service at all. He felt embarrassed then, remembering how Latika collected her sisters every afternoon. She wouldn't forgive him his cowardice. "We're all born into our lot," she murmured once. "We don't get to control how we come in. But we can choose how we go out." He wanted to show her that he could make the right choice.

He watched as she untied and retied her hair, so that for a moment it uncoiled against her back, a dark snake.

"I'm nervous," he said finally. Not even a fraction of the truth. But how could he say what he really felt when she sat here so poised and fervent? She softened, the cool pads of her fingers tracing his chin.

"You'll bewitch them all. You know this is the part you're good at." She gave him an impish smile, though her eyes remained clouded. "Anyways, you'll have to tell me how it goes."

"What do you mean?"

"They won't let me stay late this evening."

Arun knew who *they* meant. She did this when she felt slighted, turned all those around her into one nameless unit, separating herself from the rest.

"I can't believe you won't be there." The prospect of bowing out rushed back, a panic in his limbs. He could go home to visit his mother. How much simpler life would be if he just turned to his studies and let the rest go.

But Latika was still gripping his chin between her thumb and forefinger, and now she squeezed it, her nail digging slightly into the soft skin at the top of his throat. "Do it justice," she said.

The tightness of her lips reminded him of when she'd handed him her speech, a reluctance as she passed over the page. How crushed she must feel that she wouldn't be present. And then it was obvious: that she would much rather be the one up there tonight. How had he not seen it earlier? "It doesn't need to be like that, a boys-only club," Latika had once muttered when Arun and the others lingered impatiently after the union meeting, waiting for everyone else to leave. Arun had said nothing, exchanging a look with Daniel that was a mixture of embarrassment and apology, and Latika had slapped down the notes she had taken for the meeting and huffed from the room. But that moment seemed only to spur her on; she'd arrived early to every meeting since, as if running on hot coals.

He felt the hope in her gaze, on the edge of desperation, and understood for the first time why she had chosen him. Not Daniel. Not her family. She had chosen him, Arun, knowing exactly the kind of life they could have together.

Finally, he saw himself clearly. Maybe he wasn't the boundless leader, the one who sprung back from prison undiminished. Maybe his activism could be of a much more modest kind: the one who could open doors. He would give the speech where she couldn't, knowing they were her words. A warm sense of purpose flooded him. He would do it for her. A year ago he wouldn't have thought twice. In the end, it was she who he was fighting for. "You know I will," he said.

But Latika had stood from the bed and was backing away from him. He laughed uncertainly as she raised her hands like a preacher at a lectern.

"Arun," she said, her voice rising, "my ndugu, we find ourselves at a turning point. We come together as people who are angry, undaunted, and ready. We will not settle for picking up the pieces we have been given, cobbling together some semblance of peace. No, friends, today we choose to build something new. To create, with hands, minds, bodies released after too long under a broken system, a new way forward. To make a place for us all."

Arun could do little more than watch as Latika recited the entire speech she had written, her gaze cast far beyond him, out the window and across the slope of the hill, as if she were addressing the crowd, as if she were already in that other place.

Latika, 1968

THE NIGHT BEFORE HER WEDDING to Arun, Latika waited for her mother to come to her door. Her outfit was draped over a chair, a simple red fabric with a thin border of gold stitching. She had seen the teardrop earrings that Ma's mother had gifted her before her wedding and expected that Ma would be bringing her something of her own to wear. But the longer she waited, the more she understood that Ma would not be coming. She touched her wrists and felt their bareness. It wasn't jewelry that she'd been hoping for.

She was a month away from graduation, after which she would move out of the Gur nu Ghar to live with Arun, who had begun working at a law firm in Kampala. For the past year, neighbors and friends had made sly comments to Ma and Pappa—it was about time she married, did she have any prospects, best not to let a girl get too educated. At this last comment Pappa always balked. *I will not let anything come between my children and their education*, he said. But even he wanted her married as soon as she finished university. When Arun proposed, changing from his work suit into a maroon jacket for the occasion, she thought back to what had first drawn her to him—how he offered her a kind of power, a way forward when she felt trapped. And she understood that he still could. He would not deny her her work, her ambition. Her fight. With him, it could be different.

Her parents had refused. Pappa was livid, insisting it wouldn't work

145

with Arun's family. Latika knew only the basics, that Arun's parents had called hers after the prison incident, acid flying from their tongues. She supposed the rift had not healed. Arun's parents opposed too, clutching their grudge like armor, but Arun maintained that they would come around if it was what he wanted. Though Ma was furious, it was she who, in the end, insisted that it was Latika's choice. In this, Ma was unyielding. And so, the following day they would be married in a ceremony that neither set of parents would attend. She could hardly sleep anymore. At night, she thought about Pir-dada's story given to her long ago, and for the first time considered the difference between a choice and an escape.

But time was slipping away. Daniel was gone, imprisoned for inciting a demonstration against Obote's suspension of the constitution. He was likely in solitary in Luzira Prison, though no one could predict if he would resurface or just vanish. He wasn't the first. Ever since Obote began using the military, led by the brutal general Idi Amin, to quash any resistance, poets and journalists and delegates were disappearing for criticizing the government's authoritarian turn. Even before Daniel's arrest, their union meetings had languished into the night, curtains dragged across the classroom windows against the reports of Obote's spies inside the university. When Latika joined the union four years ago, they were deep in the post-Independence fervor, ripe with the promise of retelling their country's story. Now the shine was gone, dulled by the loss of loved ones to the regime, the food shortages and imprisonments without trial, the fear of speaking itself. Pappa was barely clinging to his job through Africanization, and many families from the community had lost their incomes with the persecution of Indian traders. Hope was an elusive thing, and she felt herself grasping.

Daniel had started his own underground paper, *Jicho*, after the army shot a student on campus and both the national papers and *Makerere Today* kept silent. *Jicho*'s mission was to disrupt colonial legacies, fostering a new vision. Latika had written several pieces for it, all of them published anonymously, a task that had revived her sense of purpose—though the irony of now reporting Daniel's disappearance in his own covert paper did not escape her.

Now, Latika forced her eyes shut. She hadn't changed out of her day clothes, still imagining Ma might come. She could smell the sweat on her loose tunic, her hair that snarled around her shoulders. No one would believe her to be a bride. When she and Brendah left the union meeting that day, arms linked and bodies heavy, Brendah had tapped her chin. "A bride shouldn't sulk the day before her wedding," she said. Then, softer, "Daniel would have wanted to see you happy." Latika couldn't stop the tears that sprung to her eyes.

She rubbed her face, willing sleep to come. Pappa wasn't speaking to her and Ma had turned her back. Mayuri and Kiya were caught in between, though both had cried when Pappa told them they wouldn't be attending the wedding. And now Daniel wouldn't be there. Had she chosen this? She'd gently suggested to Arun that they postpone the wedding until circumstances calmed, but the anguish in his face— already so drawn since the disappearance of his best friend—had crushed her. "We have one good thing," he'd responded, "I won't let it go." *Tomorrow will be different*, Daniel had often said. She had to believe that it would.

When she heard her door open, she turned her face into the pillow, not wanting Ma to witness her desperation. But then a warmth surged on either side of her, curling into the dips of her body. She opened her eyes to her sisters. Mayuri, to her left, held a book tucked carefully with brown paper. Kiya, to her right, twined her sinewy legs, sweaty from playing cricket, with Latika's.

"We're sorry we can't come," Mayuri whispered finally. She was fifteen, carrying her body uneasily, moving from a shy girl to a careful adult. Latika had heard her fighting with Ma about attending the wedding, her voice charged with emotion, though in the end Ma had won. She felt a twinge of bitterness that her sisters were still obeying their mother.

"We think it's stupid that they won't let us." Kiya said the word like Ma, *schuppid*, almost spitting it. Latika laughed in surprise, a wild relief breaking through her body.

"Remember how you used to chase us around the courtyard with the fugyo like a fruit bat?" Mayuri said.

"And we were your precious guavas," Kiya cackled, loudly enough that their parents would hear. Latika was grateful for this small resistance. She did remember those endless afternoons made giddy by heat, how she would pretend to gnaw on her sisters' cheeks until they howled with terror and glee. She couldn't find her words. Instead she wound an arm around each shoulder, Mayuri's rounded and Kiya's angular, and let her head grow heavy. Tomorrow, she thought, their tangled limbs sinking into the mattress, let it come.

It was a quiet function at the mandir. Latika's cousin Biju and his wife bore witness, their faces sorry. The Dalals from next door came too, a smattering of friends. Latika's neck and ears were bare. She carried herself mechanically, her smile feigned. Arun glowed in his ivory kurta, and for his sake, Latika did her best. During the ceremony she thought she saw Ma through the pandit's flame, but the heat shimmered the air, dreamlike, and she couldn't be sure. After the ceremony they met Brendah and Yusuf and a few others from the union for lunch, but Daniel's continued absence saddled the room and they ended the gathering early, the cake uncut.

That night, Arun's parents called to remind him that he and Latika must come live with them for their first married year. It was a shock after their total denial of the wedding. Arun's cheeks twitched. *I told you they'd come around*, he mouthed. Latika couldn't hide her alarm.

Slowly Arun turned back to the phone. "My job is in the city," he countered. "You'll take the car," his mother pushed. "You'll like Kariuki—the new driver." Latika waited for Arun's next argument, but it never came. With great pain, she held her words. She had already disappointed one set of parents.

The night before they were due to leave, her door opened. She was packing her trunk when Ma came in.

"Take your best saris," Ma said. "You need to dress like a wife now."

Latika jolted up, prepared to face Ma's anger once more before she left, but was disarmed by the swelling around Ma's eyes. Ma knelt on the mattress beside Latika's trunk and laid a thin gold chain on its surface.

"A woman must carry her own means."

Latika fingered the chain but did not lift it. "The wedding was a month ago." She couldn't keep her spite from slipping out.

Ma did not meet her eyes, but began to speak quickly, refolding the saris that Latika had already packed away. "You know when I got married, my mother gave me jewelry and more, more than I could need. But I've been married over twenty years now, and never once has that helped me. I wanted to give you something that mattered. And I already have. Latika, I know I never have to worry about you. You will be perfectly fine, whoever you marry, or even on your own. You always have been."

Latika didn't know if this was an apology or praise. Ma finished folding the clothes and picked up the chain. "Can I?" she murmured, slipping it around Latika's neck, the fine gold dipping between her collarbones. Her fingers lingered, parsing the knotted hairs at Latika's nape. "Maybe I should have brought a comb instead," she said, a glimmer in her eye.

Before Latika could respond, Ma brought her lips to Latika's ear and whispered, "Your father needs time to calm down. He has to show he's in control. Just wait. He'll come back." In one quick motion she crushed her lips to Latika's jaw, her breath in her ear warm and wanting. Then she stood and left the room. Latika tucked the chain beneath the neck of her nightdress. She needed no one else to see it. Feeling it there, its weight settling gently against her, was enough.

In Jinja, scrubby bushes lined the road to her in-laws' home. Latika wore a yellow sari embroidered with flowers, a jasmine bud wilting in her bun, and Arun had polished his shoes and combed back his hair. She carried a pot engraved with her grandmother's name, filled with dhokla Ma had steamed that morning. A mechanical whine trailed them, incessant and ugly. When she asked Arun what it was, he shrugged and gestured in the direction of the river, which rushed alongside the town and softened the air with its scent. "My father's factory," he said. "I barely notice the sound anymore."

His parents stood at the iron gates like two sentries, their faces round and hard as coins. An askari waited, hand on the gate, the glint of a panga visible next to his pouch of keys. Around them, bushes gaudy with cream frangipani shivered in the breeze. They lived in an old colonial mansion, salmon tiles paving the roof, white columns climbing from the carved balustrade. Latika stooped to touch their feet, and neither said a word, though Arun's father brushed his fingertips across her shoulder. His mother took Arun's cheeks between her palms. He wore an easy smile, a child's joy. Latika turned away and spied the little shed out front, the one she knew was once Bwambale's.

In the kitchen stood a thin African woman whose waist was wound in so much fabric that she appeared pregnant. Her hair was kept back in six simple cornrows that trailed off at her neck. The smell of elchi and black pepper rippled from the stove. She poured the chai for the four of them, laid out with a plate of ginger biscuits. She was not introduced. Latika only learned her name when Arun's mother took a sip, then pushed the cup roughly away, her tongue between her teeth.

"Irene," Mata-ji said, "you've curdled the milk again." She held her voice steady but it rose in pitch on the last word. Pita-ji pursed his lips.

Latika dipped a biscuit in her chai. Sodden crumbs floated on the surface. Before she could lift it to her lips, Mata-ji pointed across the table. She wore a deep violet sari that gathered over her belly, blue stones in her ears.

"You cook? Make the tea."

Latika let the biscuit dissolve in her cup. Mata-ji was watching her with narrowed eyes. Slowly Latika stood and made her way to the stove, where Irene had set a new pot atop the flame.

"Latika just graduated from the journalism program," she heard Arun say behind her.

"After marriage you should take care of your family," Mata-ji said. "When I was first married I stayed home. I was as skinny as her then. My mother-in-law taught me everything I know."

Latika's tongue felt like sand. She had applied to every newspaper in the area, pasting samples of her work into the envelopes. The silence scorched. *Jicho* hung in her mind, a starving pulse. Daniel had confided that Yusuf was part of the small but trusted distribution network. Before leaving she had written to him—*the people's eye cannot shut*—and enclosed her new address.

"I'm looking for work," she said, tipping milk into the pot. She felt the snap of their eyes against her back.

"Think what people will say. It will look like Arun can't provide. Isn't that why you married my son?"

Latika clenched her fists. When Arun needed a place to stay, her home and family were satisfactory. But now she was not good enough for theirs.

"Come on, Mummy, she's just arrived," Arun said with a nervous titter. She wanted to turn to Arun, but found herself afraid.

The conversation moved toward Pita-ji's factory and Arun's work. Beside Latika, Irene mixed the lott for dinner, fingers ocher with batter. Latika tried to meet her gaze, but Irene flicked her eyes away. Mata-ji brought up that morning's paper, which had beseeched the government to banish the Asians, calling them leeches and unscrupulous rogues. "*They should pack up and go. We should be tighter with our borders, especially to those who have one foot here and one foot there. This nation is a landlord who can choose its tenants,*" Mata-ji quoted, then slapped the paper down.

Pita-ji chuckled. "Petty jealousy. I employ thousands. This country would fall apart without us."

Over the stove, Irene became very still. Latika opened her mouth, but Mata-ji rose to her feet.

"How long does it take for a cup of tea?" Her bangles clanged down her arms as she brought her nose to the pot and gave a low, disdainful snort. "They didn't teach you that in your degree, na?"

Latika stepped in front of her, reaching for the sugar. She stirred with vigor and thought of her grandmother, who had always worked, who could never be accused of not taking care of her family. Beside her, Irene breathed through her nose like a muffled alarm.

The days stretched endlessly. Latika languished. When she needed a break from her in-laws she tried slipping out for a walk by the river, but the askari warned her against armed kondos and wouldn't open the gates. Instead, she paced the terraced gardens until her toes blistered, plucking leaves from the trim hedge, the familiar sounds of home—hawkers and horns, neighbors gathered to chat—unnervingly absent. She wrote to Brendah and her sisters, though she struggled with what to say, her mind caged in the repetitiveness of her days. Sometimes she played marbles with the young houseboy behind the porch, though at the slightest noise he scurried away. Once she saw Irene hanging washing from the shed and realized that it must be her home now. White blouses, grey slacks, a skinny tie writhed on the line. Then Kariuki, the driver who ferried Arun to and from work, emerged. He had a heavy forehead, a thin scar on his neck that disappeared into the collar of his singlet. He'd told Arun that he'd been a freedom fighter in the Kenyan Land and Freedom Army, that he'd fled to Uganda when the colonials started rounding the LFA into detention camps. He'd wanted to return after Kenyan Independence, but the land held pain now, he said.

Kariuki plucked a shirt from the line and slid his arms through the sleeves. Irene buttoned his cuffs with the ease of those who had long been companions. Alone, Latika walked back to the house.

A coldness was taking root inside her. She tried to tell Arun as he clipped his toenails one night, her eyes on his hunching back. "It's hard being here all day," she began, "and your mother..." But this was all she managed. When Arun turned to her, his lips were pouted like a small boy's. "I told you what it's like here." He sounded more indignant than understanding, as if he stood on one side of the gate, and she was fumbling to enter.

There was still no word on Daniel. Latika tried to remember him at his full height rather than imagine him confined to a cell: the fold that appeared between his eyebrows when he was focused, his capacity for both gravity and rumbling, joyful laughter. Daylight passed, and at night the sky was full of kites and bats. Latika waited eagerly for Arun to return from work, newspaper in tow, which she scoured for job postings. The gates remained closed.

Her only respite came from the letters. They made her miss home with an intensity she hadn't anticipated. She sat on the steps outside the house one evening, reading a letter from Mayuri. From it she learned that Kiya had landed a leading role in her school's play that year. *She's asking if you'll come back to watch her perform?* Mayuri wrote. Latika's fingers trembled when she read those words. How clearly she heard Mayuri's voice, disguising her own longings with someone else's, that single question mark at the end exposing her true feelings. The play was such a small thing in the scheme of the world, and yet in that moment Latika couldn't bear the thought of not being there. But she knew she wouldn't be. Her mother's words had grown clearer with distance. She was not to return until the gossip had cleared, until Pappa felt he was back in control. She didn't know how she would write back and tell them no.

Mata-ji found her on the step, stricken. Latika waited for her admonishment, idleness being the greatest offense for a new wife. "Want to go home?" Mata-ji said, indicating Mayuri's careful lettering across the page. Latika couldn't muster the energy to assure her mother-in-law that she was happy here. Mata-ji bent down with some effort, the green drape of her crepe sari crinkling, and patted Latika's hand. "Give them a grandchild," she whispered, eyes soft.

Latika considered this at night, as Arun panted above her, her nails digging into his muscled back. What did it mean to bring a child into this world, when the government had just legitimized anti-Asian discrimination, ruling that not all children born in Uganda had an automatic right to citizenship; when the best people she knew were being jailed and disappeared; when her own life had become one of both servitude and privilege. She imagined a child venturing through the neat gardens, never setting foot outside the gates. As she drifted to sleep she dreamed of the gates opening and her feet pounding the earth as she charged through, the cries of her baby behind her. She woke with a start and felt a moment's regret that she hadn't made it farther out.

Then Yusuf wrote back. Brendah too. They would do it. Latika would write; they would copy and distribute. In the months since Daniel launched *Jichu*, the network had grown, a subterranean root system thirsting for more. Latika shivered, thinking of how far her words would travel, how quietly operative she could be. The only piece missing was the middle passage, transporting the paper from Jinja to Kampala without the conspicuousness of the mail.

It could only be Arun. A year ago Latika would have been certain of his dedication; now she feared his answer. Each night he arrived spent, his energy waned. A prominent lawyer in the government was disappeared recently, reason unknown. Though Arun had tried to broach Daniel's case at work, it seemed to be a dead end. She felt him slipping back into the indifference of his old life, leaving his plate on the table after dinner.

"The least you can do is put that in the sink," she barked one night. It spilled out before she could think, but she didn't care.

Arun blinked at Latika as if just noticing her. The light caught the thick rims of his glasses. He reached for his plate, but as he lifted it from the table his fingers twitched and it smashed to the ground. Shards of ceramic, grains of rice, the pulpy stems of drumsticks skittered across the floor. Arun yelped. The blood rushed to Latika's head, her hand trembling as she swiped a clot of dal from her ankle. Simultaneously, Arun and Latika bent to gather the pieces, but Mata-ji snapped her fingers at Irene. "Clean this up."

Shame blurred Latika's vision. She refused to leave. She did not look at Mata-ji or Irene, but simply knelt to the floor. Mata-ji was cursing above her head, though Latika didn't hear the words. Then she saw her mother-in-law's wide calves sweep out, followed a minute later by Arun's socked feet. She flung the pieces into the garbage and poured water over the dishes in the basin. Irene moved to take them, but she refused that too, until they fell into a silent rhythm, Latika scrubbing, Irene rinsing.

When all was clean and Latika reached for the lamp, Irene produced an envelope from the folds of her apron.

"A letter came for you. Bwana tried to hide it."

Latika's breath quickened as she slit it open. The page was thin and the words curt. Another job rejection. Her eyes stung. She turned her face to the hallway, not wanting Irene to have to comfort her.

Latika paused on her way up the stairs, wanting to mark this opening of trust between them. "I hope you and Kariuki sleep well tonight," she whispered finally.

In their bedroom, Arun's arms shook as he folded his pants over the hanger. "In front of my family?" he burst. Latika wrenched the clip from her hair.

"Well, who am I, hm? Who is Irene to you?"

Arun's face mottled. "You are my wife, not my maid."

Latika tugged at the buttons of her tunic until one tore. "But Irene is your maid, right? So it's okay to treat her that way?"

His mouth opened and closed. "I don't...it's my mother—"

Latika scoffed. "And you? When have you defied them, for me, for Irene, for anyone?"

"I'm working all day, I don't know when you expect me to..." He trailed away as Latika threw her arms into the air.

"And Daniel?"

"Don't put that on me. What else can I do?"

Her vision flickered. "You have to do more. I can't even leave!" They were both half-clothed, both heaving. Latika slumped onto the mattress. They sat in silence, the only sound the beating of her blood. She felt a tentative hand on her back.

"I know it's hard. But fighting with my family, it's not worth your words."

"What about yours?" Latika grumbled. The tears fell now, hot and fast. His answer was clear—she didn't even need to ask. She hiccuped and thought of Kiya crying over Arun all those years ago. It only made her cry harder. Perhaps this was what Pappa had foreseen. She was trapped. She'd wanted this until she didn't. Maybe she never had. What she wanted was revolution, was love, was a partner in that fight. What she had was herself.

Arun blew softly on her cheeks. "Tell me how to help you. I'll do whatever you need."

The mattress sunk as he sidled behind her, his arms tight on her waist.

"Ndugo," she whispered. Arun kissed her mouth, her neck, bit her stomach. She grasped his hair, guiding him where she needed him to go.

She woke in the night to the patter of rain on the roof. Arun breathed heavily beside her, his arm across her back. Moonlight shifted through the window slats and stamped the wall. She had been dreaming of her mother pounding ginger to a paste. In the dream, Latika watched Ma's hands grind the pestle over the tubers, the scent sharp in her nostrils, the soup shimmering. She rose with tender wrists and her heart racing with determination.

She fished the crumpled rejection letter from under the bed. She carried her power in her mouth. *JICHO*, she wrote at the top of the page, and kept writing. Then she slipped from the sheets, wrapped a shawl around her shoulders, and left.

Her slippers sunk into the flooding grass. By the time she reached the shed, her hair was a slick rope down her back. She beat the door softly with the flat of her palm. A lamp fogged the window and the door creaked open.

Irene held her elbows, her hair wrapped in a scarf. Behind her, a gentle snore rose and fell.

"I want to ask your husband for something."

Irene pulled her lips in. In her nightdress Irene was softer, but sturdier too, the light of her own home solid around her. "Not for help—for collaboration. Yours too." She drew the page from her bag. Irene held it to her face. The light glowed through the thin sheet, catching the imprints of her pen. *Witness*, it said, *resistance. Unity, freedom from tyranny.* She had underlined, twice: *this land belongs to the African and in all affairs, political and economic, it is their word that must count.*

"You write these," Irene stated. She nodded at Latika as if remembering something. "A journalist."

Latika took a breath. "Weekly printing and distribution are already accounted for. My partner in Kampala is waiting. I just need to put these into his hands."

Irene leaned back. On the table behind her there were books, a basket of oranges, a vial of blue pills. Kariuki mumbled in his sleep, his voice rising from the shadows. He'd said they had remained in Uganda because Kenya held pain now, but there was pain here too. The British had promoted Idi Amin to commander of the Uganda Army for the sheer number of LFA fighters he had murdered. The colony hovered; the fight went on.

"We will work with you," Irene said.

In the rising silver of dawn their eyes met. Latika touched the chain around her neck. What she needed, she already had.

Mayuri, 1970

AFTER CLASS, MS. TAYLOR BECKONED Mayuri to her desk. Ms. Taylor's cheeks were pink from the heat of the classroom, though all the windows were thrown open. Mayuri neatened the tuck of her starched blouse. She was glad her teacher looked a little disheveled: it matched how she felt, her skirt too tight around her waist, the backs of her knees speckled with eczema, itching inside herself.

Ms. Taylor told Mayuri she'd been doing exceptionally well. Mayuri flushed. She still wasn't used to the new teachers who'd come in from Europe and Britain, sweeping through the halls with their airy linens collecting red dust. Rumors flew about why they were here—to escape the British weather, to find tropical love, to spread their passion for old poetry and plays—though Mayuri suspected they'd come simply because they could, pilgrims in search of who knew what.

"I'm sure you're considering medical school next year," Ms. Taylor said. Hesitantly, Mayuri said yes. She had been. She was one of the few girls in her science classes who consistently received top marks. At night she fell asleep reciting the bones of the body, its finer tendons and muscles. *Metacarpal. Sacrum. Ilium, ischium. Tibia, fibula.* It soothed her to count the parts that formed her, to name each separate piece of the whole.

She remembered watching Sonal-baa as she brewed her medicines, how she'd applied sugar to the splinters when Kiya fell from the jambu tree. It was from Sonal-baa that she first learned the names of the body parts in Swahili. *Shingo, kifundo, koo. Kope,* she'd say, fluttering her eyelashes against Mayuri's. Entwining her coarse fingers with Mayuri's small ones, *kidole.* She remembered her grandmother's thumbs, pressing the body's tender points. How they persisted until they found release.

"Mayuri, I think you should consider going abroad for your studies," Ms. Taylor said. She was craning across the desk, the tips of her blonde hair brittle. "The doors that will open for you with a degree from a well-known institution. You could have the opportunity to specialize, even to teach."

"I don't think so," Mayuri said. Sweat crept down her spine toward the band of her skirt. She dropped her gaze to stop herself from cocking her eyebrows. These teachers spoke as if it were so easy to fly away, start another life. But their families were different. Maybe the distance meant less. Maybe they trusted that they would return.

Ms. Taylor lowered her voice. "There are full scholarships. Merit- and need-based. You'd be eligible. India, England, America..."

Mayuri stretched her lips into a smile. "Thank you, miss."

Ms. Taylor's eyes crinkled. "Don't listen to what they say about you all. You Indians work hard and you deserve to stay or go how you like." She leaned closer. "And you especially, Mayuri—never late, so disciplined, unlike..." Her eyes danced toward Vicent, one of the few African boys in the class, before coming to rest on Mayuri once more with a conspiratorial smile. "Just promise me you'll consider it."

It was the European teachers who had begun making a fuss about the spicy smell that wafted in with the Indian students, picking on one boy whose mother sold tiffins in Mayuri's neighborhood. Then the African students took their lead, calling him little lamb, his mother's specialty. For the last week, the boy had stopped eating lunch, his head resting on his desk through the lessons. But Mayuri mentioned none of this. She held her smile as she walked away, promising her teacher that she would.

Kiya was waiting in the open-air compound with Adroa and Abbo, the sun winking off the tin roof of the schoolhouse. Kiya and Adroa had been friends since he and his sister Abbo joined their school during integration. Mayuri remembered when all the African children were first admitted after Independence eight years ago, at first standing together in a cluster, white socks pulled high up their knees, but soon skipping through the schoolyard with everyone else. They would go home for lunch only for Kiya and Adroa to meet up again on the field for cricket while Mayuri headed to the library.

"Ms. Taylor kept you back?" Abbo said with concern.

"She wanted to talk about my future." Mayuri shrugged.

"Makerere?"

"Abroad."

Abbo's lips parted. Mayuri shook her head, not wanting Abbo to feel hurt that their teacher hadn't pulled her aside as well. Mayuri suspected that Abbo was actually smarter than she was, but she'd noticed that Abbo's workbook had been erased and written over, while her own books were pristine. She knew that Abbo and Adroa's mother brewed waragi in the absence of a job, selling it from their home at the bottom of the hill. She thought of what Ms. Taylor had said about her discipline. It was true that she could be single-minded, more determined than anything else, but she'd seen Abbo remain absorbed in her books for hours while the other students passed notes and her own attention drifted to the window. "Not in my future," she said.

Kiya and Adroa were playing a complicated game with their fingers. Adroa grabbed Kiya's outstretched pinkie and she scowled. Mayuri checked over her shoulders. Ma and Pappa knew of Adroa as a distant classmate—Kiya was always filling dinnertime with stories—but if word got out to the aunties in the Gur nu Ghar that Kiya was proper friends with an African boy, the tales would tell themselves. Of course, these two had always seemed oblivious to that risk.

Mayuri flashed her eyes at Kiya. Kiya's bloods had begun that year, and Mayuri wanted to tell her that her actions held a different significance now, just as Latika had told Mayuri when hers began. But Kiya only grinned, said, "I hope dinner is in my future," and led them down the hill.

Around them the streets whirred, hawkers touting baskets of madafu, cyclists with towers of lumber piled on their laps. "Government grows fat while we go hungry," she overheard a man grumbling to the boy shining his shoes. They paused outside their old primary school. Mayuri glanced at the low wall painted like the sky, pastel blue spanned with murky clouds, where she and Kiya used to sit while they waited for Latika. She remembered fondly how Latika would let them pick a treat on their walk home some days, and how their adventures had broadened when Arun joined, as if the city expanded in his presence.

Latika had moved back to Kampala from Jinja after the requisite year with her in-laws, she and Arun taking the apartment next door, and though Ma and Pappa acted stiff, Mayuri sensed that secretly they were relieved. When Latika first left Kampala, Mayuri was struck by how different home felt, the alchemy of everyday life suddenly askew. She found herself resenting her sister for leaving, but then Latika's letters would arrive and, though she never said so, Mayuri could feel that she too was lonely. Then all her bitterness would drain out, replaced by a longing to be together.

The lower quadrant of the hill was where they parted, Adroa's neighborhood farther down. He flicked one of Kiya's braids. "Does your future hold cricket this weekend?"

It was the pentagonal cricket tournament—Hindus, Muslims, Goans, Africans, and Europeans playing against one another. Though Mayuri as a child had always preferred marbles and kites, Kiya lived for cricket and gilli danda, even badminton. But she shook her head. "We're dancing at the temple. It's Navratri."

How had Mayuri forgotten? Kiya always looked forward to the nights of garba at the mandir, to adorn herself with bells and makeup and gossip with her friends. Mayuri cared for none of it but the dancing. Though her coordination faltered when she knew she was being watched, she couldn't deny the pleasure of winding her body to the beat of the dhol until she grew dizzy, spinning out of her skin.

Adroa raised his eyebrows. "You wahindi always find something to celebrate."

"Want to come?" Kiya said, before both she and Adroa erupted into giggles—even they knew that was going too far.

Wherever Mayuri turned she saw someone she knew, every inhale heavy with perfume and incense. The circles of revelers danced around the clay lantern burning at the center of the room, a flurry of pinks and greens and sequins, dark hair and brown limbs. Though everyone danced on Navratri, it was the women who had always drawn Mayuri's eye, alive and radiant as on no other night, as if worshipping not just Durga but their own divinity.

Kiya had disappeared with a gaggle of her friends, Ma dancing with Varsha-foi. They had coincidentally both worn blue outfits, appearing like a pair of peacocks as they dipped their necks. When they'd emerged into the courtyard of the Gur nu Ghar in their matching skirts, they'd trilled about being twins in a past life and then linked elbows and carried on, silently deciding that neither would change. Ma was not a graceful dancer, always slightly out of step with the beat, but she seemed not to care, head thrown back and arms untethered to her body, the final effect bewitching.

Latika had said she had to attend a work dinner with Arun and hadn't come. Mayuri spied Pappa sitting in the courtyard with some of the other men, heads tipped toward each other, every so often slapping hands and cackling like children. Pappa was spending more of his time at the mandir. In a way, it felt like everyone was. Here was one place where you didn't have to worry. The paranoia of outside, the menace of lost jobs and blaming tongues, all dissolved. You could rest here, surrounded by your people, all pulling together to eat and forget.

The best part about garba was how the circle allowed everyone in, from the creakiest grandmothers in the outermost ring to the fastest dancers at the very center, where Kiya was now, body loose as water as she orbited the flames. Mayuri longed to join, but entering the center circle was like crossing traffic on Kampala Road: if you didn't force your way in, you'd never make it. She saw someone from her class teaching the steps to a pair of Ismaili girls, and a Sikh man in a turban chatting to her cousin Biju against the wall. The circle made room for all of them, and yet she was struck by the sense that she was lost.

Perhaps she danced best alone. The awareness came to her suddenly, that she felt most free in her body when no one could see her: doing the disco in an empty kitchen, twisting her fingers into the kathak mudras as she lay awake in bed. Only in those moments, responsible to no one else, did she feel gravity giving out, her body so light it might carry her away. She was not a performer like Kiya, had no desires to grace a stage. By the time the dandiya came around, her palms were slick with sweat, and the stick flew out of her hand, narrowly missing a child squatting by the cashew tree. She ducked her head, too humiliated to check if anyone had noticed.

A hand tapped her arm. A girl passed her the fallen dandiya, kajal outlining her luminous eyes and a wide gap between her front teeth. Mayuri accepted it sheepishly. So someone had seen. She made to slip away, but the girl caught her elbow and led her to the side.

"Like this," she said, lifting her dandiya and waving it before her. "One, two, one, palm."

Mayuri was entranced. She knew the movements, she always had, but in this girl's hands they appeared both effortless and achievable. The bones danced beneath her skin, *scaphoid, lunate, capitate*— Mayuri caught herself and stumbled back.

"You try," the girl said.

Beneath the girl's gaze, Mayuri's arms were heavy, shoulders rigid, nothing like the girl's swish and twirl. The girl chuckled, but her eyes were warm.

"Not like a cricket bat. It's in the fingers, not the arms."

She demonstrated again, and Mayuri saw how her fingers gripped the stick, leaving her arms free to glide through the air. There was a science to it, she could see now, the way the bones fit together, the feet always balancing each hop with a smaller step, the torso tight so the hips could roll. It was a practice born of discipline, restraint, something Mayuri knew she possessed.

"Like another finger," Mayuri said, grasping the dandiya the way the girl had shown her, "an extension of the hand."

The girl tilted her head. "I'd never thought of it like that. Try it with me."

She counted off the strokes in her head, her fingers strong and arms soft. She rocked forward and back, her weight poised between, and in the overflowing room she felt the lift of her own body, pulling up from the earth instead of bearing down. The feeling of floating. It was just she and the girl, her self-consciousness slipping away. She extended her arm and their sticks clicked together, the touch so light and yet the reverberation pulsing down Mayuri's forearm and into her chest. Her gaze kept gravitating to the space between the girl's teeth, so inviting she could fit inside it. Their eyes met. Mayuri gasped. She jerked her right arm and the dandiya thumped to the grass. The girl reached for it but Mayuri snatched it up, embarrassed at the sudden sting behind her eyes.

"You had it," the girl said delicately.

Mayuri let her arms drop to her sides. Yes, she had. For a moment, forgetting even her own skin, she had belonged.

The sun had dropped below the trees when they returned home. Ma's cheeks shone with heat and pleasure as she chattered on with Varsha-foi, their bodies loose against one another. "Did you see the way Prem was dancing? Had a few fermented bananas before he arrived, no?" Ma said, the two of them dissolving into laughter. "Arre, you vultures," Pappa said, unable to contain his grin. Kiya bounded toward the gates and curtseyed exuberantly when West, the askari, let her through. They carried home the simple delight of an evening spent among friends, more open with each other in its aftermath. Mayuri thought of the girl, the exhilaration of finding someone she could dance with. Her teacher's words about studying abroad lingered in her mind, gathering weight.

She had an abrupt urge to see Latika. When Latika moved back to Kampala, she'd taken Mayuri and Kiya for a walk and told them a story about their grandfather when he was just a boy. The story had surprised her, though to Kiya, who had only been a baby when Pirdada died, it seemed to take on the quality of a legend. Though Mayuri had few memories of her grandfather—mostly, she could conjure the outline of his skinny knees under the sheets and the perpetual scent of smoke on his pillow—the strain of his body had seemed beyond physical, an affliction in his mind. Even now, Mayuri could picture that dogged gleam of his eye. After she told them his story, Latika fell into a serene quiet, touching her fingers to Mayuri's and Kiya's hair, her usual armor falling away, and Mayuri understood that the sharing had been good for her. This wasn't gossip, where the telling made you feel wretched and powerful, but an offering, a diminishing of weight that left you more open to the world. They'd ended the walk by buying a packet of simsim from a street vendor, crunching on them as they meandered through the narrow alleys while Kiya insisted on feeding hers to a lone rooster, until suddenly she was swarmed by the whole flock. They'd teased her all the way home. Before going inside, Latika told them not to tell Ma about the mithai, just as she always had.

A kernel was forming inside Mayuri, a secret both inscrutable and absolute. If she could just share it, let it exist on its own beyond her, maybe she could feel that same lightness herself.

The heavy scent of overripe papai greeted them at the Gur nu Ghar. The ground beneath the flame tree was dotted with red blooms, shaken free by the winds. A light in Latika's apartment was visible through the bars on her window. Mayuri sped forward, calling to her parents that she would be back soon.

No one answered her knock, but the doorknob turned. Lately the neighbors had been reminding everyone to lock their doors at night, though it was so out of the ordinary that they often forgot. The inside of Latika and Arun's apartment mirrored Ma and Pappa's, the same low ceilings and damp hallway, but it was less lived in, the walls still peach rather than spattered with oil, just an umbrella and a shawl on a nail by the door. Mayuri called out to the quiet. Maybe they were caught up at the dinner. She'd give it a few more minutes. She trailed her finger over the bookshelf, imagining a library larger than the one in Kampala and friends who took her out dancing. She sifted her finger through the ashtray, but a little ash fell onto a sheet of newsprint, and she tugged it out to shake over the rug. The title caught her interest—*JICHO*, the eye. *Jicho, pua, sikio*, she recited in Swahili, then thought of the gap between that girl's teeth, *meno*. But now her eye traced over the page and she saw that it wasn't a newspaper but a typed mock-up of one, the pages held together with a paperclip, hasty scribbles with uncrossed *t*'s—Latika's unmistakable hand—marking the margins.

WRITER AND MAGAZINE FOUNDER RAJAT NEOGY IMPRISONED FOR CRITIQUE OF GOVERNMENT. OBOTE ORDERS MASS BURIAL IN VILLAGE. ASIAN APPLICATIONS FOR CITIZENSHIP DENIED. Mayuri scanned the headlines. Latika had circled the word *village* and written, *name?* Mayuri paused at the word. The pieces were linking in her head: Latika's inability to find work, and yet her constant busyness; how she held herself apart.

She felt an unexpected grief. Latika had her own secrets too. What she knew of her sister was only part of her story.

She heard a noise and shoved the paper back, dusting the ash on her skirt. Latika emerged from the hallway in a plain wrinkled kurti and bare feet. She blinked at Mayuri, who stepped away from the table.

"Oh," Latika said, "I was just..."

"At that dinner party?"

A series of small creases appeared on the bridge of Latika's nose. "Ended early." Mayuri said nothing to her lie. Latika smiled swiftly, stepping across the room in a few quick strides. "You look lovely," she said, tracing a finger down Mayuri's mirrored sleeve.

A stone was lodged between Mayuri's lungs. She gazed at her sister, trying to see past the obvious for some hint of what lay beneath. But Latika's eyes were blank. "How was tonight? I know how you feel about the crowds."

Mayuri's jaw tensed. "I enjoyed it, actually," she said, too forcefully. The words she'd hoped to share rose to the surface, but they were blocked by the stone, weak against its weight. She wanted Latika to draw the secrets out of her. She wanted her to already know, implicitly, why she had come to her, the kind of knowing that transcended words. Latika just nodded slowly, her hand slipping away from Mayuri's arm and finding the lip of the table. It was the smallest movement, a half step back, but to Mayuri it felt like a door slamming.

"I'm tired," Mayuri said. "Ma just sent me to check if you were back yet."

A moment's confusion crossed Latika's face, a flicker of hurt. But Latika was the one who had rejected her, relegating her once more to the edge. Mayuri murmured her goodbye and bunched her skirt in her fists to stop the jingling as she walked out.

Next door, Ma and Pappa had changed into their nightclothes, Ma extracting pins from her hair. The insistent clatter of water against tile, Kiya washing up out back. Mayuri's body reached the decision before her mind knew what she would say. The words streamed out, telling her parents what Ms. Taylor had said, registering in the pause after that this was the only way.

Pappa scraped a hand down his face, mussing his eyebrows so that he appeared unnerved. Even in his pajamas, his hair was always neatly combed. "Your teacher told you this?" he said quietly.

Mayuri nodded. She thought of Ms. Taylor, away from home and alone. It no longer seemed sad to her. Perhaps it was exactly what those teachers needed.

They did not speak. She felt silly in her fancy outfit, embarrassed. She hadn't thought it through. It would be a stretch, she knew: even with a scholarship, there was the travel fare, the costs of lodging and books.

She opened her mouth to say so but stopped at the last second. A stretch, but not out of reach.

Pappa expelled a long breath. He screwed his eyes shut, and when he opened them they appeared distant, though maybe it was just the fogged light of the lamps, the wear of the day. "You've always worked the hardest. Of course, of course you've been imagining this," he said finally. He wasn't smiling but his face was unguarded. "India, I think, would be a good choice."

Ma's head shot up. Pappa frowned at her, then softened. "Times have changed, na," he said. "It's safe—maybe even safer—there."

Ma's fingers were bending back the head of a bobby pin. "It's never safer to be away. You don't know what could change."

Her mother had never returned to India, dismissive when Mayuri had once asked if she wanted to. Now she seemed to be lost in thought. "Ma?" Mayuri said tentatively. "Change doesn't have to be bad, I think." Her cheeks flushed. How rarely they spoke to one another like this, unearthing their desires.

Ma set down the pin, the metal twisted irreparably. "I wish I could come with you," she said. Mayuri was surprised to hear her mother's voice filled with such sincere longing. But she let the words register and felt her muscles melt with relief.

"Maybe you could come visit while I'm there."

After a moment, Ma nodded. "Yes. Yes, it would be nice to have someone to visit."

Was it possible that her feet had left the ground? She took a long gulp of air and found that she could breathe again. "I'll tell Kiya later," she said. She would do it gently. And anyway, Kiya was popular, surrounded by friends. If she had secrets of her own, she had plenty of people to share them with.

Pappa's smile looked pained as he stood to grasp Mayuri's shoulder. His grip was strong and he shook her a little, tapping his forehead to hers. "I couldn't dream of anything better," he said.

Kiya, 1971

KIYA SPOKE TO THE BOTTOMS of Adroa's shoes. "My sister was accepted to medical school in Bombay."

She waited for him to react, but he remained half-submerged under a white Peugeot, dark grease smearing his pants.

"A few months until she's gone," Kiya said. It was easier to say it out loud when no one was looking at her. When Mayuri had broken the news, Kiya had to turn away so that Mayuri wouldn't see her hurt. Though she was fifteen, it made her feel very young that she couldn't just be happy for her sister. In the end, it was Mayuri who cried, realizing that she wouldn't meet Latika's baby before she had to leave for Bombay. It sunk in for Kiya then, that both of her sisters were leaving her in some way. She knew that it was the natural progression of things, the growing up and moving on. But nothing felt more unnatural.

There was a heavy clunk. At last Adroa scooted out from under the car, tossing a wrench aside. "Who's going to complete your assignments for you now?"

Kiya rolled her eyes. This was why she liked Adroa: in an instant he could turn a conversation, making her forget whatever she'd been moping about. "Watch out, or I'll start asking you," she said.

Adroa laughed, wiping his hands on a rag. He had picked up an extra shift at the auto shop, saving up for technical college. Mr. Singh, the owner, was often out, leaving them precious time away from prying eyes, though even still they were careful with each other, both aware that jobs were difficult to come by. Mayuri was the only one who knew about them, keeping their friendship quiet from the day Kiya and Adroa began sharing their boiled mhogo and milk at snack time. Sometimes it felt as if their entire relationship existed only in the dank shadows of the garage, infused with the perfume of fuel and burnt rubber. Once, Adroa had presented her with a stem of orange bougainvillea, and when she lifted the papery flowers to her nose she smelled gasoline. *Romantic*, she'd deadpanned, before kissing him for the first time.

"But seriously, you'll be busy being an auntie. You'll barely remember that your sister's gone."

Kiya hoped that would be true. There was a line of grease on Adroa's cheekbone, and she checked the door before thumbing it away. He leaned briefly into her hand, electricity jolting up her arm. Even now they rarely touched, afraid of who might be watching, but the heat of his skin beside her was enough to make her heart thrash.

"Or," Adroa said, "I could distract you."

Kiya grinned. "Believe me, you already do." A familiar thrill ran through her as he held her with his piercing gaze, both daring— willing—the other to lean in first. She reached for Adroa's waist, but in that instant a motorcycle sped past and they stumbled apart.

The moment was broken. Adroa shrugged at the floor. "I'll get us some cane juice," he said. "Watch the counter?"

He disappeared through the square of cold blue, his hair uneven in the back from where he'd lain on the concrete. The thick January air seeped in, rattled the fan. Then a thundering crunch, metal screeching. The pop of guns. She tore after him.

Adroa was frozen on the sidewalk. Before them, four army jeeps swerved into the road, soldiers dangling from the windows. A fifth car had already plowed into the road barrier, which twirled on the tarmac. A soldier with a rifle the length of his leg leapt onto its hood.

"General Idi Amin has seized power from the corrupt Milton Obote!

We will take back Uganda! Uhuru!" He pumped his rifle as the din of honking cars coalesced.

Adroa turned to Kiya, his face pulsing with excitement and fear.

The soldier raised a blocky radio and swiveled the dial until the familiar squabble of Radio Uganda poured out.

The Uganda Armed Forces have led a military coup while President Obote is out of country... the former president is accused of corruption in the government... we now entrust Major-General Idi Amin Dada to lead our beloved country of Uganda... the Ugandan army has sealed off Entebbe Airport and major roadblocks are in place... we are imposing a nightly curfew from six p.m. to six a.m....

Adroa whispered, "That means the bad years are over." Then, so suddenly that Kiya startled, he raised both arms and yelled, "Uhuru!"

He looked small and mad beside the army jeeps, his chest heaving, the oily rag tucked into the back pocket of his pants. The soldiers in the nearest jeep laughed and whistled. Another fired up into the clouds, the crack of his rifle shredding the sky. The gazelle stitched on his sleeve galloped as he shook his fist.

Adroa turned back to her, his eyes glassy. "Come on." When Kiya didn't follow, he closed his hand momentarily over hers. "Don't you see? The reign of fear's over. Amin is for the people. For us."

He was smearing his words like a drunk. He led her toward the street, where traffic was at a halt. People had abandoned their cars, congregating on the sidewalks in nervous clots. Kiya stumbled beside him. It made sense—Obote's regime was finished, so their circumstances would improve. But the wind carried the stench of burning metal.

An army tank ground to a halt. Kiya covered her ears. A crowd of soldiers toting spikes bearing enlarged photos of Amin spilled around the tank. All she knew about Amin was that he was the army commander, the same army that had once shot a boy at Latika's school, the same army that crammed the streets now. Kiya stared at his round jaw, the soft pout.

One of the soldiers broke from the group, tearing at a poster of Obote on the wall of a nearby building. A man in office clothes emerged from inside, waving frantically at the soldier.

"What is he..." Adroa began, but then the soldier slammed the butt of his rifle into the man's body, knocking him backward. His head hit the pavement with a wet crack. Cheers echoed, the paper Amins jousted higher.

No one was brave enough to help the man. Instead they stood motionless, eyes on the halo of blood. Kiya watched Adroa's face, some essential reckoning building there.

Behind them, the cruel yawn of metal. Kiya turned to find the owner of Khan & Khan Sweets tugging down the grille outside his shop, masking the pyramids of ladoos sweating syrup in the heat. She felt a sudden panic that he might notice her here with Adroa, that word might find its way home, before realizing that he himself was afraid. He shot her a guilty glance before he disappeared.

"We should go," Kiya said.

A white man was backing away from the street, his gaze skittering like a hunted thing. Adroa's eyes followed him. "We don't have to go."

"Adroa, this isn't—" But she was cut off by a group of boys racing past, knocking her sideways. She caught herself on the grille, the metal slicing her palm.

"Hey, hey," Adroa hollered after the group, but they were sucked into the street. He tugged the rag from his pocket and she spun it over her hand.

"Okay," he relented.

They ran. Fireworks flickered the sky. For the first time in public they held hands. The city swirled around them, for once unwatching.

Kiya grabbed the ball as it sailed by her left ear. Her fingernails flashed red. She had painted only a thin layer on each nail, so that she could scrape it off before tomorrow's appointment. But today, her hands shimmered like clusters of flame petals fallen after a rainstorm.

"Nice save," Adroa called. "You almost missed it that time." Kiya shot him a look and whipped the ball at him as hard as she could. He caught it with a triumphant thwack, then fumbled it in the air. She hooted as the ball disappeared into the elephant grass around them.

The air tingled with a merciless heat. In spite of it, the adrenaline thronged through Kiya's limbs. She loved days like this: an open field, the sky burning that in-between blue before the curtain of night was drawn. When she was a child Pappa had told her he was a top cricketer, which she'd refused to believe until he brought her to the field and taught her how to bowl. She'd returned home marveling at two things she'd learned: that her father was more than the straitlaced man he appeared to be, and that she too could throw.

"Another game?" she said now.

"Don't you need to get home to your mummy-papa?" It was Diamond, whose bare shoulders glistened, his shirt tied uselessly around his waist. Diamond always teased, but still Kiya prickled. Since the coup, amid the disappearings and the soldiers, most of Kiya's friends were kept home. And then there were the ones who'd left Uganda, flown to relatives in India or England. There were barely any Asians in the youth club anymore.

"They're working," she mumbled.

"Not for long. You people love to take our jobs."

In his words Kiya heard the echoes of the newspaper, the radio, the men gulping waragi in the midday sun. She saw Pappa's face when he came home carrying a box from his office last week, betrayed.

"At least we have jobs," she shot back, anger masking her lie. "What do precious Diamonds do all day?"

There were scattered titters from the group. The smirk slid from Diamond's face, leaving a sharp jawbone, a slack scowl. His eyes were cold. Somewhere along the way, it had stopped being a game.

"Bloodsucker," he spat.

One of the other boys began to moo. He bunched up his shirt around his nipples like two sagging teats and twisted his fists up and down. "Round 'em up," he called.

Kiya's blood rushed. Tomorrow was her family's slot for the census of Asians, which Amin had dubbed the "cattle count." If they didn't show up, they forfeited their claim to live in the country. Nobody dared speculate about what it meant that they were being carefully tallied, where the cattle eventually went.

Adroa nudged her. She could smell his baking skin.

"Let's leave," he said loudly.

"Oi, Adroa," she heard as they walked away, "what does your mother think of you going with a coolie?"

"As if she knows, you gadhedu," Kiya retorted so that only Adroa could hear. She had taught him the word for donkey in Gujarati, and now he sometimes used it instead of punda, which they both found hilarious. But Adroa didn't react. It was only as they reached the bottom of the hill that she saw his fists unclench.

She arrived home to a flurry. "Where were you?" Ma lanced, then spun away before she could respond. Kiya looked to Latika, reclining on the divan, the globe of her belly so immense that the rest of her appeared shrunken.

"Is it the baby?" she gasped, but Latika shook her head. Mayuri hurried in, her hair damp.

"They changed our census date. We have to report to the camp today." She handed Kiya a brush. "Fix up, we have to go."

Kiya slapped grass from her pants. "Why did they change it?"

"Greater chance we don't show up," Latika said, her voice flat.

A horn sounded from outside. Mayuri wedged an arm under Latika's back and rocked her to standing. Ma and Pappa spilled from their bedroom, trailing perfume and hair cream.

"Papers?" Ma said. "Check again."

Pappa patted the wad in his pocket. Though Ma had retained her status as a British subject from her time in India, Pappa hadn't been granted Ugandan citizenship yet, years after applying. No one knew what that meant. Pappa was bitter about it: "I was born here," he whispered when the pending papers arrived, "where else?"

"Chalo, chalo," Pappa urged, then stopped. "You're wearing that?"

Kiya smelled the mix of sweat and soil and the lush trace of grass on her shirt. She scraped at her nail polish as they piled into Arun's car.

"At least take this," Mayuri whispered, unhooking her earrings and dropping them into Kiya's hand. Kiya strung the flowers from her lobes, forcing them through where the skin had healed over.

Long lines of families snaked around the makeshift camp, fanning themselves and one another. The humid air churned and the sun cracked down, brutal, the ground too hot to sit on. Even families who had arrived early in the morning, as Ma had planned, said they'd been standing for hours. Soldiers bearing rifles strolled the lines, looking bored, the tents waiting in the distance.

The hours passed—stretching beyond lunchtime, then chai, edging toward dinner, the light beginning to pale. People slipped behind trees to relieve themselves and returned with heads ducked. The sharp rank of urine mingled with the smells of food unleashed from containers. Farida from the youth club was just a few places behind, pushing a wheelchair bearing her grandmother, whose head lolled. The wind caught snatches of conversation—Gujarati, Hindi, Urdu, Punjabi, all laced with Swahili—and rumbles of tired laughter. Kiya wished for her cousins to help while away the hours, but Varsha-foi's appointment was still tomorrow—according to this system, they were separate families. There was a tan dog that visited their compound daily around this hour, and Kiya grew apprehensive that no one else would remember to feed it.

Ma was in conversation with the Mehta family, whose home Kiya had grown up dipping into, all their doors open to each other. Gita-aunty was saying that her brother and his wife had left for England after he lost his job. Ma gestured to Arun knowingly; his parents too had left for London.

"Will you join them?" Gita-aunty asked.

Arun shrugged. "They want us to, but this is our home, so . . ."

"No," Latika finished.

"But look where we are—home should be safe, no?"

Kiya tuned out, her stomach growling with hunger. Leaving was not worth debating.

Pappa sweated in his grey suit, but he refused to unfasten even a button on his jacket. Latika's cheeks were deep red as she leaned heavily on Arun's arm. Ma shimmied a packet of sweets from her purse. Latika tried to refuse, then seemed to lose the energy for even that and slipped a toffee into her cheek.

Kirit from the mandir waved from farther up the line, a rose tucked into his lapel. His daughters circled his legs while his wife shuffled after them with a foil-wrapped cylinder of thepla.

"Why make us come all this way? We couldn't have mailed in our numbers?" Ma called.

"These Africans can hardly count." Kirit's laugh was halfhearted.

Pappa blotted his sweat with a handkerchief. "Still, they should trust us."

Minabhen craned her head around. "When I was that pregnant I could hardly stand up to brush my teeth. Your daughter is strong."

A few heads turned at the mention. Latika swayed and shook her head at the ground, sweat falling in her eyes. Pappa bounced a little on his toes and added that his second daughter was heading to medical school on full scholarship. "Doesn't matter what the Africans say about us if we rise like that," he said, regarding Mayuri with admiration.

"Pappa," Mayuri huffed, shifting closer to Latika and fanning her with her chunni. Kiya waited for her own praise, but it didn't come. She didn't know what he would say about her anyway. Both of her sisters were following the proper path—married and having children or pursuing a sensible degree. As a child, Kiya had harbored the secret yearning to become a film star, and even now her only interests involved being outdoors, whether on the cricket field or the school stage or at the youth club with Adroa. Nothing worthy of being shared.

"But good job you didn't miss today, or they wouldn't let you come back," Minabhen said.

A flash of annoyance crossed Mayuri's face. "Of course I'm coming back."

A guard sauntered by, his rifle gleaming. Everyone quieted. Kiya glanced at Mayuri. Her braid rested over one shoulder, and she wanted to lean her head there. She couldn't imagine her gone.

When the guard had passed, Latika lurched to the side. A feeble moan escaped from her lips. Kiya's skin crawled. She was used to her sister's anger, but not her pain.

"Not much longer," Arun murmured, straining with the force of holding her up.

"Ridiculous," Ma said loudly. Pappa bugged his eyes at her. "What?" she snapped, holding a bottle of water to Latika's lips. Latika shrugged her off, though the skin under her eyes was growing blue.

Kirit motioned to where his family stood nearer to the tent. "Why don't you come up here?" He bobbed his head, as if to say, *no problem.*

"No," Latika said.

Arun looked anxiously from her to the tent. "Latika, it could be hours still."

Latika ground her teeth. "Hours for everyone. So we all wait."

Kiya offered to find a chair and Ma cried that they just needed help, couldn't everyone see? Pappa held up his palm. His face was focused. "No problem. Let me inquire."

He stepped gingerly from the line. Pausing before the nearest guard, Pappa drew with his hands a trajectory between Latika and the tent, papers in his fist. The guard was unmoved, flicking his fingers like Pappa was a fly. Kiya could see the rise of Pappa's shoulders, the fight in them. Then he turned away. As he stepped back toward the line, the guard shot out a hand and shoved him so that he stumbled forward. His shoes caught on the torn grass and he fell to the ground.

Kiya sprinted toward him. Pappa was face down, his palms pressing the earth as if in prayer. Dirt streaked his crisp pants, smothered the shine in his shoes. He peeled himself up and spat out a whisker of grass. Their papers scattered around them, the ones demarcating who among them might still be granted citizenship and who would not. Kiya stooped to gather them, smoothing them against her so that the soil marked her clothes. Behind them, the line gathered a breath.

"Are you hurt?" Kiya whispered, but Pappa didn't respond. Ma flattened his hair with her hand.

All eyes were trained on them, and Kiya was suddenly aware of how they must look, assembled in their best clothes and yet still unruly. She was distracted by a moment of déjà vu, her first time onstage, the audience waiting for her to stammer or shine.

A different soldier approached. "End of the line, please."

Ma inhaled sharply. "We've been here for hours."

Arun pointed at the line, which had filled in their absence. "We were waiting there, between those two families."

"Yes, right here," Gita-aunty agreed. The soldier didn't seem to hear. "End of the line," he repeated. "Let's go, let's go."

He stepped toward them so that they had no choice but to move. Kiya tried to stifle the memory of the boys mooing at her that morning as the soldier herded them back.

The eve of Mayuri's departure arrived too quickly. That morning, they had sat together as Mayuri packed the last of her belongings, Kiya massaging Latika's swollen feet while Latika instructed Mayuri on how best to fold her saris. Mayuri kept dropping the fabric, jittery and glowing. "Bas, let me," Latika sighed when Mayuri bungled it once more, and Mayuri did not resist, simply handed the sari over. "I feel as if I'm forgetting something," she said, and Kiya made a show of curling her body into the trunk, refusing to leave until Mayuri tackled her, both of them falling to the rug in aching hysterics, Latika throwing up her arms at the sight of all the newly rumpled clothes.

In the afternoon Kiya left for the youth club, impatient to avoid the moments between packing that descended into melancholy. In the kitchen, Ma was barely visible behind mounds of matoke skins, flecks of besan in her hair. Earlier, Kiya had seen her buying several bunches of the tiny bananas Mayuri loved from Godfrey, the fruit vendor who passed by each morning. "Extra sweet?" Ma had asked anxiously, which Godfrey had assured her they were.

On her way out, Kiya paused at Latika and Arun's door. There was shouting on the other side, the padded slap of a fist hitting the wall. Kiya ducked below the window. "You're making yourself sick," Arun was saying, his voice straining against itself. "It's bigger than me," Latika said. There was a pause. "You're putting the baby's life in danger. And ours." The sound of paper tearing, the muffle of voices folding over each other. Kiya could picture the throb of

Arun's neck, the way Latika's tongue flicked in and out when she was angry, as if deciding which insult to throw. There was a sob, and their voices dimmed. She thought she could hear them soothing one another. She felt very aware that she was crouched outside their door, alone.

She ached for the twist of her body as she dove for the ball, her friends spread across the pitch. Even more, she ached to be with Adroa, who seemed to her now the only constant in her life as her sisters slipped out of reach and her classmates were kept home. She felt her world whittling away, then chided herself for being dramatic. Mayuri's absence was only temporary. No more of this childishness—there was a real mtoto on the way.

But Adroa wasn't at the youth club. He'd been around less, picking up more shifts at the auto shop, though whenever she stopped by he was never there. Since the coup it had grown more dangerous for them to be seen together, and they'd had to become even more careful. But she couldn't shake the unease that he was avoiding her, and the thought filled her with a new loneliness. She veered to the marketplace—spurred by the idea to find a goodbye present for Mayuri—where hawkers plucked the wings from grasshoppers on white sheets and the smells of grilled meat sizzled the air. The noise of the shoemakers hammering and boda bodas beeping overtook her thoughts, and soon she was running, the sting surging up her calves.

She rounded a corner into an empty lane, a few goats chewing at scraps, when she nearly collided with a soldier slouched against a parked car.

"Oh, sorry," she panted in Swahili, making to step around him. The soldier stood up straight, blocking her path. Sweat stained the underarms of his beige uniform.

"Where're you moving so fast?"

"Er," Kiya said, her breath catching. She motioned pointlessly up the road.

"You don't speak my language?" he asked, then threw back his head and laughed, so that his maroon beret wobbled.

Kiya tried to find someone in sight. The soldier noticed and brought his face down to hers, so that she caught the sweet-corn scent of his breath. Strands of husk, silky and blond, stuck to his chin.

"Census papers?" he said, grazing a finger over her cheek. She pulled from her pocket the receipt she had to carry wherever she went.

As he scanned the document, she tried to take a step back. The soldier's hand shot out, gripping her arm. She heard a noise like a bird, thin and meager, and realized that it was coming from her own throat.

"Everything looks in order here," the soldier said, his free hand working across Kiya's chest, pinching her left nipple, then moving down to her waist. She heard nothing now, no cars, no market sounds, only the pounding, pounding of her blood.

Time caved in, the sky dissolved. The next thing she felt was a hand at the waistband of her pants. The soldier had wadded up her receipt and stuffed it there. "All in order," he repeated, his voice quieter, and Kiya felt herself rising away, her mind taking her where her body could not. She rose until he was gone, and then she was too, carried by the familiar rhythm of her own two legs.

She found Adroa parked outside the auto shop, resting his head against the steering wheel. When he saw her, he cracked the door and jumped out. "Kiya?"

She couldn't speak. Instead she stood, nostrils flared, holding back the stab of tears.

"What's wrong?" he said. He crossed over to her and placed his hands on her shoulders, forgetting who might see. She shuddered involuntarily and lurched away.

"Oh," he said. It wasn't news anymore, to hear of girls being frisked by soldiers, pulled behind buildings, stolen from dormitory rooms at night, only to be delivered to hospitals days later, ruptured and bleeding. Kiya's classmate had had her skirt wrenched down in the market as several soldiers guffawed and marketgoers turned away.

She motioned to the garage, where Idi Amin beamed out of a framed photograph next to the smaller one of Mr. Singh, but Adroa didn't invite her inside. "You're shaking," he said. He looked troubled, as if he had witnessed the event himself. "Some of them let the power get to their heads, they're drunk on it. Most of these guys have never had power in their lives."

Kiya tried to process this. Adroa ran a palm over his head, which was newly shaved.

"Your sister is smart to leave right now."

Kiya's face whipped up. Mayuri's last night. Adroa cocked his head, but she was already retreating toward the main road.

"I have to get back." As she said it, she felt the gravity of that need, to simply be home.

Adroa moved in front of her, blocking her path. The gesture was so similar to the lone soldier's that she gasped, stumbling backward. "No," she spat.

"Let me drive you," he said gently.

She heard her own ragged breath. The tenderness of his words, the way he offered them without command, disarmed her. She turned her face away. How could she have equated him with something so hideous? His arms opened to her as the tears surged over her cheeks.

She squirmed on the plastic covering of his car seat, forehead vibrating against the windowless door. Taped to the dashboard was a tiny greying photograph of two girls, one with long braids framing her wide smile, the other with hair shorn to her scalp. Kiya remembered Abbo, the younger one, playing with Mayuri when they were small. She worked as a secretary in the city now. The older one had gone to work for a rich family, where she had disappeared, a fact that Adroa rarely spoke of, still grasping at the hope that it had been her choice.

Noticing her attention on the photo, Adroa said, "I know what it's like to have a sister leave too."

All week she had tried to banish the thought from her mind, but there it was, with nowhere left to hide. "But she'll come back," Kiya said. She had said it to comfort herself, but it landed against the picture of the smiling sisters, and Adroa's jaw tightened.

They fell silent. A lime-green bird alighted on a jacaranda. Its blossoms sprawled, purpling the ground below. A moment later they passed the Kampala Country Club, surrounded by a cement wall whose top edge was encrusted with shards of multicolored glass. Rumor was that Amin's army had taken it over, that Amin himself sat by the swimming pool in little shorts, drinking tea from tiny cups.

"They've asked me to join," Adroa said.

Kiya startled. Adroa's gaze was unbroken, watching the road. "Who?"

"Amin's army. They've asked me to join them."

She tried to take a breath, but there was no air. "But you work at the garage," she said nonsensically.

Adroa hunched forward over the steering wheel. "Not for some time. Your uncle Singh fired me."

She felt a flash of confusion as to why he'd just been at the auto shop, followed by a chill as his words settled. "*My* uncle?"

"That's why he did it, no? Indians stick with Indians. He got scared that I would try to take over or something, so he turned me out."

"You sound like Amin." She couldn't help but say it. Amin was always accusing the Asians of not integrating or intermarrying with the Africans. The last time Kiya and Adroa had talked about it, they'd shared a secret look and linked fingers under the counter.

"Well, is he wrong?" Adroa said now. Then, quieter, "He can give us a better life."

Kiya shook her head, affronted by this new attitude. She touched his elbow, desperate to bring him back. "But what about college?"

"That was a dream. This is reality. Where do you think I stand a better chance?" His eyes were stony. Kiya saw that he had made his decision. There was potential in the rifles, the promises Amin made. He'd said it himself: most of them had never had power in their lives.

"But you were just at the auto shop," she croaked. Adroa looked agitated, and suddenly Kiya didn't want to know why he'd been there. Queasily, she realized that he might have been with the army for months, whenever he said he was picking up extra shifts, more lies than she could digest. She thought of Mayuri's scholarship, of all those hours Adroa spent in the shop fixing other people's cars.

"Is it money? Because we could help you, I mean I could..."

Adroa laughed drily. "Didn't your father lose his job?"

"I just meant—"

"You think *you* can do better than *us*."

She felt the divide, newly erected. She wanted for it not to harden between them. *You people, us people.* Adroa shifted the car into third gear, bearing down on the gas. She leaned toward the window, gulping in the hot wind.

They pulled into the courtyard. Around the smoking sigri Kiya could see Varsha-foi, her cousins, and several neighbors roasting corn, preparing for Mayuri's last dinner. Kiya stayed in her seat. Their conversation felt unfinished, though there was little left to say.

"Thank you," she said finally. She meant it. He nodded, his breath shallow.

"We can still be..." he said. Kiya shut her eyes. The soldier stooped before her. She opened them fast, then cracked the car door.

Before stepping out, she hesitated. His fingers twitched toward hers. Then voices burbled through the compound and her family emerged, dressed for a celebration. On each of their foreheads, a red smudge. Kiya realized they had already visited the mandir, praying for Mayuri's safe passage, without her.

Behind them all, a thin moon punctured the sky. Kiya stepped from the car. After a moment, Adroa did the same.

Ma dashed her eyes back and forth, drawing a line between the two of them. "Where have you been?" Her voice wavered. She crossed her arms as if protecting herself from the answer.

"We were worried," Mayuri added quickly. Her skirt was patterned with silver roses, and though it was no longer safe to wear jewelry out, she had tucked a magenta flower behind her ear. But her brow was furrowed. This was supposed to be her night to gather with her loved ones and revel in her fortune before her future swept her away. Kiya hadn't even brought her a gift. For once, she didn't want the attention on herself.

"She had a run-in with a soldier." Adroa's voice was firm. All their eyes shifted over to him, except Latika's, which widened in her moon face.

"Are you all right? What happened?"

"He just asked for my papers." She swallowed the rest. Latika was studying her, fists pressed into the small of her back. Her belly hung low.

"It's good that you found her," Arun said to Adroa, sweeping his arm between them. Kiya wanted to slap his hand down. He hadn't found her. He might never find her again. Adroa shifted, one palm flat on the roof of the car.

Pappa peered at the sky. The mango tree rustled and a cluster of bats dropped from the shadows. "Come inside now. It's past curfew."

"Food is cold," Ma said. Her eyes were steely. She half turned toward the path, but took no further steps. West watched by the gates, hand resting on the lock, his face betraying nothing.

Adroa coughed. "I should go."

Kiya winced.

"You're not hungry?" Latika asked.

Kiya wrenched her eyes up. Latika gazed back, in her face something deliberate.

Adroa was still. The sky had darkened around them, their bodies illumined by the lamps inside such that her entire family was backlit, an amorphous shadow, while Adroa's face glowed.

"It's too late after curfew to drive," Kiya said. It was a final plea. It was the army that enforced the curfew, but he was here with her. He was still Adroa.

Adroa opened his mouth. Then Ma cut her voice across the dark.

"This is a family meal. No outsiders." She slid her eyes to Kiya. "And certainly no veshyas."

The word fell into silence. The metal door burned Kiya's grip. Adroa glanced at her uncertainly. She wanted to turn to him, to translate: *Veshya* as in, whore, tramp, shameless girl. *Veshya* as in, brings shame on her family while her sisters bring success. *Veshya* as in, what will people say? *Veshya* as in, this improper daughter, dirt on her hands.

Ma turned away. Kiya swiveled her head to find Adroa, but he was already inside his car, taillights flaring. She thought she caught his eyes glinting behind the blown-out reflection on the windshield, but then the engine roared, and he was gone.

"Wait," she cried, but her voice meant nothing, barely existing in the night.

Kiya clutched her chest and felt the soldier's hand there. Her body gave way. Then: arms circling her waist, Latika's belly in her hip, Mayuri's thumbs kneading her neck. She couldn't feel her legs. She let them crumple, her sisters bearing her weight.

Vinod, 1972

Vinod lay prostrate on the cool marble, his forehead to the ground. He turned one cheek, then the other, until his face came away smooth with the imprint of stone. Something held him there, a feeling surging up from below, a memory passed down, the hum of the earth. He wanted to stay in the safety of that feeling. A mantra rose up around him, and for a moment, his breath eased. He stood.

The mandir was full. His knees throbbed from the floor. Near him, two men leaned over open books, fingers turning their malas. Their expressions were furtive, lips twitching in silent prayer.

He found his friends under the low archway in the courtyard, heads tucked together. Their voices were muffled by the papery squabble of banana fronds. Vinod's bare feet clapped against the floor. The men looked up, pressing palms together. He patted Pulin's shoulder, nodded greetings to Yaksh and Naren. The circle enfolded him.

"Family okay?" Pulin asked.

Vinod bobbed his head. Mayuri was studying hard in Bombay, Kiya in school. Latika and Arun busy with baby Harilal, who was almost one. Rajni tutoring extra since Vinod lost his job. In the past he had taken pride in listing their accomplishments. But these days, he found himself counting them off like fingers on a hand, urgently reminding himself where each was. "Everyone's safe," was all he said.

Pulin's face crumpled. "My boy is in hospital." He opened his

189

mouth, but no more sound came. Yaksh filled them in: yesterday when Pulin's son was walking home from school, a man beat him with a club. He would recover, needed only a few stitches. Vinod mouthed a prayer. Pulin's son was twelve.

"Getting worse," Naren said quietly. They heard the unspoken. They rarely left home now; they all knew someone who had been disappeared, killed. Empty shoes lined the roads, neatly, the way the soldiers ordered before they forced people into their trucks. A few days ago Vinod had bumped into Okello, a former colleague. He and Rajni had visited Okello and his wife's home for dinner a few times; their children had played together in the yard while they sipped coffee into the warm night. This time, Okello looked haggard, a dark bloat beneath his eyes. He had been kidnapped, taken to some barracks, he didn't know where. They knew Amin kept underground torture chambers, a dank dungeon hidden inside a lush hill, the smell of blood and rotting flesh masked by the papai trees. Okello didn't know why he was taken there, or why he was released, only that he was lucky. "We're taking the kids to the village, to Susan's parents," he whispered. He was missing his front tooth.

"I heard about your job," Okello murmured before they parted ways, "a real shame, my brother." His face held no mockery, but Vinod stiffened. He had told no one of how he'd fought when his boss at the coffee-tea trading company informed him of his dismissal. He'd worked there for thirty-five years, but his termination letter stated it unceremoniously: Africanization. "Mimi ni wa Uganda," he found himself repeating like a child, pleading to the man who he'd once considered a friend. "And who reserved this job for you?" his boss snapped. "Go back to your mother, the Queen." The bitterness of his boss's words had silenced him. He understood then that the resentments were sown long before his time, and that they might be past repair.

"Have to keep faith," Vinod said now to his friends. The peace from earlier flooded him again. He wanted to be the solid ground they all needed beneath their feet. They parted, hands pressed together, fingers squeezed. Stay close, they said.

He walked along the river. It was his ritual after the mandir to offer prasad to the water before returning home. The bundles of blessed food had grown in the last few months, as if the sadhus were trying to dole out more luck. Since the heavy rains last week the river gushed forth, the water sucking on the shore. He could taste the humid sweetness of the low clouds, an early moon swollen behind the trees. Nearby, a crane trilled. His steps lightened, his breath melting with the rhythm of the current. *Carry me*, he thought.

He unwrapped the twist of paper and took two frosted diamonds of sugar in his fingers. *Please take care of our family.* Around him families were scrambling to leave, but he was here by the river's edge, a prayer in his palms. He knew they would be protected. He had learned from his mother an acceptance of what may come. He closed his eyes and pictured Mumma and Pappa, their first home with the braided herbs strung from the ceilings, the red of his sister Sarita's gums as she laughed. He pictured Mayuri in Bombay and felt a rush of gratitude that her ambition had taken her far away, no matter how they missed her. Crouching, he let the river skim his palm, lapping up the sugar with a hiss. He ran his fingers through his thinning hair, droplets shivering down his neck.

He stood to leave, but something near the left bank caught his eye. It was dark and slick, baying against a rock. A small, docked boat, or a wet sheet bulging from the water's surface. Then he saw it: the fingers, chunky, bloated, impossibly blue. The scream caught in his throat as he stumbled backward, falling on his side. The thing pitched as if alive. A body, face down, the naked back distended and black, black as rubber bark, black as ash, black as the smoke from the funeral pyres that burned through the night.

The streets were bare as he made his way home, but the sway of the body behind his eyelids hastened his steps. By the gate, the plastic chair where West usually perched was empty.

The lights flared in the kitchen. Harilal slept on a mat on the ground, Kiya curled beside him. The radio hummed a soft tune.

"Finally," Rajni burst, pawing his body as if feeling for holes. She had buttoned the front of her blouse wrong so that a small blip of fabric sat below her collarbone. It still startled Vinod to see Rajni without her mangalsutra, that simple string of black beads on gold thread that had bound them for over two decades now, though he knew it had not been her choice to remove it. "Where were you?"

He couldn't speak about it yet. He slid onto the stool next to Latika.

"Mandir," he croaked. Rajni swept her eyes up to the ceiling like she was looking for God.

Latika's lips were chewed red. "Arun should be back by now."

Vinod glanced at the clock, then the door. It was a half hour until curfew. They'd have to turn off the lights soon, sit in near darkness to wait. The soldiers had orders to shoot anyone seen out after seven. He wanted to tell her everything would be fine, that Arun would be home any minute now, but the body kept surfacing in his mind, the sinew binding the limbs like rope.

Then the lights blinked out. Rajni gasped and something clattered to the floor. Only the moon illuminated the room, washing out their eyes and hair.

"Get away from there!" Rajni sputtered. As Vinod's vision adjusted to the dark, he saw Latika pressed against the window. She peeled away, shaking her head.

"Lights out as far as I can see."

Vinod thought of the river and swallowed the bile in his throat. "The hydro plant," he said quietly. "I think it might be blocked." He couldn't say that it was probably clogged by bodies. The silence expanded the shadows.

The doorknob rattled. Vinod jumped up, but not faster than Latika. "Wait," he said, but she was already reaching for the latch.

"It's me." Arun's voice came through, hoarse. Latika wrenched the door open and he spilled inside.

"He's fine, you see." Vinod exhaled, though his legs were weak with fear.

Even in the unlit room, Arun looked rough. His hair fell across his forehead, the moonlight catching the dirt on his face. His shirttails dragged unevenly and one of his pockets was inside out, the white fabric poking through. A chill came in with him, though the day had been thick with heat.

"I'm all right," he said. Harilal began to cry. Rajni scooped him from the ground but Arun held his arms out. "Please."

Vinod recognized the doubt in Rajni's expression, but still she eased the baby into Arun's grip. The kajal that Rajni had taken to drawing around Harilal's eyes to ward off the evil eye marred his cheek. Arun groaned onto the stool and Latika smoothed back his hair.

"Four men," he said, gravel in his voice. "Searched me for money. Took my wallet." He looked at Latika. "Took my briefcase."

"Soldiers?" Latika said, her voice sharp.

"I don't...I didn't see uniforms," Arun fumbled, face searching. "Just kondos, I think. Just kondos." Vinod didn't see what difference it made, whether they were army or civilian fists, but Latika was momentarily pacified. He filled a glass with water and pressed it to Arun as Rajni lifted the baby back into her arms.

"Did they hurt you?" Kiya asked. Her teeth flashed in the thin light. She looked strange, her body rigid.

Arun shrugged and took a sip, but he winced as he swallowed.

Vinod thought of the perimeter of their building, the street open as water, the latch swinging uselessly against the gate. "Where?"

Arun jerked his neck, then winced again. "Parking lot. West is gone."

"Of all the days he could skip work," Rajni joked, but she sounded shaken. As if that boy could have stopped anything.

Kiya's face paled. "His real name is Otim. He's Acholi."

Vinod didn't know Kiya had befriended the askari enough for him to reveal his true name. But if he was from the Acholi tribe, there was no doubt that Amin's men had done away with him.

Latika was stuffing her feet into her shoes by the door.

"Those are mine," Kiya said.

Vinod stood. "Where are you going?" He heard the quiver in his own voice. He remembered the calm he'd felt earlier that day, how he'd spread it to the group. He tried to grasp at it, but the force of the river, the glowing body, butted it away.

Latika was shivering. She ran a hand through her hair, catching on a knot. "Just next door," she said. "Remembered I have to do something."

Arun slid from the stool. "I'll come."

Their eyes met. Vinod watched the gaze transmit between them, the unreachable language of two people deeply entwined. He was flooded with gratitude for Arun, another man in their family, one who cared for his daughter enough to protect her. He had been too hard on Latika when he spurned her wedding. Those differences didn't matter anymore; their wars had grown. Then Latika stretched a hand to Rajni.

"You should rest, Ma. Besides, it's Harilal's bedtime. We'll see you in the morning."

The door clattered, and Rajni hitched the latch. The chill didn't leave with them.

The August sun's splendor swept the night's dirt. In the morning, Vinod decided to let Arun and Latika sleep and take Harilal for a walk around the compound. He'd awoken pulsing with the resolve to carry more. The sky shimmered, mist mottling the blue. From the apartments, curtains began to open, the sounds of water running and radios powered, uncles hacking away the night's phlegm. Harilal gripped

Vinod's thumbs and staggered drunkenly, yipping. They shuffled near the gates, where Harilal reached up toward the matunda vine. Vinod tried to wrestle the vine from Harilal's mouth while peering toward the parking lot where Arun was beaten. A few of the parking spots stood empty now, reminders of the families who had left and not returned.

Something caught his eye by the left wheel of Arun's car. In the scuffle, perhaps they'd dropped something of his, unseen in the dark. He hoisted Harilal onto his shoulders, from where he tried to snatch Vinod's glasses. Focused, he tilted his neck away.

In the mist it had seemed to beckon to him, perhaps some fabric waving in the breeze, but now he saw that it was only a scroll of paper, four pages folded together. He blew off the dust. It was a newspaper he'd never come across before, titled *Jicho*. Below, a headline printed in running ink: *AMIN HAS BRITISH IN HIS POCKET*.

Despite scathing indictments of Amin's seizure of power by pan-African players, Britain embraced the news, becoming the first country to recognize Amin's government as legitimate and welcoming him to London to meet the Queen. Recent documents expose how the coup was not only supported but organized by the imperialists, and Britain continues to provide financial, political, and military support to Amin's regime. Included among Britain's offences: providing arms to Amin's military, training the Ugandan police and army forces, financing Amin's dictatorship with a £10 million loan, and most recently sending British military training specialists to Kampala. All this against a background of thousands slaughtered and more imprisoned, the systematic ethnic cleansing of two tribes, and the total military takeover of media, thought, and freedom. We must be vigilant: the imperialists have not been eradicated—they are here, striving to come back, to divide us.

Vinod swiveled his head, acutely aware of all the open windows behind him. There was one newspaper left in Uganda, government-controlled. He made sure to always keep a copy in view of the kitchen window. Last week a photographer for that very newspaper who took a photo of a mutilated body was murdered, his own body found riddled with bullets and knife wounds. This was the kind of thing that got people killed. Foolish, to bring such danger here. Balling the paper in his fist, Vinod jogged to the perimeter of the lot and flung it as far as he could. Harilal pointed where it landed, the tiny arc of his finger an accusation.

Back inside, Vinod's pulse slowed. Matoke boiled on the stove, belching sweet clouds of starch. Latika blew on her coffee by the window, Arun scanning the paper, the shadow of a bruise forming on his cheekbone. Kiya looked barely awake, sleep crusting her eyes. Varsha stopped by for a cup of rice and brought back Mumma's pot, filled with potato poha. Vinod breathed in the smell of salt, his family assembled before him, accepting a new day. The radio crooned some reggae tune on repeat as if glitching.

"Check that, Vinod," Rajni said absently, hands gilded with yellow batter to smear over timpa leaves.

Vinod deposited Harilal into Latika's arms and reached for the dial. The radio let out several honks, a burst of static. Then an unmistakable voice.

"Loyal Ugandans, citizens of this great nation, on this fourth day of August, 1972, His Excellency, President for Life, Field Marshal Al Hadji Doctor Idi Amin Dada, Lord of All the Beasts of the Earth and Fishes of the Seas, has an announcement to make," the president said. "Last night, I had a dream. It was a dream from God. He has directed me on how to solve the Asian Problem in this country. For this, I must act immediately."

Rajni rolled her eyes and grabbed a masher. "Volume," Latika said.

Louder now, the president declared it time to exterminate the cockroaches. "The railway is finished—Asians must go now. From today, you have a maximum of ninety days to leave. Any persons of Asian origin now cease to have validity in this country. Asians have milked the cow but did not feed it. I must emphasize that after the expiration of the ninety days, any of you who are still in Uganda will be illegal and will face the consequences. If you don't leave, you will be sitting on fire. I will make sure of that."

There was a crack of static, and the reggae song resumed.

Vinod reached for the dial but couldn't think what to do. It seemed the words should have upended the room, the curtains falling, coffee seeping into the rug. Yet the world remained as it was, pierced only by their breath. But his breath—it was choppy, sour. He was born here, knew no other land. This land that held so much of theirs: this home, a whole life. His mind turned circles, again and again returning to the impossibility of the words.

Kiya forced a laugh. "He's joking."

Over the stove, Rajni stood very still. His own skin felt hot, too tight. He lifted a hand to her shoulder but did not make contact. "Again?" she said, so softly only he heard.

Arun pried an orange rind from Harilal's fist. A storm was gathering in his face. "What does he mean, go?"

Voices trailed from outside. Latika opened the door. The Dalals and the Mehtas stood in the courtyard. They glanced up, brows pulling. "What do you think?" they called. "Can he do this? Citizens too?" Beyond, faces craned from barred windows and balconies. Varsha emerged from her apartment and Vinod met her gaze, vehement, like glimpsing his reflection in a concave mirror. There were eyes everywhere, searching, straining. No birds called. The hush was numbing. They held their voices low, because they knew: how a dictator's word becomes the world, how he bends reality before him, how it was not the facts that would determine their lives but the whispers, the rumors spilling between. A petal dropped from Mumma and Pappa's framed portraits, the garlands curling brown. It landed silent on the carpet. No one turned.

Vinod left the mandir in a hurry. Tomorrow, another line. His feet were sore from standing, his stomach sunken. Yesterday, eleven hours in line only to be told he didn't have the right papers. The day before, he had slept in the street when the government office closed so as not to lose his place. He didn't know what he was lining up for anymore. Thousands of them each day outside the British High Commission, the Immigration Department, the City Council Clinic, waiting for this stamp or that certificate to qualify their families for travel documents, for a medical exam, for kipande, for vouchers. The lines were endless, chaotic. People fainted in the stifling heat and guards laughed or just watched, rifles in one hand, waragi in the other. Some shoved forward, afraid of what would happen if they didn't get their papers in time.

Stories crawled through the crowds, ugly, chilling rumors. "We're his scapegoats, to get the masses on his side and distract them from all the killing," someone said. "Na, bhai, I heard it was because he wanted an Indian wife, but the one he chased rejected him. So he rejects us all!"

In the lines Vinod offered water to those around him, exuding as much calm as he could find, though his spirit deflated each time a family left before his own. Their lives were shifting at an alarming pace: seventy-two hours to leave upon admission to a country. The Mehtas had left for England. His sister Varsha had secured a passage to India, while her son Biju and his wife were heading for the United States. Their community was being fractured into little units, every family forced to think only of themselves. It was so counter to how they functioned, but it was no longer their choice. His eldest sister, Sarita, had urged Vinod to join her family in Kenya, but the Kenyan embassy declined him. He had interviewed at three embassies so far—Kenya, India, England—each one a no, though Rajni was given admission to Britain on her own, an offer she fiercely declined, the prospect of separation unthinkable. By the third rejection, he heard himself begging.

Every night a return with empty hands, to the weight of Rajni's gaze. Never mind, she would say, pushing a plate before him, reheated from yesterday because none of them could eat.

They were quantifying his existence, only so he could be stamped out. On the radio Amin read a statement praising Hitler's massacre of the Jews. He dealt with them correctly, Amin said. Their compound was emptying, the streets thinned. The truth of their conditionality dawned.

He and Rajni had begun selling some of their possessions to raise money for their flights, and Vinod found himself more embittered with each item removed from their home, as if time were running backward, his family's fortunes returning to where they had begun. Just last week he had visited the home of the Visram family high up the hill, and was surprised that they served him tea so sweet amid the sugar shortages, nodding along as they spoke of their money stowed in foreign banks, which would cushion them when they left. He'd stood atop that hill and considered what became possible at such heights. But his parents' ashes were scattered in the lands below. Even as he moved on, there they would remain.

He found his thoughts returning to his uncle Nanu, long gone, who left behind a child Vinod had never met. Vinod wondered if his cousin felt torn now between his African and Indian sides. It was cruel to be made to choose. Vinod thought there must be a third possibility—not African, not Indian, but something beyond borders, an identity forged over decades of scattering apart and, miraculously, finding repair.

Each evening before curfew Vinod returned to the mandir. A voice told him that this was futile, but he silenced that thought, kept faith in the habit. He pressed his empty palms together. Waited for the gods to hear.

The solace of the mandir faded as he pulled his car door shut.

From his window he waved to Pulin, who smiled, though his forehead remained creased, the gritty circle of kumkum streaking down to his nose. Vinod ran a finger over his left eyebrow and came away with powder like tiny pricks of blood. The red smeared against the steering wheel as he drove away.

He passed the Odeon Cinema, where yesterday he had sent Kiya and Varsha for one last film. When he suggested it, they looked at him as if he had sprouted horns. But he knew his daughter and sister couldn't resist Rajesh Khanna's apple cheeks, and they returned from the cinema looser, tittering like classmates. Vinod saw how Kiya softened into Varsha's embrace at the end of the night and knew the memory of that evening would carry long after their last goodbye.

He came up to a checkpoint and cursed under his breath. A soldier approached, cradling the barrel of his rifle between two hands.

"Kipande?" he demanded, bending so low that the butt of the gun nosed through the window.

Vinod didn't have an identity card yet. He hadn't made it to the front of that line. He tried to say so but his words shredded against his teeth. Instead he fumbled in his wallet for his census receipt and poked it through the window.

The soldier looked from the receipt to Vinod and back. Then a grin pulled across his face. Vinod steeled himself for the mockery, or whatever worse was to come.

"Vinod, my old friend," the soldier said. "You remember me?"

Vinod blinked. The soldier before him reconfigured: the wiry muscles, the broad cheekbones, the skin the very same shade as his own. It couldn't be—but it was.

"Moses?"

Moses clapped. His laugh was still a child's. Vinod wiped the sweat at his hairline.

"You've gone grey, rafiki." Moses patted his own temples.

Vinod clicked his teeth. "Been a very long time."

"Bet you can still bowl a leg-break though, eh?" The creases at the corners of his eyes formed little ripples. Vinod shook his head, chortling to himself. Relief shuddered through him. The car in front of him coughed forward and passed through.

Moses glanced over his shoulder, then bent through the window. "Get your kipande soon. You need it now." His voice was gentle, tinged with wonder, a boyish glee. Vinod nodded, still shocked to see his friend, who he'd once envied for not having to attend school—who couldn't afford to—hold such power over him now. Moses leaned back, slapped the hood of the car twice. Vinod's face collapsed with gratitude as Moses waved him through.

The wind whistled through the open windows. Vinod was nearing home. He turned the radio up, let the music stream around him. For the first time in days he was hungry. He considered stopping at a vendor for a bag of mhogo chips, that favorite snack of his childhood. He drummed the steering wheel, the nail of his ring finger perpetually stained red, the pressure to hold himself composed beginning to uncoil. In the car's empty chamber, he laughed again. It wasn't the gods who had saved him, but Moses. It was cricket, his daily pilgrimage to the field, the land—his first, most generous friend.

He saw the soldiers almost too late and slammed on the brake. They stood in the middle of the road, arms outstretched. Vinod tried to distinguish their faces, but his eyes traveled down. No, they were not arms, but machine guns.

One of the soldiers was pulling car doors open, directing men to the ground. Toka chini, toka chini. They lay in the middle of the road in a line. A man refused to leave his car, the woman in the seat beside him clutching his torso. The soldier shot his gun into the air. In the stillness that followed, he dragged the man out, throwing him down with the others. The woman in the car shoved half her body through the window, the expression on her face contorted into what could be laughter or grief.

Then his own door was thrown open and Vinod was pulled from his seat into the dense heat. A rough hand between his shoulder blades, and he was down. The dirt cradled him. The sweat of the man next to him in his nose, the desperate mutter of prayer. More were queued to his right. He was emptied, his mind a single pulse.

The shots began. The sound made him whip his neck to the left. A soldier moved down the line, aiming, firing. Then on to the next, the next. Each shot shook the earth. Vinod smelled his own urine, felt it soak the soil beneath him. For an instant it was familiar, almost sweet.

The world was acute, the light so bright, the echoes of the gun-shots more feeling than noise. Another round rang next to him. His ears throbbed. In the seconds after, he felt the breath gust from his neighbor's body. The sound was of wind through naked trees.

Now the soldier was above him, his scalp blocking the whole sky. He aimed straight into Vinod's face. Vinod didn't know if his eyes were open or closed. Something else took hold: a quiet. *If this is my time*, he thought, and with that thought came the stilling of the earth, the embrace of dirt beneath his skin, the ancient knowing that he was meant to die here and return to the land that bore him.

Then: "Muhindi, eti, muhindi." As if roused from sleep, he came to. A kick to the sole of his shoe. He opened his eyes.

A face peered into his own. The soldier pointed to Vinod's brow, where moments before he had trained the barrel of his gun.

"You are a man of God," he said, touching a finger to Vinod's forehead and then pressing it to his own. A smudge of red. The imprint left behind was smooth, warm. "Go."

The dial turned up. Life flooded in. The crickets screamed, all scorching red. Vinod was running to his father's car; he was running to the field, his chappals smacking, his friends before him, a revelation in their open arms.

Latika & Arun, 1972

A MAN CAME TO THE door that morning, someone Latika didn't recognize. The radio informed them they had seventy-seven days left. The rains had pounded the earth to a soft pulp overnight, and now the intoxicating smell of hot clay filtered through the bars on the window. Harilal sat on the bedroom floor, a line of drool dribbling down his chin. Arun draped one of Latika's embroidered chunnis over his face. He snatched it away, grinned "peeku!" and Harilal roared with delight. A tiny lizard darted up the wall behind them, the green of its body nearly translucent. Since his briefcase was taken, Arun had stopped going into work, and now Harilal was more attached to him than to her—only Arun could conjure that deep-belly laugh. She watched from the desk, papers spread across the surface, and laughed with them.

There was a knock at the door. When Latika opened it, a soldier waited. His ratty tan uniform barely reached his ankles. She realized that he was only a boy, his limbs lanky, the bulge of his Adam's apple stretching his skin taut. He dropped a letter into her hands. "An order from His Excellency," he murmured, eyes flitting left and right. Then he was gone.

She tucked the envelope into her waistband and shut the door. Framed on the living room wall was the photograph from their wedding, the sunlight dappling Arun's coif, the string of jasmines spilling from her braid. Just as the photographer clicked, Arun had turned to her, lifting his hand to smooth the flowers down her hair, and that's how they were captured then, now, forever: Arun facing Latika, eyebrows knitted, absorbed, and Latika, his subject, face washed out by the harsh light. They had laughed over the photograph, but when it came time to decide which to frame, they could not imagine a better one.

Arun came into the room, baby perched on his hip. "Who was that?"

Latika fumbled with her kurti to make sure it bore no trace.

"Just Ma dropping by. Dinner's almost ready." She spoke quickly, her voice even. She wasn't sure why she lied, but as she did a thrill rose up her spine. The boy had no doubt come for Arun: she was an Asian woman, passive, homebound—what business could he have with her? And yet he had given her the envelope, his mind clearly elsewhere. He couldn't have known what that would do to her, for that power to be placed in her hands.

Arun's body relaxed. He set Harilal down, where he tottered forward on unsteady legs. "I'll just get ready." Latika nodded, relieved. His trust was immense.

That night, as Arun slept on a stomach full of Ma's cooking, simpler now because of the food shortages, Latika opened the envelope. The letter bore a waxy red government stamp, typed on thick cardstock.

Mr. Arun Jani,

Under strict word from His Excellency, President for Life, Doctor Idi Amin Dada, you are hereby ordered to cease publication of your weekly press, JICHO. This order is on the basis of the anti-Government sentiment, false allegations about His Excellency's presidency, highly seditious material, and incitement of civil disobedience in JICHO, which has become one of the principal radical newspapers in Uganda. This order for termination of JICHO is effective immediately.

She read it twice, shaking, then stowed it inside Harilal's pillowcase, where he slept with his face turned to the wall, his breath shuffling the still night air. It was the only place she could think that no one would check.

For so long, Arun had argued with her to end the paper. It was dangerous, he said, for all of them. Their family came first. *Justice is bigger than our love*, she found herself screeching, over and over, his face darkening—with hurt, guilt—every time. Sometimes, after those particularly scalding fights, he would soften, tucking a sheaf of papers into his briefcase on his way to work. She would bite his ear, wind her arms around his waist, overwhelmed by the intensity of her own gratitude. But by nightfall his resolve would have swung back, his face paving over, his days an endless pendulum between fight and retreat. Each argument was a reminder that the scope of his desires had changed. A family. That was what he fought for now. She felt trapped in a choice she had never wanted to make.

She picked up the phone and called Brendah, then Yusuf. Neither had received a letter. They would lie low, they said, would halt production for a few weeks. Be careful, they warned, but she appreciated how neither of them counseled her to stop. Like her, they were bound—to Daniel, to the resistance, to their pledge to keep fighting. They knew that silencing was the dictatorship's tactic when threatened. Their very existence represented a danger. The letter confirmed that those in power were afraid.

She thought of Irene and Kariuki, wondered how far back the government could trace *Jicho*, though they'd left no trail. But the last she'd heard of them, they were packing up their shed after Arun's parents left, returning to their family land in Kenya. She thought of Ma and Pappa next door, asleep and unaware, and for once she was consoled by the frontier of secrecy she'd built between them, knowing it would shield them from harm. She thought of Arun, his name embossed on the letter. His face swam before her, the fruit of his cheeks, the thoughtfully tousled hair, how the sun gilded his skin yellow gold. She knew he would be all right—he always was. He'd said so himself: he glided through life, his every step cushioned from before he was born.

She stayed up the rest of the night at her desk, lit by one kerosene lamp. By the morning she had finished it: it was longer than usual, nearly seven pages. From the letter she knew that she had accomplished something greater than she had imagined: the paper was being circulated, accessed by thousands. The regime controlled what the people read, but she could reach them another way. In the people's eye, she was seen.

Arun dragged his feet across the tarmac, the street lined with makeshift government tents and harried, straggling families. The September rains hadn't come, and dust clogged the air. The lines filled his days, his dreams. At night he tried to pack, though his hands refused to cooperate. But now his time had come. His gut twisted at the idea of leaving, so much that he nearly dipped out of the line before the British embassy that morning. Quietly, the officer scanned his papers, then granted a refugee card for Arun and his two dependents. *Watch the newspapers*, the officer said, *they'll announce the flights there. Your ticket is valid for the next seventy-two hours and then it expires.* Arun left the tent sick with disbelief. He was afraid to tell Latika, though she must have known it was coming. Seventy-two hours left to tie up a life.

He spied Vinod emerging from a wending line. Rajni and Kiya were being x-rayed in the medical tent down the street, hoping their bones qualified for asylum somewhere. "We have good teeth," Vinod told Kiya that morning, when she struggled to pull herself out of bed.

Vinod raised a hand to Arun. His hair was greyer, mussed at the temples.

"They tore up our papers."

Arun blinked. "What?"

Vinod told him the officer asked for their birth certificates and passports, then tore them up, saying they weren't citizens anymore. "You don't argue with a machine gun," he said, his eyes momentarily hard. Then his face dropped. "We're stateless now."

Arun grasped his father-in-law's shoulder. It was all he could think to do. That morning he'd awoken to glass smashing, and when he looked outside, his car was gone. And now, Vinod's identity.

Beneath his hand, Vinod slumped. Arun held his news in his mouth. Guilt flushed his cheeks. It was all luck, random chance. Vinod prayed for his whole family every morning. Arun heard him counting off the names, including his own, and even his parents'. If anyone deserved the blessing, it was Vinod. He shifted his body closer, holding Vinod up, the only comfort he had left to offer. A breeze loosened the air, the crickets unrelenting.

When he reached home, Arun found Brendah sitting with Latika on the couch, Harilal in her lap. Yusuf was perched on the edge of the coffee table, his pants hiking up above his ankles. Arun drew the curtains hastily. Just being together now could draw the ire of African soldiers and the suspicion of Indian neighbors.

"They came to help pack," Latika said, though the apartment appeared the same, the cupboards crowded, the record player missing along with a few other belongings sold to raise money for her family's flights and the community fund.

Brendah's eyes glittered as she stroked Harilal's earlobe. "Your auntie Brendah will miss you."

Yusuf's knee was jumping against the table leg. "The students just held a rally against the expulsion of Asians. The union leader issued a letter to Amin saying his policies are blatantly racist."

"Brave."

"No one can believe it. No one wants you to go."

Arun laughed through his nose. If only it were true. Amin knew how to win the people over. He was reallocating all the Asian shops and homes and businesses to local Ugandans, *real citizens over aliens*—who would protest that? The day before, Arun was walking home when a pair of men began jeering at him, patting their stomachs and saying that they would become mafuta mingi now.

Brendah sighed. "It's true, ndugu. Only Amin's elite will benefit. We just foot the bill."

Harilal let out a cry, short and sharp, like he'd been bitten. Yusuf reached over and chucked his chin in the way of older uncles. His action disarmed Arun. Latika kissed Harilal's face and hummed the tune that Arun usually sang to lull him to sleep. When Arun was a child, one of their maids, perhaps Irene, used to sing it as she swept. *We will never be silent / until we get land to cultivate / and freedom in this country of ours.* The melody was imprinted in his body, though the lyrics had only come back to him later, as if from underground.

In the bedroom, Arun tried to fold his clothes: work shirts, bundled ties, the things he no longer needed. He knew he must tell Latika about England, but witnessing Vinod's dejection that afternoon had caged his words. Latika was already struggling with the possibility of their separation, how as his wife she was considered Arun's charge rather than theirs.

His maroon blazer was draped over Harilal's crib. As he grabbed it, he knocked the pillow down and something slid from the case: a thick, embossed card. He lifted the cracked government seal, read the notice dated over a month earlier. Sweat broke out across his forehead. He couldn't see straight, had to sit, rest his head between his knees. Anger gripped him, at this reckless woman, her betrayal.

In the *Uganda Argus* every day, the reporters wrote of Amin Dada's humane measures to restore justice, how he was merely pruning the tree of the nation, doing away with the dead and rotten fruit. In the pages of *Jicho*, Latika responded in full force. Where others were sinking into their powerlessness, her determination only grew.

Enough, he had pleaded for months, *we've done our part, let's end this now*. And yet she wouldn't. Something in her kept fighting, beyond him, beyond even herself. He pressed his face into the blazer, the one he'd worn the night he proposed, and not for the first time he wondered if he'd been all she believed he would be.

He leaned back against the wall, tipped his head around the doorframe. Latika sat on the floor too, Harilal between her legs, a bottle in his fist. Their gazes met. His heart clambered for her, even still, even now. Her face opened as if she knew. And in her eyes he saw the reflection of his own, the fear and the fire, the unrelenting life in her that he had first admired. How deeply she believed in people's goodness; how deeply he believed in hers. He knew, then, that he would bend to her, until the end: she had always been the stronger half.

On the television that night, a British politician bragged that his country would take in as many of the 80,000 Ugandan Asian refugees as they could pack into their little island. Latika sucked her teeth as the politician described Amin's methods. "He says it like Amin's army invented torture and violence. As if the British Empire didn't do the same."

Arun pushed out his chest. "Come, poor exiles, enjoy the riches of my nation, grown wealthy on your backs."

Latika snickered, deepening her voice. "We left our broken systems behind there, now come enjoy ours here."

Arun whistled and pulled on his cigarette. He reclined with his feet on the table, exposed. "I think that's where we'll end up, though." He knew this had to be the moment. "Isn't it funny, after everything, we move to the master's house."

Latika looked at him, his meaning taking shape in her eyes. Then she laughed, so loud he worried she'd wake Harilal. But he kept snoring in the surprising way of babies. Arun laughed too, cackled really, eyes leaky. They bellowed, ribs expanding to break. Their fingers entwined over Harilal on the couch. They kissed, and she came away with ash on her bottom lip.

There was a bang, like thunder. The next minute he was on the floor, a knee on his back. On the ground beside him, the cigarette glowed like an eye. Latika was shrieking, guttural cries he'd never heard before. In her arms, Harilal panted. Tan army boots, laces chewed and muddy. Mud tracked into their home—that was what his mind latched on to, the cleaning it would take to scrub the stains from the carpet, to sanitize for Harilal's curious fingers, his perfect teething mouth.

Three, maybe four men dragged him outside by the arms. His bare feet scraped across the compound. Latika threw herself forward, voice choked with tears. "Take me instead, it's me you want," she was screaming. Arun craned to see, his head twisted awkwardly against his shoulder. His breath was constricted, emerging in sharp hiccups. One of the armed men guffawed, but then he backed away. Maybe because of Harilal, clutched to her hip, or maybe because he saw the wildness, the absolute abandon in her eyes.

They were pulling him away now. Arun tried to right himself before they shoved him into the car, just enough to see Latika and Harilal one more time, but then a sack engulfed his face, he tasted rust, and all went black.

Thirty. Latika woke with the number pounding in her temples. Thirty days since Arun. Each day a lifetime.

Beside her on the mattress, Harilal stretched his balled fists toward her and cooed, "Mama." His voice was a memory of Arun. His fingers opened and closed, tugging a clod of her hair, baring the small nubs of his teeth. She purred Arun's lullaby but choked on the word *freedom.* She pressed Harilal's cheek, warm and sticky with drool, to her breast.

She was hollowed. Her insides burned as if she had drunk gasoline, though she had hardly eaten for days. Her clothes hung limp on her shrinking frame, blisters bursting across her toes. But still, she would go searching, leave Harilal with Ma and wander the streets. She would ask everyone she passed if they had seen Arun. Spectral, she would haunt the alleys until she found him. She would scale every hill, so many more than the seven the British had decided flanked the city's land. Rome had seven. Kampala: immeasurable.

She had heard that Amin's security forces drove prisoners in circles for hours before depositing them at the barracks so that they would lose all sense of place. He could be right here, in Kampala. He could be behind the banana grove, he could be by the river, hidden in the brush. She would climb Makerere's clock tower to look. She would scream his name until he heard her. Until he called back.

The curtains were still half-torn and limp, the sheets stripped. The photograph from their wedding askew on the wall, Arun's thick sideburns grazing the curve of his jaw, the glitter of his eyes startling even through the grainy print. He had been impenetrable, so polished. She had believed so fully in the idea of him that she'd overlooked what lay beneath. She had thought nothing could break them. But he was just a man.

Brendah and Yusuf had gone into hiding. Daniel had never resurfaced. With Arun gone too, Latika had nowhere to turn. She almost confessed to her family, choking just before the words emerged. "It was me," was all she could say. Her father had stared at her for a long while. "You wrote that paper," he said finally, and though she wasn't sure what he had seen, she did not deny it. But her mother had drawn her into her arms, rocked her gently, and whispered, "You can't bear that burden alone." In her mother's embrace, a part of Latika that had long ago shriveled began to uncoil.

With only two weeks until Amin's deadline, Ma and Pappa were making arrangements for them to leave. Now that they were stateless, they qualified for humanitarian consideration. They said something about a Canadian visa, waiting for their passage. They were gentle with her. You have to start getting ready, they said. We've made all the plans. Just start to be prepared.

She knew what they were saying. The regime had made it clear what would happen to those who stayed. She had no choice but to go. So she nodded, murmured that she would ready her bag. In the evenings she rolled Harilal's clothes into little cylinders, disappeared his toys one by one. They saw this and thought she was okay, she was grieving, moving forward. They thought she was simmering, cooling. But they didn't know. They couldn't see. That it didn't matter.

That already, she was sitting on fire.

Rajni, 1972

RAJNI CLUTCHED THE TRANSISTOR RADIO to her ear. *The Ugandan Asians have three days until the deadline*, it said. *The time is almost up.* She flung the radio onto the mattress and called out for Vinod and Kiya, for Latika. Outside, a hazy sun was beginning to breach the horizon, the top of the Nandi flame tree glowing embers. Soon, it would be ablaze.

The phone had rung incessantly all night. She knew without answering that it was Mayuri in Bombay, heart breaking as she understood that she would never return home. She heard Vinod pick up, his reassuring voice. They were all broken now. At least Mayuri didn't have to see it—at least, apart, she was safe.

On the floor, her parents' blue suitcase was filled with her family's clothes, some photographs, the steel pot engraved with Sonal's name. Their most precious valuables were sewn into the hems of their saris: the gold hoops that Sonal had given Kiya years ago, the teardrop earrings from Rajni's wedding that her mother had slipped into the same suitcase before she left Karachi, the river stone from her brother. Everything else—the camera, books, school reports and framed degrees—would remain. They were allowed one suitcase only. Their money, all of it, was frozen in the bank, sucked away, save for fifty pounds that they were permitted to take. They were to leave the keys in their car, their house unlocked.

The day before, Godfrey the fruit seller had passed by the compound, and for an instant when he called to her, Rajni believed that nothing had changed. Then she stiffened. She remembered when neighbors in Karachi, once amicable, transformed overnight. When she refused to approach, Godfrey had pushed a bunch of bananas through the gates. "Like sugar," he said softly, before continuing up the hill.

Rajni glanced in the mirror above the dresser and saw the outline of her mother. The wide nose, the dip above the lips. Time was flattening before her. She had already left once. She had already escaped. How many times could a person be made to endure? But she was a mother now. At last she understood her parents' sacrifice, which she had once thought a betrayal. You persisted for those you loved. For her children, she would do the same.

She bundled her kurti in a corner of the room and began to drape her sari. Vinod hurried inside, pursed his lips, and snapped the suitcase shut. Behind him, Kiya stood in the doorway.

"They've increased the roadblocks. We should go sooner."

Kiya's face was a child's, so close to shattering. The neighbors had reminded her that young Asian women traveling to the airport were at the greatest risk. Rajni remembered when she too had been called a risk, a whole lifetime ago.

When they stepped for the last time from the door, Rajni made sure not to look back.

"Latika," Vinod said.

The Gur nu Ghar had emptied, almost everyone gone. Their foot-steps echoed on the pavement, the absence oppressive. A rusted child's bike was tossed near the guava tree, a cricket bat leaning on its frame like a bodiless leg. At the very edge of the compound, in the Dalals' old apartment, a family had already moved in. Rajni had watched through her window as they towed their canvas bags up the lane. She had wanted to find their faces greedy, their children snotty and the parents spiteful. Instead, they seemed timid, at most hopeful. Between the curtains she watched the youngest boy pull a blossom from the frangipani bush, his black fingers spilling gold.

Rajni crossed to the next apartment. Inside, Latika sat on the floor in a simple white kurti, her feet bare, a small sack at her side. Harilal, on her lap, was swaddled in a scarf the color of sand.

Slowly she stood, hefted Harilal to her hip. She met Rajni's eyes, and Rajni saw an expression there she couldn't put into words. Something that had closed.

"Ready?" she called brightly, and before Latika could answer she turned and walked back toward the car. Latika followed her out. She gave the sack to Kiya, who swung it over her back. Then she turned to Rajni.

"I can't leave him," she said. In the quiet that followed, Rajni understood who she meant. Her ears clanged, the sharp echo of a bell. Behind her, Vinod and Kiya stirred, the truth of it dawning.

"He's not coming back." Rajni's voice was forceful, the time for sentiment passed.

"Chalo," Vinod called, urgent.

"I can't."

Rajni's body was vibrating, never more alive than now. This was her family, *her* family, hers. She would not lose them again. She lunged forward, gripped Latika above the elbow, her nails tearing skin. She was tugging at a tree, ripping it out by its roots. She split branches, tore leaves. She was out of control. Begging, unable to hear her words over the haste of her blood.

Latika's eyes were steel. Slowly, she unhooked Harilal's arms from her neck and held him toward Rajni. Harilal made a sound of protest, jammed a fist into his eye.

"Take him."

Kiya dropped the sack. "Nonononono," she moaned, surging forward, grasping at Rajni, at Latika.

Vinod made a dying sound. His knees hit the earth with a smack.

215

"Ma," Latika said, and Rajni heard the command, and the desperation, and the absolute, unshakable faith. "Please."

"You want to die?" Kiya screamed, shoulders quaking. "Ma, tell her! You want to die?"

Latika's face did not change. Rajni recognized the perseverance in Latika's eye, the face of Pirbhai. All her daughters had inherited his determination, and Sonal's will. It lived in their blood, their bones.

The world tilted. Rajni held Latika's gaze as she reached out for her grandson. She had never done enough for her first daughter. She had never relinquished her hopes for a son. But she too had carried the guilt of leaving her brothers behind. In this way at least, Latika took after her.

Harilal curled into the crook of Rajni's arm. For a heartbeat, Latika's fingers lingered where Rajni's hand met Harilal's body. Then she coiled her arms around herself like a rope.

Somewhere, Rajni had always known the borders of their attachment, that this girl was of her but was not hers to claim. Latika turned and walked back into her apartment. In the second after the lock clicked, Harilal began to cry.

Rajni didn't know how they left. She didn't know how long Vinod banged the door, how terribly Kiya screamed. There was no narrative her mind could follow. She didn't know why there were scrapes down Vinod's arms, or when Kiya's face bricked over, at what point she threw herself into the back of the car. She knew only that she held her grandson to her body, a part of her daughter, of her lost son. She thought of her brothers, the protection they had asked of her, all the ways she had already failed. With Harilal's weight against her breastbone, she felt a moment's clarity. Latika had left them long ago. It was only for Harilal's sake she had come back.

They sped through noiseless streets, the hour of their flight approaching, a steady stream of cars nosing toward Entebbe. They were waved through the first two checkpoints, ordered out of their car at the third. Harilal clutched Rajni's blouse as if she might let go.

Vinod held their documents in an envelope as the soldiers threw open their trunk, dragged their suitcase into the street, and kicked it open. Rivers of saris spooled out, Vinod's work khakis, a slash of blue in the dust. The remains of their life, strewn about like debris after a parade.

Their car jammed the road behind. The soldiers directed others out, the solid thunk of four, five cars popping their doors. They trickled forth, a disheveled stream. Cockroaches, Amin called them, and Rajni saw it now, how they chose survival, how they refused to be killed.

The morning moon hung like a dirty fingernail in the sky. In the cluster of families and soldiers, Rajni recognized Mr. Singh from the auto shop. The light from the waking horizon skimmed their faces, silvering the black and brown. They stood in two groups, uniformed and not. There was a time when they would have stood together, clucked at the lines in the market, picked up their children from school. But with their freedom had come their separation.

A soldier broke into the group, a bottle of waragi in his fist, and ripped the muted orange turban from Mr. Singh's head. Mr. Singh's eyes disappeared into the folds of his skin, the fabric unraveling by his feet. Rajni turned her face, but she couldn't stop seeing the masses of dark hair coiled atop his head sprung loose. The soldier grasped him by the neck, smashed his bottle against a car, and began to shear the hair with a wide shard. The sound was of fur tearing. Mr. Singh's body was rigid as the soldier scattered the tufts across the road, a farmer fertilizing his crops.

Vinod heaved into his hands. Rajni held Harilal so tightly he should have cried, but he remained silent, observing with glassy eyes. If the gods were watching, they too had turned away. The soldier tossed the bottle on the road as if bored with his own actions. Mr. Singh keened on the ground. Shaggy tangles of hair bunched around his ears and were gathered in his fists. He turned his face to the sun as if in prayer, but his lips remained shut.

There was a cough of gas, an engine whirring. Rajni spun around in time to see their car slashing down the road without them.

Harilal twisted and strained toward the ground. His cry was enraged. Kiya reached for him, but her arms were trembling, and Rajni held him away. Kiya's expression fell to disbelief. "Ma," she whispered.

For the second time that morning, Rajni felt the boundaries of her being calcified in her daughter's eyes. She shifted Harilal, a new weight in her arms, the burden of Latika's trust.

Vinod slapped at his pockets. "We have to make our flight," he was saying, again and again, craning his neck as if the soldier might come back. Harilal cried in juddering gulps, pinching at Rajni's neck. Rajni pitched forward, searching for something to steady herself. Flecks of copper glimmered in the red dirt, snatching at the sun. She lowered her face. She wanted to remember nothing else, only this: the light in the soil, all that it had nurtured.

A pair of heavy boots snuffed out the light. Rajni looked up into a face that she knew. Adroa did not smile. His eyes were dimmed. Fear constricted Rajni's throat. Fear and shame.

In that moment, Adroa shook his head so subtly that Rajni might have imagined it. But Kiya clamped her lips, her face desperately open.

"Come with me," he said.

They piled into his jeep in silence. Rajni had stooped to gather what she could from the dirt, and now she clutched Sonal's pot in her lap. Adroa blitzed forward; time bent and began again. The dust swirled, resettled. In the back seat Kiya stared out the fly-streaked window, bereft. Harilal drifted to sleep, his face lined with fatigue. Before they hit the checkpoints, Adroa made them crawl under the seats. When they emerged, Rajni felt a part of herself slip from her skin and rise into the bruising sky. Around her she saw infinite hills rising to fogged peaks. A spill of jacaranda across a compound fence, the glowing bulbs of a matunda vine. A sweep of bats turned to spirits in the milk-white moon. Lake Victoria spread sapphire, the water cresting pearls. A railroad the length of thousands of bodies, beneath it the ruins of other homes. The ashes of their ancestors united with the dirt, the land hatched with scars. The land—seized, unclaimable. Before them, somewhere waiting like a silent mouth.

PART THREE

1974–1992

Rajni, 1974

RAJNI SCRAPED THE MUSH OF sand and decomposing leaves from her shoes. A slick wind threaded through the gap between her scarf and collar. October in Toronto was chilling. Somehow the children never felt the cold: their coats were flung about everywhere, sweaters draping the blue monkey bars, boots kicked off by the gaping maw of the slide.

From the playground, Harilal charged toward her, frosted clouds puffing from his cheeks. The back of his hair stuck up with sweat, and flecks of paint freckled his knees. Dahlia surged behind him, eyes green as the listing pines.

"Juice," she commanded, one hand outstretched in wait.

"Joosh," Harilal echoed.

Rajni frowned at them both. Dahlia understood first, stuck her hands behind her back, cocked her head. "Pretty please."

"Mumma, joosh, please."

"Apple today," Rajni said, extracting the semi-crushed pouches from her bag. Dahlia and Harilal grabbed at them, piercing with vigor, sucking greedy as bees. "Juicy-juice, juicy-juice," they sang, hips jerking.

Dahlia rubbed at her ponytail, mussing it further. Her hair was the color of the unripe strawberries that Vinod once brought home from his shift at Dominion. Sick fruit, Rajni thought, slicing into the pale white hearts.

Dahlia finished first, wiping her mouth with the back of her sleeve and bouncing in her rubber boots. Harilal sipped delicately, rocking in the wind. Dahlia was a year older than Harilal and stood a few inches taller, lithe and wiry, with hair so fine it never held the lacy clips her mother fastened into it—Rajni was constantly repinning them. At three, Harilal was sturdy, the block of his body barreling across the park, the collar of his shirt puckered from where he chewed the fabric.

Harilal pointed at the dribbling water fountain where a cluster of pigeons burbled, their plumes splayed into dusty crowns. Pale birds, pale fruit, the sky never quite ascending to that vibrant, godly blue. Rajni's own skin was more muted now, and Vinod was certainly greying. Rajni had attempted to dye his hair before one of his job interviews, knowing his age would work against him. They'd felt like children, Vinod crouched bare-chested in the coral tub as Rajni slapped on the color, some cheap packet she'd bought at the drugstore, resulting in drippy stains down Vinod's forehead. They'd laughed bitterly until something cracked open and they roared unrestrained, their sides aching, for what felt like the first time. Though the color had washed out quickly, now Vinod let his hair go steadily whiter without complaint.

Harilal lowered his juice and made kissing sounds at the indifferent birds. Dahlia had gnawed her straw down to a pulp and removed it from her lips with two fingers like a cigarette. Rajni tutted.

"Are you a movie star now? Time to go." She stood from the bench, layers of jackets and shawls settling over her sari like feathers ruffling back into place.

It was at this park that she first met Jane and Dahlia. Midsummer, the sun thick on her back, she watched Harilal dump a plastic bucket of sand under the gathered shade of an oak tree. On the nearby benches other women clustered, brown and chattering, wearing salwars tucked into their running shoes or patterned dresses reminiscent of kangas. She was friendly with them, exchanging smiles and huffing in solidarity when their charges fought over toys, but these women were young, fine-boned, their youth draping their cheeks. Beside them, Rajni felt the weather in her joints, the weight that had clung to her middle ever since Kiya's birth—the faded luster of herself.

That day a white woman in a blue blazer and kitten heels approached Rajni's bench. Her hair was pulled back with a plastic headband as if she were a child, though her eyelids were crinkled with wear. A girl emerged from behind her, pulling at a lollipop with wide, watery lips.

"I'm looking for someone who can help part-time. Dahlia goes to school but we'd need you for the days I work late. You seem a little older than the other ladies and we like that, someone more experienced." The woman's lips were upturned but her face was expectant. In the silence, she gestured toward the next bench. "Dahlia chose you herself."

Rajni looked at the little girl named Dahlia, who exposed her blue tongue as she grinned. She kept her eye on Harilal under the tree, and now she stood, collecting her purse and extending an arm toward her boy.

"I am not an ayah," she said. She had meant to say *nanny* but she forgot the word. The sentence came out mongreled, souring the air, the woman's face pinching, then smoothing, politeness papering over her distaste. Magnanimous, Harilal panted over and took Rajni's hand.

Dahlia kicked her heels as they walked home. Harilal sped forward, stopping only when Rajni yelled to watch for cars. Then he threw his head back over his shoulder, his expression deeply bored.

They passed Dahlia's school, where Rajni and Harilal collected her four times a week. The windows twinkled with paper streamers and cut-out snowflakes, the jungle gym yolky with fresh paint. Often, Dahlia emerged with glitter on her fingers, or rubbery strands of glue that she peeled and flicked to the pavement. "Harilal will start here next year," Rajni had exclaimed when Jane first brought her to the school, but Jane told Rajni to check her address. "You're in a different catchment area, I'd bet."

At Jane's building, Dahlia and Harilal bickered over who would press the elevator button until Dahlia conceded. "Because you're younger," she said, tipping her face like she was doing him a service. Harilal smashed the button with his whole fist. Rajni held them both to her as they rode the elevator, whispering a silent prayer while the children yipped in this tube that clanged them up to the sky.

At the door, Jane's skirt suit hugged her slim thighs. It seemed she never changed from her work outfits, the trim blazers and straight-leg pants. She kissed the top of Dahlia's head, then Harilal's. Behind her, the television flashed against the wall, a laugh track burbling. Rajni had herself watched this television family laugh countless times. She could picture the straw-haired children slapping the table while the mother, with hair coiffed perfectly into frosted waves, pulled a roast chicken from the oven, its skin glistening with fat. When they first arrived, Rajni would watch the family constantly at the YMCA—a shock to see the television in color for the first time—obsessed with their gleaming house and their ordered, predictable life. She preferred the show to the news, which looped footage of soldiers in maroon berets as the anchor recited words like *ethnic cleansing* and *mass deportation* and *reign of terror*. Only later would Rajni realize that these words were referring to what had happened to her.

"Catoons," Harilal stated.

"Mom, can Hari pleaseplease come watch TV with us?" Dahlia whined.

"Would you like to come in?" Jane was speaking to Harilal, leaning toward his wiggling frame.

"No, thank you," Rajni answered, though she too missed watching television since moving out of the Y.

Jane lifted her shoulders. "You know you're always welcome. Your family too. For dinner?"

Rajni busied herself tugging up Harilal's coat zipper. She felt uncomfortable turning down so many invitations—back home, such things would never pass unspoken, would always find their way out through gossip or explosive fights that ended with chai in the court-yard. Here, life was hemmed in, never quite honest.

"My husband mostly works nights," was what she said.

Jane's eyebrows hooked just like Dahlia's. "Still at the parking lot?"

Rajni shifted, sweating under her jacket in the warm hallway. She listened for the clanking of radiators, the banging that dragged her awake every night, imagining army boots against the door. She heard only a soft hum, like a languid cat.

"For now." She hated thinking of Vinod in the little glass cube at the parking lot, the bullet holes wadded up with duct tape, though the overnight hours paid better. He didn't have the vigor or the muscle of the askaris back home, and here they didn't arm him with a dagger, just a walkie-talkie that grumbled static. *We just keep going*, Vinod had said, and in those words Rajni heard Vinod's father. In her toughest moments Rajni reminded herself that her parents too had been made refugees and forced to start again. After Partition they'd settled in Ahmedabad, and though communicating with them had grown difficult in the aftermath of her brothers' deaths, Rajni wished now she could ask them how they had gotten through.

Jane shook her head, then hopped up brightly. "Oh, I almost forgot." She disappeared behind the door and returned with a paper bag. Rajni peered inside—a winter hat, navy blue and patterned with one white maple leaf, a thick pair of gloves, an envelope with the week's payment wedged between. "For your husband. Nights are getting colder."

Rajni crushed the bag to her jacket. Jane's forehead was still knitted. "I know the winters are harsh, but this is really a great country." She chuckled, her fringe curtaining her eyes. "Though of course you know that, after what you've been through." Rajni was reminded of the border guard at the airport when they arrived in Montreal. *It's a shame you people had to arrive in the wintertime,* he said, casting an eye over her thin sari, the yellow scarf bundled around Harilal's body. They all liked to mention the grim weather, how unwelcoming it must be, as if that were the real challenge. Then, she'd barely registered the ice slick across the tarmac, the way the sky gathered, pregnant, before dropping clouds of white. But Rajni had no desire to measure this nation against any other: she had lost her country when she lost her family, her brothers and her daughter. Now she stood before Jane and her waiting, wavering smile.

A painful goodbye doesn't change the love that precedes it, she thought to say. You've obviously never walked home in a dust storm until your clothes turn red, or been feasted on by mosquitos in the equatorial heat. She almost laughed, but caught herself, bobbing her head from side to side. She knew this confounded the Canadians, not knowing if she was smiling or frowning, nodding or shaking her head. More and more, she found herself reaching for this gesture, taking pleasure in the way it baffled, a wry substitute for what she really wanted to say.

By the time they emerged from the apartment block, the sun had dropped behind the trees. Jane had called them back before they reached the elevator to ask if Rajni could work extra hours tomorrow. She was up for a promotion, she said, her cheeks pinking. The buildings crowded in as they walked toward their neighborhood, disappearing the sky, the scent of pine replaced with gasoline and potatoes frying. A few street-lights had winked out, casting them in shadow. A motorcycle scorched past and Harilal tracked it with shining eyes. Rajni pulled him toward her, his toes catching on the cracked sidewalk.

On their street, laundry hung stiff from lines strung between balco-nies, and a moldy mattress suffocated the lone patch of grass, dimpled as if someone had slept the night in its damp folds. Rajni shuffled Harilal past the exposed pipe that leaked yellow liquid into the road, its sulfur stink so strong in the summer that they kept the windows shut. A neighbor lazing on his balcony called out as they passed. "Hey, little man." Unlike in Jane's building, Rajni's neighbors were a motley crew, Sri Lankans and Somalis and Ethiopians and Vietnamese, that Ukrainian family down the hall and the Guyanese grandmother with the jumble of herbs cascading from her windows. In a way it reminded her of the compound in Kampala, all those languages in one place, neighbors dropping off food at Eid and Vaisakhi and Diwali alike.

"Race you!" Harilal shouted when they reached the staircase. Rajni huffed after him. A part of her loosened as she entered the shelter of their hallway, unbuttoning her jacket so that the drape of her sari swept out. Mrs. Bose waved from her door, an apron flopping over her waist. When they moved in, Mrs. Bose had given Rajni and Kiya a plastic bag full of her own saris and kurtis. When Rajni tried one on she was reminded of who she'd been not long ago, though the memory felt distant, and she drew on lipstick for the first time in this country before striding down the hall to embrace her neighbor.

Rajni flicked on the lights. Vinod sat at the table, blinking in the sudden yellow. Relief coursed through her to see him sitting there; even now, she panicked when he came home later than planned.

"Pappa," Harilal squealed, clambering onto Vinod's lap.

"Surprise," Rajni smirked, handing Vinod the paper bag from Jane.

Vinod laid the items on the table before him and chortled. "More gloves." He traced his finger over the maple leaf, scratching at the white stitching. Rajni clucked. Between the winter clothing donations they received when they'd arrived at the military base and Jane's frequent gifts, they had duplicates of everything.

She swept an empty glass filmed with orange juice into the sink and carved the bruise from a dark-spotted pear, attempting to impose some order. Pulling the blinds, she was greeted by the giant graffiti sprayed on the opposing wall, an unreadable splotch of yellows and pinks that had affronted her until she noticed the way it made Harilal's eyes shine each time he passed the window.

"Kiya home?" Harilal asked.

"Not yet." Vinod never used English with Harilal, and often snapped at Rajni when she did, as if in language they could still hold some claim to the place they'd left. They were raising a child together once more, but now they were slower, had less patience for Harilal's chatter and games. And here there wasn't a multitude of aunties and neighbors ready to step in, children flitting from door to open door. Latika had always been the one to collect her sisters from school, cut them fruit, retie their braids. Rajni may have been overwhelmed then, but she'd never borne it alone.

Vinod was fiddling with the radio, his constant companion, a weather report blathering on. "A letter came," he said.

The dishcloth slipped from Rajni's fingers. She was aware of the days Vinod spent by the phone, collecting coins to make calls to a number that was long disconnected, writing endless letters to Latika's address that he posted in secret, though Rajni always noticed the dwindling stamps. For a while she silently replaced them, until she didn't. False hope, she told herself, though a part of her prayed he would continue to write.

Vinod's eyes widened. "No, no. From my sister."

Rajni turned to the stove, not wanting Vinod to see the tears that prickled her eyes. He averted his gaze too. It was impossible to speak of this thing between them, so massive that they could barely see one another around it. If it weren't for Harilal, Rajni feared they may have stopped speaking entirely.

"Varsha?" Rajni said, setting the rice to boil and prying the lid from the tub of dal she had cooked last night. She scraped it into a pot, dribbled in hot water to stretch between them, squirted ketchup for the mithu-murchu she always craved.

Vinod hummed yes. Varshabhen and Narenbhai had made it to Gujarat, moving into a house with other Ugandan refugees. From her previous letters it sounded cramped but comforting, the kitchen always bustling, papai trees down the road, Swahili and Gujarati mingling in every room. "She's trying to get Mayuri to come stay with her for Diwali break. Apparently Mayuri said she has too much studying."

"That girl. Too focused." Rajni blistered with envy. If she were so close, she wouldn't think twice about visiting family. How different life would be if they simply had someone nearby, some company for Kiya, cousins for Harilal, voices to fill the emptiness.

Vinod grunted. "No such thing." Rajni had heard Vinod telling the neighbors that they had a daughter in medical school, pride tingeing his words. *Top marks*, he would say, *heart surgery, sometimes her teachers ask her to take over their lessons*. Rajni allowed his embellishments, touched by the return of Vinod's exuberance.

It was Vinod who had convinced Mayuri to stay put. "Let me come," Mayuri had pleaded on their first call from Canada—her voice cracking with fear and relief to finally hear that they'd made it somewhere safely—and on many calls since, and each time Rajni heard the omission at the end, how she never said *home*. She would leave school, Mayuri said, she wanted to help, to just be with them. Vinod was the first to say no. "Your degree," he said, "that's the biggest help." He didn't say the next thing, that she was the eldest daughter now.

Steam fogged the windows. The lock rattled and Kiya walked in. She hooked her coat on the back of the chair rather than in the closet, making Rajni twitch. Her hair tumbled down her back in messy ringlets, her grey T-shirt soaked black at the stomach from her job as a dishwasher at a diner near her school.

Rajni drew a fork through the rice. "Dinner almost ready."

"Already ate."

Rajni clenched the lid of the pot. Kiya often claimed to have eaten at the restaurant after her shift, where she dined for free. *Baked potato*, she'd said when Rajni asked what she was eating, *beans, I don't know*. But if anything, her body was shrinking, her waist narrowed, jawbone sharpened.

"I told you to stop that."

Kiya refused to look at her. She peeled her socks into her boots and left them there, two wilted stems. "It's not a big deal."

The dal smoked and spat. Rajni slammed off the heat, her arm glancing against the searing rim of the pot. "You'll eat what I make."

Kiya's nostrils flared. "You can't control everything we do."

"I'm your mother."

"You were *her* mother too." Kiya's voice was acid. Her head tilted momentarily toward Harilal, who glanced up from the floor, where he was rolling a rubber ball between his splayed legs.

Rajni gripped the countertop, her fists white. Kiya blamed her as if Latika's decision had been her own, as if she had decided to let her daughter die. She shivered, remembering how they had banished Latika after she married Arun, their own pride marring their love. She saw the accusation in Kiya's glare: they were here, without Latika, because of her. Her body deflated. *I tried*, she thought. *I'm trying now.* "At least sit."

Kiya shrugged, a gesture so uncaring Rajni had to look away. "Homework."

Vinod turned off the radio. "She has to study," he said. After past arguments, Vinod had reminded Rajni that Kiya joined high school at

232

an age when groups of friends were already solidified. She was eighteen now, and if she kept her grades straight she could graduate in a year. In Kampala she had been the most social of them all, always dashing out to rehearsal, the cricket pitch, or a friend's. And always, she'd had her sisters. Now she kept to herself.

Kiya strode down the hall, ruffling Harilal's hair as she passed. "See you in there, Tweety," she murmured. Half a smile tugged at his teardrop lips. Harilal loved that yellow bird, from the first time he watched cartoons at the Y. Rajni had found a T-shirt emblazoned with the big-eyed creature in the children's bin at the thrift store, a perfect fit as if made for him, and though it was senseless to buy clothing that he'd outgrow in a few months, she bought it anyway.

When Kiya's door shut, the walls shuddered. Rajni tore three bowls from the cupboard, but Vinod stilled her with a hand, the moons of his fingernails bluish against her skin.

"I need to sleep before my shift." His voice was soft, as if he knew that it would hurt. Rajni remembered the early months of their marriage, when Vinod had been so attentive she'd almost felt embarrassed, coming home for lunch every day, taking her for evening walks around the town that was once new to her. Now she barely saw him at all. She had taken that time for granted, his attention and her youth.

Rajni didn't turn around, simply slung one bowl back into the cupboard, wincing at the ceramic clank. Harilal padded over, straining up on his tiptoes to grasp something out of reach. His fingers grazed the flame-orange cereal box, the ballooning eyes of the tiger egging him on. The bedroom door clicked shut.

The morning Rajni met Jane, Vinod had shaved and creamed his hair for his interview, his back rod-straight. Dominion was hiring a distribution manager, which seemed close enough to Vinod's import-export experience that he told the rest of them to be ready to celebrate. Rajni had insisted they pray before the shrine in their cupboard, feeding Vinod a spoonful of sour yogurt before he stepped out, knowing bhagwan had saved her husband more than once. Instead, the interviewer offered him a job bagging groceries at the checkout. "Take it or leave it, I've got a line of people behind you," the man said. Vinod returned with a red name tag jammed in his fist. Rajni couldn't help thinking that the old Vinod would have pushed harder, but he looked so dejected that she swallowed her rancor. In a few years he would be sixty. No one chose to start again at that age. The radio was constantly whispering in his ear about rising unemployment, and no amount of hair dye could mask the truth of their circumstance.

The next day, in spite of the rain, Rajni took Harilal to the park, where he slapped in puddles until she saw Jane, until she lowered her hood and raised her chin and said, all right.

At Jane's the next evening, it was her husband, Dale, who opened the door. Dale had a pad of fat over what was probably once a muscular body. His hair was receding so that his forehead bulged, but his eyes were clear as mints. Dahlia squeezed past him, rubbing her face against his hip, catlike.

"Jane's running a little late." He hesitated. "Come in?"

Rajni shifted her gaze to the top of Harilal's head, which shone from soap and hair oil. She didn't know if Dale would pay her the overtime, or if Jane would see it as a snub of her duties if she left. She knew what Vinod would say: it's good for them to see us working harder.

"Thirsty," Harilal said.

Dale clapped. "We can fix that."

Rajni reached down to pry off her shoes but Dale shook his head. Neither he nor Dahlia had removed theirs. Rajni hoped Harilal wouldn't sit on the floor. Framed paintings that looked like they'd been scribbled by Dahlia splashed the room with purples and dribbly blues. Rajni's bangles clicked as she moved, her sari swishing against the carpet. The noises felt out of place, inappropriately loud, and she hitched her skirts. Harilal found the sink and stood below it. Dale tapped the top of Harilal's head like an egg.

"Smart one here." He filled a plastic cup and eased it into Harilal's outstretched hands.

"Slowly," Rajni urged, watching water soak the mouth of his shirt. He fingered the blue-glass knob of a low cupboard as he drank. Rajni wished he was old enough to read the caution in her eyes. "Don't touch," she murmured.

There were things everywhere, trinkets and books and mugs with coffee stains browning the rims, a stack of crusted plates beside the sink. Without thinking, Rajni passed her hand over the table, sweeping crumbs into a pile.

"Been hard, with Jane working more," Dale said. Rajni dropped her hand, dusting it on the back of her thigh.

Harilal drained the glass and huffed as if he'd just run laps. "I'm hungry," Dahlia called from where she stood before the TV. Harilal wandered toward her, eyes pasted to the screen.

Dale didn't move, then seemed to realize it was his home and blew a stream of air. "Ah, let me..." he muttered, opening the fridge and pulling out two loaves of white bread, mayonnaise, olives, an open jar of jam, some carrots that appeared to be stunted, a carton of grapes, whole milk, and what looked like an old container of pasta, the shells fused together into one solid block. He surveyed the table. Rajni felt an involuntary jerk when Dale reached for the leftover pasta.

"I could..." she offered.

Dale backed away from the counter, laughing quietly. "Probably best."

Rajni untwined the bread and laid two slices out. She ran water over the miniature carrots and grapes, found a butter knife in a drawer. Dale hovered as if uncomfortable, though with her hands occupied Rajni felt finally at ease.

"So you're settling in okay?" Dale asked. Rajni spread jam thick on a slice of bread, which pillowed beneath her fingers. She thought of the sag of Vinod's neck, Kiya's words like spears. Of Latika, a grief that could never settle. The answer Dale wanted wasn't the one she could give. Mmm, she hummed, pretending to struggle with the lid on the peanut butter.

"Me and Jane, we can't imagine. Been here since my great-grandparents came over, when there was nothing but grass for miles."

The knife sliced cleanly through the peanut butter. Rajni had tasted it once before and been alarmed at its smooth texture, though its sweetness was an unexpected delight.

"That's lucky," she said, beginning to halve the grapes. Dale looked confused, irritated.

"What's that?" He rubbed the back of his neck. "They worked hard to settle. Nothing handed to them." Half a grape slid from her knife and skittered across the table. Dale caught it, popped it in his mouth. The red skin clung to his teeth. "Eat or be eaten, eh?" He laughed.

Dahlia bobbed near Rajni's hip, scratching the baby hairs at her temples, her face gathering into a pout. "I'm reallyreally hungry."

Rajni set the plate in front of her. Dahlia grabbed half a sandwich, stuffing the soft crust into her mouth. The peanut butter and jam worked like glue. Harilal watched from the edge of the table, his eyes following her fingers from plate to mouth, the way she touched each grape before deciding on a carrot. Rajni cupped his face into her body, her two bangles clinking.

"We should really go," she said.

There was a flurry of noise and Jane emerged from the hallway, keys jangling.

"Sorry, I'm so late, you must all be—oh." Her eyes landed on the plate, Dahlia's contented chewing. Rajni inched toward the hall, one hand around Harilal's elbow. She felt her presence in their room, taking up too much space. Just the payment, she thought.

"Thank you so much," Jane said. She reached down and plucked a carrot from Dahlia's plate, gnawing toothily. "You're really...I got the promotion!" A bit of carrot speckled her lip. Dale and Dahlia cheered, and Harilal clapped, enthralled by their joy. Rajni added her congratulations. In the cranked heat Jane slung her blazer across a chair, exposing her wrinkled blouse, sweat sheening the silk. Rajni kept her cardigan pulled over herself, her back pooling, aware that she was allowed only certain kinds of mess.

"Cake!" Dahlia screamed. Jane echoed the request. Rajni felt old, her bulk bearing down on her knees. Part of herself receded as they whirled around her, as Dale grabbed his keys to run out for cake and Harilal's tongue dropped from his mouth and Jane insisted that they stay.

By the time they reached home, Vinod had left for the parking lot. Harilal lumbered, half-asleep as he plodded up the stairs. Rajni cradled two paper plates shielding a massive slice of chocolate cake, baby-blue icing that spelled out *ATS!* Her voice was hoarse from singing "Happy Birthday," upon Dahlia's insistence, heedless of the occasion. She stood before Kiya's door and knocked, the plate held before her, an offering. Kiya eyed the cake but didn't take it. Just as Rajni turned to leave, Kiya cupped Harilal's lolling head and peeled him off Rajni.

"I'll put him to bed," she said softly.

Rajni regarded her daughter, in a grey sweater when once she'd worn only the brightest hues, and remembered that, like Kiya, she too had been subdued by the losses of her hometown, her brothers. But her spirit had come back, hadn't it? She tossed her head and waggled her eyebrows. "If you need me, I'll be finishing this cake before your Pappa gets home," she said.

Alone at the table, Rajni turned the radio to a music station and let her shoulders sway to the tune. The dal she had soaked that morning remained in Sonal's steel pot, the sickly sweet of the frosting still coating her teeth. In their family, Mayuri had the sweet tooth. They would call her tomorrow, Saturday being the day they made long-distance calls, when they would inquire about her studies and the rains and when her exams were and what had she eaten, all they could think to ask except what they couldn't say.

They learned through Mayuri that their people were dispersed around the globe. Mayuri, being the only one who hadn't moved, received their calls, flung across the world, seeking each other's whereabouts, saying ahiya chu, ahiya chu, I'm here, I'm here, I'm here. Varshabhen and Narenbhai in Gujarat, Saritabhen still in Kenya, Biju and his family in Missouri, the Dalals and the Mehtas in the UK. They'd spoken a couple of times to Kantabhen, Arun's mother, in London, breaking the news that Latika had stayed behind. When Rajni told her, Kantabhen was silent for a long while before saying, "That girl was always selfish." "She stayed for your son," Rajni had replied, heat building in her face, but Kantabhen seemed not to hear. After that, their calls were infrequent, just a perfunctory hello at Diwali. Latika was the one call that never came, that never would. Rajni wanted to scoop her people between her palms like so many crumbs.

She burrowed the spoon into the dry sponge. She couldn't think of Latika, of Arun, of Kampala. Instead she thought of the pitch of Harilal's voice when he asked for something, the slope of his sleeping head. The anxious flare of static from Vinod's radio. The way Kiya turned from her when she reached out. How the sunlight, at a certain hour of the day, flushed the apartment rose-gold. The prick of hot oil spattering her forearms, the choke of cigarette smoke in the stairwell. These moments evoked not memories but a sense returned. She had closed the gate on the past, but this feeling she couldn't control: it flooded in, alive, and once arrived, it never left.

On Monday, Dahlia didn't emerge from her school. Rajni waited as Harilal plucked at the grass that butted through the pavement. Dahlia was usually one of the first to flail through the doors, eyes scanning until she spied Rajni, and then her lopsided grin. The minutes ticked, the children strapped into backpacks dwindling. A gentle-faced teacher recognized Rajni and came over, checked his clipboard, checked again. "Dahlia didn't come to school today," he said.

They sped down the street, Rajni turning scenarios over in her mind. On days when Dahlia was sick or had a forgotten appointment, Jane would call in a panic, asking if Rajni could please take her for the day, she would pay overtime, she just needed to get to work. The silence chewed at Rajni. Her gut lurched up the elevator, Harilal screeching with glee.

No one answered on the first knock. On the second, Jane peered through the door, holding it open only a few inches. She wore a downy robe, a thick shower cap clamped over her skull, her face denuded. It was the first time Rajni had seen her not wearing a suit. A smell slipped out with her, chemical and rank. Harilal clapped a hand over his nose and Rajni stepped in front of him.

"It's Monday, I didn't hear from you—"

"Dahlia couldn't go to school today."

Rajni was unused to being interrupted by Jane, who usually listened with such fierce attention that Rajni felt scrutinized. "She's not well?"

Jane's painted fingernails gripped the edge of the door. "Lice."

Rajni sucked in a breath. A drop of whitish goop slid from beneath Jane's shower cap, edging toward her eyebrow. Harilal was tugging his mittens off with his teeth, and Jane's gaze fell to him. Her face sealed.

"We don't...it wasn't...my house is," Rajni stuttered. Instinctively, she fanned her fingers through Harilal's thick hair.

Jane sniffed. "I missed my first day in the new role." Rajni stiffened. The accusation shot between them. Oblivious, Harilal meowed, licked the back of his hand, and pretended to groom his forehead.

Jane slipped behind the door. She returned holding out a plastic bag, her arm stretched as far as it could go without her stepping forward. Slowly, Rajni took the bag. Inside, she saw a bottle of thick white liquid, a slew of medicinal names under the shampoo brand, and a fine-tooth comb.

She looked up and saw herself the way Jane did. She saw Jane, leaping toward her success, and Dale, at ease as she sliced grapes at his table, and little Dahlia, demanding, and herself, shrinking in their home. How they all became the stories they were told.

Her hands had tugged Harilal down the hall, her elbow jamming the elevator button, before she realized that Jane was still waiting for her thanks.

Outside, the city was expanding, metal cranes swarming the sky. Below the potholed roads, the frosted grass, life crawled, teemed, died and resurged. Harilal led the way, his body more attuned than hers to this landscape. The air was milder than usual, the sky a plush grey. The 91 bus rumbled down the road, headlights blurring in the fog, and Rajni flung out an arm.

"Where we going?" Harilal asked as she slipped the cold coins into the ticket box, smashing his nose into the hazy glass. In their first year in Toronto, Rajni had walked everywhere, her thighs slimming and heels hardening, explaining that she was getting to know the city that way, though in truth she was disoriented by the new systems, fearful that she'd do something wrong. It was only when she and Vinod had to travel by bus together that Rajni's confusion had shown, faltering with the change at the ticket box. If Vinod had noticed her embarrassment he made nothing of it, though she thought he exaggerated his motions ever so slightly for the remainder of the ride, pulling the yellow cord to indicate their stop, waiting behind the line before thanking the driver and stepping out. He didn't comment when she began to ride the bus after that, though he must have known. He, too, allowed her her dignity.

When they neared the stop, Rajni let Harilal yank the cord. She left the plastic bag on the seat behind them.

They tumbled into a thick snow, fat flakes swirling around their faces. They ran across the street toward the empty beach. A slick wind blew off the water, blasting their hair back. And then they were by the shore, the beach covered in a skin of sugar. Before them, the lake stretched to a horizon that was at once pink and lavender and gold. Harilal tipped back his head and caught a snowflake on his tongue, and Rajni mirrored him. A crest of sunlight broke the clouds, and below their feet the sand glimmered with so many creatures, come and gone from this lake that belonged to none of them.

Harilal was laughing, stretching a cupped hand to the sky. "Look, Mumma," he said, and Rajni looked, and saw the messy, the beautiful, the wild improbable light.

Mayuri, 1977

S HE SCANNED THE CROWDS AT the Toronto International Airport for
a familiar face. There were women clutching stiff bouquets of flowers and men wedging cardboard signs over the railing, children darting
across the floor like mice. Nearby, a family embraced around a pile of
plastic-wrapped suitcases. When they parted, Kunal stood in the space
between. His hair was recently trimmed, buzzed too close at the sides,
and his T-shirt was tucked into his dark jeans. He raised a hand, face
lifting. Her husband. The word crusted in her mouth, and she felt no
rush of emotion as she lugged her suitcase toward him, her shoes stick-
ing on the tile. Her blood was beginning to recirculate, the sensation
trickling back into her swollen feet. And yet, a part of her was absent
since losing Latika, a limb that had never regained feeling.

Kunal rushed to close the gap between them, untwining the bags
from her arms and drawing her into a loose hug. "Welcome home."

She pulled away and smoothed her braid over her shoulder. If she
spoke, he might smell the twenty-two-hour journey on her breath,
might turn his face away in regret. Instead she cast her eyes around the
room, as if dizzied by all the cold light.

His car stunk of leather and grease. She wanted to crack a window
but didn't want to offend him, so she kept her forehead pressed against
the cool glass, watching the city spin past. She had known him a
week. Her parents had called her late last year, a proposition eager on

their lips. They had found someone for her, they said, an electronics technician who had come to install the television at their apartment. He was tall, kind. Raised in India but worked long enough in Canada to have won permanent residency. His parents were worried about their son, all alone in Toronto, and were desperate to find him a match. "He's Canadian," Ma insisted again, and in the urgency of her voice Mayuri saw the pathway rolling out before her.

When she first talked to Kunal on the phone, she found him to be mild, generous. He spoke in a halting way that verged on nervous, but he listened intently, offered encouragement for her qualifying exams. The second time they spoke, he told her about Toronto, the roads as wide as a river, the shops that sold everything from Chinese noodles to imported British teas. He described her parents' apartment, the little boy who announced himself as Hari and strung his wiry arms around Kunal when he clicked the new TV set on for the first time. The sting of jealousy spurred her to call her parents. She hadn't seen them in six years. Her guilt was bottomless. In the space of the dial tone she thought of Ruhi, the shimmer of her teeth in the light off the sea, the way her skin always smelled of salt. Then Ma picked up, and behind her Hari was screeching, and behind him metal was banging, throbbing like an animal in a cage. "Hello, hellohellohello," Ma called.

"I'll do it," Mayuri said.

Kunal flew to India for the ceremony. They filled out paperwork printed with a red maple leaf in the top right corner of each page. After the wedding they spent four days in a hill station in Sikkim, a quick honeymoon before Kunal's vacation days ran out. Each night, in the silver eye of the Himalayas, Mayuri turned away from him, feigning sleep or bashfulness. *I just need to know you first*, she repeated, a mantra that tinkled the wind chimes strung outside their window.

"Shall we go straight to your parents'?" Kunal said now. He smelled clean, like soap, nothing fancy. He kept bringing his fingertips up to his clipped hairline as if hoping it had grown back.

While they waited for Mayuri's papers to come through, Kunal played the part of the good son-in-law, allowing Ma to fill his freezer with containers of batata and thepla. Each time he mentioned visiting them she felt ill—with envy or relief, she wasn't sure. Through his words her longing for them surged, a constant, thankless clock. She imagined them the same, frozen in a past and place that were gone. Only now, in Kunal's car, did she feel her own skin, how far she had stretched from the self they knew.

She shook her head. Her hair was knotted and her teeth needed brushing. "Tomorrow. I'm tired."

Kunal nodded and flipped his right blinker, veering to exit the highway. The industrial buildings blurred past. April in Bombay was relentlessly hot, the sky hoarding moisture for the coming rains so that her cheeks were always a little glazed. Here, the air bit her fingers and a cold fog slithered around the lampposts, clouding the yellow light. From her parents' calls she could describe Toronto's monthly weather patterns in great detail—January, terrorized by ice; February, grim; March, slushy; April, the kind of wet that lives in your joints. After six years apart, she knew more about the weather in Toronto than any of their lives. They had hardly even spoken of Latika, and never of Kampala. Now she had landed here, in this smoggy chill, her new home. She dipped her head to her knees.

"Feeling sick?" Kunal asked, inching a hand toward her. She suddenly couldn't bear another moment away, overcome by the need to be with the only people who could understand.

"Actually, can we go home?" she said, holding her voice steady.

He flipped off the blinker, not needing to ask her which home she meant.

She had met Ruhi in early 1973. For months, she had fielded calls from family and friends, their voices scattered across the world, seeking her out like the only map. The community ruptured, the love radically disoriented. Ahiya, tya, ahiya, tya, she became a signpost, the whereabouts of each community member pinned in her mind. It was the privilege of being rooted, at least partially; of having been away. She could scarcely focus, the words sliding over the pages of her textbooks. Even with all the calls, Latika was never one of them. "That's because she's dead," Kiya said on the phone once before hanging up. But Mayuri couldn't see it, how one day Latika could be eating at the table, pregnant, bursting with twice the life, and the next day, gone.

Living in India unsettled her. She felt she was peering into a bent mirror: so much was familiar, and yet everything was slightly misshapen. When peers and strangers learned she was from Uganda, they often wrinkled their noses, confused by this new caste she hailed from. When she recounted this to her parents on the phone, Pappa laughed incredulously. "Too Indian for Africa, too African for India," he said. Mayuri relished having the space to sink deep into her studies, the late nights with her hostel mates cooking seero on hotplates, but a part of her remained an outsider, searching for her place.

Ruhi worked in the library, the stud in her nostril glinting against the rows of dusty covers. Mayuri noticed her behind the desk more than once, how her hair fell choppily over her forehead as if she'd cut it herself, the small, hooked nose, how she continued reading while checking out books for the line of students, oblivious to their impatience. Mayuri found herself scanning campus for her, searching the sea of heads in the lecture halls, the women's hostel when she retreated for the night. She didn't know why, only that her eyes roved every room she entered, and always came away disappointed, and then flustered by that feeling.

One night near exams Mayuri stayed in the library until closing, drifting at the table between frenzied studying and hazy sleep. She woke to Ruhi's fingers tapping her elbow, light and persistent as a woodpecker. "What do you study?" Mayuri asked as Ruhi locked up, the night a warm curtain around them. Ruhi showed her teeth, which were worn small like a child's. "Not a student," she said. "This is just my bread and butter." She cocked her head to the line of palm trees, behind which the Arabian Sea rolled its salty neck. "Real life is out there," she said, in a way that felt less a judgment than an invitation.

Mayuri and Kunal pulled into a parking space between a series of low apartment buildings, balconied cement blocks with signs of life all around—overstretched clotheslines, plastic tricycles, a basketball rim groaning from a tree. She jumped as an empty shopping bag scurried over her foot. Kunal touched her shoulder and guided her to the door, where he dialed a combination of numbers on the panel and waited for a buzz. Mayuri smoothed her hair, her vision a blur.

She thought she'd have a moment to prepare herself, but when Kunal pushed through the fire escape door at the top of the stairwell, there they stood.

"Hi Ma, Dad," Kunal said, taking his hand from the small of Mayuri's back to press his palms together. Mayuri stepped forward.

They surveyed one another. Mayuri absorbed how Ma had aged, her body bloated outward, a chunky knit sweater buttoned over her blue sari, and Pappa, who next to Ma seemed even smaller, the skin clinging to his cheekbones and the tendons of his neck, a red ball cap squashed on his head. She was aware of herself too, the pilling leggings and shawl that smelled of airplane food, the way her body over the years had expanded and firmed. The beat of her blood drowned out the noises of the building, all sensation gone.

Then Ma's arms were around her, her smell of shampoo and cooking oil, the bristle of Pappa's stubble against her forehead. Her body returned, though not entirely. A feeling leapt inside her, swirling somewhere between pure joy and grief, the two sharing a border easily crossed.

"You've gotten so thin," Ma said, dabbing her eyes. She'd taken care to wear lipstick and earrings, and though Mayuri remembered that Ma had loved to dress up, it made her feel like more of a guest. "I have to feed you up. Look at me now, all this bread."

Mayuri's shoulders trembled with laughter, her eyes watery. Pappa tapped her chin with his fist.

"The doctor returns," he said.

Mayuri shook her head. Years ago, after she called her parents pleading to leave school, Pappa told her that he'd once hoped to attend college in India. *My family couldn't manage it then*, he said. *But you're there now. An education is something they can't take from you.* His words struck Mayuri. Never before had Pappa mentioned such a desire, never even indicated that he might have hoped for something else. She decided then she had to stay until the end, and it eased her guilt just the slightest, knowing that she was living out an ambition for them both.

She turned her gaze to the carpeted hallway, where a few doors were opened, curious faces peering out. "Where's Kiya? And Hari?"

Ma and Pappa exchanged a small glance, but Ma quickly turned down the hall. "Chal."

Mayuri blinked as they entered the apartment, adjusting to the weaker lights. The walls were tinged a pale yellow, perhaps once white but dimmed with age. It was smaller than they had described on the phone. She could smell something rich with peanuts and ginger, and Ma hurried to the stove. A table and four chairs crowded next to a brown couch, dimpled with use. At the table, head bent over a bowl of plain rice, sat a boy Mayuri had never seen before, with thick hair and eyebrows, a wide mouth framed by delicate lips, in a T-shirt with a cartoon bird peeling on the front.

"Come meet your big sister," Pappa said.

Rice clung to the spoon clutched in Hari's fist. "I have another big sister?"

Mayuri was prepared for the ways he would look like Arun, but not the ways he echoed Latika. In spite of his accent, the long vowels and lazy *a*'s, his mouth moved over his words just like his mother's, his lips pulling up at one corner, an accidental half smile.

It was almost comical, the idea that her parents could have a daughter her age and a son his. He was already six, this boy whose childhood she had missed. *We're not telling him*, Ma had cautioned on their last phone call before Mayuri's flight, a statement that left no room for questions. Faced with him now, she wanted to say how much he resembled his parents, to have Ma agree that he had Latika's mouth and Arun's build, to confirm that Mayuri hadn't forgotten. "Do you remember me from the phone? I'm Mayuri."

Hari squinted like he was thinking hard. "Oh, yeah." He shrugged one bony shoulder, looked sheepishly at Pappa. "I guess I forgot."

They were all watching her now, their eyes pinning her down. She was afraid to move, to disrupt the gears shifting in Hari's mind. She was afraid of saying the wrong thing and peeling back the fantasy they had built around him.

"I live here now," she said. She realized only afterward that it wasn't true.

Hari dropped down from his chair, the pads of his feet thudding on the carpet. "You could share my room."

Kunal laughed, though Mayuri wished he wouldn't. Her body sighed toward Hari, a small opening in the fabric of her family that had woven tighter without her. Before she could correct her mistake, the door clattered behind them. Mayuri turned to find Kiya, flared jeans torn to reveal bony knees. They met eyes, Kiya's darkly rimmed, carefully blank. Mayuri lost her breath. She stepped forward, but in that moment Kiya turned away, shaking off her jacket and tossing it over a vacant chair.

"Hi," Mayuri gasped, at the same time as Ma snapped, "Say hello," as if she were speaking to Hari and not a twenty-one-year-old woman. Kiya glanced at Mayuri only briefly.

"Nice of you to join us," she said tartly. When she brushed past toward the bedrooms, the air smelled of stale perfume.

Pappa touched Mayuri's shoulder. His eyes were pained. "You're looking tired, dikri. Why don't you lie down."

"She needs to eat," Ma said. "You'll stay the night?"

"Of course," Mayuri agreed, at the same time as Kunal said, "We'll eat, then go. She has to unpack."

Ma seemed discouraged but said nothing. Mayuri looked from Kunal to her parents, all making decisions about what she must want. No one asked her. But if they had, what would she have said? She had wanted to come home, to the smell of leaking jambu and murchu frying in batter, to her family, whole and singular, around the table. *Does that still exist?* Ruhi had asked her, and she had wanted it enough that she extracted herself from their tangle of limbs, shrugged her shirt over her shoulders, put enough space between their bodies that Ruhi would understand what Mayuri needed to believe in order to go. Though from the hurt that gleamed in Ruhi's eyes she understood that even if she wasn't choosing what to leave for, she was choosing what to leave behind.

With Pappa sitting a foot lower than the rest on a stool and Hari playing on the couch, they crowded around for dinner. Their elbows brushed. Kiya picked at her plate, but Mayuri ate hurriedly, indelicately, her stomach bottomless. The meals in the canteen had been surprisingly delicious, the kadak chai and steaming tiffin, but at the first mouthful of Ma's sweet kadhi she felt that her last meal had been six years ago. Every time a space opened on Mayuri's plate, Ma filled it with more, beaming at her with such satisfaction that Pappa exclaimed, "Oi Raju, it's rude to stare in Canada!"

"What else do I need to know?" Mayuri laughed, turning to Kiya, who had remained silent for most of the meal. "Help me, na, since clearly Ma can't."

"Arre," Ma said, scandalized. Kiya's lips twitched, but she stuffed a bite of potato into her mouth. Mayuri reminded herself that Kiya might just need time to thaw, but she couldn't stop herself from trying to coax out the gossiper she knew was in there.

Kunal told a story of how he'd offended an elderly woman by sitting next to her on the bus when the rest of the seats were empty. He'd thought it would be impolite to sit far apart from her—he didn't want her to think he believed himself above her—but after several bus rides he'd understood that, here, personal space was the highest civility, and an unspoken rule relegated the brown youth to the back of the bus, the white elderly to the front.

Hari popped his head over the arm of the couch, reaching out to grab Mayuri's attention and tracing a finger down her sleeve. "I can show you the bus stop. And my school. The park—I'll teach you the monkey bars!"

Only now did Kiya meet Mayuri's eye, her face lightening ever so slightly. When Kiya returned her bemused smile, Mayuri knew they were in the same memory.

When she couldn't eat a morsel more, Mayuri retrieved an envelope from her bag. She had pieced together that her family hadn't been able to bring much with them, few of their belongings making it to the airport in Entebbe. Aside from a print of a sunflower field framed above the television, the walls were bare. Mayuri cleared a space on the table and fanned out the photographs she had carried with her to Bombay all those years ago, propping them on the windowsill in every hostel room she occupied. Her parents had mailed her a few photographs after Hari was born, and despite being the most recent, those were the shabbiest from how often Mayuri held them to study her nephew's face.

Ma sucked in her breath. Pappa stood to rinse his fingers, then returned and lifted a photograph from the pile, cradling it as if it were a small animal. In the photo, Latika, Mayuri, and Kiya sat on a woven blanket in the grass, only Kiya looking at the camera, a few heavy branches of the flame tree leaning into the frame. Long creases formed around Pappa's eyes, but he continued to stare.

"I thought you might not have any," Mayuri said.

Kunal leaned over Pappa's shoulder. "Who's the third girl?"

Mayuri's eyebrows drew together, but Ma plucked the photo from Pappa's hands and swept it with the others into the envelope. Her lips were pursed as she crossed to the fridge and stood on her tiptoes to slide the envelope on top.

"I think everybody's tired," she said, still facing the fridge. Pappa's head hung low, his empty hands splayed on the table.

Mayuri didn't move. It dawned on her now that the silence about Latika was not just around Hari. She looked to Kiya, who was shaking her head stonily, once again rejecting Mayuri's gaze. A weight smashed down on her. All those years away, what she'd longed for was simply this: to sit with her family and, together, hold what was gone. Now she felt as if she were being strangled. But Kunal's question hung in the air, answering hers. They would not even speak her name.

Mayuri stood, her legs weak. Hari watched her from the couch. Ma peeled away from the fridge.

"You've had a long flight. And Kunal, driving all that way." She spoke each word deliberately. Her eyes were sunken but defiant, holding Mayuri at a distance.

Mayuri nodded slowly. She was remembering the night Arun arrived at their home, the first time she'd seen Latika as a separate entity, not just her sister. Watching them grow closer, Mayuri's greatest fear had been to lose Latika to Arun. She'd feared it enough that she'd told her parents about the protest, though its meaning was beyond her. But her words had done the opposite of bringing Latika back. "Then we should go."

A moment's disappointment danced across Ma's eyes. But just as quickly she turned, pulling an old yogurt tub from the cupboard and spooning rice inside. Without a word, Ma held out the container of food as she opened the door.

Thirty minutes away, Kunal's apartment building had an elevator and a pot of zinnias wilting by the entrance. The peal of subway cars clattering down distant tracks cut through the windows. The solitude of the sound raised the hairs on her neck. Kunal wedged her suitcase into the bedroom, which was neat and spare. She stiffened, each of them standing on opposite sides of the bed.

"I left you room to decorate," he said, motioning to the blank walls disrupted only by red curtains over the sooty sill. "I want it to feel like yours too."

She met his eyes and softened. He hadn't asked her to explain anything, and for that she was grateful. Gingerly, he perched on the white duvet.

"Thank you for all of this," she said, sitting too.

His eyebrows pulled together, confusion flickering across his face. "You're my wife."

Mayuri wrapped her arms around her shins. The word sunk deeper. She was not cargo, not a self traded for another. To Kunal, she was not just a product of a careful calculation in which she could enter the country of her family's residence without years of applications, large checks, and demeaning tests, the probability of rejection a pale specter. Kunal had been lonely for years, Kunal wanted a family, and now she was his wife.

She remembered when Ma and Pappa refused to accept Latika's decision to marry Arun. Mayuri hadn't understood the gravity of what Latika had done then, making her own choice. But Latika had always been the fighter, the most stubborn of them all. Mayuri had lost their last days together. She had lost the chance to see her sister as a new mother. She had lost their home, though she was absent for the violence and fear that had shredded them apart. *You don't have to be selfless*, Ruhi said, when Mayuri admitted that she felt she had no right to disappoint her family, to choose something against them. That word, *selfless*, how Ruhi's eyes saw something so much greater than she was. *No, I'm being selfish by going*, she replied, and tried to quantify the fracture, to clarify how accepting Kunal was so she would not lose one thing more.

Kunal said it once more that night, *my wife*, as his fingers found her skin beneath her nightdress. She brushed his hands off her stomach. "I'm so tired," she said, her face in the pillow, and for a moment his grip tightened and she knew he was not finished. Then he sighed and rolled away. She held her body rigid until she felt the kick of his dreams.

Her parents never mentioned that dinner, and Mayuri didn't see the photographs again. She understood what was expected of her: to not trouble the veneer of this new life her family had created in her absence. She had gone away, and this was the price if she wished to return.

Hari took to her faster than she could have hoped. When she stepped from the red bus onto their street she felt buoyed knowing he would be waiting, thrilled to have a captive audience for the hockey cards and picture books he toted home from the school library. *My-my*, he called her, which made her laugh, and when she laughed he would meet her eyes and laugh too, the gaps in his smile wide and gummy, which made her gut flutter. He showed her his homework pages, the colorful stickers peeling up beside his name, which invariably said

Hari, the *–lal* dropped. He told her he liked it better this way, though she questioned how much it had really been his choice. When she told him stories he would prop his chin on his knee, entirely transfixed, and when she said she was a doctor, he lifted her hand and placed it on his chest, asking if she could feel what was inside his heart. Yes, she told him, I can feel it all.

But she wasn't a doctor—or at least, not here. She received a letter in the mail informing her that she did not have degree equivalency. Her father had been wrong: they had stripped her of her years of medical training, house jobs, night shifts, and exams. On her spousal visa application she had accrued points for her profession, and how quickly the country had invited her in, an absolute gain. Only after arrival did the door close. She could retrain for two years at a local university, the letter said, pay full tuition and redo her residency. "We'll find a way," Kunal urged. Instead, Mayuri secured a meeting with an administrator at a local hospital. She wore a brown pantsuit and practiced smiling with all her teeth.

The administrator wore beige heels that she clacked against the floor throughout the meeting. Mayuri explained that she had experience in every kind of ward, sometimes seeing hundreds of patients a day in the government hospital. But instead of impressing the administrator, this seemed to further perturb her. "That's the problem, the difference in our systems and all," she said. Mayuri lost focus as the woman lectured that they were just trying to keep their patients safe, noting that the woman's fingernails were also painted beige, tuning in again only when she said the hospital had a shortage of medical assistants, if that was at all of interest. In Bombay, the medical assistants took patient histories, fetched pills in little white cups, filled out insurance forms, and disposed of contaminated supplies. When Mayuri clarified that this meant the same here, the woman told her she'd be able to start quickly, what with all her experience.

Beneath the table, Mayuri clenched her fists against her ironed suit.

Through the high window the sun slit the smoggy horizon, not unlike the sky in Bombay, where she could have stayed on to become a doctor at a teaching hospital, maybe picking up a cone of bhel puri on her way home, extra onions but no tamarind, the way Ruhi liked it. Above the table she smiled back, though she couldn't bring herself to show her teeth.

In Bombay, Mayuri would often leave the hospital to find Ruhi smoking by the bicycles. She was prone to wearing dresses that just grazed her knees, and always only black. The color of death, Mayuri joked once, parroting the aunties who clicked their tongues when black fell into fashion, but Ruhi didn't laugh. *Don't immortalize an idea that should die*, she said. Mayuri never saw where she lived, though she knew it was only with her mother. They avoided campus too, only meeting there around Ruhi's shifts, when she would slink to Mayuri's room after closing the library. The hostel warden was a middle-aged man who didn't like to see young women traveling home alone at night, so he acquiesced when Ruhi came to stay at Mayuri's. Those nights, they fell into each other's mouths, backs slick with humidity, hair tangling, and in the mornings, Mayuri would wake with coarse strands wound around her fingers, white lines scored into her flesh. But mostly they spent time in the light. They would sit on the beach for hours, salt furring their teeth, talking until the sun sipped the water, until men flocked and called names, never suspecting that their eyes yearned for one another. That when they grabbed hands and ran away, kicking seawater and spewing curses, they were somewhere inside themselves thankful, glad.

When she reached the apartment, it was not Hari but Kiya who answered the door. She shifted aside so that Mayuri could slide in, where Hari watched cartoons standing up. Mayuri stroked his hair and he leaned into her side, lingering when she made to pull away.

Kiya and Mayuri sunk into chairs, the table between them. Mayuri was surprised to feel nervous around her younger sister.

"Imagine after all those years, they want me to go back to school," she said.

Kiya tilted her head. Mayuri sensed an opening and rushed through. She explained the letter, the meeting at the hospital. She felt as if she hadn't spoken since she'd arrived in Toronto. Kiya focused on her words, and Mayuri's nerves drained, feeling the novelty of speaking to her sister as an adult, and yet the familiarity of her presence. She wanted to keep talking forever, to make up for the years gone. She mentioned the strangeness of living with Kunal, but noticed a shift in Kiya's body, her eyes frosting over, and halted.

"You don't get to complain," Kiya said.

"I'm not—" she began, but of course she was complaining, sounding like a spoiled child.

Kiya cricked her neck to glance at Hari. "It's been hard."

"I know."

"You don't."

Mayuri pursed her lips. How many times today would she have to prove herself? "I lost everything too."

Kiya was shaking her head, slow and constant. "You didn't see it. And everything after. You were off studying while we were all just trying to—"

"I wanted to come back. I didn't want to be gone, I didn't even get to say—"

"And you didn't see how they left her. I couldn't stop them on my own," Kiya finished, the rush of words expelled. The blame settled between them. Mayuri didn't want to consider whether she could have persuaded Latika to leave had she only been there, if Latika's absence now was in part due to her own.

"You aren't responsible for that," Mayuri murmured, eyes stinging.

"Then who is?" Kiya shot back.

"She made a choice."

They were silent. Kiya exhaled slowly. Her face looked smaller.

Mayuri thought of her grandmother, who had left her family in Kenya in order to support them. The skin of her fingers was always coarse when she patted Mayuri's cheeks. *Selfless*, Ruhi had said, and now Mayuri wondered if Sonal-baa had ever wished to turn her back on her duties, to simply choose herself. She would never know what her grandmother wanted, but she knew the life she had lived. It was inbred in Mayuri, perhaps, to yield herself for those she loved.

"You can't imagine," Kiya breathed.

Sitting across from her sister, the years hardening between them, Mayuri saw that nothing could return the time she'd been gone. No photographs or conversations around the table could claw back what was lost. Her family wanted her to lead them forward, not unearth what they had stowed away.

She shut her eyes and imagined. Taking the medical assistant job, making a salary her family could use. Talking to Kiya not with the memory of who she once was but with curiosity about who she had become. She imagined telling Hari stories of Latika, memories he too could carry. She imagined being the eldest child, holding responsibilities, being who they needed. She imagined stepping up, out, until she was inside her family once more.

"Let me try," she said.

Kunal ate his rice dolloped with plain yogurt until the dal turned a ruddy pink. Ruhi preferred hers slathered in ghee and pickle until each grain was coated red, her fingers slick and stinging. Kunal flossed after brushing his teeth, and only after washing his face with the same soap he used for his body, so that in the mornings his cheeks crackled like paper against the bedsheets. Ruhi rubbed oil into her and Mayuri's hair before rinsing in the bath, tipping Mayuri's head back and pouring cupfuls of lukewarm water over her scalp. Her fingernails scratched the tender skin at the nape of Mayuri's neck, but always she formed her hand into a visor over Mayuri's forehead so the water never dribbled into her eyes. Kunal bathed with a bucket and cup too, but always efficiently, so perfunctorily that traces of white foam sometimes clung to the insides of his ears. These days, Mayuri preferred the shower.

With each new fact she learned came another she erased. She undid them quietly, letting loose the skin she had previously stitched. When the spring turned to summer, the sky opening for heat, Kunal held her face between his hands. "I'm your husband," he said, and it was not a command but a plea. She closed her eyes as his body engulfed hers, his cheek warm and dry on her neck. She imagined. Ruhi in the draw of her breath, in the surprise of her voice, the shock of pleasure within the pain. Ruhi in the scent of herself, in the musk and toothpaste and salt. Ruhi in the pull of nails down skin, the pressure of teeth, the insistence of tongue. Ruhi in the desire to immortalize the long gone.

In the quiet after, Mayuri heard her voice rising from her body. "I had an older sister," she said, and felt Kunal's attention sharpen. She let the voice emerge. She recounted the moments she had witnessed and imagined the ones she had not. She recalled when Latika would bathe her and Kiya, the Dettol dispersing through the water until their bodies disappeared like mountains behind clouds. Kiya would cry at her sore red skin, but Mayuri would emerge sensing her own vitality, grateful to feel each limb—painfully, joyfully—tingling back to life.

Hari, 1978

GRADE TWO WAS BETTER THAN grade one because you weren't the littlest anymore. Even though Hari's toes squished inside his shoes, which Pappa had painted over with black polish to hide the scuffy parts, and even though his hair smelled like the coconut oil that Ma had scraped through it until his parting glistened in the mirror, he didn't fuss, because tantrums were for grade one.

Ma made him eat a spoonful of yogurt after his cereal for good luck. It puckered his lips, but then Kiya sprinkled a little sugar on top and the granules crunched sweet in his teeth. Then Ma surprised him by saying she would walk him to school. He looked up from where he was tying his laces on the floor, two loops, crisscross. Normally Ma sent him off to school with Mr. Bose and his kids, or else with Kiya when she was around. But Ma's lips were stained pink and her sari was the one with the silver beads sewn into swirls above the hem, and she smelled flowery and a little spicy, like she was going somewhere special. Then Pappa came out of the bathroom and his hair was combed down. His navy vest with the little CANADA POST patch was snug over a tomato-red tie, and his eyes were crinkled.

"Pappa took a night shift so he could walk you this morning," Ma said. The two loops fell out of Hari's fingers. He couldn't remember Ma and Pappa ever walking him to school, both of them beside him like celebrity bodyguards.

The sidewalk was his red carpet and the neighbors leaned out of their balconies to watch him go. He spun his fingers at them the way the Queen did on TV. Ma did the Queen wave too, and Pappa asked what kind of wave the king did, which nobody knew, so instead he puffed out his arms and flared his nose and marched like King Kong.

When they got to school, Ma and Pappa stopped. Pappa's chest sunk in and he held his King Kong hands behind his back, and Ma scratched crusty cereal milk from Hari's cheek and then put her Queen palm over her purse, and they walked inside. Kids stumbled all over, hugging and jumping and already breaking into their after-lunch snacks. Hari led them past the gritty hall, where the kindergarteners tracked in sand from the playground like kittens, to his new classroom. The door was papered with giant cut-out bees and a banner that read GRADE TWO IS BUZZING WITH FUN! He read the sign out loud, and the teacher standing by the door clapped. "Very good!" she beamed, and Pappa patted Hari's shoulder and Ma stroked his hair.

The teacher had a nut-brown ponytail with a big fringe and polka dots all over her canary-yellow skirt. She was smiling so wide, but her cheeks were a little tight, like maybe she'd been doing this too long.

"Welcome, we're so happy to have you. I'm Ms. Zielinski. Just call me Miss Zed or Zee." She stretched out her hand to shake. Hari mashed his laugh behind his fingers, watching her pale hand grip King Kong's, then the Queen's.

"He'll do very well in your class," Pappa said, swapping his *v* and *w*.

Ms. Zed nodded hopefully. "And how long have you been here?"

"Long time," Pappa replied, knuckling the ridge of his name tag under his vest.

"One year," Ma said at the same time, tugging up the zipper on Hari's backpack, which was true too, because that's how long Hari had been at this school.

Ms. Zed looked a little confused, her lips sliding into a frown. Behind her, Hari saw TJ and Ronny and Anh on the rainbow rug, and Melanie drawing on the chalkboard, and a handful of kids he didn't know.

"Ja, ja, diku," Ma urged, seeing him leaning toward his friends.

"Have fun today," Pappa said in Gujarati, and Hari smiled because that meant it was their secret.

In the classroom, a blond boy Hari didn't recognize was dragging his finger over a little xylophone to make tinkly music. Hari wanted to play but remembered that in grade two you had to be more polite, so he turned to Ms. Zed and said, "Can I please go inside now?" She opened her arms like a crossing guard, and he started in before he remembered Ma and Pappa in the hall. He turned around and saw their soft eyes and proud shoulders and worried lips, so he stuck out his hand for a shake, holding his laughter inside his mouth.

After lunch, Ms. Zed pulled Hari aside and crouched down in front of him. "This afternoon, you'll be going to a special class," she told him.

Hari looked at TJ, who was tugging on his jacket for recess. "Just me?"

"You'll make new friends there," Ms. Zed said.

The special class was down one flight of stairs in the basement. The lights down there blinked with little clicking sounds every few seconds. Ms. Zed held his hand for the walk over and told him soon he'd be walking there all on his own, every afternoon.

The special classroom was bigger, but there were no desks or instruments crowding the shelves. Instead, the wall was filled with a giant alphabet, a red *A* taped above a picture of a bitten apple, *B* with a loaf of white bread, and all the way to the grinning zebra. Hari shivered when Ms. Zed let go of his hand, the chill of the basement tiles cutting through his corduroys when he sat on the floor with the other kids. The girl next to Hari, small with two black pigtails, grabbed his arm to tell him something, but when he turned to her she only grinned and said a word he didn't know, her tongue pushing through the giant gap in her teeth. Seated on the only chair in the room, the teacher clapped loudly, her hair a white cloud around her ears. "Miss-is Phill-izz," she said slowly, placing a hand on her collar. "Now you," she said, pointing around the circle.

"Mrs. Phyllis," Hari repeated, though most of the other kids said nothing. The boy to Hari's right said it too, and he and Hari passed a nervous smile between them. The boy had huge watery eyes and skin darker than Hari's and a little bit of construction paper stuck to the soft fuzz of his hair.

Hari learned his name when it was his turn to tell the group. SOLO-MON! they all yelled back, catching on fast. MAY-LEE! ABDULLAH! SAMIYA! TENZIN! When it was Hari's turn, he didn't hesitate. "Harilal, but you can call me Hari," he said, thinking of Ms. Zed or Zee. Mrs. Phyllis raised her chin at him, peeking through chunky glasses. "All right then, Hari," she said, and the group mumbled something back, the energy and the name lost in all the words. "Ha-lee," the pigtailed girl beside him whispered into her lap.

Afterward, Mrs. Phyllis made them sing the alphabet, and then each of them had to stand beside the first letter of their name and pronounce the word in the picture. "Heart," Hari said proudly when it was his turn, and Mrs. Phyllis gave him a thumbs-up. Some of the other kids didn't understand, just repeating their names over and over or choosing a random letter from the wall. "Your name isn't Gabdullah," Hari said to Abdullah, who had chosen to stand beside him, but Abdullah only blinked at Hari and then traced the giraffe in the picture with his wet finger. Back on the rug, Hari and Solomon sat side by side, both of their hands shooting up whenever Mrs. Phyllis asked a question, grinning in surprise at each other every time they got an answer right. "This is so easy," Solomon whispered in Hari's ear, while the rest of the class fidgeted and looked on with foggy eyes.

Hari waited until Ma and Pappa were both home before he told them the news.

"They put me in a special class today," he said as Ma swirled her tea and Pappa stood on a chair to change the lightbulb that always hissed.

"What kind of class?" Ma asked, fishing out her teabag and dropping it into Pappa's mug, reaching behind her for the tin kettle.

Hari thought, chewing on the rim of his shirt. "A class for extra-smart kids, I think, because me and Solomon got all the answers right."

From the chair, Pappa looked down with eyes shining in the new light. "Gifted! My boy."

Ma squeezed Hari's cheek, then scooted his glass of milk over the counter. "Now let's grow your body to catch up with your big brain."

Hari shrugged a laugh. He thought about the zapping hallway lights and the way the other kids looked around the room like they couldn't remember where they were. A little cold milk dribbled into his lap, shivering his back, reminding him of that dark stairwell with Ms. Zed, and the nagging feeling that this class wasn't so special like she said. But Ma was grinning while she phoophooed her tea and Pappa was lifting the phone to call Mayuri and Kunal, the news sparkly on his lips, the tired gone from his face, so Hari said nothing, just drank and drank until he'd drained the whole glass.

The best thing about the special class was Solomon. Hari couldn't wait for the afternoons. They always sat with each other, and because the basement was creepy, Mrs. Phyllis let them go to the bathroom together. They would race each other there and then run the sink and mold Hari's hair into spikes or slick it all the way back, water soaking the neck of his shirt, until Mrs. Phyllis made a rule that your bathroom buddy couldn't be your best friend.

On days when Mrs. Phyllis was tired, she would sigh and tell Hari and Solomon to separate. "Sep-a-rate," she would sing, making the word into a whole sentence. It happened enough that the other kids caught on, the word taking shape in front of them, chanting it all together when Mrs. Phyllis glared at Hari and Solomon with that tone in her eyes, and they would have to stand and pick their way over the crisscross legs to opposite sides of the rug, their heads hung to their chewed collars. One time Hari whispered a joke to Solomon, and it made him snort so loud that Mrs. Phyllis jerked up from the book she was reading them, her eyes icing over. "Solomon," she said, all cold and clippy, which was worse than the yelling they were all used to at home, "do you have something you'd like to share?" On the rug, they all bristled. Solomon shook his head, but his lips were still twitching from Hari's joke. Hari waited for the chant to rise up, *sep-a-raaate*, but instead Mrs. Phyllis crooked one finger at Solomon and curled it in. He stood like she had hooked his collar. "You'll sit in the corner until you're ready to be serious," she said. Solomon stepped off the rug, his eyebrows knitted. Hari dropped his eyes to his lap, knowing he had started it but that somehow, this time, he got to stay put.

Mrs. Phyllis had a beach ball in the shape of a globe, bright blue and pink and bumpy where there were mountains. The game that day was to name where you were born and then Mrs. Phyllis would show you where it was on the ball. Hari learned where Vietnam was, and also India, but a few of the other kids didn't know how to answer, so Mrs. Phyllis would guess for them. "China," she said for May-Lee, who nodded uncertainly. "China," she said for Tenzin. When it was Hari's turn, Pooja from India turned to look at him with a gloss in her eye. "Uganda," Hari said. Mrs. Phyllis looked at him hard, her forehead suspicious, before turning the ball a few times, her fingernails sliding over the plastic until she showed the class with a triumphant smile. It was a little smear inside a bigger blob, pine-green and bumpy on the edges.

When it was Solomon's turn, he stood up to show her himself.

"Ah ah ah, use your words, not your body," Mrs. Phyllis tutted.

Solomon, still standing, shrugged. "Toronto," he said.

Mrs. Phyllis cocked her head. "No, sweetie, that's where you live. Tell us where you were born. B-o-r-n."

"Toronto." Solomon was getting annoyed. Hari could tell by the way his knees were a little bent, like he was ready to pounce or duck.

Mrs. Phyllis blew a long breath. Her fingernails traced over the globe again, harder this time so that they left behind thin lines slashing up all the countries. "Somalia," she said finally.

When Solomon sat down again, his leg jittered against the floor. Hari nudged him to stop. Solomon sat quiet for the rest of the afternoon, picking little scrolls of skin from around his fingernails. Hari sat quiet too, pulling faces when Mrs. Phyllis wasn't looking to try to make him laugh. Solomon did laugh, but it was more like a sigh. In that class, neither of them were used to being wrong.

It was getting boring lately, always the alphabet and the same name song every afternoon, and sometimes Hari found his eyes glazing over as Mrs. Phyllis yapped on. Instead, he would lean back on the rug and tell himself the story Mayuri always told him, the one about the girl with hair like snakes who lived in the blue mountains with her family.

When the girl was little she found out she could pull fruit from the earth with her bare hands, dates and matunda where the soil was parched. She used to share the fruit with everyone, especially the people who couldn't grow food of their own or didn't have any land, and even if she herself hadn't eaten that day she would give up her share. Really, the girl didn't believe in shares, just that she had been gifted with bountiful fingers and so it was her duty to keep giving. One day, the girl pulled a papai from the earth, but when she peeled open the skin she found not sweet flesh but a baby. She loved the baby, taught him to dance and mash plantains, but she was scared that the soil would swallow him back like a seed she wasn't supposed to have. She started hiding the baby between the scraped-out rind of a melon whenever anyone came by. One night the girl was so busy that she forgot the baby inside the melon. In the morning, she found that he had eaten his way out of the rind. After that, the girl gave the baby to her family and made them promise to protect him forever while she traveled the land and made sure everyone else was fed too. The family was sad to say goodbye, but they loved the girl and so they let her go. In time the baby forgot the girl, but for the rest of his life he loved the sweetness of papai and the bitter of melon; he loved it like his own mother.

Sometimes Hari would ask Ma or Pappa for the story, but neither of them knew it. Pappa's stories were always about the giant iron snake that ate up all the trees in the forest, or about Hari's grandfather who sailed on a little boat to make a better life, and they always ended with a lesson that Hari was supposed to guess, like *You can do anything if you work hard enough* or *Always stick together* or *How do you build a railroad? One track at a time.* Those stories bored Hari. Only Mayuri knew the good one. But in the special classroom, Hari realized he knew it too.

Kiya had been staying at her friend's for so long that Hari hadn't had a chance to tell her all about his special class. He was jamming his fingers around the TV buttons after school, trying to clear away the blue static, when she walked in. Ma stood up and stared at her like she'd thought she was never coming home. For a minute Ma's eyes were soft jelly, and then they froze over.

"Where have you been?" Ma said.

"She was at her friend's," Hari reminded her, because maybe Ma forgot what she had told him. Ma and Kiya both looked at him, their eyes the same, confused and hard. Then Kiya dropped her scarf and walked to the bedroom and closed the door. The static growled and Hari wanted to call Kunal and ask him how to fix it. In the summer before grade two, Kunal drove Hari to the zoo and bought him a half-melted freezie and made faces at the silverback gorilla in the plastic trees, and Hari had laughed until he vomited electric-blue sugar onto his sandals. After, Kunal used his handkerchief to mop up Hari's feet, then gave him the option to keep wandering the African Kingdom or drive back home. Hari was always asking when Kunal would come over next, but today he wanted to talk to Kiya more, so he powered off the TV and watched the blue-grey swap to midnight-black and left Ma still standing at the table, holding the edge like she was scared she'd float away.

Kiya sat at the foot of her bed, kneading her feet like she'd run a marathon. Her college textbooks were piled up on the ground. Hari had pawed through them while she was gone, finding words he knew like *teacher* and *classroom* and *children*, but mostly words he couldn't sound out. She looked up and tried to smile, but her shoulders sagged forward.

"Can I have a minute?" she said.

"I gotta tell you about—"

"I'm going to take a bath now."

"—the special class they put me in at school."

Kiya stopped kneading. "What kind of class?"

Hari spoke fast because she looked like she really needed that bath. He told her about Solomon and May-Lee and how Mrs. Phyllis said everything twice and the word wall with the giant letters and how that afternoon all the kids sang *sep a rate*, even the kids who never spoke any words at all.

Kiya was watching him with her back on the wall. He waited nervously for her to be proud like everyone else, but he had a feeling she might not. She started shaking her head, and her mouth wouldn't break a smile. "Hari, you shouldn't be in that class," she said.

"Why not?" He hoped his whine didn't sound like he was in grade one, because he really wanted to know.

Kiya was rubbing her forehead with her fingers, and then she was rising from the bed and leaving the room. Instead of going to the bathroom she picked up the phone from the kitchen table and flipped through the yellow book with a wet thumb. Hari watched her from the doorway, her lips moving with words he couldn't hear, glancing back at him every few seconds with eyes dark and sad, and wondered if in grade two you could still pull your sister by the arm and talk and talk until she listened.

The next day, Hari ate his lunch so fast his belly ballooned in his shirt, lining up at the door before the afternoon bell had even rung. He wanted to get downstairs as soon as he could. All morning he sat in the back, quiet and waiting to go. He'd written out the spelling words lightning fast, and his writing was a little sloppy, but the answers were all right. He thought about another story Pappa liked to tell, about the time Hari's grandpa escaped a man-eating lion by working in the dirt so quiet that the lion didn't notice him and ate his noisy friends instead. When the bell rang, Ms. Zed pulled Hari aside, crouching down again with her knees in the carpet. Her eyes were creamy as the peacock-blue pencil crayon in the twenty-four pack.

"You won't be going to Mrs. Phyllis's class anymore," she said.

Hari's jaw fell open. "Wha'd'y—why not?"

Ms. Zed chewed her bottom lip. "Hari, that's a class for children who are learning English. Are you learning English?"

Hari shook his head, but he didn't understand, because him and Solomon spoke English in that class all the time.

Ms. Zed's cheeks turned poppy red. "Why didn't you tell me? I just thought, when I met your parents, they couldn't...and your mother..."

She wasn't making sense. Hari's fists shook and a noise came out of him that he hadn't tried to make, a huffy growl. Ms. Zed's eyes flickered, turning slate grey.

"There's no need to be upset. This just means you get to spend more time with your friends here." She pulled a scrap of paper from her pocket and peeled off a glittery sticker, of a banana in sunglasses saying GOOD EFFORT! Then she took Hari's hand in her peach one and pressed the sticker under his knuckles.

"See? All better." She looked at him the way she did when kids spoke out during silent reading time. Hari felt hot in his cheeks and neck. He glanced at the sticker and couldn't decide if he wanted to show Solomon or throw it away.

"Can I use the bathroom?" he blurted. He forgot it wasn't polite to not listen before speaking. His body was shaky and his athanu sandwich flopped in his belly.

Ms. Zed sighed. "Be quick."

Hari was down the basement hallway before he remembered to check for shadows in the stairwell. When he neared the classroom door, he stopped. They were singing a new song today, one about Mr. Blue who lost his Shoe in his Canoe. Every word rhymed with *blue*: *clue*, *true*, *new*, *stew*. Hari knew what word he'd whisper to Solomon, and he knew how hard Solomon would laugh. But through the propped door he could see Solomon on the rug, bobbing his head as he sang, May-Lee twinkling her fingers beside him, Mrs. Phyllis tacking the rhyming words up on the word wall. They were all in a circle, elbow to elbow to elbow to Mrs. Phyllis's shins in her chair, squashed together so close it looked like if one of them came away,

269

they would all fall apart. Hari wondered if Solomon's teacher would pull him aside too, if at this second his sister or mother was calling the school to tell them there had been a mistake. But now Mrs. Phyllis was making her eyes cartoon-big, singing *what will he DO?* and Solomon was laughing, his head leaning against May-Lee's, the rug fire-orange, the space where Hari normally sat between them squeezing shut like an eye. He took the stairs back two at a time, a single tube light blinking out overhead.

That night, Kiya was late coming home from college and Pappa was napping before his shift. Kunal came over to fix the TV and Mayuri hovered around the stove in her grape-violet hospital scrubs, speaking quietly with Ma. Kunal was on all fours behind the TV stand, his face blurred by the furry light. He asked Hari to press a button and twitched the antenna and slapped the top of the TV, leaving a handprint in the dust. "I already tried that," Hari told him. Before walking home, he'd peeled the sticker from the back of his hand and stuck it to the inside of his shirt, his own secret. He felt its shine against his chest, tickling his skin where the edges peeled up.

There was a pop like a firework and the TV exploded into sound, the evening news shimmering onto the screen. Kunal wiped his forehead and Ma cheered, striding over with half a carrot in her hand. Hari hopped on his feet as swirling clouds swept behind the news anchor. His fingers jerked in his pocket, wanting to switch to cartoons but not wanting to lose the signal again.

"No wonder you're in the gifted class. You watch *Global News at 6*!" Kunal said, ruffling Hari's hair.

Hari lifted one shoulder. "Not in that class anymore."

Kunal rocked back on his heels, looking suddenly worried. "What happened?"

Hari let his shoulder drop. "It was for kids who can't speak English. Ms. Zed made a mistake."

Kunal sucked in his lips. A string of grated carrot dropped from Ma's knife and slapped the floor. Ma's eyes shrank small and her face lost a little color.

"Why would she do a thing like that?"

In his pockets, Hari's hands became fists. The sticker caught on the soft hairs of his belly and snagged. He remembered what Ms. Zed had told him, the stringy words she fought to put together. He remembered when King Kong and the Queen waltzed him to school, how they curled up inside his parents so that Ms. Zed didn't see. He knew something that Ma didn't, a truth inside him that he could share or keep. Ma was watching him close. Hari wanted the Queen again, the one who billowed through the streets. He saw her disappearing and wanted her back.

"They mixed me up with someone else," he said. The lines around Ma's eyes melted and Hari knew she believed him. For a second he did too. He stooped down and pinched up the strand of carrot, and he almost offered it back to Ma, but then he strode to the garbage can and chucked it away himself.

Kiya, 1981

KIYA COUGHED AT THE CHALKBOARD dust as she erased the multi-plication tables. Behind her, the head teacher uncapped three pens—pink, orange, blue—and began marking that day's spelling tests with an air of self-importance that made Kiya roll her eyes. This was the realm of being a classroom assistant: clicking the lids back on the markers, tying chewed laces before recess, photocopying assignments so mundane she had to stop herself from sighing along with the students when she handed them out. It crushed her to see them slumped in their seats, eyes on the clock. In those moments, she reminded herself that she'd taken the job to stay close to Hari, prompted by the incident with his second-grade teacher a few years back. Hari was ten now, young enough to still find her presence thrilling rather than embarrassing, and she cherished the moments when she would glimpse him in the lunchroom or running down the hallway with Solomon. After she lost her last job, her parents were surprised when she told them she was offered this one, and though she acted stung by their reaction, privately she was satisfied. For the first time since the hard years—that's how Kiya thought of them, the nightmare years, the angry years, the lonely years—she felt as if she'd done something right.

She sidled toward the hallway to collect Hari, pressing a finger to the point of her earring as she passed the head teacher's desk. A week ago, the teacher had taken Kiya aside, urging her to dress the part. *Animal prints, apple earrings, something that says: look at me, I'm alive!* she'd said, the pink Easter bunny on her own shirt glaring at Kiya's dark sweater and slacks. The teacher's words shook loose a memory of when Kiya had been a student in Toronto, ridiculed by her classmates for wearing a salwar in those first few weeks of school before she'd had a chance to get new clothes. She'd left the conversation fuming, browsing the stores bitterly—because what did it mean to be *alive* when she hadn't slept in years? When she spent so many nights in the dim cave of that club on Yonge that the bartender knew her by name? When she did this simply to be gone, to dare her parents to say anything to her rather than stew in their silence? Perhaps *alive* just meant: more than her sister. Yes, she was so *alive* that she left the apartment some nights to run barefoot down the street, as if her feet might take her somewhere better. Even then she showed up to breakfast duty each morning, and wasn't that enough?

Between combing through the racks of pastel cardigans, she'd thought of her father, who left for work each morning with his pants creased down the center and every shirt button fastened, a kind of armor. But Kiya was exhausted by all the pretending. She'd left the mall with a pair of fake shark-tooth earrings that she'd worn to work every day since, gloating when her students touched them in awe.

The juice she'd snagged from the snack cart stirred in her stomach and she lurched toward the staff bathroom, making it just as the acid scorched up her throat. Staring at the orange liquid in the bowl, she knew she could no longer avoid reality. She fumbled in her purse for the pregnancy test she'd carried around for days.

Several minutes later, minutes in which the world seemed to dim, the lines stared back at her. She slouched against the door and was overwhelmed by the strange feeling that someone would burst in and cut the scene. *I'm a fraud,* she thought. The Kiya out there was a fake, gossiping in the staffroom and handing out granola bars in her hazardous earrings, while the real Kiya crouched here, unwittingly pregnant, with not a single person to turn to.

She yanked the earrings from her lobes and flung them at the mirror, where they clattered dispiritingly into the sink. When they left Kampala she'd been reckless with anger—so much anger that she hadn't known where to put it. She'd turned it on her parents, the hard years widening the rift between them. Then she'd lashed out at Mayuri, refusing her attempts at repair until that door had all but closed to her. It startled her how strongly she had the urge to call Mayuri now. In a way, it had felt safer to be alone.

A silhouette of a man came to mind, his features darkened by night as he traced her palm on the cab ride to his place. She couldn't be sure it was his. She recalled how, when Latika announced to their parents that she was pregnant, the distance that had grown between them collapsed. Latika's hands fluttering around her flat stomach as Pappa's claps echoed through the hall, Ma's joyful tears. Kiya wondered if there was a version of this story that could bring her closer to her family. She imagined telling them, the light in their eyes when she named them Nana and Nani—but no, they were already grandparents. More clearly, she could picture their faces falling, the chill of Ma's stare as she rebuked Kiya for being a veshya, again. In quiet moments like this, her heart often stuttered as she remembered the soldier's cold eyes as he gripped her. "You can't touch me," she mumbled to herself, over and over until her breath slowed, but still she felt stained, that ugly, timeworn story of her own shame resurfacing. She realized then that the nightmare years hadn't ended.

By the time she left the bathroom, she was late. Hari would be waiting for her to collect him, his cheeks bloated with worry. He grew anxious when she wasn't there right on time. *I thought you weren't coming*, he told her once. *I thought something happened.* She wished she could tell him he had nothing to fear. Instead, she tried her best to always be early.

Voices spilled out from the open gym as she rushed past—*From the top!*—and despite her haste she paused before the play rehearsal, attention caught by the children clutching their scripts. They spoke haltingly at first, but as Kiya watched, they settled into their roles, voices projecting louder and limbs loosening. She could remember the exhilaration of that first moment onstage, when the play shifted from practice to reality, when you yourself transformed. She felt an abrupt clutch of jealousy, a reminder of her own youth interrupted, and almost turned away. But her gaze fell on the drama teacher at the center of the gym. The seriousness of her face as she mouthed the lines, the pride glittering in her eyes, stole Kiya's breath, muting her envy into a quiet desire.

The teacher noticed her wavering by the door and flapped an arm. "Are you here to assist?" Kiya snapped to attention, not knowing how long she'd stood there watching. The teacher's stance beckoned, and Kiya's feet faltered as she hurried away.

Outside, Hari waited by the steps, his forehead heavy and lips gathering. The image of Latika closing her apartment door behind her flooded Kiya's mind, but she blinked it away and threw up her arms. Solomon stood next to him, flipping through a pack of cards. When Hari saw her, his face broke, all that fear melting off as he nudged Solomon goodbye. Up close, she noticed the sheen of tears in his eyes, though she rarely saw him cry.

He grasped the red straps of his backpack in his fists. "It's 4:02," he said.

"I'm sorry." She held out her hand for his backpack. For a moment he seemed uncertain, a flicker of reproach twisting his lips. Then he slipped his hand into hers. How uncomplicated his love for her could be; she squeezed his fingers, grateful.

When they reached home, she tried phoning Mayuri. Just a patient calling a doctor for advice, she told herself, though she despaired at the beep of the answering machine, mumbling a few words before hanging up.

"Do you think there's a horror movie on?" Hari said.

She laughed. "You wish."

A few nights before, she had scorched the rice while looking after Hari. To make it up to him, she let him watch a horror movie on TV until past his bedtime. He said nothing, crunching the blackened grains and peeking out from the blankets during the movie, but that night he complained of a bellyache and asked if he could sleep in her bed, and she knew then that she'd done something wrong, whether the dinner or the fright. In the morning she snuck him an extra rock of gur on his oatmeal, winking when Ma's back was turned. Now she wondered at what point he might stop forgiving her.

She sliced bananas and grapes and sprinkled them with sugar, trying to satisfy a craving. They propped the bowl between them on the couch and ate with their fingers. But the taste she wanted sat just out of reach, the dish an approximation of a memory she couldn't reel in. Hari pulled his homework from his bag while Kiya pawed through the small pile of mail she'd collected on their way inside, sorting absently through the sales pamphlets and flyers for waste removal.

Her fingers stopped. The letter was thin, addressed to her, a cluster of stamps consuming half the envelope. In the left corner, so close to her name, was his: Adroa.

She hadn't heard from him since they'd left Kampala. Despite Pappa's radio obsession, she had avoided the news, not wanting to risk hearing any more of Amin's brutality. Even on the days when she imagined Adroa might still be alive, she didn't expect to hear from him again. Once, on a whim, she'd written to the address of the home he'd grown up in, a tacky postcard of Toronto's skyline, letting him know she was safe and hoping that he was too. He'd never responded. Whatever was between them had broken when he joined the army. The expulsion order came mere months later. They'd never had a chance to mend.

Beside her, Hari's pencil was poised above his workbook, though his eyes were locked on the TV. She slit the envelope and held the thin blue page flat against her lap.

Kiya—

I'm sorry it took me this long. I've thought about writing since I received your card, but I couldn't bring myself to. I've been thinking of you, since the birth of my daughter. Her name is Dembe, and she nearly has all her teeth. I've been thinking about what world she was born into, and how different it is from the one we grew up in. I've been thinking of everything she won't know, everything I will try and fail to tell her, and everything I won't. All the things that didn't happen, the could-have-beens. What I mean to say is that I acted so my daughter could have her birthright, which is a place that she can live and walk and know that she is welcomed and equal and free. And I've been thinking about how you deserved that, too.

I've only been able to imagine these things since Amin was ousted. All the collapse. The river—I wish I could erase it from my mind. My sister's disappearance spurred me to join the army, out of denial, maybe, but also as a way towards answers, which come with power. It's taken me years to admit that the very army I joined was likely a part of her end. I see it now, the destruction, but I also see why I'm still here. I made choices to stay on the side of the living. I did what had to be done. For so long I avoided writing you because I didn't know how to admit to you that I wouldn't have done anything differently—because I felt, like most of us, that there was little else I could do. We adapted to a reality where we had so little control. But I know that I betrayed your trust, and that every morning I put on the uniform, my loyalty was to the country first. I made a choice that divided us. I became what you feared.

After you left, I went back to your neighbourhood only once. This was maybe a year or so after the expulsion. That's when I saw your sister in her apartment. I recognized you in her. I could never have expected that, how her face would make me feel. I thought I was seeing a spirit. She told me she was getting out of the country soon. She seemed broken in the way that we all are. I hope she relayed my wishes to you.

Kiya could no longer see the page. The room had dissolved, reality peeling away. Latika, alive. Her sister, long mourned, now returned. She couldn't piece it together, the letter in her lap and Adroa's amends and the sister she grieved who perhaps still lived, away from them all, another impossible betrayal.

She shoved the letter back into its envelope. The milk commercial that Hari loved flashed across the television and he howled, seeking out Kiya's eyes as if wanting to share the moment of delight. Despite the chill coursing through her limbs she felt her lips tugging up, her impulse to reassure Hari assuaged when he turned, still giggling, back to the screen.

The lock clicked behind them and Pappa walked in, his red tie neat down his shirt. "Kem cho?" he called as he set the kettle to boil. Hari waved but remained near the TV. Kiya stood, the letter clutched in her fist. Most times they existed like ships in the night, never lingering with each other for too long. Pappa breathed in the steam and closed his eyes. His face was lined, the hair sparse around his crown.

"Pappa," she said. His eyes fluttered open. She couldn't say the words. He squinted at her, perhaps noticing the quiver of her chin.

"I think Latika..." she said. Pappa's eyes ballooned and he jerked his head toward Hari. Kiya dropped her voice to a whisper. "I got a letter." Slowly she held out the envelope, then hesitated, the letter suddenly an artifact, her only link to Adroa, a long-held ache for him revived; embarrassing proof that in spite of everything, his life was in order, while she continued to wander, her sweat in so many beds, severing every connection she had, unable to watch Hari for even one night without making mistakes. But nothing was sacred, not even this relic of time lost. Pappa stared at the page, his eyes flitting back and forth. A strangled sound rose from his chest. Trembling, he bowed his head to the table.

It became real then. Kiya's hands flew to cover her ears. She knew acutely the sounds of her parents' grief, the unbearable tenor that each of them reached. Soon Ma would be home. Kiya didn't want to witness her mother's last unscathed moments, where she could hold her sorrow at a distance. Pappa's eyes were bloodshot when he lifted his neck, his gaze fixed on the back of Hari's head. The memories came for her. She felt her old rage surging. Latika had held the door closed while Kiya screamed. Latika had listened to the battering of her parents' fists, and still she had chosen to stay. Pappa was scraping his hands up and down his face, then reaching for the phone. He stood quickly.

"Hari," he rasped, eyes unfocused, "why don't you go play outside?"

Hari ripped his eyes from the screen, breaking into a grin. Kiya had seen Hari's concentration when he smacked a basketball on the tarmac with the other kids from the building, how the joy rippled across his face when he made a shot. She wanted nothing to take away his childhood. Her impulse was to run, to protect herself from what was coming. *Like Latika*, she thought as the door shut behind her.

As a child, Kiya had been the fearless one, the one who smashed the scorpion in the storage room with a slipper and scaled the jambu tree without checking for snakes. The one who was unafraid to love Adroa. She had so relished this role that she'd never spoken her true fears aloud. How to say she was afraid to sleep, to dream. Afraid to feel that anger again. Afraid she might always feel stateless. Afraid that she had become someone else, not daring and bold but listless and fragile. Now that she wanted to speak them, she didn't know how.

Unbidden, her last hours at Entebbe came back to her. Adroa avoiding her gaze as they left his jeep, the panic breaking in his eyes when she turned back to look at him. The three most ordinary revelations she hadn't said to him: *Thank you, I'm sorry, goodbye.* How she'd hardly reacted when the soldiers inside the airport searched for gold beneath her blouse, demanded bribes from Pappa, nearly split her family apart. The moment of liftoff, crammed on the airplane floor with the other young people, the din of terror, then the silence of relief. How she broke open as they rose up, knowing what she'd left behind. *I saw you in your school play*, the boy next to her murmured when she struggled to breathe, his hand on her shoulder, a cut over his eye. *You were good*, he said. *You were honestly good.*

Kiya hadn't known where she was going until she stood outside her sister's apartment. When the door swung open, Mayuri sucked in sharply, her face immediately closing. Her hair was wrapped in a cream towel and her cheeks shone clean in the glow of the window.

"You're here."

Kiya wrung her hands. "Did Pappa call you?"

Mayuri looked confused. "I got your message...sorry I didn't call back."

Kiya motioned to come in, and though Mayuri huffed, she stepped aside. Her blue scrubs were draped over the radiator, a pile of earmarked textbooks on the counter—Mayuri retraining. Four dirty plates were stacked in the sink as if she and Kunal had just hosted friends—signs of an ordered, tidy life. Kiya folded herself into a corner of the couch, steeling herself as the silence calcified between them.

"Adroa wrote me. I think Latika's alive. He saw her. She was planning to leave Uganda."

Mayuri's lips parted and closed without sound. Eventually she began to splutter—"What? When? How can—?"—half-formed questions falling around them.

"A year after we left. He went to our compound and she was still there." Having laid the cold facts bare, Kiya shut her eyes and tried to recount the rest. She described Pappa's reaction, Hari's obliviousness, her own anger, how for years she'd blamed everyone for turning away.

When she opened her eyes Mayuri was on the couch next to her. The towel had slipped down her hairline and the floral scent of shampoo draped them both.

"They'll find her. They'll call everyone we know again." Mayuri's voice was flat with disbelief.

"And Hari?"

Mayuri shook her head, but the truth of it seemed to be dawning on her now, and her voice quavered as she spoke. "You know they won't tell him anything." She swept her eyes up, covering her mouth. "Hai, bhagwan," she murmured into her fist.

Kiya twisted her toes into the carpet. "I was just thinking about her this morning, I was just—"

Mayuri caught Kiya's hands, her grip firm. "I know. I'm always thinking about her too."

The tears fell now, her wrists shuddering in Mayuri's grasp. She couldn't remember the last time Mayuri held her. She couldn't remember the last time they spoke Latika's name between them. She had lost not one sister but two. But she'd made it here, to Mayuri. She didn't have to stay gone.

Mayuri's shoulders rocked. "I can't believe it. They have to find her."

"Maybe she doesn't want to be found," Kiya said.

"Maybe she needs to be."

Kiya dropped her head. The curtains swelled in the breeze, and the words rose within her. "I'm pregnant."

Mayuri blinked rapidly, sat back, and then leaned forward once more, as if the news were sweeping through her. "Are you sure?" She paused. "Whose is it?"

"I don't know."

Mayuri was silent for some time. A bus groaned outside. Through the window, the moon hung in the dark bend of the sky. "What do you want to do?"

The knowledge about Latika tangled with an image of Adroa's daughter, her toothy smile, and of Hari on the school steps, the scars of his abandonment clear in the worry on his face, his need for her to simply be there, his trust that she would try, again and again and again. An instinct was rushing forward, a need to shelter from the forces that still haunted her darkest dreams.

She hunched over. Her body was forever changed. But inside it, something beat. It couldn't return to how it once was, but it could create something new.

Mayuri rested a hand on the back of Kiya's head and drew her fingers through her hair. "You know, I never wanted children. Not after what happened. I didn't think I could bear it—I'm not strong enough to make those kinds of choices. But you are."

Kiya let this sink in. Latika, gone, newly unearthed, was everywhere, the context to each word they spoke. The space between them clamored with the truth that Latika had relinquished Hari and never come back. Already Kiya was wildly protective of what was inside her; even now, letting her child go was unimaginable.

"You think so?" she said, swallowing thickly. She wanted to be brave enough, to still be that person who had once graced the stage. She wanted to know that someone thought she could.

"Who else knows you better?"

Kiya remembered a time when the greatest arguments between them had been over which snack to buy after school, Mayuri's sweet tooth aching for the mandazi, Kiya pining for something salty. It was Latika who settled these arguments, and often Kiya won since mhogo chips only cost ten cents. She said this to Mayuri, who looked at her strangely.

"No," Mayuri said slowly, "it was always you who let me win. You used to say my sweet tooth was bigger than your salty one."

Her own words floated down to her as if from a dream. She wanted to stay in this moment forever, the one where Mayuri brought her back. She ran her finger over the outline of the earrings in her pocket, the ridges pressing into her thigh.

"I thought you'd be a mother before me," she said, drying her face. "I'm not like you. Warm. Maternal." She paused, a new lightness returning between them. "Nice."

Mayuri lifted her shoulders. "No, but you'd do whatever it takes to defend your own."

Kiya sensed a passage opening before her. She understood why her feet had led her here; that in some sense, she had always been on her way back. Mayuri crossed to the fridge, drawing out an assortment of items. Kiya watched as she sliced grapes and apples, cracked a tin of pineapple, reached for the sugar. She brought over two bowls and set one in Kiya's lap, the pieces of fruit bobbing in sweetened milk.

"No papai or matunda, but..." she said.

Kiya brought the spoon to her lips. It was the exact taste that she had longed for earlier, the tartness of the fruit and the bite of skin softened by the milk. She ate hurriedly, spoon after spoon, until all the fruit was gone, and then brought the bowl to her lips. She emerged panting, Mayuri chuckling.

"Latika was wild for fruit pudding when she was pregnant. Ma would make it for her almost every day." Mayuri took a sip from her own bowl, then looked at Kiya. "We'll tell them when you're ready."

Kiya heard the *we* that encompassed her, that held her even as she transformed.

Latika, 1981

I AWOKE TO AN IMAGE of my sisters: Kiya, hair always defying her braids, and Mayuri, that softness in her face. I had dreamed that we were playing marbles in the courtyard of the Gur nu Ghar, a line drawn in the red dust between us, and I could feel the dirt under my nails and the fire ants scorching my bare feet. I tried to shrug the memory off as I rose, but I sensed it would linger, casting a pall over my day.

I brushed my teeth and fixed my hair before work, but the dream colluded with my reflection in the mirror, and I glimpsed my ghost, the woman who existed before. Her sunken gaze and the tilt of her chin, her large hands and a spark in the eye. She was a girl finding her place, a woman in a lineage of drifting women and climbing men, a line that never settled. But that woman could be no more. I blinked and she was gone.

The only remnant of my past life that I had carried with me, knotted in my chunni on the flight from Kampala to London, was Arun's lighter. It sat now in my kitchen cupboard with my bowl and spoon, a boxy silver thing with his initials engraved faintly along the bottom, and every morning I held it in my hand while I ate my plain porridge. It was a reminder of what I had done to Arun, to Harilal. Its weight in my palm called forth the memory of my grandfather, the choice he had made and perhaps wished he had not. And my thumb caressing but never flicking the wheel was a daily test of my conviction: if I could

285

hold this lighter and not spark it, I could go another day without my family, another day without causing harm.

The shadow of the dream followed me until that afternoon, when I found a rolling pin under the till of the newsagents' shop. My hands grazed it as I was reaching for a new cylinder of coins, and when I brandished it like a club, Zera doubled over in laughter. "Come get your morning paper with a side of paratha?" I said.

Zera had been spooling twine into a ball—the shop saved everything, each elastic band and length of string that came in with the newspapers stowed away—and now it came apart in her hands. "Now look what you've made me do," she said, but her voice was light.

I took up the ball of twine as Zera explained, punctuated by little huffs of amusement. She had first brought the rolling pin to work in September of 1972, the week of the anti-immigration demonstration as the first of thousands of Indo-Ugandan refugees started to pour into the UK. Local authorities were begging that no more refugees be sent to them, saying they were swamped—an invasion, some called it, the National Front taking up the mantle. Zera and Maaz had fought over whether to keep the shop open that week, but they couldn't afford to close, so she had found her own way to feel safe.

"And you've kept it here all these years?" I laughed.

"Well, has anything changed?"

The comment sobered us both, though Zera giggled once more as I stowed the rolling pin away. "Oh, that felt good," she said.

I sensed the specter of the dream receding and agreed.

From outside, we could hear the clamor of hungry crowds gathering, the pub on the corner throwing open its doors. Maaz was running errands, but soon he would arrive to take Zera home for lunch. Later, they would collect their children from school, a young girl and a lanky boy who ran the paper route most mornings.

I handed Zera the fattened wad of twine. Like Zera's, the tips of my fingers were stained black with ink.

"Come with us today," she said.

I shifted my eyes away. Most days I worked through lunch, taking a sandwich at the till, while Zera and Maaz went home. Occasionally, they brought me back a roti rolled with onion pickle or a flask of chai boiled thick as cream, but these days I ate plainly, food seasoned only with salt or a little lemon. I never accepted their offers to come eat with them. I didn't think I could bear to be in their home, amid the sounds of oil spitting and children shrieking, to witness a gathered life. When I first started working in their shop years ago, soon after arriving in London, I'd told them of a fictional family: a bad divorce, no children, parents long perished. The words spilled out as if by choice, though I'd been as surprised to hear them as Zera. But I had become my present self, responsible to no past, no person or place. I had become something separate. In many ways it felt like the truer truth, that I was simply alone. Alongside the guilt of erasing my family came relief: if my family ceased to exist for me, I could cease to exist for them, my son's life renewed in my absence. Still, Zera made it a point to invite me wherever she could.

"I told Randy I'd eat with him," I lied. Now I'd have to visit the greengrocer's next door to save face.

Zera eyed me, and for a moment I thought she would protest. Then she sighed. "One day I'll get you home."

I was glad when the moment passed. It bothered me to think that Zera might see me as cold, when I stayed away to keep her from harm. Come any closer, and the borders of my control could blur. If only I could tell her that it took all my energy to fight that instinct to go home—though where that home was now, I couldn't say.

It was that instinct that first drew me to the shop. The familiar smell of ripe fruit and laundry that marked the East London neighborhood, lines of kurtas and cotton nightgowns strung between apartments. It was a cleansing breath after the signs on other shop windows: WE DO NOT HIRE ASIANS; NO DOGS. I'd paused outside the greengrocer's, admiring the great mounds of hairy dried coconuts rustling in the wind, when I heard voices coming from the newsagents' next door. It was unmistakably the accent of my people, that lilting brew of Indian and East African, the hard *t*'s and long, curving vowels, but pared down, clipped into a British cadence. I'd peeked inside, struck by the smell of ink and hot paper from the printing press in the back. Later, I'd learned that Zera and Maaz were Indo-Kenyan, having left a few years before Amin's expulsion order, when the Kenyan government began denying Asians work permits and their family lost their living.

I told them I'd been a journalist back in Kampala, and either they believed me or took pity on me. "You're sure you want to work here?" Maaz had said, indicating the dusty stacks, the leftmost window of the shop taped over with brown butcher paper to cover the cracks. But I felt as if I'd struck gold. In those early months in London, I'd moved about carefully so as not to be noticed by anyone who might send word to my family, though my body gravitated toward anything that reminded me of them—the curry houses and sari shops, the mandir. How deeply I yearned for them, the way a bone still aches long after the fracture. But I knew I could not give in. After Arun, after Harilal, I couldn't trust myself any longer. I had left Harilal with my mother, knowing that she would protect him fiercely, and I imagined she might see that I was doing the same. The newsagents' came as a small, necessary relief.

When Zera and Maaz left for lunch, I bought a banana from Randy next door. The ink on my hands marked the fruit but I ate it anyway, wiping my fingertips down my slacks to try to erase the stains. I thought then of Pir-dada, how he had set sail for another country and left his family behind. For years his mother and siblings in Gujarat had no idea where he'd gone, no sense of whether he was alive or dead. I'd been too young to know if this aggrieved him, but I knew he was a man who believed a life could be remade. Perhaps that was what he had seen in me, that day he shared his story. I imagined sitting on the edge of his mattress again, the obscuring shelter of the mosquito net around us, and recounting my own. I imagined he would understand.

The street outside had grown drizzly and grim. I tossed the banana peel and listened to the patter of rain. Perhaps that evening I would see a film, or stop by the library on my way home. My apartment needed cleaning, the windows dense with grime. Or maybe I would stay late, let Zera and Maaz leave early and lock up myself. My favorite hour was just before closing time, when through the gritty window I watched the mist darkening the sky, swirling around the lampposts like crickets, like the nsenene that vendors in Kampala would capture at sundown with paper bags under the lights, then fry up with chili and onion and sell from carts along Buganda Road. That was the hour I felt most at home. I waited for that light.

In Kampala, too, I had waited. For Arun, I kept telling myself, forcing myself outside to search for him day after day. But soon the search became empty, rote. Lost woman, they called me on the streets. Or maybe, ghost woman. At first they harassed me. With every Asian gone, there was more hostility for those who remained. I heard that most were sheltering in the mandirs and gurudwaras. I passed the shuttered tailor's where Pappa's work suit was made, the mithai shop where I would bring my sisters after school for a treat, sugar dusting the floor like ash. Mr. Singh's auto shop taken over by soldiers, the drive-in cinema where my family used to congregate with friends on weekend nights, the quiet made eerier for how it had once rung with music and laughter. I wandered, ignoring the taunts and jeers, until I became a part of the landscape, like the broken doors and the cloy of decay, like the knots of vultures by the river. The phone lines were down. Roadblocks at every step, tanks like great beasts asleep in the sun. Shots through the night, soldiers with their guns and pride. Each boarded-up shop and abandoned flat carved into my heart, a dark accumulation.

Even still, life rolled on. Teenagers corralling to watch television in the hot streets, the marketplace just as fragrant with chapati and eggs, the matunda vine in the courtyard heavy with fruit. Once the kerosene lamps ran dry, I ate bread dipped in Carnation condensed milk by candlelight. Many times, a kind someone tried to lead me to the UN tent, where they awaited stragglers like me. A young man on a bicycle offered me money to help me leave. Each time, I resisted and walked myself back home. But the emptiness was beginning to consume me.

Next door, I could hear music and children's cries, the trickle of water running in the mornings. The sounds of a new family. They didn't try to take my home. But I knew that they were afraid. Not of me, but of what I had become. A haunting. Through my window, I saw a small boy, yellow shorts and cropped hair, a mottled dog nosing his ankles. When he saw me, his face turned ashen, his scream muffled by his hands. *Roho*, he breathed behind his fingers. *Spirit woman.*

I watched the Nandi flame tree turn from bloodred to orange to unremarkable brown, the fire sputtering and letting go. I felt myself losing my grasp on the world, on myself, my only anchor the familiar terrain beneath my feet.

Then one day Adroa came to my door. He was alarmed to find me there. I wondered what had brought him back, but what else binds us to the places that have hurt us but love?

"Just one person in this whole apartment," he said. He perhaps meant it sympathetically, but I heard it with bitterness. I understood then that there was nothing noble in holding on. His words brought into focus my dusty sofa, the chilling stares that followed me home, all the houses vacant or reoccupied, everything telling me what I already knew inside: there was no longer a place for me here.

"I'm sorry," he added when he saw my grimace. "Your husband."

From the way he said it, I could tell he believed that Arun was forever gone. I studied his face, his guarded posture, and knew he had seen too much to conclude otherwise.

The certainty released me. I felt my conviction, already so frayed, dissipate. The thought occurred to me that the best thing I could do was disappear too. Erase myself just as my people had been erased from the streets, and let the world churn on.

I remembered the night they took Arun—Harilal and I curled on the floor as if stranded in the ocean. If I let go, I knew one of us would sink. He pressed his wet face to mine, gripped my ears with surprising strength. My anger welled. I blamed him for what happened to Arun: because of my baby, they didn't take me. And I was terrified then, that I could tether such a weight to my child. Was that the night I let him go? I'd done it as a mercy. It was not my own life I wished to remake, but his.

Adroa looked pained, and I sensed there was something more he wanted to say. "Your family is okay?" he asked finally, a flicker of hope in his eyes, wavering on the edge of a great and wild despair. I recalled the last time he was here, the night he drove Kiya home, and the person I had been then: someone literally full of life, someone who wouldn't lie down to wait for death. And I thought: *I will not turn you away again.*

"Take the apartment," I told him, and felt a new conviction return.

I had no passport, but I was given a refugee card for the United Kingdom. On my last morning I plucked a matunda from the vine, broke the purple skin with my thumbs, and scooped the tart flesh. Each dark seed in my teeth, whole and separate, all joined together by that supple membrane the color of a Ugandan sunrise, the only one I'd ever known.

It was just before that tender hour when the sun dips beneath the trees and the streetlamps erupt. I was in the shop alone, Zera and Maaz at an event at their mosque for the evening, and I was about to lock up for the night when a crash split the air. Shards of glass sprayed like sand, catching the light. I leapt to the door and thought I saw a jacketed figure dashing away, a slash of white in the black road. The brick had landed cleanly in the aisle before the till. My lungs were shuddering so violently I had to squat down and cradle my head between my knees. For a moment my protective myopia vanished and I saw that this country didn't want us, just as I did with every slur uttered in the trains and grocery lines, the letters painted on brick walls. The response from the leader of the National Front after a Sikh boy was murdered by a police officer while pulling weeds in his mother's garden, which Zera read aloud from the paper the next morning: *One down, another million to go.* Maaz had shaken his head and said, *but in this country we have the rule of law, not the rule of gun*, but of course they were operated by the same hands. How else to explain the petrol-bombing of clubs and theatres where our people congregated, or the group of Indian children brutally attacked by three skinheads in Brick Lane and who were arrested instead of the attackers when the youngest called the police for help. My mind was spinning out, and I took long, slow breaths until I could feel my feet on the ground. I considered calling Zera and Maaz, but they were surrounded by their people, praying and eating and crowding together to forget the cold. I would not break them apart.

In that moment Arun came to me, appraising me with his generous gaze. *Uhuru*, he had repeated that first night I met him, until it became what he symbolized. I imagined him finding me here, among the remnants of glass and stone, away from everyone I knew, away even from myself. *Uhuru, just like you told me*, I imagined telling him. But no matter how hard I tried, he would not crack a smile. His expression was not the carefree, admiring one from our earliest days together, but the one at the end, the day he found the notice in Harilal's pillow: heavy and knowing.

Rain blew in slantwise through the wrecked glass, prickling my skin.

Latika, 1981

I pulled on gloves and brushed the shards into a garbage bag, swept the dirt out the door and taped butcher paper over the window. Zera had told me the other window had cracked from the cold. We all protected each other how we could.

When I was finished, I stood at the entrance, surveying this space that was not mine but that I cared for deeply. The brick, the weapon, I dusted off and left by the door; we'd been in need of a doorstop. In that moment I felt an impossible gratitude. I had swept the trouble away. No one need know of the destruction: in its aftermath, I'd keep us safe. We could go on.

Vinod, 1985

THE FIRST TIME VINOD VISITED the open house, he came alone. He'd found the sale ad in the newspaper and made the phone call while Rajni was out. In the smeared newsprint, he traced the tiny photo with his thumb: a small redbrick semi-detached, three steps climbing up to the eggshell door, a square of grass in the back leading to a shared alleyway. It straddled the divide between Toronto and Scarborough and was part of the developments that were cropping up around the new Scarborough Rapid Transit line that was soon to open. Each day, train cars stuffed with immigrants would clang from the suburb toward the city for work. Vinod felt its promise like an answer he'd long awaited.

When he told Rajni, she fell quiet. The idea of moving unnerved her. They'd had their share of resettling; let them ignore the thin walls of the apartment they'd moved into over a decade ago, the tired rooms that were more cramped now that their granddaughter was in the mix, for the sake of staying put. But beneath all that, Vinod knew she yearned for permanence. He felt it too: the desire to stake a claim that no one could deny.

Before him, the RT line was under construction, workers in orange vests flicking cigarettes across the tracks. He watched them for a few minutes: the domed helmets that sheathed their heads, the way they called to one another before turning their focus back to the rail.

Vinod pictured his father, a shirt tied over his hair, his back to the uninterrupted sun as he worked. He remembered the day Pappa was hired by the government Transport Department and came home with a bag of sweets in his hand. His father had known it was not just a job but a ladder. A chance. And now they were here: on firm ground, equal by all measures. *We did it*, he thought, as a drill exploded into motion, the scream of iron against screws.

Across the street was a plywood wall papered over with advertisements for a series of townhouses. MINUTES FROM THE NEW RT, the sign boasted. DIRECT LINE TO SCARBOROUGH TOWN CENTRE MALL! Vinod paused, unsure which way to walk. A man smoked on the stoop of a convenience store nearby, his arms dangling over his knees. His skin was a deep brown and sheened with sweat, the afternoon having taken an unseasonably muggy turn. Vinod called out for directions.

"You visiting?" the man asked, giving Vinod a once-over with keen eyes. His accent was lilting, musical.

Vinod bounced up on the balls of his feet, unable to rein in his enthusiasm. "For now."

The man leaned in conspiratorially and jerked his head toward the advertisements.

"What a mess. Shops going under. They just bought out my buddy Al's motel. You know him? He opened it twenty years ago."

Vinod nodded. "But the rail, surely it'll make life easier."

The man ashed his cigarette on the pocked step. "Sure, for them people. Not for us."

He puffed deep, smoke spiraling from his nose. Vinod stepped back to avoid the cloud. His maternal grandparents had once run a shop by the railroad in Kisumu, a little hovel of a dukan that flourished as the traffic through the area rose. They had been thrifty, his grandparents, and sharp, moving to Kenya with the knowledge that a railroad would bring new settlements whose residents would need flour and oil and soap to live. He came from a people who did more than sit on a stoop and complain. *I made choices to stay on the side of the living*, Adroa had written in his letter to Kiya, the line streaming into Vinod's mind as he stood before the man on the other side of the pavement.

"We're looking to buy," Vinod said.

The man cocked his head back, appraising Vinod with slit eyes.

"I see." He dashed his half-smoked cigarette over the stoop and creaked to his feet. On the step he stood more than a foot taller than Vinod, who boxed his shoulders higher. For a moment they lingered, a warm breeze shuffling the air between them.

"I should get to it, then," Vinod said, turning up the road.

"Other way," the man said. Vinod spun a full circle, sheepish, nodding his thanks. "Good luck with that," the man called as he walked away, though Vinod couldn't tell if his wish was sarcastic or sincere.

A double sink in the kitchen and a finished basement, Vinod described over dinner. Rajni pursed her lips as Vinod went on, the house expanding in his mind as he spoke.

"We're moving?" Hari said.

"Only you," Rajni replied, pinching his cheek. Hari laughed and swatted her off.

"Imagine—your own room. And a driveway to play basketball. We can put up your own net." Despite Hari's new teenage indifference, his eyes shone.

Rajni grunted. "Your father spends too much time watching television and getting these fancy ideas."

Vinod had spent many nights with their account books, noting calculations in the margins. "We can manage it," he said. Meetu was smashing chickpeas into her plate with her thumb. *If not for them, then for her*, he thought. For his grandchildren to grow up rooted was the greatest reason of all. "And the train!" Vinod said, tickling her under the chin, to which she responded with a wet *choo-choo!*

"Bas, Vinod," Rajni said after dinner, grabbing a fistful of sopping potato peels from the sink catch and slapping them into the bin.

Vinod poked her hip, trying to coax out her playful attitude from earlier. "But how about—" he began, remembering the park a few blocks away and imagining Meetu on the painted swing set.

Rajni jerked away, glaring. Trails of soapy water slithered toward her elbows. "The last thing we need is to get our hopes up again."

Vinod softened at her last word. He couldn't describe how it had felt to lose everything they had worked for at the age of fifty-five; to start again. But Rajni had started over twice. If he hungered for stability, she was famished.

"It's not just hope. I saw it. It's real." He spoke gently, his voice melding with the running water. She reached for the faucet and screwed the tap shut. When she turned to face him once more, he caught the spark of possibility flaring in her eyes.

That night, after Rajni had gone to bed, Mayuri splayed her fingers on the table in front of Vinod. "We want to help," she said.

Vinod squinted at her clear fingernails, then caught her meaning. "Na, na, na."

Kunal glanced at Mayuri. "It would be good for all of us."

"It wouldn't be right," Vinod said. If he knew anything, it was that there was an order to things. Parents provided for children. Children did the same when they had children of their own. His eyes fell on the space between Kunal and Mayuri, a whole kitchen chair separating them. He no longer urged them to have children. But in Mayuri's desire to take control of her life in ways that only she could, he had always recognized something of himself. When he first arrived in Toronto nearly thirteen years ago he'd been terrified, overwhelmed by the towering buildings and bus lines that crossed every which way. He'd thought then of his boyhood wish to leave home and travel overseas for college, and laughed at himself for thinking it so easy to begin again. Perhaps he'd been braver back then and grown cautious with age. But Mayuri had found her way.

"Pappa, please," Mayuri said, "let us give you this."

Vinod saw in her face the same expression he had witnessed when she first joined them in Canada. *You owe us nothing*, he had wanted to tell her then. Yet now he sensed it wasn't so much what she felt she owed, but what she believed they all deserved.

Vinod tugged the final box through the doorway, the arches of his feet throbbing. He was a few years shy of seventy, his eyesight dimmed by the time evening came such that he had to squint at the television. But today, he was young, his energy boundless. Today, he was the body he'd once been, makeshift cricket bat in hand, smacking golf balls all the way back to the country club. Today, he was moving his family into their new home, a place where they could take root and grow.

Meetu ran up the path and clutched the back of Vinod's calf with ragged fingernails. "Go inside?" she said, her curls spilling out of the ribbon that Kiya was forever retying. She was three now, already talking as fast as a train, but Vinod still cherished the memory of that day when she had first called him Nana, her second word.

"Tu ja, dikri," Vinod said, "I'm right behind you." He watched her skip to the door, stunned for a moment by the simple beauty of her spirit. It was innate in children, that fire for life.

The door of the van sucked shut, and Rajni appeared at his elbow. That morning they had fought while packing the last of the boxes, bickering over how much tape was necessary. It was a silly argument, the kind their marriage barely registered anymore, but this morning it papered over the surprising pain of leaving the apartment that had held so much. The neighbors who had jammed the hallway with balloons when Meetu was born, who accepted containers of Rajni's dhebra and later returned them packed with pepper soup and string hoppers; the doorframe nicked with pencil marks recording Hari's growth, soon to be painted over. Now, standing before their new house, Rajni squeezed Vinod's arm, and through the layers of sweaters and coats he felt the solidity of her hands.

He told Rajni he'd catch up with her. When she was inside, he pulled the envelope of photographs that Mayuri had given them eight years ago from his bag, the first one yellowing around the edges. For years he'd made it a ritual to slip it out when no one else was home.

His three daughters in the grass. Had they ever really been that small, all of them crowding in his lap like kittens? He could scarcely make sense of it now: one a doctor and a wife, ever determined, carving a way forward for the rest of them. In the last few years, it was she who supported Hari with his studies and spun elaborate bedtime tales for Meetu. And his youngest—what was it she called herself? An *educator*. Not quite a teacher as Rajni had been, but still. He'd gone to watch one of the school plays she'd directed and kept finding himself turning to watch his daughter instead, the hope illuminating her face. And a mother. Meetu's birth had softened the soreness between Kiya and Vinod, and even Rajni. Kiya had told them she better understood what they'd taken on. He'd expressed his shock at the pregnancy and agreed when Rajni confided in him that Kiya had needed a firmer hand. But privately he could think only of his beloved uncle Nanu, whose child their family had shunned without taking the chance to even know him. Hadn't Vinod too been restless and unruly? Hadn't he loved an open field and the beat of his legs below him?

He looked, finally, to Latika. In the picture her eyes darted to the side, and Vinod liked to imagine that it was at him, dancing to make his daughters laugh while Rajni clicked the camera. But he knew her gaze had always been beyond them.

If she lived, it was not in any place they could reach. Their calls around the community had proved fruitless, tearing the scab from their grief only to let the wound weep. Though Rajni continued her search, Vinod found it too painful to swing endlessly between the belief that Latika lived elsewhere and the fear that she didn't, that she hadn't made it out after all. Now he'd sealed himself off, an abscess around the fracture. He could not pretend to understand his daughter. He could not make her look at him. He could only hope that one day he might have the chance to ask what she had seen.

He heard Rajni calling and tucked the photograph back in its envelope, heavy with the weight of love, and folded it away once more.

In the yard, Mayuri was readying the fire for the puja, Kiya swiping at Meetu's prying fingers before relenting and letting her suck the syrup off a glistening jalebi. Hari was touring Kunal around the garden, unaware that Mayuri and Kunal had paid part of the down payment, an offer that Vinod had eventually accepted so long as they kept it between them.

The fire hissed. Rajni raised the tray, her finger inked red, and marked Vinod's forehead, powder catching his eyebrows. He swallowed his memory, steadied his feet against the ground. Since Uganda, Rajni had thickened in her faith, offering food to their cupboard shrine morning and night, believing that without the gods, they may not have survived. Perhaps she was right. But since that day in Kampala, Vinod's faith had grown another skin. Faith, to him, was routine, the steps each morning from shower to mala, the portioning of prasad to each of his family members, the prayer on his lips whenever the phone rang. It was community: the masis who left tubs of khichdi outside their apartment when Rajni came down with the flu; the moment he saw his childhood friend Pulin in the mandir in Toronto, the way their eyes grew boyish and wet across the room. It was the certainty that some things remained and others dissolved. But to Vinod, faith was not survival. That day, over a decade ago, his survival had reminded him of a time when his religion was the land that nurtured him. In Kampala he woke to the call of the muezzins and the church bells and the mandir bhajans, but it was the crow of the rooster that got him out of bed. He felt it, ancestrally, moments before what should have been his death: not a call from the gods above, but a pull from the earth below.

Mayuri dug the shovel into the hardened earth, and into the hole, Hari and Meetu settled the tiny sugar maple sapling Vinod had bought from Canadian Tire. "Home sweet home," Hari said in English, pressing the soil into place. Vinod startled. How could this boy know that they'd once bestowed that name on their old home, the Gur nu Ghar, that beloved compound of joy and grief.

Vinod closed his eyes, let the feeling settle. They had it now: a place of their own.

Home found them. Vinod relished it, sanding down a wooden bench for the back alley, the tile above the stove already flecked yellow with hardar and oil. Pulin and his wife, Naina, visited, bringing with them cassava from the Jamaican grocer and a clay Ganesh statue that now guarded the door. Rajni still believed that nothing belonged to them, insisting they wrap the couches in faded bedsheets and scrub the walls and hinges and her own children as if someone might otherwise take them away. There was a guest bedroom in the basement that Vinod once found himself thinking of as Latika's room, and since then he took pains to avoid it.

But Vinod couldn't shake the sensation that something wasn't right. He stood outside the house, eyeing the brittle tips of grass on their patch of lawn, the smattering of pebbles forming a walkway toward the steps. He wanted the whole house to gleam with the pride he felt.

On the block, his house would be twice as beautiful, would unfailingly earn its place.

He exchanged a terse nod with the neighbor, Mr. Clark, who was hurrying out to his car. When Rajni brought his family a tray of mithai their first week in the neighborhood, the man brought it back untouched. Nut allergy, Vinod assured her, dipping into the pista barfi himself. "Yes, maybe they only eat cashews," Rajni joked, "or those bleached almonds." He had to admit it was unsettling not to know their neighbors, but he batted away Rajni's implication. "They like their privacy here," he reminded her, "no gapasapa over chai."

Hari loped up behind him, his hair awry and jacket musty with sweat. He stunk in a way that Rajni hated and Vinod treasured, that in-between manner of boys becoming. He'd begun to move his body differently since turning fourteen, baring his chest, limbs splayed wide. He was nearing in height to Vinod, and his voice crackled and pitched like an old radio, the dial twisting toward Arun.

Vinod turned from the thought of his son's father. He remembered the start of that school year, when Hari had come home seething that Solomon had been streamed into the nonacademic program, Hari making wild plans to confront their teacher. Though Vinod was proud that Hari remained in the academic track, he was so alarmed by Hari's outspokenness that he'd neglected to voice his delight entirely, instead warning Hari not to jeopardize his own path to university. It worried him, this streak in his son.

Hari lowered his backpack and joined Vinod in scrutinizing the front of the house. "Color's weird," he said, pointing at a spot above the windows where the painted slats shifted from white to a murky grey, chipped to expose the naked materials beneath.

Vinod clapped his shoulder. How easily those young eyes could see what his couldn't. "We'll paint it."

Hari twisted his lips. "But it's fine."

"Fine isn't good enough. Help me get the ladder."

Hari didn't move. Vinod shot him a look. "You think I can climb myself?"

Hari groaned, sounding less a teenager than a little boy. Vinod too had been young once, steadfast in his belief that all was well. He saw it in Hari's easy walk, his bellowing laugh, the carefree way he rolled out of bed before school, sometimes wearing the same shirt as the day before. How trusting this boy was, how open to the world that had hurt him in ways he didn't remember.

Hari dragged the ladder from around back and set it against the side of the house. It wobbled slightly, the ground beneath choppy with ice. The sky was darkening, winter swallowing the day. Hari was sullen, his back to Vinod as he cracked the lid off the old paint pot. Ignoring his theatrics, Vinod steadied the base of the ladder, and Hari, with a long sigh, began to climb.

"Make sure you get every inch," Vinod said when Hari paused to blow air into his fingers, stiff with cold.

A hollow wind rattled the eaves. The lights inside blinked on, casting a ghoulish glow across Hari's wide forehead. He looked down at Vinod, his eyes glassy discs, no longer angry but tired.

"One more coat," Vinod said. Unnecessary, maybe, but it was important to push through, stretch the body just a little bit more. Vinod almost laughed—was he becoming his father? Maybe at one point the thought would have repelled him, but now he was glad. His father had known that nothing was guaranteed.

Hari's face hardened, an indignant expression taking over, one so like Arun that Vinod's hand faltered at the base of the ladder, his wrist clanging against a low rung. He sucked in a pained breath, and in that moment Hari's body arced back, his grip giving way to gravity, and then he was falling, hurtling to the ground by Vinod's feet. The sound was of branches snapping. On the ground Hari lay still, frozen as Vinod's breath. Then Hari's eyes flew wide, his mouth tearing at the air, fingers reaching toward the awkward twist of his leg.

Vinod slapped against the fogged window and dropped to the ground. Hari stammered about his ankle, his eyes screwed shut. Then Rajni was beside them, her body carrying all the heat of their home, and together they were hoisting Hari to his feet, Vinod slinging Hari's gangly arms around his neck as Rajni flew back inside to grab the keys to the car.

The hospital waiting room brimmed with unnerving beeps and rumbling coughs. They found a space between a man buttressing his chin with an ice pack and a woman wiping the crusted nose of her toddler. When the nurse came for Hari with a wheelchair, both Rajni and Vinod stood to follow. The nurse held out a hand. "We're packed inside," she said, and wheeled their son away.

Rajni gripped the lips of her coat, squashing the fabric. With icy fingers, Vinod kneaded his neck, cricked from staring up at Hari perched on the ladder.

"What were you thinking?" Rajni cut her eyes to him before turning to the wall. Vinod bristled. Not here, among so many ears.

"He was helping me. He needs to learn to take care of things," he said calmly.

"He's your child. We're supposed to take care of *him*." She whipped her head toward him. The woman with the toddler shifted away from them in her seat. Despite the throb in his neck, Vinod tipped his face toward the television on the wall, squinting to focus on the reporter before a courthouse. Something about a Native group launching a case against the government, declaring that the Crown had illegally acquired their land two hundred years prior. Vinod let it fade out.

"If it was up to you, you'd still be spoon-feeding him," he muttered to the TV. Rajni's coat rustled as she straightened, though he refused to face her.

"What's that supposed to mean?" Her voice dropped to that quiet, dangerous place.

"It means he's becoming entitled, like—" Vinod stopped. Arun's face danced before him, the persuasive, irresponsible laugh, the righteous diatribes. A face that invited trouble. But with the thought of Arun came the twin memory of Latika, and how Vinod had turned her away. He had rejected her wish to marry and had let her move to Jinja, and she had returned changed and hardened. He hadn't been there when she needed him. What else was a father for? A vein of anxiety pulsed through him at the thought that he might have now spoiled something with Hari. Bones would heal, that Vinod knew, but what of trust?

Rajni seemed to hear the end of his sentence. She leaned back in her chair. "I have to protect him," she said finally. Vinod sensed what she too wasn't saying. But there was no better protection than being prepared for what might come.

Vinod let out a long breath. He had been the one to lose hold of the ladder, long enough for Hari to miss his footing. Had he pushed Hari too far? He had only wanted to teach his son what his father had taught him, that if he worked hard enough, he could find freedom. He had wanted to show Hari who he believed they were. But no, that wasn't entirely true: he had wanted to prove his place not just to Hari but to himself. He thought of the man smoking on the stoop and saw now that their only difference was how he'd thought himself better. Perhaps the ladder had never been in his hands.

Rajni was breathing heavily. They'd been married nearly forty years—he knew what she needed to hear.

"Bhagwan is protecting him," he said.

A nurse wheeled Hari out after midnight, and he left the hospital with a pair of crutches and a cast-bound ankle. Hari paused to squint up at the side of the house after Vinod helped him from the car, the ladder still leaning against the wall. Vinod looked too, but could find no flaw in the surface, though the leftover paint had already frozen in the can, the brush bristles dried at irreparable angles. But he could say nothing. In his anxiety he could see their lives spooling out before them, his son pulling away from the father who pushed him too hard, the distance widening until it was too great to cross.

Hari leaned hard on one crutch. "Paint job looks great," he said.

Vinod searched his son's face, drowsy with painkillers, trying to find the resentment that he knew he deserved. But he found nothing. Across the way, the RT jangled across the tracks. He followed Hari into the house, bending to help him untie his one shoe, and wondered if the crack between them might be repaired, or at least forgotten.

Latika, 1986

IN THE MORNING, I FOUND a letter on my pillow. I had been seeing Theo for just under a year, but now the side of my bed he slept on was empty—he must have snuck out in the night—the only remnant a letter explaining that he and his wife had decided to give it another go. *I wanted to tell you last night*, he wrote, *but instead I decided to let us have one last good memory.*

I balled the letter in my fist, surprised by my own anger, by the hole opening in my chest. The intensity of my dejection chastened me. Though I had become involved with a few men, Theo was the only one who stuck, a married lecturer who I met, of all places, at the laundry. I caught him trying to stuff soiled clothes into the dryer rather than the washing machine. He'd laughed at himself when I corrected him, and it was this streak in him that charmed me, how he wasn't afraid to admit his flaws and try again. I suppose in the end, that was our downfall. With Theo I was free to withhold what I needed to, knowing that he was doing the same. Most nights we spent apart; he had his children and maybe-wife, I had my past. I never told him of Arun, though I felt the space his presence occupied between us. Even still, I had let myself tumble further than I intended.

His note reminded me of the letters in my dresser, pages penned to Brendah that I knew I'd never send. I remembered lounging in Brendah's room in Mary Stuart Hall, the only women's residence and the

307

ugliest building on campus, and in the letters I grasped at that thread between us, embellishing them with *dearest comrade* and *my sister*. Writing to her let me exist for a time in that comfort of waiting, keeping at bay the painful truth that our separation was permanent. Though many times the thought had occurred to me to write to my family, I had never been able to pen them a single letter, not even to languish in my drawer—the words would simply not come. Now Theo's note snapped me from my reverie and reminded me of the woman I had once been.

I was unanchored. I'd left the only place I'd known, and now I had the perpetual feeling of treading off a dark landing, the bottomless jolt of missing a step. On the plane to Heathrow, I'd sat next to a woman named Hansa in a peach sari, who offered me a plastic container of bhajias. I was grateful for the companionship, but just as my finger grazed an oil-soaked piece, Hansabhen jerked the box back. "They're not batata," she grinned, and broke one in half. Inside: a gold coin. She had rolled all her valuables in batter and deep-fried them. It was how her family, who had left Uganda in the early days of the expulsion, had managed to smuggle out some of their jewelry. I marveled at the woman's cunning, this creative act of survival. Hansabhen told me she had refused to leave her family home in Mbarara when her daughter and son-in-law were fleeing. But she soon began to understand what it meant to lose the heart of the place you once loved. This, I understood. She was bursting with months of latent affection for her grandchildren, the airplane seat barely able to contain her. "My daughter sings like a filmi star," she said. "I bet my grandchildren are missing my stories." I nodded along, the cold blast from the overhead vent drying my nervous sweat.

When Hansabhen asked if I was joining my family, I said I had none. That was my first erasure. By the time we careened onto the runway, Hansabhen had invited me to stay with her until I could get on my feet. She said that when her family landed, they were put in a resettlement camp, given clothes and baby formula and help to find jobs. "But the fuss is over now," she said. I wondered if it had been the same in Canada, if my family had found winter coats and work. My reluctance to leave Kampala had prevented me from figuring out what would happen once I arrived elsewhere. Hansabhen dug deep into the greasy container, tore a bhajia in half to reveal the black seeds of matoke, and handed it to me. With oil marking my lips, I accepted her offer.

When we arrived, I saw what she meant. The country had moved on. If once they had proclaimed heroism, opening their arms to the deluge of refugees, now they were turning their backs. We became the next burden. We were spread out intentionally so as not to swamp any one area, broken further apart. I remembered the advertisement printed in the *Uganda Argus* during the expulsion, pleading with soon-to-be refugees not to settle in the town of Leicester. When I asked Hansabhen which town her family lived in, she looked at me blankly.

It was called Ealing. The council block where they lived was a squat compound the deep brown of decaying leaves. The ground before it seemed to have been torn up, requiring a walk through fetid dirt pocked with muddy pools. In the one-bedroom apartment, Pankaj, Hansabhen's son-in-law, explained that this council estate had been slated for demolition until the influx of refugees with no place to go. The walls inside were covered in yellow paper that peeled away from the baseboards, the ceiling flowering with mold. A table, three chairs, a defunct fireplace, no light within, a dusty radiator that felt cold to the touch, and some kerosene lamps took up the majority of the space. Two small children darted around my legs, and a boy with shaggy hair loped in not long after, handing Hansabhen a plastic shopping bag. Inside was a pair of house slippers, hide-brown with curls of synthetic sheep's wool peeking from the insides. "The cold feet are the hardest," Pankaj said. Hansabhen smiled and patted his hand, then placed the slippers in my lap.

I forced myself to push away any thought of my own parents in a dim room like this. I couldn't imagine what they'd had to bear to resettle the family, let alone the extra burden I had bestowed on them, a whole life. I knew my father would have tried to shoulder that weight alone, but I had to believe that my decision was for the best. My father had always made love the center of his world.

The sky was a washed-out lavender, drizzling quietly, the chill of the air the first shock I encountered in this new place. But for a moment, despite the damp, the dark streets, I was comforted by the full room. Then they were gone. Pankaj worked seven days a week in a meat-packing plant. The shaggy-haired boy bagged groceries after school. Pankaj's wife was still looking for work, roaming the main roads every day with her youngest on her hip before the children returned. Now she plopped Pinky on Hansabhen's lap, pulled a brown checkered coat over her shoulders, and left the apartment.

Hansabhen remained in a chair, her lips a thin line. She didn't seem able to move. All day she stared vacantly out the streaky window. For ten days I stayed with her, taking care of Pinky, organizing the furniture to make room for the growing family. Pinky reminded me of Kiya when she was small, oblivious to all but her own adventures, and I had to stop myself from worrying about what bigger exploits my sister might be navigating now.

I wandered the streets, peering into shopfronts for employment signs or fetching gas for Hansabhen's family, surprised in some areas by all the shades of brown around me, as if I were back on Kampala Road at Diwali. Here we were, the brown swamp, pouring through the streets, hailing from wherever this country's hands had once reached. *Stick with your people* was a common refrain in the council block, but the boundaries of our people had shifted again, expanding around all whose histories were linked by violence and domination, our present united by our collective grief.

At night we ate in silence. Once, Hansabhen told a story of the time the workers in her late husband's maize mill had revolted, refusing to work their shifts but coming back for lunch with hands outstretched. "My husband told them, how can we feed you if we have no maize?" she said. Her canines glinted, her palms cupped to form an empty bowl. "You can't eat memories, Ma," Pankaj said gently, gesturing at her plate, the edges of her rotli scarcely picked. Her cheeks went slack. I recalled how gleefully she'd torn into the bhajia on the plane. Slowly, she left the kitchen, the bed creaking in the next room. After, we kept eating as if she'd never been there.

I saw what happened when Hansabhen arrived: she couldn't get away from herself. She was stuck in the loss of something she could never have again. The grief had shackled her to the place in her mind. *Look around you*, I wanted to say. *Open your eyes.* I wanted not to be bound by what no longer was. Every observation about my new surroundings only made me more aware of where I was not—with my family, elsewhere and together. But sorrow was a luxury I couldn't allow myself. *Justice is bigger than our love*, I had repeated to Arun when he threatened to leave the movement, and now it was turning back on me: greater than my own anguish was the possibility of a better life for my son. If I gave in to myself and reached out to my family, I risked disrupting that fragile chance. The only way forward was to pretend the rest wasn't real, to fully believe in this new existence.

Here, I remained on the periphery, and so it was simple to detach myself. On the eleventh day, I placed Pinky in Hansabhen's lap, made two butter sandwiches on white bread that I set by the window, and left the apartment to find a job, a flat, and another life.

When Zera and I left work that evening, she insisted I come to her place. I had told her about Theo and knew she was worried about me returning to an empty flat.

I had been to her house several times by now, reluctantly sucked in during a snowfall, when the roads cranked to a halt and I couldn't get home from the shop. "Only took an act of God to get you here," Maaz joked that time. The warmth of their home and their ferocious hospitality threatened to wear down my conviction, but still I held on, eating sparingly at their table and maintaining my distance from their children. It would be too easy to be pulled into their orbit, the daily drama of a little family, imperfect but happy, that might diminish my resolve. But after that morning, how close to Theo I'd allowed myself to become, I knew I had to restrain myself once more.

"Oh, just come, will you," Zera said when I declined, chiding and consoling me in that particular way of older sisters.

"You don't have to worry about me," I said.

Zera stiffened, her features closing. "And who says it's about you?" she shot, then turned her face to the street, blinking rapidly.

It dawned on me that she was inviting me for her own sake. Only then did I realize that I had become something for Zera—more than a friend, an anchor perhaps. A sick feeling swam in my stomach, that I had let go of my principle enough to cause her pain.

But Zera had started up now, her pitch rising. "What is it? What is it about us?"

I could have told her that the sight of her children brought into focus every stage I had missed in my son's life: the tantrums over dinner, the brilliant moment when the words click into place and the child begins to read, the early teenage pout masking that simple longing to be heard. I could have said that the way she and Maaz moved with one another, intimate in the most ordinary sense—the refilling of an empty water glass, the brushing of a wayward eyelash—surfaced moments that even now I could not face. I could have said she had already been too good to me, without knowing who I had once been. But in that instant I drew a blank, unable to conjure a single memory that might answer her question.

"It's only me," I answered.

Now Zera was walking away, her shoulders tucked low. I thought of my flat, starkly hollow save for a few unsent letters, written and unwritten. Of the need in Zera's eyes, her disappointment so vast she could not speak it. My gut twisted, telling me this rupture was necessary, inevitable even. But I couldn't let her go. Before she could disappear into the station I hurried after her, calling her name until she looked back.

Hari, 1988

"Hari, you're burning everything," Mayuri scoffed, grabbing the spatula from his grip and plucking the puris from the hot oil. It was true that one side had fried more than the other so that they were a rich brown, but Hari had always liked them a little crisp.

"Oops," he said sheepishly, as Mayuri elbowed him away from the stovetop. Kunal, who was folding napkins at the table, shrugged in sympathy. It was Ma's sixtieth birthday, and they'd banished her from the kitchen until the party that night.

The guests would be arriving soon—Pulin-uncle and Naina-aunty, some neighbors from the old apartment, and a few families from the mandir. Varsha-foi, Pappa's sister, was visiting from India, a tiny woman with shrewd eyes and a big laugh that Hari recognized from their phone calls over the years. When she'd arrived, Mayuri had gasped and remarked how much she now resembled Sonal-baa, to which Varsha-foi responded by swatting Mayuri's bottom like a child and proclaiming herself still young. She asked if Ma remembered the tan dog who would visit their compound for a breakfast of roti and milk, told Hari that Pappa had been a star cricket player, and over dinner one evening she mentioned something about eating by candlelight during curfew in Kampala, after which everyone at the table fell silent. Her presence in the house alerted Hari to how little he knew of not only his blood relatives scattered around the

314

world, but also about his own family here, all the lives they'd lived before.

That morning, Hari and Kiya had knocked on their neighbors' doors to invite them over. They'd left the Clarks for last. Hari was sort of friends with the Clarks' son, Will, or at least they were the same age and had been bored enough one summer to start kicking a ball around and slurp freezies in the back alley. But Will's father scarcely acknowledged Hari's family whenever they called across the driveway, his mother sometimes waving with an apprehensive smile. Will shrugged when Hari mentioned this. "They don't like change," he said. Why invite them? Hari had asked Ma that morning, but she was insistent that it was offensive not to, that you couldn't have a party and not summon your whole street. She refused the isolation that this country tried to impose on her.

When the door opened to both Mr. and Mrs. Clark, Kiya explained that there would be food and music and no need for gifts. Mr. Clark stared down at their feet on his stoop, and Hari became acutely aware that he was barefoot. "Happy birthday, then," Mr. Clark said flatly. Mrs. Clark twiddled at her necklace. "Tell your mother I wouldn't believe she's turning sixty," she said with sincerity, though she too made no mention of their invitation. Kiya scuffed her chappal on the WELCOME doormat before they left. Hari hobbled away as the pebbled pathway pricked his bare arches, a familiar, nameless feeling gathering inside him.

"You can help me instead, Hari-mama," Meetu said now. She was small for six and stood on a kitchen chair, frosting in her hair as she attempted to ice a crumbling Victoria sponge cake with a spoon. A gentle tune floated in from the living room where they'd relegated Ma, listening to her favorite Hindi music cassette, discordant with the chaos in the kitchen. Dishes buried the sink, and flecks of coriander dotted the countertop, the windows fogged with steam. Plastic plates and cups tumbled from giant Dollar Store bags along with a string of silver tinsel that Meetu had insisted on. A red stain bloomed on Mayuri's turquoise kurti from when Hari had stirred the tameta-peas shaak with too much vigor. She'd seemed ready to curse him out that time.

"Who thought it was a good idea for the kids to make the food?" Hari chuckled.

Kiya tutted. "The only kids I see here are you and Meetu. And she's making less of a mess than you."

Hari backed away, sensing they were about to banish him too. "I'll go check on Ma."

"*Don't* let her come in here!" Mayuri screeched.

Hari bulged his eyes at Kiya, but she shook her head in silent warning. Seeing Mayuri, usually so composed, completely beside herself made him want to laugh. He supposed she never did settle for anything less than perfect.

Ma was sitting on her hands in the armchair by the cassette player. Despite their protests, she had already passed through every room with a mop, and that morning Pappa had washed the windows and hidden new traps behind the cupboards, though no one but him had heard the mice.

"They set the kitchen on fire, didn't they?" Ma said, but Hari didn't have to lie because there was a knock at the front door. Ma stood, seeming equal parts relieved and nervous, and shook the pleats of her burgundy sari into place. She'd spent longer than usual getting ready, emerging spiritedly with blush gilding her cheeks and a swipe of ruby on her lips, a jeweled clip pinning her hair in a low bun. "Not a day over thirty," Hari said. Ma touched her collarbone and for a moment appeared timid, but then she let slip a giggle. "You should have seen me at that age, your father couldn't stop staring." She paused. "Where is he, anyway?"

Hari found Pappa in his bedroom while Ma welcomed the guests. He was hunched near the dresser, gazing at something cupped between his hands. He'd combed what remained of his white hair so that it curled softly around his ears and buttoned his shirt to the very top. When Hari said his name, he leapt up and thrust whatever he'd been studying into the top drawer.

"Guests are here," Hari said. Pappa blinked slowly. Hari waited; his father was growing older, and there were moments when it seemed he was disappearing inside himself. But when Pappa stepped away from the dresser, his face cracked into a grin.

"Let's hope they brought dinner with them, na?" he said, drumming Hari's cheek as he ambled past him.

Hari was about to follow him when the dresser caught his eye. Atop the jumble of socks and stockings inside, he found a scattering of black-and-white photographs slipping from a worn envelope. They were small and square, some faded almost to yellow. He'd never seen them before, and he couldn't help but sift through them now, his eyes scanning the grainy trees with unbelievably wide leaves, the girls in looped braids and boys in starched shorts, the familiar hooded eyes of his family gazing back at him.

He recognized younger versions of Ma and Pappa—Ma's hair longer, her waist slimmed, and more than once, her mouth hanging open mid-speech. Pappa was more filled out, his skin gleaming with sun. Hari paused on a photograph of Pappa leaned against a tree bursting with blooms, sunglasses shading his eyes and his arms loosely crossed, and wondered if he'd ever seen his father so at ease. He thought he could identify a younger version of his sisters, Mayuri's round cheeks and Kiya's long chin, and he tried to guess at their ages, hoping he would appear in the mix.

In several photos there were people he didn't recognize, an elegant young woman and startlingly handsome man appearing often, perhaps neighbors or distant cousins. There was a photograph from what looked like a mandir, dozens of people perched on the temple steps and spilling into the open courtyard, foreheads painted with kumkum, a few women carrying baskets of fruit as if about to distribute them. In the bottom row, Hari thought he could make out his parents and Kiya, and next to them a young woman holding a baby. He squinted, wishing it were larger. The woman was blinking into the sun, a small smile on her lips, Kiya leaning into her shoulder, Ma lifting her hand to shade her eyes, Pappa smiling wanly, behind them all the sky unbroken. Hari examined the bodies curved around each other and realized that this was what his family had been severed from. They'd belonged to something bigger once.

With a brief unease, Hari wondered why he hadn't been shown these photographs, why he hadn't even known they existed, though he'd never asked. But he'd never felt he could. The silence spoke for them. They had unwillingly moved away and willfully forgotten. This was what he understood of exile.

He heard a flurry of laughter, the tinkle of the bell as someone offered a plate to bhagwan. Soon, they would be eating. They treated these moments together as sacred. Hari recalled the chaos of earlier, all of them packed into the kitchen, and sensed that beneath the turmoil lived an ancient, restless joy.

The party was incandescent. Fifteen families filled their home, mostly brown of all shades with a smattering of others from the old apartment or Pappa's work, arriving with cellophane-wrapped daisies and too much perfume. Meetu flitted between legs with her magic wand, banishing greedy fingers from her cheeks, but it was Ma who commanded the room, slipping like water between the guests. Hari dawdled by the food table, drinking cup after cup of green pop from the liter bottles that Pulin-uncle and Naina-aunty brought from the corner store they owned downtown. Varsha-foi rested by the stereo, bobbling her head to the music and smiling dreamily when Pappa introduced her. Solomon dropped by, handing over a tray of store-bought cupcakes that were devoured faster than any of Mayuri's homemade ladoos, making her scowl.

The chutney was oversalted and the puris—admittedly—a little tough, but the guests ate happily, and Ma's eyes were warm with approval. Over the years, his parents had gathered these friends between them, some old but most new. In the full room, the photograph from the mandir in Kampala took on new meaning in Hari's mind. Perhaps some measure of what was lost might be found again.

He was sitting through a lecture about his future from Pulin-uncle when he heard a knock. Though he saw Ma rise, Hari leapt up too, eager for an escape.

Ma reached the door before him and opened it to Mr. Clark. Her eyes grew round, but quickly she rearranged her features and opened her arms, her pallu fanning out like a wing.

"So glad you could make it," she said, beckoning.

Mr. Clark remained on the front step. "I've come to ask you to turn it down."

Ma dropped her arm, crushing the fabric. "We've disturbed you?"

"My son has a college entrance exam tomorrow. He can't focus. I told your children this morning that we'd need the noise kept in check tonight."

"I'll get him to turn it down," Ma said. But Will hadn't mentioned any entrance exam—as far as Hari knew, he was out with his crew like every Saturday night. Annoyed, Hari stepped forward.

"And one of your guests' cars is parked on our drive," Mr. Clark added hastily.

Ma was silent now, her body still. She barely glanced out the door to check their driveway. Mr. Clark peered past them into the light of the hallway, where guests ate leaning against furniture, a gaggle of children playing clapping games near the kitchen, the low throb of the stereo crooning out a Hindi film tune. For the first time Hari saw the scene as his neighbor did, and he tried to blink the vision away.

"You all can't just take over the road," Mr. Clark said.

Hari's jaw tensed. "What's that—" he began, but Ma stepped in front of him, blocking him with the bulk of her body, although the top of her head barely grazed his nose.

"Thank you for dropping by. We hope next time you make it inside," she said calmly, and closed the door.

"He lied, Ma. He didn't say anything about his son."

For a moment Ma looked pale. Then she shook her head. "So what? Everybody lies."

Hari laughed incredulously. "So, don't you see? He's trying to scare us. We should turn the music up." He brandished his arms by his head, throwing his voice toward the open window. "Let them hear! The dotheads are dancing!"

Ma rounded on him, eyes flashing. "You think it's a game, acting out like that? Bas," she said suddenly as Pappa approached. He held a plate with a slice of cake, waving his fork around the hallway.

"Having fun, party girl?"

Ma thumbed a dot of frosting from Pappa's mustache. "Lovely."

"Remember, Raju, when we first came to Toronto? How lonely we were, fighting always just to make some noise. You remember how afraid you were the first time the sun set before five o'clock? You thought something was wrong with the sky." Pappa whooped, gesturing with his plate so that the buttercream wobbled.

Ma shook her head, but she couldn't mask her smile. "Feels like a thousand years ago."

"Exactly." Pappa nodded at the door. "Did someone come?"

Ma straightened her sari. A memory swam back to Hari: Ma fixing her hair before a door in a carpeted hallway, pulling Hari away from the racket of cartoons erupting from inside the apartment.

"Just the Clarks sending their birthday wishes. They said the house looks wonderful."

Pappa lifted his chin, pride in his shoulders. Hari stared at Ma, but she refused his gaze, pointing at Pappa's plate. "Aren't you going to feed the birthday girl some cake?"

Hari watched as they walked toward the kitchen together. The blood rushed in his ears. He wanted to blast the volume and run shouting through the street, to show the neighbors he wasn't afraid. He bristled thinking about how Ma had turned on him, as if his anger were an indulgence she could graciously decline.

He thought of the photographs stuffed in a drawer and knew then that he wouldn't ask about them. Whatever fissures their losses had left, his family had taken great pains to fill them. Maybe it was their secrets that allowed them to keep going. Who was he to unstitch the wounds? Someone had started singing "Happy Birthday," and more voices joined in, Meetu's the loudest of all. Hari locked the door and slipped back into the warm column of the hall, his family waiting.

Latika, 1991

THE EVENING OF THE GARBA, I pinned my chunni in place before the mirror. My chest fluttered, my body already remembering the steps. Zera had pleaded that I take her to dance. She wanted her daughter to share her memories of Navratri in Kenya. I hadn't stepped foot in a temple since leaving Kampala; it was too tied to the vision of my father arriving home each evening with red dusting his forehead and an ease in his step. But I was no longer afraid of being recognized, age having done its work, and I couldn't deny the desire calling out to me, to dance once more.

Suddenly I could see Kiya's lithe limbs, Mayuri forgetting her shyness in the stamping of feet, Ma swinging wild and unrestrained, the pulse of the room around us. I pressed a blue chandlo between my eyebrows and, after a moment's consideration, drew a dot of kajal behind my ear as my mother used to do to shield us all from the evil eye. I felt the contours of her then, the woman I'd been. A part of her had always wanted this, a life separate and unbound; still, she had had the protection of her mother, the twin pillars of her sisters, the knowledge that if she ever spun out too far, the ones who knew her best would reel her back. Even then I had battled with that tether, believing it was tying me down rather than rooting me in myself. For a fleeting instant I wished to feel it within me again, that grounding, solid tug.

The phone rang and I answered eagerly. Zera's voice was too quiet.

Her mother had taken very ill, she said. She and Maaz and the children were driving to stay with her parents for some time.

"I'll come with you," I said without thinking. The silence on the other end undid me. I leaned my forehead against the mirror, cheeks burning. I had never met Zera's parents; it would have been absurd for them to bring me. Yet somehow, I had expected it.

"I'm sorry," I mumbled. Zera said my name gently but nothing more. An awareness was sweeping through me, turning my skin cold. In this second life, I had kept myself apart, every *us* whittled down to just me. But even as I had sought to remain beyond the pull of anyone's orbit, my heart had taken its own lead, finding its way to love.

"There's something I need to tell you," I said. Minutes before, I had been picturing my mother as she'd been twenty years ago, but now the truth struck that she too had aged; I had no sense of her health, the state of her body and spirit. I couldn't remember how I had arrived here, pressing my heels into the rug as Zera promised we'd speak when she returned home. "You can always tell me," Zera said, and I understood then that I had found in Zera a true friend, someone who might say, *You can let it go now*, or at least, *I understand*—the kinds of assurances a sister would offer.

I had to sit to calm myself, my chunni falling out of place. I was winded by a memory of my family in the courtyard of the Gur nu Ghar, passing a bottle of cola back and forth while the neighborhood children ran circles around us. I'd sat among my people, sharing drinks and time, the partitions between us so slim they were hardly there. But every border was imagined. Only now did I remember that I hadn't danced with my family on our last Navratri together in Kampala. It was I who had exiled myself.

My conviction dissolved once more. Was it déjà vu, this feeling of letting go? I was in Kampala again, in the apartment with Adroa, the moment I understood I would leave Uganda. My commitment to what had felt like the right path began to recede, and in its place, the longing

I had tried to keep at bay for these many years flooded in. It was a hunger so simple and necessary that it led me out the door.

The recreation centre where the garba was held was reminiscent of a school gymnasium, but between the bright lights and bodies twirling with abandon, the speakers pounding with such vigor that I witnessed an elderly uncle remove his hearing aid, the room was transformed. Everywhere, people were clutching each other and clapping and finding their place in the many circles orbiting the room. No one knew that I had come alone, or noticed that my steps were unpracticed, or minded when I lost my breath and had to step out for a break. If once I'd believed the circle had edged me out, it did not hesitate to accept me back.

I had just looked up from the drinking fountain when I saw her. The woman was familiar, not just in the way of older masis, how the flesh of her upper arms drooped in soft folds, the mangalsutra peeking from beneath her mirrored outfit. Though the rest of her face was bright, tenderness and sorrow hung in her eyes, so that they held more weight if you knew to look. She readjusted her blouse with a confident sweep of her hands, and I remembered her running a tape measure across my shoulders and around the hump of my pregnant belly, fitting me for a new outfit not long before Harilal was born.

I approached the woman, drying my mouth on the back of my hand. "Uganda?" I said in a breath. Her eyebrows rose. I told her I'd lived in Kampala, that I remembered her from the sari shop in Nakasero. I'd been pregnant, I said, and had come with my mother. The words dropped out of me all at once, the hunger taking over.

The masi's eyes widened. She pressed her hands, suffused with the scent of cooking oil and detergent, to my cheeks, then held up one pinkie finger like a lonely branch. "You were three times as big then. Now you're like this."

I was so surprised to be recognized, I couldn't help but laugh. It burbled out, nervous and elated, the kind of laughter that marks the end of a long, exhausting fight.

"Was it a son or daughter?"

I answered without thinking. "A son."

"Next time bring him."

It was a simple invitation, the most natural thing to say. But it revealed to me how the seams of my carefully fastened reality were coming undone. Standing at the garba, the rings of people circling the room, I was overcome with the realization that it could not be danced alone. Once, I had believed in the power of the collective above all else, had known that our greatest chance lay in coming together. How hard I had fought to join the union, how deeply I felt that that was where I belonged. And the masi had known me as that woman, embedded in the unit of her family, dragged to the sari shop by her mother, fitting for an outfit several sizes bigger to accommodate her growing belly, her sisters eating roasted makai on the street outside. She had seen us.

I felt myself drop into her skin, this flicker of the woman from before. I sensed an old conviction returning, tugging me back along an ancient, invisible line. I thought again of my grandfather, his story that lived with me like a ghost. And I imagined for the first time that perhaps there was more to the telling than I had known. Not just to free himself. Not just for penance. He was baring to me his truest self, the one he had tried—and failed—to efface. He was telling me, simply, to remember. He was showing me that the fire was mine now, the choice of how to go on.

The woman must have noticed my expression. She gestured to the bustling room and turned to leave, but I grasped her arm and asked, at last, for help.

When I was exiled to Jinja after my marriage, it was my mother-in-law who offered me a way back to my family: *Give them a grandchild*, she'd said. But the masi didn't know Arun's parents, who had come to London long ago. Though Kantabhen and Samirbhai had moved in with some distant relatives on arrival in the UK, twenty years later I didn't know where they might be.

"Give me your number, I'll find out and call you," she said.

"No need, it's all right," I protested, but the masi regarded me as if I were a petulant child and reached for an old receipt in her purse.

My eyes stung from this simple generosity. When I passed over my number, her hand closed over mine. "I still recognize you," she said softly, as relieved, it seemed, as I.

The following weekend, I took the train to Birmingham. Grassy hills speckled with sheep sped past, whorls of smoke filtering across the window as the carriage purred over the tracks. On the phone, Mata-ji was oddly calm. "I knew one day you'd come," she said. She told me her husband had recently passed away, that her nephew had moved to America and her sister lived down the street. She filled the silence so that I wouldn't have to. It was startling how time had continued heedless of our choices, how it simply carried on.

I arrived at a compact brick house. It was wedged between two identical ones, barely separated by a strip of grass. Above, a low sun hid behind an apple tree, the leaves bitten and faded.

I held my breath on the step. Here I was, in the final moment I could turn away. I could still choose to leave, to let the past rest only in memory. Then the door opened, and there stood my mother-in-law in a floral housedress and slippers, loose flesh pouched beneath her cheeks and chin. Arun's eyes—elongated, flecked with amber—peering out at me.

I reached to touch her feet, and Mata-ji pulled me upright with both hands. "Avo, avo," she murmured, not smiling but inviting me in all the same.

The kitchen was lined with houseplants, curling ferns and fine-stemmed mint, jasmine flowering in a pot on the tiled floor. The dining table overflowed with browning bouquets of yellow roses, cards with teddy bears and clouded suns expressing their condolences. "I'm so sorry," I whispered, surveying the table, all the love it couldn't contain.

Mata-ji stood in the soft light of the window, her arms hanging by her sides. Arthritis bent her fingers into unnatural claws.

"Thank you for calling me," she said. The faintness of her voice, her body yielding in her simple clothing, so inconsistent with my memory of the refined woman I had known, was unnerving.

"I'm sorry it wasn't sooner," I replied. There was no way to explain it. I had no language for how far I had traveled, running from myself.

"You lost more than me," Mata-ji said. I shook my head, uncomfortable with the stacking up of sufferings, but I could feel Mata-ji seeing me, the self I had crafted, who only now was beginning to step into all the skins I had shed, and I knew what losses she meant.

We drank sugary chai at the table, boiled with ginger and mint. Mata-ji cleared a space between the flowers and laid out a plate of plain digestive biscuits, which she ate by nearly dissolving them in her tea before sucking off small bites. I couldn't help but visualize the woman whose house had gleamed by the hands of her servants, who had believed that my histories were inferior to her own and not good enough for her son. Mata-ji appeared to have forgotten all of that, prodding a second biscuit onto my plate.

"I wasn't sure if you'd want to hear from me. You didn't exactly want me before." My fingers were trembling and I curled them into fists.

Mata-ji slowly nodded. "It wasn't about you. I wanted what was best for my own. Isn't that all any of us hope for?"

"I think we defined *our own* differently," I murmured.

Mata-ji seemed to consider this, her eyes grown wide, but she said nothing. I let my gaze follow a fruit fly drifting on the current from an open window. Of course I had wanted the best for my own. I had wanted it enough to fight for it, enough to make choices for Arun too. But I had not known that every choice has a shadow. I recalled the day when I realized Arun had read the letter to cease and desist, the moment I understood I had gone too far. I had made myself relive that night for months after giving Harilal up, to convince myself that I was right to leave him. Mata-ji had not been wrong: in the end, I wasn't good for her son.

"Meetu's almost ten. And Hari, nineteen, can you believe it," Mata-ji said. I stared at her, not registering the unfamiliar names. Slowly it dawned on me: *Hari*, the *–lal* dropped entirely. I could picture so clearly the pinch of Mata-ji's lips the first time she visited the Gur nu Ghar, how Pappa told her twice that he had hired the askari himself. I had believed then that the chasm between them could never be crossed. And yet here was proof that my families had found a bridge.

"You came to me first," Mata-ji said.

I swirled my tea. Mata-ji had lost her husband, just as I had lost mine. "It was easier to pretend," I said slowly. "I think I couldn't face a future where he was gone, so I created a new one."

"I felt that too. How do you go on living when the best part of you has died?" Mata-ji's nostrils flared, eyes sharpening, and for a second I recognized the woman I had known, chiding me to be grateful that at least *my* son was alive. Then her face mellowed once more. "But then I would think about my son, really think about who he was. And I knew that the only way to let my Arun live was to remember him."

It was startling to hear his name spoken out loud. When was the last time I had let my tongue do the same? I thought then of my mother, who had carried the guilt of leaving her brothers all through her life. But I knew both their names, my would-have-been uncles: Harish and Mohan. I knew this only because my mother had told me, had not let their memories die. Perhaps it was this that had allowed her to live, that brought her back to herself, again and again.

"Tell me something about Hari," I said, his name emerging from my lips for the very first time.

Mata-ji sent me off with my family's number and address, copied out in my own writing because of her arthritis. "When you're ready," she said, drawing a finger over her lips to indicate our trust, the firm hand I had once known softened by age and loss.

I kept the note folded in my fist the entire train ride. When I reached home, I tucked the slip of paper under the telephone, next to Arun's lighter.

Over the months that followed I sometimes touched the note as I passed by, hearing Arun's voice, which had never ceased speaking to me, telling me what I needed to hear, even when I could not listen. For the first time in years, I found myself recalling the day we had driven to Lake Victoria, on our way from Kampala to Jinja to tell his parents that I was pregnant.

My stomach rolled with morning sickness and dread. Ma had packed us cloth-wrapped cylinders of pudla that we ate on the hood of the car, its grille studded with road butterflies that streaked our clothes with orange dust. Arun stroked my forehead. Whatever nerves he too might have felt, he masked with his joy and his steady, open love. Arun always saw the greatest possibility in our togetherness; I hadn't understood that then. I was only beginning to see him now, not the idea I'd fallen in love with but the man he really was. Fighting looks different for everyone, and he had fought and fought.

Inside me, our child was just a flicker. But that day I felt his warmth.

After a while I slipped from the car, thighs squelching with sweat, and walked to the edge of the water. My head was light and body heavy. The clay between my toes was red and indulgent, and I wondered then if my grandfather had stood here when the railroad reached the lake. My grandmother too had lived by this shore, and on their first journey from Kisumu to Kampala they'd known only to follow the lake west. With Pir-dada's eyes on the shoreline, and Sonal-baa's on the star-punctured sky, they had found their way.

Fish glittered between my calves, kissing skin from my heels. My family had scattered both grandparents' ashes here. Ma's face was glazed with tears, and when it came time, Pappa's fists stayed curled like he couldn't let go. I had peeked between my palms at what remained of my grandfather, the parts that resisted burning, that couldn't be erased. The powder fine as sugar and laced with splinters of bone, glinting like Pir-dada's smile—his good, solid teeth. I wished I could tell him that you could not free yourself alone. But I thought of him journeying to Kampala with Sonal-baa, the map only complete between the two of them, and imagined that he already knew.

The water had soaked my skirt above the thighs, and I dipped down to my waist. Arun called out to me, *easy*, until I caught his eyes and showed him my wet shirt clinging to the barest rise of my belly, and his alarm fell to laughter.

We came upon a young woman and an older one standing in the water, droplets gilding their shoulders like amber. A small girl squatted where the froth met the shore, the bottom of her shorts sagging with sand. "Hapana," she said to the grasping tide, and the women tittered and sighed.

Arun stood with pants rolled to the calves, running a hand over his hair such that the water slicked it down. "You'll be ready one day," he said with kindness. The girl gazed up at him, then touched one wet hand to the crown of her head.

Day after day, I felt safer touching the note by the telephone.

For years I had tried to imagine speaking to my family, accounting for my absence, and every time I would hastily push the thought away. Now I imagined reaching out to my son. I couldn't picture who he was now, and I couldn't hear his response. But I imagined myself trying, knowing nothing belonged to me but that possibility. I guarded the spark and felt its growing flame.

Rajni, 1991

Rajni found Mayuri digging in the alleyway behind their strip of townhouses. It was the kind of early May day that banished all memories of winter, and Rajni carried a tub of supplies for a barbecue with Pulinbhai and Nainabhen that evening, with extra plates for the neighbors who were certain to drift through.

She was alarmed to see her daughter, in her sagging hospital scrubs, spearing the dead grass with a shovel. Mayuri had been coming over more often lately, after work and on the weekends, gazing around the living room as if she'd forgotten where she lived, but today she had bypassed the house completely.

"Planting the corn for dinner?" Rajni said. Mayuri startled, running a hand over her ponytail threaded with early greys. She looked momentarily embarrassed, but quickly composed herself.

"I'll change before they come. Just wanted a little time out here." She gestured at the patch of earth beneath her, whose soil she had begun to overturn.

Rajni watched her scrape at the dirt. *A mother always knows*, Sonal had said after Rajni had confided in her—cautiously, not wanting to come off as fragile to her new family—that she was straining to care for her daughter while mourning the loss of her brothers. Sonal had not chastised her, nor had she offered instruction. She had simply told Rajni that she had known something was amiss, and that when Latika was in need, Rajni would know too. Rajni had walked away soothed, not by Sonal's counsel but by how her mother-in-law's words had claimed her as her daughter. Of course, Rajni had not always known when Latika was struggling. But her inattention then had only made her more attuned to the shifts in her other children now. She felt her spirits darkening and swept the thought of her eldest daughter away, focusing on Mayuri before her.

"You've been stressed," Rajni said with gentleness. She'd tried to broach the topic once before. Kunal rarely came with Mayuri anymore, and Rajni sensed that there lay the issue. But Mayuri had dismissed her question, saying she just needed a change of pace, that the hospital was closer to here than to her home, the commute tiresome. "So many answers to one little question," Rajni had said, to which Mayuri had gritted her teeth in a way that told Rajni she was in no mood to be teased.

Mayuri shrugged. "I couldn't find methi in the grocery store the other day, and I thought, why not plant it myself?"

"A good idea," Rajni agreed, stopping herself from returning to the real subject. Children didn't like being interrogated by their parents. You had to edge around the tender topics, and even then, you couldn't always know what might cross the invisible lines they'd all drawn between them. If she wished Mayuri would confide in them, she had to admit that they'd never been good at speaking their hurts. Like that Jenga game Meetu loved, forcing them all to play round after round: you could pluck out one hurt, turn it around in your fingers, but who knew which would be the one to bring all the others tumbling down.

Kiya and Vinod stumbled outside with arms full of the remaining barbecue supplies. Vinod seemed disconcerted by Mayuri's appearance, exchanging a troubled glance with Rajni, though Kiya barely registered her presence.

"I have to go back in, Meetu's crying over . . . something," Kiya said, blowing a stream of air up into her hair. It seemed that every night Kiya was ferrying Meetu to this practice or that, baking brownies for her class bake sale, then staying up long after Meetu had gone to sleep to plan lessons for her own students and make costumes for her plays.

"I tried to help with her long division but she said I used the wrong method. *But look*, I said, *the answer is right!* And oh, that made her upset," Vinod explained. Mayuri speculated that Meetu was frustrated to be doing homework on a sunny Saturday, which made Kiya glare.

"I was trying to keep her occupied so I could help Ma prepare for tonight. Which you're doing by, what, throwing dirt everywhere?"

Rajni looked between her two daughters. Maybe the hurts didn't need to be spoken out loud—maybe they simply needed to be tended to. She put on a show of dusting the barbecue, casually mentioning over her shoulder that all the work was done and they'd be more help getting out of the way for a few hours.

Vinod knocked his forehead. "Good idea, Raju. Both of you, ja, leave us the baby and go. We're tired of you moping around here!"

Despite herself, Mayuri's cheeks twitched.

"Do not let her hear you calling her a baby," Kiya warned, but she tipped her head at Mayuri, a glimmer of promise passing between them.

Rajni wasn't sure where her daughters went, but they returned just as Pulin and Naina arrived. "I still need a business partner," Pulin said to Vinod, who was ragged from playing badminton with Meetu. Since Pulin and Naina had taken over the downtown corner store, they were always complaining about the price of work. "Oi, gadhedu, you just want to sleep on the job," Vinod said, laughing, and the two of them slapped hands in some private joke that Rajni had never understood.

They grilled corn and rubbed it with chili and lemon, charred burger buns and topped them with potato patties. As predicted, the smell of it was its own invitation, neighbors drifting down the alley, Mayuri scooping ice cream for the children who appeared, the cones puddling in the evening heat. Rajni remembered all those nights in the courtyard in Kampala, gathered around the sigri to roast maize and mhogo until the fruit bats darkened the sky. Her earlier thoughts about Latika hovered at the edges of her vision, throwing into contrast the joyful scene before her. In moments like these she understood that she was mourning not just the past but the future, everything her daughter wouldn't get to see.

The young ones stayed out into the night, turning up the stereo while Meetu scrawled the alleyway with sidewalk chalk. Inside, Rajni clicked on the burner for chai, their old friends gathered in the kitchen. Their lives had twined together over the years, buying bootleg Bollywood videos with a side of paan from the shops in Little India, holding a puja when they bought the convenience store and celebrating over packets of candy. It was Pulin's son who Hari had turned to for advice when applying for university, Naina's friend who colored Rajni's hair in her home. Countless nights like this one, growing into a family beyond blood.

Now, Naina and Pulin exchanged a glance. "We have something to tell you," Pulin said, just as Hari came inside, opening the fridge and digging around.

"We're thinking of going back," Naina continued. "To Uganda."

Rajni turned from where she was glugging milk into the pot. Since Museveni became president they had heard whispers that Uganda was turning over a new leaf. Just recently, he had announced that he was inviting the exiled Asians back. Repatriation, he called it, which Vinod had immediately looked up in the dictionary. *The return of someone to their own country.* The definition had haunted Rajni since then. She knew Vinod considered Uganda his own country, but the country of Rajni's birth had been split as she left it, for another that she'd been severed from. Nineteen years on, she still felt tentative about their life in Toronto, treading lightly as if waiting for the ground to shift.

"For good?"

Naina splayed her fingers. "We're going to reclaim the house. Probably to sell and bring the money back here."

"But maybe to stay," Pulin said softly. He chewed the ends of his mustache. "We never told you this, but Amin's government gave me a pass to stay on after the expulsion. Said my work was an asset to the Ugandan people."

Vinod's lips parted, and Rajni could see him trying to process this admission. She'd heard rumors of this happening, and with a lurch she wondered what might have been different if Pulin had remained, if it could have changed something for Latika, to have someone trusted close by.

"But you didn't stay," Vinod said.

Naina clicked her teeth. "He wanted me and the children to leave without him. I told him, *if it's safe enough for you, it's safe enough for us*." She winked.

"After our son was beaten..." Pulin drifted off, then drew a circle around the room with his finger. "I don't regret leaving together. But I can't help but wonder what it might be like to go back."

"It doesn't feel right," Rajni said. When she'd heard the announcement, she had waved it away. It was something they hadn't known to hope for. But those same whispers of a new country, a better government, had circulated in the first days of Amin's rule too. It was impossible to foresee how a person might change, what power and money could permit. Pulin had been allowed to stay only because of his work. Going back or living here, it meant the same: tolerated for what they could give.

"You mean, they're giving back what they took?" Hari spoke with his mouth full, eating old rice and karela straight from a yogurt tub.

Naina frowned. "We lost more than anyone can return, na?"

"But going back, after everything..." Rajni muttered. She looked to Vinod but his eyes were fixed on Pulin.

Pulin nodded. "That's why we're thinking of just reclaiming. Won't be much, but—"

"But it's something," Naina finished.

Rajni dipped her face toward the pot. She imagined it for a moment, disembarking at Entebbe, the courtyard with the colossal flame tree, their picture frames on the apartment walls. But she knew better than to believe that any of it remained. The home they had known existed only in memory now, unbound to the earth.

Hari drummed his knuckles on the table. Just days before, Vinod had hidden the coffee can behind the couch, declaring Hari too wired. He had an energy beyond the rest of them, the volume of his youth turned up, able to carry any conversation regardless of the subject. *An ease*, Mayuri had described it once, and Rajni agreed: there was an effortlessness in the way he occupied space. He was now the same age Arun had been when he came to live with them.

"Have you thought about it, Pappa? Ma?" Hari's face was rosy. It was a game to him, as simple as hide-and-seek, the lost returned; the gravity of the losing, the grieving, the searching, all overlooked. But reflected in Hari's glow was Vinod's own, the glitter of his eyes alighting on a once-distant hope.

"It is something," Vinod said quietly. "We could . . ."

His eyes floated up to hers. Rajni willed her expression not to betray her. If nothing else, she wanted him to have this: a moment of unhindered belief in himself, in a world that healed what it broke.

"You had a house, na?" Naina offered. In that instant Vinod's shoulders slid, the hope dissolved.

"We could reclaim the car," he mumbled. He did not look at Hari, his face drawing closed. Turning, he resumed pulling teacups from the cupboard. Rajni took them from him, thinking of Mayuri and Kiya that afternoon, stealing a few hours away from worries beyond her knowledge. Life was no easier anywhere else—the troubles would follow wherever they went. But here, at least, they were together; here, they could carry the weight for each other.

The perfume of warmed sugar draped the room. Vinod accepted a full cup from Rajni. She could not consider any country her own. None but this kitchen filled with their friends, that strip of soil out back, the bed they shared each night.

"We live here," she said firmly.

Vinod lifted his face to hers, the glow fighting to return.

The call came the next morning. Vinod was in the back with Meetu, weeding around the sugar maple. Rajni grasped for the phone, her other hand flicking beads of batter into oil to test its heat. It was Kantabhen, Arun's mother. In the years after Adroa's letter they had begun speaking frequently, although once the hope dissipated, the calls were again relegated to a yearly greeting at Diwali.

"My husband passed some months ago," Kantabhen said, and Rajni felt a stab of regret. She had only met Arun's father once, when the pair traveled from Jinja to Kampala before Hari was born. They had been stiff then, inspecting the cups before accepting tea as if expecting to find them crusted with dirt. Rajni murmured her condolences.

"I want to speak with my grandson," Kantabhen said. It took Rajni a few seconds to understand who she meant. Her own body had adapted to its extended motherhood so that *grandchild* evoked only Meetu, her hunger for stories and her self-assured cackle.

"He's not home," she lied. Hari knew Kantabhen only as a distant auntie, akin to the Dalals. The woman had hardly been interested in him. In her more generous moments, Rajni thought she could understand. When Hari's likeness to Latika revealed itself—the curve of his smirk when he laughed, that rise of his chin—Rajni wanted to turn away. For Kantabhen, perhaps, it had been too much.

The line crackled. Rajni fixed her eyes on Vinod's bent back, the sun lacing his bald scalp. Then Kantabhen began to speak. She explained that she could reclaim her husband's soap factory under the new repatriation scheme, but that many years ago her husband had transferred the deed to Arun's name. With Arun gone, the property fell to Hari, the next male heir. "I want to give it back," Kantabhen finished.

Latika had once described to Rajni the fluted columns and pink roof tiles of her in-laws' house, the floral smell of the factory that wafted through the area. "What do you mean?"

"The way we lived there—we made mistakes. My husband wouldn't pay the workers overtime, and I..." She trailed off, then began again. "We knew we weren't wanted there, so instead we made it so that it wouldn't matter what anyone thought, because we owned it all, we were on top. Of course, in the end, that didn't matter."

Rajni said nothing, trying to reconcile the openness of this woman with the one she had known. She thought of the look on Vinod's face the night before, yearning to reclaim something that had never been his. They had risen to the middle of the hill, between the colonial mansions and the tin-roofed shanties, but always with the belief that the top was within reach. And how they had tried to climb, thinking it could secure their futures, erase their pasts. Even now it was painful to admit that they weren't wanted, but there had been no greater fire beneath their feet, spurring them up and on.

"Why now?" Rajni asked finally.

"I always felt I needed Latika's permission, since Arun was her husband, and Hari her son. Even back when we weren't on good terms, I wanted..." Kantabhen paused, and Rajni wondered why Latika had never mentioned that she didn't get along with her in-laws.

Then Kantabhen's meaning clicked together, and Rajni clutched the phone with both hands, her words tripping in the effort to come out.

"What do you mean, *back when*?"

Kantabhen's breath was audible. "She came to me."

It took all Rajni's strength not to hang up. For so many years she had believed that Latika was gone, but what she'd really wanted to believe was that she could stand behind her choice to let her daughter decide her own life. The fragment of herself that had never stopped hoping, the one she had tried to smother with time and distance, reared a deep, ragged breath.

Vinod coughed when he stepped inside. The oil was ruined, scorching the air. He turned to Rajni with a question on his lips, but saw her—face drained of color, phone cord limp in one hand, a scrap of paper clutched in the other—and knew the answer before she could speak.

In the kitchen, Vinod's face had caved in, eyes sunken beneath wiry brows. "All this time," he repeated, cradling his forehead. Between them on the table was the notepaper with Latika's information. Someone had seen her. She was no longer a ghost.

"We have to tell Hari," Rajni said. The world had lifted, revealing the bones beneath, the secrets that they had kept intact for all the years that Hari had been theirs. He was nineteen now, boyish in his gait, his sloppiness, his joy, but still: grown.

Vinod looked up so swiftly his head bounced against the back of his chair.

"How can we?" His nostrils flared. Rajni knew what he was afraid of. Already, one of their children had chosen to leave them. Who was to say Hari wouldn't do the same? At the start they had believed that Hari was too young to tell. The distance between child and grandchild had seemed insignificant when their whole lives had overturned and crumbled like parched soil. And yet, over time it simply became easier to maintain the fiction. To protect Hari, they had told each other, though if Rajni was being honest now, they were also guarding their own hearts. Years may have passed, but the ache of Latika's departure had hardly dulled.

"He deserves to know." And all this time, hadn't she deserved to know that her daughter was alive? An indignation was breaking through her, at the injustice of Latika's silence, at all the years submerged in uncertainty.

"You said it yourself—we have to protect him," Vinod sputtered. His eyes were feral now, pleading. A marriage could do this, could allow such corruption in the name of family. When Latika handed over Harilal for the last time, Rajni had taken not only her child but her trust: that she could care for him better than his own mother. It came naturally to her, the same way her father had made up stories of drums and djinns to shield her brothers from the truth of the violence outside all those years ago. She had clung to that belief, that they were also protecting Hari, that this was love. But she too had been grown, just like Hari was now, and her parents hadn't sheltered her with deceit. No, in the face of the truth, they had given her a choice.

She tented her fingers over her eyes. "We don't get to decide anymore." Vinod's cheeks crumpled. "No," he said, "no, no, no," his body quaking, speaking not to her but to himself, to the hopelessness of leaving anything behind.

Rajni stood from the table. She had left her first family, and behind her they had shattered. The cleft between her and her parents had never healed. Latika, as a baby, had drunk in that loss, had suckled the milk of her mother's splintering. Of course, then, she had inherited that possibility; of course she had left.

That night, Rajni awoke to an alert mind. From the thin light coming through the curtains, she could tell it was not yet midnight. She had hardly been asleep at all. A plate jangled, flung hastily into the sink.

Her heart beat steady. She draped a shawl around her shoulders and slipped from the room, grateful to hear Vinod's continued snores as she shut the door behind her. She felt her way to the kitchen, gliding as if still in a dream. At the threshold, she paused, seeing Hari illuminated by the cold light of the fridge.

He shut the fridge and startled. He wore his shirt unbuttoned, hanging loose by his hips, a wrinkled T-shirt exposed beneath. Pressing the carton of milk to his forehead, he asked why she was still up. She pictured herself gone, and Hari drinking milk with the lights off, the normalcy she was about to upend.

"Ma, you feeling okay?" Hari said.

Rajni wondered if he would still call her that tomorrow. He took a step forward. She held out her hand to stop him, needing the distance to continue.

"I had another daughter," she said. So this is where she would begin: with the extending of her body. That's what it was to have a child: to give up to the world what had once been solely yours.

Hari's mouth made a shape, but no sound. Rajni's weight was in her arm, the doorframe, these walls.

"Before Mayuri—my first. Her name was Latika. She married a man named Arun, and they had a baby the year before we left Uganda. A son."

"In 1971," Hari said. His shoulders were rising and falling in double time. "You mean…"

Rajni nodded. Darkness crept in around the edges of her eyes, blurring reality. She forced herself to continue. "Your parents," she finished.

Hari's Adam's apple pulsed beneath his stubbled skin. His eyes never left hers, glinting like chips of amber. "The photograph," he said, and Rajni's mouth fell open, realizing how little control they had really had. "I don't understand," Hari murmured, though she could see that he did.

"Your father was a political activist." She paused, the truth she had long ignored surfacing. "They both were, your mother too. A couple months before we left, Arun was imprisoned. At that time prison meant..." She stopped, unable to breach the insulation of silence.

Hari swallowed. "Death," he said. Rajni toed the cold tile. "And... her?"

"She wouldn't leave him behind. We didn't think she was alive. Only today I heard for sure that she is." Rajni inhaled and tried her best to explain that Latika was in London, that Kantabhen had called, what she was asking. She spoke until Hari dropped his gaze, his lashes betraying the tic of his eyes. His shoulders were vibrating, edging on the precipice of a great fall.

"How could you not tell me?" he said quietly. He passed a hand over his face, and when he released his arms there was no precipice, only descent. Rajni stumbled forward.

"Diku, we thought it was better this way—"

"You were wrong," Hari roared.

Rajni pressed a hand to her neck, wanting to cry, wanting not to deserve his anger. He was backing away, shaking his head as if she were a child. More monstrous than a child: a mother who had failed.

"Get away from me," Hari spat. "I don't know you, I don't even know..."

Rajni's shoulders curved in. She gripped the counter to stop herself from advancing and pushed her voice out, speaking through its tremor.

"It's your choice if you want to speak to either of them—your grandmother or your mother." She unfolded the damp shred of paper from her fist. The words hung between them like the past, which was not some distant place but a continuous story, woven through skin, the landscape to even their deepest silences. Hari was crouched by the window, shielding his head as if under attack. Rajni backed away until she could no longer see him, holding herself apart, knowing that love, like fire, needed oxygen to survive.

Rajni & Vinod, 1991

A MONTH AFTER THE BARBECUE, Pulinbhai had a heart attack. The next day they visited him in the hospital, where he seemed to be recuperating, although he passed later that night. The failed hope devastated all of them, but Vinod saw it coming. As he perched on the hospital bed next to his oldest remaining friend, Pulin's papery fingers had grasped his. "We've fought hard," Pulin told him. "Like donkeys," Vinod replied, eyes stinging as Pulin strained to laugh. After he passed, Vinod filled in the rest. His friend was telling him he was ready to let go.

After the funeral, Rajni and Vinod dropped by the downtown convenience store that Pulinbhai and Nainabhen had run and lived above. The shop, closed since Pulin's death, was already in shambles, half-opened boxes blocking the aisles, crushed packets of raisins scattered like rat droppings. Upstairs, Nainabhen sat in her white sari amid piles of her husband's books and sweaters, her face stricken. "I can't stay here," she said. Rajni tried to fold some of the mess away. "Take a break," she urged, "until you feel ready again." But Nainabhen turned her face to the wall, hung with photographs of her children and grandchildren, her husband always behind the camera and therefore glaringly absent. Two tickets to Uganda booked and unused, a hope Pulin carried to his end.

Nainabhen would move in with her son and daughter-in-law. She

343

would clear out her apartment but wasn't yet ready to pack up the shop, her husband's pride, the culmination of their years of toil and uproot. Vinod wrung his hands. He recalled how just weeks before, in his kitchen, Pulinbhai had asked for a partner. He turned to Nainabhen with an offering.

Rajni and Vinod moved into the apartment above the shop at the end of June, just the two of them. They kept the doors locked for several days while they unpacked and scrubbed, elbow-deep in bleach. On the weekend, Kiya lugged chairs up the stairs and Mayuri broke down boxes, Meetu inventing songs as she repainted the front door. Hari stayed away. In the weeks since Rajni revealed their secret, Hari had swung between explosive rage and cutting silence. Each night, Rajni and Vinod would meet in bed with heavy bodies, everything they'd tried to shutter now blown open, too exhausted by their own guilt to offer one another anything more than simple words of comfort. "And you say *we're* the hush-hush ones?" Rajni quipped once, when Hari refused to speak to her, and after that he began spending more time out of the house, often not returning until everyone had retired to sleep. Let's just *talk*, she wanted to say to him, though she knew she had lost that right.

When their daughters questioned their decision to take over a business at their age, they spun their hands and made jokes. "We're not dead yet," Vinod said. "I like the glamorous city life," Rajni laughed. They would catch eyes and know that they were still a good match in life. But they both knew that they had chosen this departure not to begin something new, but to leave something behind.

They left the house for their children. That was the more honest truth. Meetu, at age nine, no longer wanted to share a room with her mother. Even still, they saw the worry take over Meetu's face when they left: that desperate longing for togetherness in a world that had split them apart; that duty, unrelenting, to each other. Mayuri moved in too, after Kunal moved out. She'd flown to Bombay for a medical conference, and when she returned to find Kunal packing, she claimed her room next to Kiya's. She had already been spending even more time at the house after Hari learned the truth, prompted by how he'd erupted at Kiya, accusing her of disloyalty. Rajni wondered if it was this stress that ultimately broke Mayuri and Kunal, their long-fraying relationship finally collapsing beneath the pressure, but Mayuri insisted that wasn't the case. "I couldn't love him," she'd confessed. Rajni had wanted to shake her daughter then. How hard she'd had to work to love Vinod when she first moved to Uganda. And after her brothers were killed, how hard she'd had to work not to resent Vinod for what she felt he'd taken from her, though now she saw that there was no certainty in anyone's survival. "Don't be silly," she'd snapped, but Mayuri stared back, her body poised as if ready to receive consecration. "You're not listening. I said I *couldn't.*" Something in Mayuri seemed to ignite as she spoke, and her spine lengthened. Rajni understood then that her daughter didn't require her blessing, or perhaps anyone's.

Meetu moved into Hari's room and Hari shifted to the basement bedroom, the one they had always thought of as Latika's. He needed space. That's what they told each other, all the times Vinod tried to speak to him, all the times Rajni left bowls of peeled clementines outside his closed door. In a way, Hari had been the easiest of their children to raise because his needs were always plain—he had wanted, simply, to be loved, and yet now he rejected their every attempt.

They left because they understood what their children needed to go on. And perhaps it was what they needed too. They never spoke about their hope that Latika would see a place for herself in that house if she ever returned. They made dust of their own loss. Though for years they had tried and failed to find Latika, now that they had her number, they could not be the ones to call. That was Hari's decision to make.

Behind the till, they kept the framed photograph of Pulinbhai and Nainabhen before the shop's yellow sign, pride beaming from their unsmiling faces. *Satisfied*, Rajni would think whenever she glanced at it, and would feel a hint of it herself. They wondered if customers ever noticed that it wasn't them, but they didn't mind being mistaken for their friends. They had come here separately and found each other again, drawn closer by necessity and loss and a history that lived between them.

At the start it was frenzied, the shipments and daily inventory and the sticky cashbox. Each night Vinod collapsed into an exhausted slumber while Rajni lay awake, counting items in her head. They began to snap at each other once again, as they had decades ago. It was unsettling to find themselves back where they began, the sharp edge of old resentments returned. Alone with each other over dinner, they sometimes allowed themselves to wonder if they were in over their heads.

But the thought never took root. The shop gave them purpose, a routine to supplant the memories of everything that had come before. Over time they grew fond of the place, its ketchup chips and the hot coffee dispenser that gurgled steam through the day. And its regulars— the businesswoman who picked up a newspaper on her way to the subway every morning and the father who brought in his daughter on Saturdays to choose a treat and give his wife a break. They found a new rhythm, eating their toast at dawn before opening, cranking the radio as they propped open the door. Here was a place where they were necessary. Here, they were wanted.

Soon Rajni began boiling extra tea in the mornings for customers and deliverymen, frying cereal chevdo late into the night. While Rajni cooked, Vinod read the paper and listened to the radio at the same time, so that he would never run out of things to say. He found himself cracking jokes, surprised at first when customers would laugh, until he remembered that as a child, in another land, he had been the class clown. They told everyone of their children, though they spoke little of themselves: their daughters the doctor and teacher, their son in university, their granddaughter gifting them a vocabulary they had never learned. They told stories not of their origins but of their future. Their house had been an anchor, but the shop was a raft, carrying them on when it was time to go.

Hari came in one day, in the last stretch of summer. In the two months since they'd seen him, his stubble had grown thick and his hair chaotic. Vinod, behind the counter, had to stop himself from asking if Hari had made a decision, or remarking on his lack of shaving, or giving in to any of the other tics that might turn his son out the door again. "I was in the neighborhood," Hari mumbled, as if he needed a reason to come. Vinod held his breath. All those endless conversations with customers and now he couldn't speak. Instead, he spun his hands at the crowded aisles. "Pick anything you like," he said. Hari trailed his fingers over the plastic-wrapped brownies and the dusty collection of plants by the door. Rajni emerged from the staircase bearing a tray. When she spotted Hari she made a noise, muted as if underwater. "You came back," she said, but so quietly that it appeared only Vinod heard. Then she shook the tray. "Masala peanuts, garam garam." A half smile rose on Hari's face as he reached to her for a handful and plucked a liter bottle of Coke from the cooler.

Rajni blinked. He had to be remembering the same moment as her. They'd been sitting across from each other at a cafeteria table in a mall, Hari's feet barely grazing the ground, Rajni observing him as he slurped from a Coke can with a straw. He'd drunk noisily, stopping only to burp into his sleeve, at which point Rajni pulled a coin from her pocket. "Get me some peanuts," she'd said, thrusting her head in the direction of the vending machine. When Hari returned, she tore the packet with her teeth and shook the contents into the can, the peanuts crackling and bobbing like tiny boats. Then she tipped her head back, crunching and smacking her lips. "Try it," she urged as Hari looked on in horror. When he took a cautious sip, his face curled in shock. "No waaay," he breathed. Later, Rajni would hear him saying it as praise—*no way* when the Toronto Maple Leafs won a game and *no way* when Kiya brought home doughnuts from work—but in that instant Rajni heard it as rejection. She took the can, downing the rest, and hiccuped loudly. Her eyes grew round with alarm and she checked over both shoulders. But Hari couldn't help it: a giggle burbled out of him, tumbling into a laugh, giddy and drunk. Rajni's eyes widened even more, her finger rising to her lips, but Hari wouldn't stop, his body rippling with its own force, snorting until she was sure the Coke would pour from his nostrils, and then she was laughing too, cackling really as she wiped the napkin over the table, sweeping up Hari's mess and her own.

He had been that young once, never judging her, wanting her comfort, her arms. They'd had laughter between them, a tenderness that throbbed. Now it had frozen over. But Vinod reminded her of what he said at the start of every winter when she dreaded the cold months ahead: it would thaw once more.

Now they watched as Hari funneled the nuts through the mouth of the bottle and took a long drink. They observed him in the kind of silence that he had raged against before they moved out, pointing fingers at their betrayal. When Hari set the bottle down, Vinod said, "Don't spoil your appetite—stay for dinner?" The shift was instant, Hari's face paving over. Vinod had ruined it, said too much, unable to hold himself back. Slowly, Hari screwed the cap, then raised the bottle in a toast so that brown foam rose like a tide. "Thanks," he said flatly, the bottle swinging between two fingers at his knee, the sea inside churning as he walked out.

That night in bed Rajni turned to Vinod, seeking him out. It had been so long since she'd felt that appetite, a need to fill the emptiness that loomed. But in the dark of their new home, reality blurred; she was nineteen again, a new bride, her family gone and she, alone, fighting to keep herself going. Vinod grasped her, feeling not the beginning of their lives together but the trickle toward the end, the desire to cling a little tighter. Their weight on top of one another, gasping, a remembrance on the edge of joy. Afterward, Vinod slept deeply and Rajni rose to begin the next day, bathing slowly and setting the milk to boil.

They didn't speak of Hari's visit, that night or the nights after. If anything, it cemented what they knew to be true: it had had to be them who left. In Mayuri's garden Rajni had tried planting the seeds of a matunda she'd bought at the Indian grocer, but even the plants bore allegiance to their soil; they couldn't grow somewhere they didn't belong. Neither she nor Vinod could deny that their home had shifted, the space for them diminished.

When they moved out of the house, they kept pieces of their old bedroom intact: the hangers of ties and sequined saris they no longer had occasion to wear, the drawer of baby teeth and birthday cards and finger paintings. They did this to placate their children, as if the home were still theirs, their leaving only a temporary step away. But what they knew of leaving was that you couldn't go back. As they had driven off, fingers linked over the gearshift, they had felt an old wisdom shaken by the act of departing. They left to keep their family whole, something their ancestors had understood. But this time, it was their choice. Vinod's grandparents had known it, and his parents, and Rajni's too. Even Latika. How the leaving was protection, a kind of survival. How sometimes, holding on required letting go.

Mayuri & Kiya & Meetu, 1991

MAYURI ROSE EARLY ON HARI's twentieth birthday, her hands already preparing for the day. She would set out half a banana for bhagwan, slice the other half into Meetu's cereal, water the garden before the sun grew too strong, all the consoling routines she'd begun after Kunal left and she moved into her family's house. On her way to start the laundry she passed Hari's room, only to find his door ajar, his blankets rumpled, Hari gone. Her stomach clenched. She'd noticed him growing sullen as his birthday approached, but she hadn't expected him to disappear. She was on the verge of rushing to alert Kiya when she noticed Hari's basketball shoes missing by the front door, a wake of mud in their absence.

She exhaled. Pressing her fingertips to her temples, she reminded herself that this day had always carried more emotion than she could shoulder.

She lit a candle for Latika by bhagwan's shrine, her fingers fumbling with the match. Unlike Kiya, Mayuri had never fully accepted that Latika was forever lost to them. And yet, it was only these rituals of mourning that gave her relief—an acknowledgment that, though Latika lived, she remained absent from their lives. Mayuri wanted to offer something special to the shrine today, something her sister had loved, but the cupboards seemed starkly empty, yellowing celery and leftover lasagna glaring back at her from the fridge. Already the day was slipping

350

beyond her control, and she shoved the fridge door shut with a clank, then worried she'd woken Kiya and Meetu.

They were still finding their rhythm in the house, made new not just by all the departures and returns, but by the memory of Latika finally being allowed inside. They let Hari move how he needed to, conscious not to treat him any differently—nothing less than a brother. Though Hari's fury had simmered since those first months, it had taken on a restless edge—his knee jittering, his laugh quick and dry, his temper taut to snap. Some days Mayuri would come home from work to find him smoking outside, a habit he'd recently acquired, his face daring her to protest. She could see the child seeking solace wrestling against the adult wanting to carve his own path. She didn't tell him that the smell that lingered on his clothes was familiar, that she found comfort in the occasional whiff of tobacco and menthol, a relic from another time.

The first time Hari lashed out at Mayuri for keeping the truth from him, she'd grown defensive. "I tried telling you," she'd retorted. "Don't you remember all those stories?" She'd felt something breaking loose within her, feelings that had long been dammed—righteousness, love, her own sense of justice—boiling her blood. But the bewilderment in his eyes had stung her, and she wondered then if she'd fooled herself. She'd returned home to Kunal shaken, newly seeing the distances between them, the truths she'd kept hidden even from herself.

When she returned from Bombay to find Kunal wrangling a suitcase shut, she recalled how she'd avoided unpacking her own bags for weeks when she first moved to Toronto. Though Kunal had been a friend in her loneliest moments, the trip to Bombay had reminded her of a self she had almost forgotten in the ensuing years of work and marriage. Amid the familiar smells of sea and smog, she'd recognized that this was the only place she had given herself a kind of sovereignty.

She was attempting to find her way back to that other self, the one with her own center of gravity. The ache of Kunal's leaving haunted her, but she carried the salt of Bombay in her hair, the memory of her first arrival, of how expansive she could be if she let herself.

Footsteps pattered down the hall and Meetu appeared with pillow lines webbed across her face. "I heard a noise," she said.

Mayuri sucked air through her teeth. "I was having too much fun in the kitchen."

Meetu's eyebrows pulled together. "No, earlier. I heard Hari-mama leave."

Since Ma and Pappa moved out, Meetu had become apprehensive, repeatedly asking when they would return. Mayuri recognized in Meetu the same need she'd noticed in Hari when she moved to Toronto, elated whenever she came over and clinging on when it was time to leave. It had crushed her each time she'd had to go. She smoothed back Meetu's tangled hair.

Meetu leaned against her, then pointed out the window. "Darlene's out there already."

Mayuri followed her finger to see Darlene in the alley, soft lines gathering around her eyes. Anticipation fluttered Mayuri's lungs to see her standing there, her cheeks growing warm.

The sun flared through the glass and Mayuri was struck by an image of Latika as a young girl shaking a tomato in her fist like a prize. Perhaps in their grandmother's vegetable patch—but why then the scent of eucalyptus in her nostrils, the tickle of mowed grass on her shins? Fetching a bowl from the cupboard, she turned to Meetu with an idea.

As she watched Meetu dart outside, Mayuri caught Darlene beckoning her to join. She made to fix her rumpled shirt, then dropped her hand. She'd become more aware of her body as she neared forty, the softening of her cheeks and the rounding of her waist, but with Darlene she felt the tentative pleasure of settling into a skin made beautiful by time. As they had grown closer, she sensed a long standing discipline coming loose in herself. She'd been resistant at first, not wanting to slap a bandage on an open wound. But now she saw that before the bandage came the salve, the sugar drawing out the poison.

Meetu dropped cherry tomatoes into the steel pot, her fingers grazing the little letters scratched on the side. Mayuri-masi had asked her to pick them for bhagwan, but she decided to keep a few aside for Hari-mama. She'd heard him leaving his room that morning and had followed him to the front door. "You didn't say bye," she said from the shadow of the hall, making him jump. "You always say goodbye," she insisted, because he did, even when he was upset. He only whispered that he'd be back, his face tired and guilty.

The bean vines spilled down the alley, the garden Mayuri-masi had started in the spring now in full bloom. The neighbors had taken notice, collecting herbs or giving advice or just pausing for a second to admire the slash of color against the peeling garage doors. Meetu had felt possessive of the garden at first, but she was starting to enjoy the way it made people linger.

Darlene popped a yellow tomato in her mouth and made a sour face, then grinned. She was the caretaker for the old man down the road, and she often took her breaks out here, she and Mayuri-masi talking close as they dug in the soil, laughing at nothing or just working in a soft quiet. Darlene had brought a baggie of seeds for a squash plant whose name she only knew in her language. She was born and raised in Trinidad, her skin brown like theirs, and she explained to Meetu that her ancestors too had been scattered like seeds from their first home, but her family had found a way to grow in another land. Meetu sifted her fingers through the damp earth, awed by all it could hold.

Kiya emerged into the kitchen, showered and dressed, to see Mayuri and Meetu with Darlene out back. She watched them for a moment through the young branches of the sugar maple, Meetu talking with a hand on her hip because these days she knew it all, Mayuri waving a cloud of midges away from their heads. Though she'd made it clear to her parents that Hari didn't want to celebrate, they'd insisted she collect something from the corner store. She'd conceded, aware that the gesture was as much for themselves as for Hari. With a jolt she realized she had hardly thought about Latika all morning, her mind trained on the tasks before her. When had her grief grown this new skin? she wondered; when had the sharp point of her anger blunted, so that some days were hardly pierced by it at all?

As she drove toward her parents' shop, her thoughts turned toward Hari. When he'd begun unloading his frustration on her, blaming her for choosing Ma's side, she'd felt all sense of time crumble. In Hari's torment she glimpsed a version of her own, shocked out of her youth into a cold and uncaring future, one that didn't include her sister, where her only measure of control was how far she could push everyone away. *The nightmare years.* She pondered now if she had ever woken up, or if she'd simply learned to expect the shadows at every turn.

Still, beneath Hari's rage she sensed an anxiety pulsing. She'd done her best to quell his fears of being abandoned on the school steps, but after Ma's revelation, such assurance was beyond her power. When Mayuri moved in, Hari turned on her, Kunal's departure a stroke too far. "What did you do?" he yelled, though seeing the hurt on Mayuri's face he grew remorseful. "Can I call him?" he asked Kiya later that day. "Will Mayuri be upset if we still talk?" Kiya had laughed, maybe a little meanly, but she had seen Mayuri's dejection and felt protective. "Really Hari, he's not leaving *you*." Hari seemed embarrassed then, and Kiya regretted what she'd said. She had only a shaky memory of the day Arun was banished from their home by her parents, but she remembered feeling distraught. No goodbye could be so clean; there were casualties, aftershocks. Even if Hari's sadness was marginal to Mayuri's, it was not lesser.

She knew Hari's heartache might linger for years. She tried to remember this when he was gruff with her still, when her own exhaustion reared and rancid words rushed to her tongue. In the hardest moments, between Mayuri's mourning for a relationship lost and Hari's for one never had—when Kiya's own loneliness swelled, when she feared that maybe she'd squandered her chance at a great love—she thought of Latika and caught a glimmer of understanding. To have a life of your own making; surely everyone felt that hunger. But if anything, the tremors in their home only triggered Kiya's instinct to hold them together, something she had never expected to find in herself. She pulled up to the corner store, inhaled, and stepped out. What was love but one long act of forgiveness, of choosing to return, again and again.

Meetu found Hari-mama smoking out front. He was glum and sweaty, and when she asked him how many three-pointers he'd scored, he shrugged. Meetu had seen Mayuri-masi out here with him before, closing her eyes and breathing in the same way Meetu liked to sniff Raju-nani's perfume. "*So* sweet," Vinod-nana liked to say, pinching Meetu's cheek and then kissing his fingers, "just like your name says." "I'm *not* sweet," Meetu would scowl, wiping her cheek, their little game. Vinod-nana would smack his teeth and say, "You're right—salty too," and then they would laugh, knowing that her name meant both.

Now Meetu watched her uncle clamp the smoke in his teeth and stopped herself from asking why he wasn't celebrating and what had happened that morning and didn't twenty feel old? She wanted to describe to him the spider spinning its web between the cucumber plants, how all day it had worked at repairing the segments that were torn. But then Hari-mama said he had something to tell her.

"You had another aunt and uncle that you never got to meet," he said. "Listen to me, I'm telling you the truth because nobody else will."

His eyes were hard and foggy. A bubble rose in her stomach, between a giggle and a cry—she didn't understand his joke and his face wouldn't break. She smashed his smoke ring with her fist and he leaned back and snorted like she wasn't there, and then his shoulders were shaking and he was slapping the wall, saying, gone, gone, gone. Meetu was sure then that he was going to leave, afraid that everyone would disappear and no one would say goodbye. And then she was running inside to tell someone, feeling like she'd seen something exposed, something he truly, deeply needed her to see.

The screen door clattered open and Meetu charged toward them, face streaky, Hari panting behind her. Kiya tried to decipher what her daughter was crying—*aunt, the truth, gone*—the meaning stitching together before her. Mayuri gasped and Kiya shook, yelling like she hadn't in years, *you had no right, you had no right*.

"And you had no right to keep the truth from me. All this time and nothing," Hari shouted, kicking a chair.

"It wasn't our choice," Mayuri said, but her voice quaked as if she no longer believed it. Despite her anguish, she felt a moment's awe for Hari, who had found the words himself.

"Or maybe we just weren't ready," Kiya cried, realizing in that moment that it was true.

Hari cursed so furiously that Mayuri leapt. Meetu began to sob, clutching Kiya's waist. As Kiya witnessed the scene playing out before her—Meetu distraught over something she couldn't comprehend, Hari cracking under the weight of a lifetime of secrecy—she was struck by how deeply they were both shaken by a history they didn't know.

The outburst seemed to drain Hari. He collapsed into a chair. "I only thought about her as my mother, not your sister. But I guess that would be hard to talk about, what you lost."

Mayuri nodded. She could feel the tension losing hold, the reality that for so long she had wanted to unpeel finally showing. She thought of how Pappa had always avoided the room Hari now slept in, how once he had slipped and referred to it as Latika's room, then vanished into his mind for the rest of the day. Despite everything, they had never entirely given up hope.

Kiya untangled herself from Meetu and told her that Hari was right, they'd had another sister and they would tell Meetu about her one day.

Hari rubbed his eyes. "You could tell us about her now," he said hoarsely. They regarded him, inviting them into their own memories, which was perhaps the only way inside. Kiya opened her mouth, but then Mayuri blew her nose and said, "Not until we've had some cake."

It was a yellow sheet cake, the gift that Kiya had picked up from her parents that morning, with the words JUST ANOTHER DAY iced in white. When she saw it, Mayuri laughed from her belly. "Definitely Pappa's idea." Even Hari cracked a smile.

Tongues relaxed with sugar, it was easier to speak.

"So, what were they like?" Meetu asked, and Kiya was buoyed by her daughter's boldness, even if she'd also inherited a fear whose lineage she was only now beginning to understand. Love and separation had always been connected.

Arun was worldly, Mayuri began, funny, intelligent. "And handsome," Kiya added. "I acted a fool around him." They simpered as they had when Arun arrived. Hari's eyes lit up.

"And...her?"

Mayuri paused. "I always think of what I overheard Latika and Arun discussing at night. The rest of us were asleep, but I could tell her eyes were wide open."

"Arun lived with us until the protest," Kiya explained. Hari's gaze darted between them. "However different they were, they shared a deep sense of purpose. And whatever the costs, they would fight together for a safer future."

"For all of us," Mayuri added, throat tight. "For you."

Hari glanced up, his face opening. "Protest? What was happening?"

Mayuri was remembering the moment she'd repeated Arun's plan to her parents, the word she hadn't understood until she spoke it out loud. Even then she'd felt its immense power in her mouth. She'd been taught that such an idea was wrong, the word souring on her tongue, but now she wished she could go back and tell her younger self that it meant nothing but a way to persist. Hadn't they all needed that chance?

Kiya gazed into her palms. Her throat called back the feeling of silence, of never revealing what had happened to her, never voicing her desires, Arun disappearing for daring to speak. The answer to Hari's question was too great to express, and in its expanse she lost her bearings, veering to places she did not want to return. Her mind grew obscured, her chest strained with held breath. "It's not that I've forgotten," she said finally, "it's just that I can't always remember."

Mayuri took Kiya's hand and pressed her thumbs into her wrist. "Sometimes that's the only way through."

Hari was quiet, watching the inexpressible pass between them. "Maybe there's another way," he said after a moment, a smoky rasp in his throat.

As Mayuri and Kiya turned to him, Hari swept his hair, dark as ink, from his forehead, his eyes clear and unwavering, opening to an idea at once ancient and new.

Later that night, Mayuri found Kiya in the backyard, a cigarette between her fingers.

"You too?"

Kiya smirked and blew a thin stream from the corner of her lips. "Just one."

They had stayed at the table until Meetu's body sagged with sleep and Hari carried her to bed. Picking at the cake, they had told stories of their family as it once was. Hari listened closely, saying little, while Meetu added fanciful stories of her own. They mingled together, the past and the future, old homes and new. They summoned names that they hadn't spoken in years, not just Arun's and Latika's, but names of friends and teachers, of their school and their city, of the hills and rivers that once held them. They spoke them into being, cautiously claiming them back.

They had plucked the thread that unspooled the rest, and now they were feverish with everything more they could share. They felt lighter, though some memories were still too tender to touch. Some, they knew, would never be spoken.

Mayuri leaned against the screen door. "You know, I've been thinking—we have her number."

Kiya stared. "You mean we could call."

Mayuri said nothing, just left the thought between them.

At the end of the night, when the plates were cleared and they made their way to bed, Hari turned to them. "I had a good birthday," he said. They sensed there was more he wanted to say, but for now, it was enough.

Hari, 1991

HARI JOGGED TOWARD THE PARK, basketball clamped in his arm-pit. He hadn't cut his hair since his parents moved out and now it flopped into his eyes, a defiant marker of time. He'd visited the court all summer long, his feet finding respite against the sunken asphalt as his life toppled around him, but he'd had less time since the new school year started. Now his steps quickened as he caught sight of his friends.

He'd left home in a funk, brooding over the previous night, when his parents had come to the house for the first time since moving out. Ma had heated food from the yogurt tubs she'd brought, Pappa instructing them with the latest phony advice he'd absorbed from his radio shows—blend cucumbers with lemon for blood pressure, always say goodnight to your spouse before bed. He'd winked at Ma when he said that part, making Kiya fake-retch and Meetu crow with delight. But Hari had turned away in confusion, finding their charade maddening and yet unable to deny his relief at their return, that same feeling he used to have when he finally spied Kiya after school. He'd wanted—expected—to feel only anger still, but watching his parents dance around the painful subjects, which he'd always assumed was just the way they moved, he kept recalling his sisters on the night of his birthday, soothing each other as they'd attempted to share with him experiences beyond words. He'd gone to bed tense and woken up

360

impatient for the sting of rubber against his palms, ignoring his mound of coursework as his feet led him to the court.

A few younger boys he'd seen around were shooting hoops, Marcus leaning against the chain fence as Sami set up a speaker.

"Prof makes it back," Marcus called out, though he too was in college now, and Solomon taking night classes. Sami's father had even been a professor back in Sri Lanka, but somehow only Hari ended up with a nickname. Hari rolled his eyes and broke into a grin. Then he popped the ball hard at Marcus, and Sami hooted, backing up and opening his stance.

By the time Solomon arrived, Hari's shirt was soaked through, his feet wrecked from pounding the asphalt. They jostled down the court, the baked concrete smell surging around them, their bodies everywhere at once. Hari didn't give Sol a second, chest-passing him the ball the moment his shoes touched the court, Sol charging past and pulling up for a jumper. Hari whooped, the unease of the morning melting off, his muscles singing and his limbs syrupy and numb.

The sun was at its highest when they took their first break. While they chugged water bottles by the fence, Sol recounted the latest shenanigans at the diner where he flipped burgers. "My mom said she's tired of eating burgers so often. 'Solomon, why didn't you take a job at the Indian restaurant? You know I love that mutton curry.'" Sol slapped his thigh.

"I thought you were applying to other jobs, though?" Marcus said.

"I have been." Solomon shrugged, his face dropping for a second. Then he cut his eyes to Hari and smirked. "I think my mom just misses you. The good boy."

"The prof!" Sami yelled.

It had always been a joke between them, how Hari left Sol behind in that ESL nightmare, how Sol got to play around in woodshop while Hari broke his head over calc, how their mothers sent Pyrexes of food back and forth with no idea that their sons were skipping gym to smoke behind the bleachers together, and still, Hari was the example.

"Switch with me then. You can come play pretend with my parents. They're so fixed on acting like everything's fine, they probably won't even notice."

Hari had narrated to his friends all the details he was only beginning to see: his mother's insomnia and his father's obsession with setting traps for mice that he insisted were in the walls; the age gap between him and his sisters; and how he could count the number of stories he'd heard about their lives in Uganda on one hand, repeated like they came from a jukebox. "Mine are that way too. *Clean slate*," Sol had crooned in his mother's accent. Their group of friends was from everywhere and nowhere at once, their parents born in Jamaica and Hong Kong and India and Sudan, so Hari knew that they would understand. But he didn't know how to express what lay beneath: the loneliness of mourning something he had never known. As his friends snickered now, he thought once more of Mayuri and Kiya battling against their own memories and felt a shiver of guilt. In the weeks after that night, Hari had tried to do his own research, thinking he could find some answers himself. But after hours in the library, he'd come away with little more than a few sentences in the history books about Amin's dictatorship in Uganda—nothing before or after—and not a single word on the expulsion. As the silences resounded, Hari began to wonder how far back they ran.

"Hey." Solomon boxed Hari's shoulder, snapping him from his thoughts. He shook his head to clear his mind, gauging from his friends' faces that he must have been absent for some time. "You good?"

Hari opened his mouth but couldn't find an answer. Instead, he pushed off the ground and stole the ball from Sami, ducking around him and taking a shot that missed horrendously and clanged off the fence. He heard his friends stirring behind him, likely exchanging looks, but he didn't want to think about any of it anymore, wanted only the relief of his body in motion, to revive that earlier peace. He focused on the dribble of the ball before him until they joined him, and then they were on, playing until a light rain began and the court cleared out, until steam rose off the wet concrete and the moon glared and they could practically feel the area residents calling in their nightly noise complaints.

A few weeks later, Hari was working at the kitchen table when Sol called him to come play. The sunlight through the window warmed his forearms, drawing his attention away from his textbook and toward the jumble of vines out back, the leaves of the sugar maple just blushing orange, and Hari had no trouble ditching the report he was supposed to be writing.

They met at the Tim Hortons by the park, where Sol ordered two double-doubles and a doughnut, slapping his change down on the counter before Hari could pay. They hunched over their creamy coffees at a table shared with another family, whose kids were losing their minds, standing on the chairs, the parents switching between English and Vietnamese so that Hari caught only snatches—*enough, quiet, hey!*

"*Honey Cruller?*" Hari poked at the crackled icing, trying to make Sol laugh. "You know it's Boston Cream or bust for me."

"Fine," Sol said distractedly, waving the doughnut at the screeching kid next to him, who grabbed for it with both hands.

Hari watched as the kid scraped the icing off the cruller with his fingernails before looking up at his mother. The way his eyes sought her out reminded Hari of the last time his parents had come over, which they'd begun doing weekly now. This time, he noticed how Ma held her breath when he spoke, how Pappa's eyes followed him around the room. It wasn't that nothing had changed for them; they were just waiting to see a change in him. Since then, his thoughts had hovered around the phone number that Ma had given him. Until now it had felt irrelevant, the idea of wanting to connect with someone he didn't remember absurd when his actual relationships were falling apart. But now he realized what it meant for his family to relinquish that power to him. No matter the costs to them, they were trying to make things right.

Sol drained his coffee and confided that his boss had accused him of stealing tips that week, to which he had retorted that there were no tips to steal in this dump, and his boss had threatened to fire him right there. "Wish he had," Sol snorted, though his voice was heavy.

Hari appraised his friend with a stab of concern, but Sol shook his head.

"Don't look at me like that. I'm fine."

Hari raised an eyebrow. "If you say so."

"I'm just tired," Sol said, gritting his teeth, and Hari knew it was the kind of tired that had nothing to do with sleep.

Hari stood abruptly. "Let's go," he said, and Sol rose too with a relieved sigh.

They raced each other there like they were still eight years old, Hari's hair falling in his eyes, both of them eager for the solace of the park.

"Free court," Sol whistled when they arrived, but then he stopped cold, Hari following the line of his gaze.

The basketball hoops were gone. The empty backboards glared back at them, white and scuffed like two bloodshot eyes, ragged holes charting the places where the rims had been taken down. Hari's stomach hollowed. His neighbor Will had told him about the public hockey rink he played at downtown, complete with its own change rooms. Probably no crumbling curb, and certainly no city employees padlocking the goals overnight. Hari recalled all the noise complaint notices they had jeered at, every warning that their joy was too much. His limbs surged with heat, with the desire to feel that burn of relief in his muscles he'd come to rely on.

Solomon threw up his arms, and in his stance Hari witnessed his own rage and dejection boiling over. This was it, their hardtop cathedral, their sanctuary, their daily ritual to soften every ache. He thought of Mayuri digging in her garden every morning, and Kiya taking a breath at the window as she watched Meetu rule the alley with her friends. Of his parents when they dragged him to the mandir on the weekends, which for them was not just a place to pray but to gather, to belong to something greater.

Sol met Hari's eyes, and for a moment they stood speechless, the truth dawning on them both, the injustice pulsing between them.

The weight of it crashed down on Hari. "Let's get out of here," he growled.

Sol's shoulders tensed. "And go where, exactly?"

Hari thumbed at the bare backboards. "What's the point in staying?"

"The point?" Sol rounded on him now. "The point is that we're here. The point is that we deserve better. The point is that you're not noble for slinking off and pretending like it's nothing." He laughed, but it was vacant. "Or is Professor Hari too *good* for that?"

Hari was stunned into silence. A rip that could have formed between him and Solomon long ago was threatening to come apart. He thought then of his mother on the night she told him the truth; of his sisters still struggling to speak now. He was beginning to see that, for his family, keeping quiet meant a ground stable enough to stand on. But what use was a solid ground if they couldn't all move freely on it, if his best friend now wavered before him, on the brink of splitting away?

"The lions eat the noisy ones," Hari murmured.

Sol cocked his head, caught off guard. Then he smirked. "Not if they all make enough noise," he said, and Hari was reminded of why they were friends.

If they were at risk of tearing apart, there was a stronger thread that had held them together all these years, one woven from trust and time and love. The same thread that his family was trying to offer him now. A thread, a tether, a life rope thrown into the sea.

Sol flicked his gaze to the hoopless backboards, and Hari turned with him. He did not want to break away on his own. If they rose, it could only be together.

Before he could think, Hari gripped the ball, flexed his knees, and launched. The ball smacked the center of the backboard with a boom so resounding a puff of birds scattered from the trees. Solomon stared, something resolving behind his eyes. When the ball bounced back, Sol grabbed it, aimed, and released up, the noise vibrating their teeth. Hari whistled and followed, and on they went, the ball shuttling between them, each impact echoing louder, boom, boom, boom.

Rajni, Vinod, Mayuri, Kiya, & Hari, 1992

T HE CHIME TINKLED AS AN elderly man entered the shop. Hari recognized him as the man who came in to buy milk, as he was doing
now, lifting a purple bag from the fridge.

"How's your dad this week?" he asked.

Hari accepted the creased bill. Pappa was in bed upstairs, the radio
drowning out the rattle of his sunken chest. Since his stroke, every
day was different. Despite Hari's and his sisters' protests, Ma and
Pappa were unwavering in their refusal to give up the shop. Their
stubbornness was nothing new, but the way they'd both repeated the
same reason—*it's better for all of us if we stay*—had revealed it was less
about their allegiance to the shop than their resolution to remain for
Hari's sake. Once he recognized he wouldn't convince them to return
home, he moved in instead. Pappa's stroke had apprised him of the
fragility of his parents'—his grandparents'—bodies, and despite all that
had transpired over the last year, he found himself reassured to be there
with them now.

"Been all right this week," Hari replied, thinking of the day before,
when Pappa had stayed alert for the entirety of a cricket match,
narrating his predictions until Ma mimed turning his volume down.
Though Hari had been apprehensive about sharing space again, the
routines demanded by the shop and Pappa's health allowed them to
fall back into a familiar rhythm. "It's all in the past," Ma had said when

he moved in, a longing in her face. Hari understood then that decades of protecting themselves in this way could not be so easily undone, and that perhaps some feelings could never be named.

"Best be careful out there today. Storm brewing," the customer said.

The May sun glared through the window, cutting shapes on the shop floor. Hari tilted his head at the man, who chuckled.

"I mean all that protest business. The police are cordoning off the main streets. Radio said it might turn ugly."

Hari dropped his eyes. By now his friends would be getting ready for the rally, rolling their signs into backpacks. They were all going, marching down Yonge to the sit-in at Bloor. Hari imagined thousands of people bottlenecked up the road, just minutes away from here. The plans began as a solidarity rally for LA after the four police officers caught on video beating Rodney King were acquitted. But just three days on, Raymond Lawrence was murdered by the Toronto police, and the white officers who had killed Michael Wade Lawson in a Toronto suburb were acquitted; the plans by the Black Action Defence Committee swelled with urgency. "*Canada the Good* just loves to quietly shake its head," Sol had said when he came back from the affinity group meeting, before reporting that he was in the middle group, the one that would prefer not to make police contact but would offer themselves up if need be. Hari had thought of that day when the basketball hoops were taken down and known that he, too, would be there.

Hari handed the man his change. He had heard the news reports too, the claims that *race had absolutely no bearing on what happened*, but he no longer trusted the official narratives—his own life had shown him not to. That, he knew in his bones.

The man sorted the coins in his chapped palm, dropping half into the tip can and pocketing the rest. "Take care of your old man," he said, the chime jingling him out.

Above the till, the photograph of Ma and Pappa outside the house was tucked into the garlanded frame of Naina-auntie and Pulin-uncle's photo. It felt strange to see Pappa standing on his own in the picture, no walker or cane. Hari smoothed its curled edges as he grabbed his pack of cigarettes.

Inside, the air had felt muggy, but out here on the sidewalk he found it had a slight underbite. Perfect for a rally. He sucked in the smoke, nerves rattling. Ma and Pappa had raised him in the shelter of their fear. They had taught him all they had learned to survive. But he had always known that survival was not enough—they deserved to flourish and sprawl out, to speak, to dream. He could not stay silent; his life had been molded from the consequences of a mother and father who had not.

Rajni set the rice to boil for Vinod's lunch. The night before, he had eaten a little rotli softened with dahi, though this morning he had refused even water. She sighed. They could take no day for granted now. Despite all they'd been through, Vinod remained buoyant. He had an inner sheen that kept glowing. Only after his stroke did Rajni understand that he was not the youthful man he'd once been, though when he'd first woken in the hospital she was startled by the determination in his eyes. After the stroke he spoke only in Gujarati woven with Swahili, his carefully honed English gone. She felt the breadth of every day acutely now, the uncaring passage of time.

Downstairs, the shop door chimed. When Hari said he wanted to move in, she'd put up a fight. *Focus on school, we're managing, it's not your responsibility to worry.* A part of her truly meant it; they'd left, after all, to give him space. She'd been a young mother, and then an old mother, and she wanted to believe that she'd learned something between. But she couldn't deny her hope when Hari voiced his concern, or her relief when he came back.

Vinod's radio squabbled against the whine of his snores, turned on even in his sleep. *I had reason to fear for my life*, a voice was saying. Rajni had heard about the demonstrations even before the news reports. Solomon had been calling frequently, and Rajni had once overheard Hari speaking to him about it, the phone cord stretched taut into the bathroom. From this, she deduced that Hari would go. She had not been so astute two decades ago, when Latika was furtively preparing for the same. But no matter how fearful she was at the thought of him attending, she forced herself to say nothing—such was the toll of the silence she and Vinod had imposed. He had returned to her; she would not push him away again.

Not long after Hari moved in, Rajni asked him to write a notice for the shop about the reduced hours during Vinod's recovery. "Don't say he's sick," she warned. *Due to the needs of our family*, Hari wrote instead, words that pleased Rajni, as if her family were a little sprout that simply needed water and sun and soil to grow. "You write well," she told him, at which Hari perked up and replied, "I suppose my mother must have too. She was a journalist, right?" Rajni was taken aback, this being the first time they had spoken of Latika without tears or anger, and she understood with a twinge of jealousy that Mayuri and Kiya must have been sharing stories with Hari. And yet, in the face of his simplest query, she felt herself clamming up, growing defensive. "Bas, the shop is waiting," she'd said instead, distressed by the memories stirred by his question, even as she watched his face fall.

Why should she remember? she'd asked herself that night, trying to ignore the renewed distance between herself and Hari. Let her daughters speak if they wished, but no narration could bring back the past, and no story could revive those who were gone.

And yet, since then the memories had begun rising to the surface more often, and she noticed that they did not always trouble her; once, in fact, remembering a silly game she used to play with her brothers in Karachi, she had laughed. It was almost enough to want to tell someone, and yet she found that she couldn't, having already shut the

370

pathway with Hari and not wanting to disturb Vinod in his delicate state. Still, the desire grew in her, steady with time.

She snapped the ironing board open in front of the television and was draping one of Hari's T-shirts across it when the phone rang. She snatched it up, not wanting to wake Vinod.

The voice on the line spoke mechanically. "Hello, this is the neighborhood business association. We're advising all businesses in the area to close early in light of this afternoon's demonstration. Police are informing citizens to be wary of activity after nightfall. We advise you to vacate the premises before then, as roads may be congested and unforeseen events may occur."

Rajni hung up. The language was vague but its meaning clear. She could close the shop now, bring Vinod to her daughters' for the night. But she imagined Hari out there while she was far away, returning that evening to an empty apartment, shaken and alone. The thought was worse than anything that might happen. She passed the iron over the wrinkled sleeves, pressing away the lines. She would not close the shop or flee the premises. A defiant pleasure coursed through her. They would stay.

She skimmed her eyes over the flowered curtains, Hari's backpack limp against a chair, the framed certificate on the wall that Vinod was gifted upon his retirement from Canada Post. It was the sixth place she'd lived since bidding goodbye to her parents' house in Karachi. Some days she felt that all the leaving had left her unable to settle. Other times, when making breakfast for her family or sinking into bed beside Vinod after a long day, she believed that anywhere could become home.

The phone rang again. Rajni wondered if she should have said something the last time, but when she lifted the receiver, it was not the same voice.

"Hari? Oh, hello auntie." It was Solomon. Rajni remembered him at seven or eight, when Hari first brought him over. She thought it was miraculous that after all the years, the moves and changes, the two had remained friends. She used to tell them this sometimes, when they were dribbling a ball outside or wolfing down sandwiches at the sink, holding her laughter in her cheeks as Hari flushed with embarrassment.

"He's downstairs. Shall I call him?"

"No, no, I'll get him later." Solomon paused. "Everything okay with uncle today?"

Rajni squeezed the phone between her shoulder and ear, flattening the fresh crease of Vinod's pajamas. "He didn't sleep much last night. I thought he—" She stopped herself. Solomon didn't want to hear the details of Vinod's failing body, the shifts in his lungs from morning to night. Even when speaking to Mayuri and Kiya, Rajni was careful with what she shared. Children didn't want to be reminded that their parents were mortal; there was no need to cause them alarm. Some things were still better left unsaid.

"I hope he's resting. Hari tells me how hard he works. And you too."

Rajni knew Solomon would be out there that afternoon, and maybe the rest of their friends, boys with curly hair and smooth skin and loud yells and sloppy smiles, boys Rajni had witnessed in and out of their childhoods. "Thank you, dikro," she said, momentarily forgetting that he didn't speak her language. "And you. Stay safe."

The line grew quiet. Solomon was probably wondering how much she knew. "That's just what we're trying to do."

She waited for him to hang up before she let go of the phone. A gentle warmth flooded her. She considered what he had said. And she thought then of Adroa, that boy who had shepherded her family from harm even as he joined the army that booted them out. Rajni had never welcomed him, even after he sent the letter alerting them about Latika; her hospitality, even in her mind, could not encompass him. His family had lived at the bottom of the hill, his community separate from hers. But they had wanted the same things, hadn't they: to feel safe in their homes, to know they were cared for, to have a little more. Amin had promised the Africans a better life, just as the British had promised the same to Pirbhai long ago. Their pain was not the same pain, but they had lived on common ground.

The pile of laundry was undiminished, the pressure cooker spitting steam. Some days were a fight, and others like this one, simple, her purpose clear. She had always tried to keep her family safe. And briefly she could see that her children had striven for this too: Latika, Hari, even Mayuri and Kiya, finding ways to repair what was broken, to preserve what might otherwise be lost. The desire rose in her again to speak this aloud, and she was met with the realization that perhaps it was not about bringing back the past, but rather bringing it forward.

She thought she heard Vinod rustling in the bedroom, the patter of toes finding the floor. She dropped the freshly folded pajamas and hurried to meet him.

Vinod woke, startled from sleep by the heat of the sun. His arms jerked to shield his face, and from this he knew that he was healing. He could clearly see the outline of his feet under the sheet, the photographs on the dresser, the light streaming in through the crooked blinds. He eased his legs over the side of the bed. Rajni didn't like him to walk alone anymore, but he didn't want to call on her every time. The other morning he had noticed the delicate shape of her skull beneath her thinning hair. There was frailty in them both.

He walked to the mirror and lifted a tremoring hand to trace the slumped corner of his mouth. Eating his dinner last night, he hadn't noticed when he'd begun to drool. Rajni caught the strand of saliva with a sheet of paper towel, folding it swiftly away. But he'd felt it deeply. His body was betraying him. All his life he had kept his shirt tucked, his hair combed, hiding his lips behind his fingers when he chewed. He had been raised to never show himself as anything less than spotless. There were so many ways the world had attempted to take his pride, but in the end his own body was trying to rob him of it.

Rajni swept in, batting her arms. "Arre, I told you to call me."

Vinod plodded past her into the hallway. His mind was sharper today, his limbs light. He made it to the couch and sat down with a sigh. Rajni threw a blanket over his legs, fussing at the edges.

"Raju, please."

She stood back abruptly, wounded. He hadn't meant to say it so tersely, but these days finding the words drained him. He was tired of feeling like a child. Not even a child—as a boy he'd been the funny one, the fast one, the god of the backspin. The memory of his young body came rudely, almost like a violence. He thought then of Pulin, his last words to Vinod. Indeed, they had fought. Vinod had refused death over and over, breaking his body in the hope that he could earn his rightful place. He had never imagined an alternative, for his father had never stopped striving for somewhere to call his own. But Vinod had always known where he belonged: on the field, with his friends, stolen golf balls flying between them. *Asians milked the cow but didn't feed it*, Amin had said, and all his life, Vinod had prided himself on how much he'd fed the cow, in Uganda and Canada both. But was it not enough some days to sit with the cow, stroke her flank, water the grass she grazed? It struck him that this might have been what his father desired all along, a little place to simply exist, freely, and with dignity.

He opened a newspaper over his lap and smoothed the pages, though his eyes couldn't focus on the words. When he had his next good day, he would like for his daughters to bring him to the house, where he'd sit in a deckchair in that garden they'd planted, the radio narrating a cricket match, the sun gracing his face. The thought filled him with optimism. Maybe this was his body telling him he didn't have to keep fighting. Maybe his fate, now, was to rest.

Hari came up from the shop, in a rumpled sweatshirt and slippers.

Rajni handed him a bowl. "Maybe he'll eat if you give it," she said in a voice loud enough that Vinod supposed he was meant to hear.

He looked doubtfully at the watery dal. "Am I too old for bhajias? What about french fries. Jalebi-gathiya?" He laughed at his own joke, his breath rattling. "I still have all my teeth, na?"

Rajni rolled her eyes. "Okay, big man. Today khichdi, tomorrow jalebi-gathiya." She flashed her eyes at Hari, who made to turn on the TV, but Vinod stopped his hand. They'd used that move on Hari countless times, the chatter of cartoons distracting from the spoon as it moved from bowl to mouth. He'd rather talk while he sensed that brightness behind his eyes. He wanted to share something with his son, let himself be known.

"We've always had good teeth, Hari. Have I told you about the time—" He faltered, seeing Hari shift beside him. The nerves hushed him. He still worried sometimes that he would say the wrong thing.

"You should eat, Pappa," Hari said, his eyes imploring. "I want to hear, it's just—I have to go."

The grin slid from Vinod's lips. He tried to hold it, though with the numbness in parts of his face he couldn't be sure. He had wanted to tell the story of the time he nearly lost a tooth to a cricket ball. Or was it his friend who was hit in the mouth, that boy with the yellow uniform? He wanted to recreate everything, just for a moment, Kampala and the neighborhood and his friends. He shook his head. He could let it go. "Bas, bas, forget it. Tu ja."

Hari looked uneasy. Vinod sighed, dug a heaping spoonful, and swallowed it down. He wiped his lips with a paper towel just in case, then lifted the spoon again with his eyes on Hari, who raised his hands.

"If you're sure." For confirmation, Hari glanced up at Rajni, who stiffened over the iron, her fingers dancing too close to the steam. She jerked her arm back, shaking.

"Careful!" Hari said.

Rajni clenched her fingers into a fist, dropping it behind her back. "You too." She hesitated. "I know...I know you'll keep yourself safe."

Hari studied her uncertainly. After a moment, he said gently, "Not just myself."

Vinod peered from his wife to his son, an unnameable exchange passing between them. He was aware that much was transpiring beyond his grasp these days, and though the young Vinod inside urged him to stay attuned to every situation, a newer, quieter voice whispered that he could let himself sit back.

For a moment it seemed that Rajni would speak again, but then Hari turned to the hall, shoving his feet into his sneakers.

"Bring me back something fried and crunchy," Vinod called as Hari opened the door, a soft gurgle beneath his voice as the dal settled in his throat. He thought he heard Hari laugh as he walked out. Vinod looked into his palms, his thinning legs, the breaking, healing body of an old man, and felt himself smile.

It was time to plant the seeds. Mayuri waited for this part, sorting through what they'd salvaged from last year's crop. They'd asked Hari to help, but he said he was busy today. No matter. It wasn't that more hands were needed, simply wanted. The garden asked for it, the leaves made greener, the carrots sweeter, by the touch of many.

And there were many. Kiya, Meetu. The neighbors. Darlene. Naina-aunty came by often, slow on her feet now and quieter without Pulin-uncle, but spouting old songs after a little time rooting in the dirt. Once, Kunal, when he dropped by to fix the television—Hari had called him, though Mayuri was certain he could have solved the problem himself—and despite Mayuri's vexation at Hari she'd been glad to see Kunal healthy, reassured when he accepted a bundle of mint, knowing he liked it in his tea.

And Hari came too, with Solomon and their friends, or the boy next door, a friendship grown stronger when Will took a semester off from university and admitted to Hari that he was lost. These boys who wandered but never questioned their place. Mayuri admired the way they gave themselves space to *figure it out*, how they didn't doubt that a future lay before them. She herself had never had that certainty, her life governed by a set of prescribed rules. As a girl she'd struggled to find her place, but now she wondered if it wasn't something to be found but created. Back then she'd believed the sea was the start of the rest of the world, but here she was learning the possibilities of coming back.

Kiya saw Mayuri gathering the tools and went out to join her. She'd had qualms about planting the garden again this year. It was she who'd dealt with the neighbors who called it an eyesore and an encroachment on shared space, who blamed it when their children were stung by bees, who worried it would invite "thieves and junkies" to loiter. What she knew of paradise was that it was until it wasn't. She was sure it would bring more conflict, that these relationships might sour over time.

But a line kept returning to her from Adroa's letter, forever in her memory. *I acted so my daughter could have her birthright, which is a place that she can know she is welcomed and equal and free.* Kiya saw her daughter moving through the space as if it was hers, but also not hers, tending to the plants with the consideration of someone who understood some things could never be owned. Her birthright: a place to grow and share a meal, to feel safe and nourished. Kiya still carried a loneliness she believed she might never shake, a sister unfound, a letter unreturned. But she no longer felt unmoored; the shape of her desires had grown beyond her. Now she wanted for all of them: herself, her family, this home she shared with the two great loves of her life.

Latika had told them the story of how their grandfather had torn down homes, breaking ties with the land with every rail laid down. But Mayuri had told her another story, of how their grandmother had given him a home, spent her life healing those around her with herbs she nurtured from the soil. One didn't cure the other, but taken together perhaps they made something greater. Watering what was once burnt. This place was exactly their birthright: for every bite of sourness, a little sweet.

Their voices, together, were a wave. They volleyed rhymes around the crowd, timed by the beat of their feet. *No justice, no peace, no racist police. From LA, to TO, racism has got to go. Hey hey, ho ho.*

Hari marched. The record shops and dive bars of Yonge Street bobbed past. To his left, Solomon raised his fist, the pure afternoon light catching the rise of his cheekbones. To his right, Marcus and Sami, the cardboard sign between them shaking above the mass: LET'S UNITE SAME BOSSES SAME FIGHT. Inside, Hari carried a haunting, alive only in blood, which had taught him to sing, to resist, to move. If he felt severed from who he had been, in this crowd he was connected, his body a part of the whole, his voice finding the chants as if he'd always known them. The photograph of his family outside the Kampala mandir danced across his mind, all of them joined together. He saw his parents, their eyes wet with hope, with the belief that they had transcended their place: just look how hard they worked to get there, just look at who they were not. Beneath every fable they had told him, of his great-grandfather and the railroad and the lions, was a desire for better—for him, for their family, for their people. The same belief that propelled thousands onto the streets now, that saw them fighting for a future, refusing to leave. Separation was in their blood, but so, too, was this.

Along the sidewalk, a line of people stood eerily still, pale blades of forehead gleaming. One of them hoisted his sign higher: *We denounce the racist murder of WHITES.* Hari did a double take and caught the tip of a hooded face ticking toward him. In that instant, someone roared into a megaphone so that the air swelled with noise, bellowing over and over: *Our liberation is linked! Our liberation is linked!* Hari found his voice in the reverberation of others, in a cry so furious it refused fear.

The signals at the intersection blinked uselessly, cars honking without end. The warmth of the sun-soaked tarmac seeped through Hari's jeans, though the sky had paled toward evening. Their bodies filled the road, barely contained between the traffic lights, the sign for Bloor Street rocking in the wind.

What do we want? Justice! Behind Hari, a man beat a leather drum, the wail of his song otherworldly. *When do we want it? Now!* Hari turned to Solomon just as Solomon swiveled toward him, his mouth singing open, and there were tears in his eyes, like tiny beacons, and Hari felt the wetness on his own cheeks, as if they were one body, their pain, their power, linked. *The people! United! Will never be divided!* A siren bleated, the blue flash of emergency lights. On the ground, their arms were entwined, and now they tightened together, squeezing out whatever space might be used to tear them apart. *The people! United! Will never be defeated!* Hari could no longer hear his own voice or even feel the crags in the road against his skin. They were a collective, a movement against history, carrying with them not only their pasts and their presents but their insistence on a future. *The people! United! Will never be divided!* A voice over a loudspeaker, a warning to clear the area immediately. Their chants rose louder, drowning all else: no horns, no sirens, just their words and their bodies and the ground beneath them. *THE PEOPLE! UNITED! WILL NEVER BE DEFEATED!* In the periphery, a platoon of horses emerged like a mirage, uniformed officers hovering above. A quiet pulse rippled across the group, a heartbeat of silence. They held each other down. There was an ancient logic to it, that to hold together meant to thrive. To survive. *THE PEOPLE! UNITED! WILL NEVER BE—*

They got the call while Meetu was preparing for bed. Kiya startled at the shrill of the phone. A minute later Mayuri flew into the room, her face drained of color. "Hari's missing."

"What?" Kiya and Meetu both said together.

In the light of the lamps the whites of their eyes were brighter. Mayuri twisted the phone cord around her fingers.

"Ma called. Hari went to the protest downtown. It should've been over hours ago. They're going out looking for him."

"They—Pappa too?"

Mayuri nodded tersely. "They'll be gone by the time we get there."

Meetu was pinching Kiya's arm. "Missing?"

Kiya hushed her. "He's probably fine." It was true, it had to be. The ground swooped out beneath her, the room dissolving into another—walls pocked with mosquito guts, bars on the windows, a warm, ripe breeze slipping through. She blinked, but the image lingered.

Mayuri was tugging one of Kiya's jackets over her shoulders, the sleeves too tight. That day, when Latika didn't collect them from school, when Mayuri repeated the word *protest* for the first time—no one was hurt, but something else had happened, Arun taken, Latika changed, Ma unbearably angry. She saw Meetu's jeans for tomorrow laid out over the dresser and tossed them on the bed.

Kiya and Mayuri exchanged a glance, and in that second they felt the weight of their fear between them, made heavier by generations.

"I'm sure Hari's fine," Kiya repeated, speaking his name to remember where they were.

"Hurry," Mayuri said. Despite her worry, her throat stung with gratitude to be here with her sister, this safety they'd nurtured between them. She opened the door, a prayer beneath her breath.

Officially, the rally was over. When they stood, their limbs creaked like ships unmoored. They tried to shuffle forward, but horses clogged the intersection. They were barricaded. A shiver snaked through the crowd. Someone began a chant, the call and response feeble at first, but gaining bulk as it went on, muscling through the choked road. *Whose streets? Our streets. Whose streets?*

The horses followed, the uniformed men. They moved silently but their presence was felt, spectral, guiding the group toward an end that was not of their choosing. The crowd responded with noise, declaring themselves still here.

Our streets. The specter landed. Harsh lights, red and blue, sparkled off the glass shopfronts, glancing off faces frozen by their glare. An arm of people broke away, charging toward the sidewalk and slamming a newspaper box to the ground. Then the horses descended, batons cracking down as the officers hurtled between them. Hari jolted back into his body. His neck prickled with terror that what they had made was broken, and with rage at everything tearing them apart. He could hear his breath and Solomon's, ragged between chants. Marcus ducked as a rock sang past his face, crashing into the window of a store. *Whose streets?* Everywhere, scrambling, yelling, tripping, fear ushering fear. A horse swerved between Hari and Solomon, teeth bright as bullets against the fast-blooming night. "Let's go home, let's everybody just get home," a man was insisting, his hands flapping in surrender or plea. *Yes*, Hari thought, *let it be over, let us go home.* But until they could all feel that sense of refuge here, there could be no such thing.

Someone snatched Hari's shoulder and he shook free, but the hand seized him again, and when he turned he found himself scowling at Sol, dust and spit streaking his chin. Hari heard laughter and realized it was his own, rippling out in desperate waves.

"Stay with—" Hari began, but his voice was stunned by a clink, a burst, and then a searing fog, eating the air, scraping his eyes like ragged fingernails. He gagged, falling to his knees. Then an arm tugging him upright. They were running and crying and choking on their own breath, the air gone, the panic swelling to breaking.

Hari hooked his collar over his nose, clutching the hand that he knew he couldn't let go. His lips felt as if they were peeling away, shedding to reveal a dark jelly of blood. He tried to open his eyes but was met with a searing pain. He was blinded. The calm of that realization was followed by horror, his chest seizing as he tried to feel his way unseeing over *whose streets? whose streets? whose streets?*

He stumbled on. *NO*, he heard, or was it *GO*? He couldn't tell but it didn't matter because it was a voice, a reminder that he had one. *Solomon*, he screamed, but it emerged as a croak, brittle and unheard. *Solomon*, he shrieked again, *Mayuri, Ma*, and then they were spilling from him, names falling like embers on the road. His throat was raw with yelling, each name a prayer unanswered, all of them with him, his family come and gone. Behind his eyelids he saw a body huddled in a dank chamber, soles cracked as the soil they would become, and a tree blooming red as flame, and a boat dimly bobbing across black waters, propelled by the belief that it might one day arrive.

He opened his eyes. The chemical fog hung like a white sheet in the night sky. A stop sign bent at the knees, a car choked in fire, the bodies jostling for safety from the air and batons and hands that beat, beat, beat and held them down.

His gaze landed on the street sign before him. And he knew, then, where his loyalty lay. He scanned the roads for Solomon, a tether in this life. But the bodies blurred impossibly. He ran, eyes streaming as he clawed his way home.

She could see nothing. Sirens and shouts, the sounds indistinguishable. Her legs ached, her breaths shallow. Rajni reached for Vinod, clutching his cane. She shivered in her nightdress; they hadn't even thought to change. How long had they searched? Hours or years. Time blurred, moments collapsing upon each other.

They wouldn't find him. She had let her fear overtake her, shaking her beyond thought. She had forgotten where she was, imagining bats in the sky and a river swollen red. She had thought she could find her children, grab their wrists and pull them back home.

She could smell smoke. Strange colors floated through the air, silver and shimmering. A young woman with braids ran toward them, arms held open. "Are you lost?" she said. "Let me help you." Rajni tried to explain that they were near home, that they were looking for someone, reaching for the right words. The woman's eyes were warm, crinkling at the edges. "Can you find your way?" she asked.

Rajni didn't know why this made her knees tremble. The woman's arms were still outstretched, and Rajni saw in her the desire not just to shelter them but to shepherd them into a safe and boundless future. Vinod was gazing at the woman too, his eyes distant, a smile growing on his face. "You were right," he murmured, his Gujarati soft. "My daughter, you were right."

The woman's face grew bewildered. Rajni turned to Vinod, wanting to pull him away, but not wanting to end the dream he had stepped into. Then she heard her daughter's voice, clear as a foghorn, a sound calling her home. She turned to see Meetu racing toward them, Mayuri and Kiya behind.

"My daughter's come," Rajni wheezed. The woman nodded, the streets thundering, and she was gone.

Vinod pointed up ahead, their street sign glinting against the black sky. Rajni stumbled on the curb and Vinod gripped her elbow, his fingers surprisingly firm. Together they ducked through the throngs of people, finding their way back.

He knew the truth before he saw it. The windows were blown out, the sidewalk radiant with glass. A pall of smoke churned to the sky. The shop was burning. Hari charged forward until he saw them, small and huddled at the edge of the road. Pappa sloped over his cane, Ma quivering in her nightdress. And next to them, Mayuri and Kiya and Meetu. He reached them and collapsed across their arms, his eyes raw as their faces shifted from shock to relief, as Ma rubbed his neck and Meetu slammed into his gut.

He peeled off his sweatshirt and wrapped it around Ma's shoulders, then wedged his arm around Pappa's waist. They were both still, eyes locked on the shop. Hari wrenched his gaze away to look with them. The brick was blackened and ash drifted through the air. The yellow sign had melted, belching acrid fumes, and the newly painted door was scorched to reveal the warped wood beneath. Around them the city swirled, unsettled and awake.

"When?" Hari said. "How?"

Ma spoke slowly, her eyes never leaving the building. "We were already outside."

Mayuri coughed. "They went looking for you."

The neighbors were no longer dumping buckets of water. Instead, they too had congregated on the sidewalk, arms limp by their sides.

Meetu pointed at a small puddle at the shop entrance. "It won't all be gone." Kiya pushed the hair off her face, but she said nothing.

Mayuri shifted nearer to Ma, tears slipping into the corners of her mouth. Kiya drew Meetu's face into her side, Meetu's hand still looped with Hari's, his arm still supporting Pappa. They clung to each other as if on a life raft. And yet for once, they were rooted in place.

They watched as if they could see everything disappearing. Hari blazed. "We have to do something. It'll keep burning—"

Ma clicked her teeth. "It's done."

He turned to her, eyes bulging. "How can we just stand here?"

Pappa choked then—but no, he was laughing, phlegm rumbling as he rocked. The light flickered his eyes, his wide teeth bared in wonder. "You sound like her."

Hari stared. Mayuri let out a sob and Kiya was laughing too, soot smearing her cheeks. Ma laced her hand in Pappa's, gripping his shaking fingers with her swollen, hardened ones. Her expression, in the pain, was resolute. "We know how to rebuild. So we do it again."

"No," said Pappa. "Now, we rest."

The fire had taken what it would. Hari had missed the moment it ripped into their home, the igniting and devouring, the tails of orange and simmering blue. He had come only in time to witness the smoke as it rose above the paved land, the ground below charred and readied, the slow, determined birth of something new.

They had arrived here: almost whole. They would leave again, find another place. They would let it burn and insist on something better.

Epilogue

ON A ROCKY OUTCROPPING OFF the shore, a young man and an older woman stand. Around them, the lake holds the bloated moon. They have come here to speak, if not honestly, then at least alone. They recognize each other in the slope of their foreheads, the smile that is only ever half. But beneath that too. They both know something of what it means to come apart.

They speak of people remote and unknowable as the land before the water. The woman has traveled far, and yet in all the movement a part of her feels restored. Encircled by her family, she knows that she has come not just forward, but also back. When their conversation falters, they take in the stillness around them, how the waves make silence with sound. They let the tide crest over their feet and remember what the water has carried and what it has swallowed.

The water, at first, is a shock, a chill that seeps and burrows. They curl their toes and laugh, nervous and stunned, but then their skin eases, their muscles give way. The woman has just finished telling a tale, imparted to her long ago. She watches as the words settle into truth. She shares it not as a release but an inheritance, a history they carry. They speak of fires old and new. She cups the lake in her palm and lets it trail down her wrist.

The man slips a little on a rock slick with algae. The woman, leaning, rights him in a gesture unpracticed and natural. Her fingers linger, uncertain of when to let go. She recalls a moment in a distant country, another hand in hers. Her husband beside her, walking toward home, the eye of his cigarette blinking between a smile. The young man witnesses her remembering. He recalls losses that he cannot know. Beneath the water's surface, his heels mark where they stand, on the rocks between the shore, not quite land nor lake, but something in between.

Their feet, toughened by sand and stone, arrive where they began, at an ancient knowing. Beyond them, the tide continues. The water shifts the sand, reassembles the shells, sucks the stones to pebbles. The waves break and mend, break and mend. A reminder, as they stand together, that what the water takes, it returns.

Acknowledgments

This book would not exist without my community, who carried me over the many years it took to write it. I wrote this book mostly in Tkaronto. The final chapter of this novel contains the chant "*Whose streets? Our streets!*" as a record of the protest chants common at the time, but this is all occupied Indigenous land. I'm grateful to the land that feeds and sustains us.

My deepest thanks to Sarah Bowlin, my fearless agent, who answers my questions before I even know what to ask and whose faith in me changed everything. I am so grateful to you and the entire Aevitas team.

To my dream team of editors, Seema Mahanian at Grand Central, Anita Chong at McClelland & Stewart, and Becky Hardie at Chatto & Windus: I don't know how I got so lucky as to have three such brilliant minds working on my book. Thank you for meeting the work with such care and for pushing me to make the book truer with every revision.

I'm grateful to the whole GCP team, especially Andy Dodds, Theresa DeLucci, Albert Tang, Mari Okuda, Kristen Lemire, Rick Ball, and Simone Noronha for the passion fruit cover of my dreams; to the M&S team, especially Kristin Cochrane, Jared Bland, Stephanie Sinclair, Kimberlee Kemp, Gemma Wain, Kim Kandravy, Ruta Liormonas, Tonia Addison, Sarah Howland, Anyka Davis, JR Simpson, Jessica Reid, and Jennifer Griffiths for the glorious cover design; and to the

Chatto team, especially Suzanne Dean, Asia Choudhry, Priya Roy, and Rosanna Boscawen. Warmest thanks to Muhammed Sajid for the radiant UK cover art.

To the writing teachers over the years who made me believe I could do this: Faith Adiele, Lisa Ko, Megan Giddings, Shyam Selvadurai, Chelsea Bieker, Arif Anwar—in whose Introductory Novel class at University of Toronto Continuing Studies the spark of this book came alive—and Ingrid Rojas Contreras, in whose Novel Workshop I first articulated the questions at the heart of this book.

To the writing workshops and residencies where I found community and had the fortune to deepen my craft: VONA/Voices of our Nation, Tin House, One Story Writers' Conference, and the Millay Colony. Deepest gratitude to the Toronto Public Library for the books that shaped me as a writer and the space to work. Gratitude also to the Canada Council for the Arts, the Ontario Arts Council, and the Toronto Arts Council for the crucial funding and support.

To Sharon Bala, who has shown me the meaning of true mentorship. This book would be entirely different without your dedication, belief, and willingness to read draft after draft. Heartfelt thanks to Zalika Reid-Benta and Diaspora Dialogues for this life-changing opportunity.

This book is based on history and events spanning India, East Africa, England, and Canada over nearly one hundred years, but I have taken many liberties for the purpose of fiction. My intention was to convey the essence of these times and places through the lens of my own imagination. As such, the chronology of certain events has been altered and some historical inaccuracies exist in service of the story. For instance, the proceedings of both Idi Amin's 1972 expulsion announcements and the events of the 1992 racial uprising in Toronto have been compressed for the sake of the timeline. I did extensive research for this book and must deeply thank the following authors for their scholarship and literature: Ngũgĩ wa Thiong'o, Gaiutra Bahadur,

David Dabydeen, Maria del Pilar Kaladeen, and Tina K. Ramnarine, Amrit Wilson, Yasmin Alibhai-Brown, Aanchal Malhotra, Robert G. Gregory, M. G. Vassanji, Peter Kimani, Nisid Hajari, Mahmood Mamdani, Z. Lalani, and Shezan Muhammedi. I owe much also to the 2017 documentary *It Takes A Riot: Race, Rebellion, Reform*, produced by Simon Black, Howard Grandison, and Idil Abdillahi, about the 1992 Yonge Street Uprising in Toronto.

The lyrics on page 208 that Arun remembers Irene singing to him as a child come from a Mau Mau liberation song as quoted in *Never Be Silent: Publishing and Imperialism in Kenya 1884–1963* by Shiraz Durrani, and which originally appeared in *The Urban Guerrilla* by Mohamed Mathu, ed. Donald Barnett (Richmond, BC: LSM Information Center, 1974).

Few historical records about this period exist, and I owe the greatest debt to those who gave their time to speak with me about their experiences and memories. My heartfelt gratitude especially to Manubhai Chaturbhai Patel and Priyanka Patel, Bhupen Tanna, Sudha and Usha Trivedi, Dhiren and Kalpana Oza, Ashoka Kavi, Mina Jani, Tushar Trivedi, Amit and Dipti Oza, Sikandar, Gulshan, Sadrudin, Didar, Zarina, Lutaf, Sultan, and Shakufe Virani; Rashida and Moonira Ukani; Najma, Saqueeb, and Natasha Rajan; Mahedi, Tayreez, and Karim Mushani, and Nazlin Jivraj for introducing me to your generous family. Without you all, this book would not exist; thank you for refusing to let this history disappear. A special thank-you to my aunt, Dipti Oza, for connecting me with so many community members, for all your help with the translation and transliteration of the Gujarati and Swahili in the book, and for having the memory of an elephant.

To Amanda Churchill, for reading early drafts with such sensitivity, for walking this publication journey together, and for the most encouraging WhatsApp thread that could ever exist.

To Joanne Szilagyi and Jody Chan, writing group of my heart, for reading the most fledgling drafts of all these chapters, for holding my writing and my feelings with such tenderness, and for always bringing dinner. Joanne, thank you for urging me to go with my gut—this book is better for it.

To Pauline Holdsworth, for reading countless full drafts, partial drafts, half chapters and everything between, for being the first person to tell me the novel was ready, and for reminding me what is possible.

To pruneah Kim, for all those hours and days writing beside you, for every morsel of reassurance you've fed me, and for always reminding me of all that we deserve. To Constantine Harmantas and Jehan Husain, oldest friends and first-ever readers of my stories, I'm so glad we stuck together. To Richa Sandill, Jenny Tran, Rekha Mistry, and all the friends and family unnamed here who have nourished me over the years—I could not have completed this novel without your grace and kindness.

To Jody (again), my tether in this life, my home for so much of writing this book, and even still. You help me find the words, but with you I don't need them. To Nithin, first reader and listener, I will never know a more generous heart. Thank you for being the most steadying force through it all and for expanding my capacity to love. To Maria Papachristos and in loving memory of Thomas Papachristos, who taught me what it means to have grandparents. To my ancestors whose labors and journeys made it possible for me to be here: I wrote this book toward you. To my brother Manish, for believing in books, and in me, and for making me cackle exactly when I need it. To my mother and father, for your example of quiet strength and deep devotion, and for all your ways of loving that go far beyond words. My dad was always the first to call me a writer. I hope this ghadedu did you proud.

About the Author

Janika Oza is the winner of the 2022 O. Henry Prize for Short Fiction, and the 2020 Kenyon Review Short Fiction Award. She has received support from The Millay Colony, Tin House Summer and Winter Workshops, VONA/Voices of Our Nation, and the One Story Summer Writers' Conference, and her stories and essays have appeared in publications such as *The Best Small Fictions 2019 Anthology*, *Catapult*, *The Adroit Journal*, and *The Cincinnati Review*, among others. She lives in Toronto.